Barga... the Billionaire

*He'll make her his own
– no matter how high the price!*

**Three thrilling, contemporary romances
from three beloved Mills & Boon authors!**

In May 2009 Mills & Boon bring you
two classic collections, each
featuring three favourite romances
by our bestselling authors…

BARGAINING WITH THE BILLIONAIRE

The Blackmail Bargain by Robyn Donald
The Billion-Dollar Bride by Kay Thorpe
How To Marry a Billionaire
by Ally Blake

WON BY THE WEALTHY GREEK

The Greek's Seven-Day Seduction
by Susan Stephens
Constantinou's Mistress
by Cathy Williams
The Greek Doctor's Rescue
by Meredith Webber

Bargaining with the Billionaire

THE BLACKMAIL BARGAIN
by
Robyn Donald

THE BILLION-DOLLAR BRIDE
by
Kay Thorpe

HOW TO MARRY A BILLIONAIRE
by
Ally Blake

MILLS & BOON®
Pure reading pleasure™

*Harlequin Mills & Boon Limited,
Eton House, 18-24 Paradise Road, Richmond, Surrey TW9 1SR*

BARGAINING WITH THE BILLIONAIRE
© by Harlequin Enterprises II B.V./S.à.r.l 2009

The Blackmail Bargain, The Billion-Dollar Bride and *How To Marry
a Billionaire* were first published in Great Britain by Harlequin
Mills & Boon Limited in separate, single volumes.

The Blackmail Bargain © Robyn Kingston 2005
The Billion-Dollar Bride © Kay Thorpe 2004
How To Marry a Billionaire © Ally Blake 2004

ISBN: 978 0 263 87130 2

05-0509

*Printed and bound in Spain
by Litografia Rosés S.A., Barcelona*

THE BLACKMAIL BARGAIN

by

Robyn Donald

Robyn Donald can't remember not being able to read, and will be eternally grateful to the local farmers who carefully avoided her on a dusty country road as she read her way to and from school, transported to places and times far away from her small village in Northland, New Zealand. Growing up fed her habit; as well as training as a teacher, marrying and raising two children, she discovered the delights of romances and read them voraciously, especially enjoying the ones written by New Zealand writers. So much so, that one day she decided to write one herself. Writing soon grew to be as much of a delight as reading – although infinitely more challenging – and when eventually her first book was accepted by Mills & Boon she felt she'd arrived home. She still lives in a small town in Northland with her family close by, using the landscape as a setting for much of her work. Her life is enriched by the friends she's made among writers and readers, and complicated by a determined corgi called Buster who is convinced that blackbirds are evil entities. Her greatest hobby is still reading, with travelling a very close second.

PROLOGUE

HARD blue eyes narrowing, Curt McIntosh surveyed his sister. 'All right, you've hedged enough. Tell me straight, is Ian having an affair with this Peta Grey?'

Gillian flushed. 'Don't you look down your nose at me like that! You remind me of Dad when anyone dares to contradict him—high-handed, intolerant and dictatorial!'

His voice stripped of everything but the authority that underpinned its deep tone, Curt stated, 'Nothing you say is convincing in itself. Do you have proof that Ian is sleeping with this woman, or is he just being a good neighbour?'

One glance upwards blocked Gillian's first impetuous response. Not a muscle had moved in Curt's formidable face, compelling in its bold, predatory beauty, but she chose her words carefully. 'I shouldn't have said that—about Dad.'

'It doesn't matter.' He pinned her with a steely gaze. 'And you're still avoiding the subject.'

She flounced around to stare at the view outside his office window. In summer Auckland was thick with jacaranda trees, and the one in the Domain over the busy city road was an airy dome of lilac-purple. Its beauty did nothing to relieve the sick turmoil inside her.

With a spurt of defiance she exclaimed, 'Peta! What a ridiculous name for a girl! I'll bet her father wanted a son.' She gnawed on her lip before finally admitting, 'I know Ian's not just being a good neighbour. There's something else between them.'

Her brother's straight black brow shot up. 'What?'

'Awareness,' she retorted, temper flashing for a second.

7

'Is this the intuition women are so famous for,' he said drily, 'or is your fear based on something concrete?'

Gillian reined in her anger. It wasn't *fair*; she was four years older than Curt's thirty-two, but the extra years had counted for nothing since he'd turned fifteen and shot up to well over six feet. Those extra inches had given him an edge that his intelligence and tough ruthlessness had honed into a formidable weapon. Although most of the time he was an affectionate brother, when he went into intimidation mode she took notice.

She said unsteadily, 'You might not know much about love, Curt, but don't try to convince me you don't understand sizzle! You were only sixteen when you seduced my best friend, and you haven't been wasting any time since then—'

Shrugging, he broke in, 'Is that all you've got to go on? An awareness of sizzle?'

She flushed at the satirical note in his words and shook her head.

Dispassionately he said, 'It happens, Gillian. It's the way men are; we see a beautiful woman and the hormones begin to stir. An honourable man doesn't follow it up if he's already committed. I've always believed Ian to be honourable.'

'Oh, how you testosterone brigade stick together!' She forced herself to be calm because he distrusted emotional outbursts. Eventually she said in a more temperate voice, 'Curt, I'm Ian's wife. I love him, and I know him very well. Trust me, whatever it is that Ian feels for Peta Grey it's more than a quick, easily forgotten flash of lust. I'd accept that if she was gorgeous, but she's not. She's not even pretty.'

'Then what are you worrying about?' Curt demanded,

adding with cool logic, 'Ian's not likely to throw everything away on a plain woman. What does Peta Grey look like?'

'She's striking,' Gillian admitted resentfully, 'if you like tall, broad-shouldered, *strong* women. And that's one of the reasons I'm worried—she's not Ian's type at all. The only times I've ever seen her in anything smarter than a T-shirt and jeans and gumboots have been when we've invited the neighbours around for drinks or a barbecue. She scrubs up pretty well then, but she's so…so *rural*. All she can talk about is her stock and the measly few hectares she calls a farm.'

She paused, then added with bleak honesty, 'Which is more than Ian and I seem to have to talk about now.'

Curt examined her closely. Small and slight, his sister breathed urban sophistication; on her own ground she'd hold all the weapons. 'So what does Ian see in her?'

Eyes glittering with frustrated tears, Gillian snapped, 'She's tall, and I imagine her mouth and green eyes make her sexy in a kind of earthy, land-girl way. Apart from that she's got lovely skin, brown hair usually dragged off her face and tied with string in a ponytail, and a reasonably good figure.'

Curt inspected his sister from the top of her expertly cut hair to the slim Italian shoes on her narrow feet. 'She doesn't sound like competition. Why would Ian fall for her?'

'Oh, you know Ian—he's always had a soft spot for people who work hard. Probably because he had to haul himself up by his bootstraps.' After a short hesitation she said reluctantly, 'And she's a battler—she's only got a few acres besides the land that Ian leased her, but she manages to scrape a living from it.'

Curt had thought nothing of his brother-in-law's decision to lease a small area to his neighbour. Cut off from the rest of the station by a large gully, the land hadn't been fully utilised. Now he wondered why it hadn't occurred to him to suggest it be planted with trees...

He said judicially, 'You're sophisticated enough to know that men don't fall in love with every woman they admire. There must be more than that to it.'

Her desperation showing, she retorted, 'She's at least ten years younger than I am—she can't be much over twenty-three or -four. And a couple of months ago I noticed that whenever he talked about her—which he no longer does, and that's a bad sign too!—something about his voice set every alarm off.' She looked her brother full in the face. 'You're not the only one in the family with good instincts. I know when my marriage is threatened, and believe me, Peta Grey is a threat.'

Curt's brows drew together but he tempered his voice. 'If you want me to do something about it you're going to have to give me proof, Gilly. So far, you haven't.'

She spread her hands in a gesture that held elements of both appeal and despair. Elegant, manicured hands, he noted, with Ian's engagement and wedding rings making a statement on one long finger.

'I don't think they're lovers yet,' she admitted, 'but it's only a matter of time, and I want us out of Northland before—before it happens. A few months ago Ian was talking about a job in Vanuatu managing your rice plantation there. He seemed intrigued...'

The words trailed away as Curt said quietly, 'Gilly, be reasonable. I can't just move him on without some proof that it's necessary. He's doing a good job on Tanekaha; he's hauled the station into profit under budget, and he's a skilful manager of staff.'

Tears welled in her eyes, but even as he found his handkerchief she fought them back with a flare of anger. 'Oh, see for yourself! I hate showing you these—I'm ashamed I even looked at them!—but if you want proof, here it is.'

She groped in her bag, hauled out a couple of photographs and hurled one onto the big desk. '*Now* tell me I've got nothing to worry about!'

Curt picked up the photograph. His brother-in-law stood facing a woman, a hand lifting to her face.

'Check out this one too,' Gillian said savagely, plonking another down on the desk.

If he'd had any doubt at all, the second shot banished it. This time both the people in the picture had turned towards an out-of-focus blur that might have been a bird swooping low, and the guilt stamped on Ian's face would have convinced anyone.

Frowning, he examined the woman's features. Certainly no beauty, but deep in his gut something stirred, a primal appetite that hardened his voice. 'Who took the shots?'

'Hannah Sillitoe—Mandy's daughter. She got a digital camera in her Christmas stocking. Mandy dropped in to see us on their way back to Auckland after the holidays, and of course Hannah spent every moment outside taking photos of anything that would stay still long enough.'

Curt dropped the shiny images onto his desk. 'How did she get these?'

'She thought she saw a native pigeon fly into the big puriri tree by the stockyards. She's an adventurous kid so she climbed the tree, but she couldn't see any sign of the bird. She was on her way down when Ian and Peta came out of the old barn and stopped to talk.' Her hands clenched by her sides. 'Hannah was intrigued by the way the sun caught Peta's hair, so she snapped them. The flash must have startled the pigeon because it swooped from the tree and flew towards them.'

Curt nodded. 'Go on.'

She indicated the second photograph and finished in a voice brittle with humiliation, 'They both swivelled around. Hannah tried to get a picture of the bird, but got that instead. When Mandy saw them she thought I should know what was going on.'

Curt asked brusquely, 'What happened then?'

'Hannah said they went off in different directions.'

He examined the photographs again, reluctantly admitting they were pretty damning evidence. Everything about the two figures shrieked intimacy—their closeness, the way they inclined subtly towards each other, their unconscious mimicry of stance and posture.

And being a man, he could understand what Ian saw in Peta Grey. The faded T-shirt moulded breasts voluptuous enough to stir a eunuch's blood, and beneath the faded jeans her legs were long and lithe. Her coolly enigmatic face challenged the camera, and her mouth was sultry enough to tempt a saint; what would it take to shatter that air of control and release the passion beneath?

Of course, you might find nothing but naked self-interest there.

Anger smouldered to life inside him. 'Does Ian know you've got these?'

'No, and I'm not going to tell him,' Gillian returned with spirit. 'I'm not that stupid.'

Curt noted the way the sun shone on Peta Grey's hair. The elemental fire in the pit of his stomach burned hotter, transmuting into something more complex than anger. When Gillian spoke he had to yank his gaze from the photograph to focus on her.

'Curt, why don't you come up and see for yourself? Believe me, if I'm wrong I'd be so relieved and grateful.'

Her voice broke on the final word and the smile she'd summoned wavered, then tightened into a grimace as she fought back tears. 'I'm sorry to lump you with this, but there's no one else I trust enough. And no one I can talk to.'

Which was his fault; Gilly had supported him when he needed her, and her love and faith had been punished. Neither of them had spoken to their parents for ten years.

Curt slung an arm around her shoulders and drew her against him. She sniffed valiantly, but eventually surrendered to harsh, difficult sobs, clutching his shirt with desperate hands as she gave up the fight for control. Like him, she'd been conditioned to hide her emotions, so she was terrified at this threat to her marriage.

'All right,' he said quietly when her tears began to ease. 'I can come up next week.'

He'd planned a tryst in Tahiti with his current lover, but this was more important.

Mouth quivering, she reached up and kissed his cheek. 'Thank you,' she said soberly. She stepped back and grimaced at his shirt. 'I've made you all wet—and streaked with lipstick. Have you got a spare shirt here?'

'It doesn't matter, but yes, I have.' He lifted her chin and met her eyes. 'If I think you're wrong, what will you do?'

'Find a counsellor, I suppose,' she said drearily. 'I'll need it, because…oh, because things have been going wrong since before Ian noticed Peta Grey.'

'What things?'

Gillian paused. 'Oh, you might as well know everything. Since we found out that the reason I can't get pregnant is an infection I caught in my wild youth. I never pretended to be a virgin when we met, but as long as I didn't rub his face in my love affairs Ian didn't seem to mind. Discovering why I couldn't conceive is rubbing his face in it with a vengeance, Curt.'

'I don't imagine he was a virgin either when he married,' Curt said forcefully.

'No, but he wasn't careless enough to let himself be made sterile. Ian wants children, and once we got the results he started pulling away.' She dragged in a deep breath. 'He blames me, of course. And like all you men, he's possessive.'

'I don't consider myself possessive,' Curt said brusquely. 'I don't share, but that's not possessiveness.'

'You've never loved anyone enough to be possessive.' His sister gave him a trembling smile. 'Ian might even still love me, but he wants a family, and he—he might be looking for someone who can give him one.' She pulled away and finished steadily, 'Someone who isn't infertile because she slept around.'

Astonished, Curt asked, 'Are you telling me that this Peta Grey is a virgin? How do you know?'

'I don't. There has been gossip, but apparently her father was a very controlling man—he didn't let her go out with boys. Her mother was delicate so Peta left school the day she turned sixteen, and acted as nurse, housekeeper and farmhand until her parents were killed in a car accident a few years later.'

'You seem to have been gossiping to a purpose.' Curt's distaste sharpened his voice.

Gillian shrugged. 'I heard you say once, *Know your enemy*. In a way I feel sorry for the girl. She's spent her life on that little farm working all hours of the day and night to survive.' She looked up, entreaty plain in her lovely face. 'I don't wish her any ill; I just don't want her to wreck my marriage.'

'Has it occurred to you that if Ian wants her, you'll be better off without him?' Curt knew it had to be said, even though his bluntness drove the colour from her face. 'He made vows. If he breaks them, will you ever trust him again?'

Trust Curt to voice her worst fear. Gillian had to stop her hands from twisting together in futile terror. 'I need time,' she told him intensely. 'I love him, and if there's any chance that he still loves me I'll fight this—this *fling*. He's a sophisticated mature man, and she's a…well, she's a *nothing*!'

'If he thinks he's in love with her, any hint of interference might persuade him to leave you.'

'You always did make me face consequences,' she said in a low voice, 'and yes, I accept that. If he does leave, I—I don't know what I'll do, but I'll deal with it. It's the wondering and waiting and uncertainty that's tearing me apart.'

'I'm not a miracle worker,' Curt warned her.

'You'll fix it,' she said eagerly. 'You've always done what you set your mind to. I have complete faith in you!'

That, he knew. Her faith had cost her dearly. 'What exactly did you have in mind?'

Gillian rushed on, 'Couldn't you make a play for her? If she's like ninety-eight per cent of womankind she'll fall at your feet in worshipful delight.'

'You grossly overestimate my effect on your sex,' he said drily. 'Is that what you want me to do?'

Her anxious eyes searched his face. 'I—well, probably not. Nobody, especially not Ian, would believe that you'd find a girl like her attractive.' She gave a twisted smile. 'Your preference for beautiful women is too well known. But there must be some way out of this, because I'm certain she's not in love with him.'

'How do you know?' Curt asked ironically. 'And don't tell me it's women's intuition.'

'Ha! That's rich coming from you!' Now that he'd

agreed she was confident again, her eyes gleaming and her smile reckless. 'Everyone believes you dragged Dad's sinking firm out of the mire and into the stratosphere with brilliance and sheer force of will, but you told me once that most of the time you followed your gut instinct.'

'And sometimes I ignored it,' he said sardonically.

'Well, intuition's got nothing to do with this. You got to the top because as well as being brutally clever you're good at reading body language,' she said crisply. 'So am I. And her body language tells me Peta Grey is *not* in love with Ian. She wants out of being stuck away on a little farm miles from the nearest village, with no money, no prospects except hard work, and no chance of meeting a decent man. Except married ones!' she finished bitterly.

Curt glanced down at the photographs, his gaze caught and held by Peta Grey's challenging face with its lush, firmly disciplined mouth. His protective affection for Gillian warred with a darker, more subtle instinct that warned him of danger if he didn't keep out of this.

But looking after his sister was a habit too strong to be broken. He leaned over and wrote something in his desk diary. 'All right, I'll see you next week.'

She let out a long sigh. 'Thank you,' she said in a voice that quivered. 'I'll be eternally grateful.'

'I'm not promising anything,' he said abruptly. 'Can I take you out to lunch?'

'I'd love to go out to lunch with you, but I'm already booked with a couple of old girlfriends. Besides, I bet you've got some high-powered meeting with important people.'

'Guilty,' he agreed, with the rare smile that dazzled even his sister. 'But I'd have cut it short if you needed me.'

She came up to him in a small, scented rush and pulled his head down to kiss his lean cheek, then rested her head on his chest for a second. 'I knew I could rely on you,' she said, and gave him a gallant smile and left.

Frowning, Curt watched her go, then called his secretary. 'Have John Stevens contact me as soon as possible,' he said, hard eyes missing nothing of the traffic heading towards the magnificently columned Museum. Shining like a white temple in the summer sun, Auckland's tribute to its war dead crowned a hill that commanded the city and the harbour.

At any other time he'd look forward to a week on Tanekaha, but even apart from the loss of time with Anna he didn't expect to enjoy this stay. He swivelled and picked up the photographs again, gazing not at his brother-in-law but at the woman so nearly in Ian's arms. The sun shimmered in lazy golden fire across her head; at her feet he could see a hat, as though an ungentle hand had pushed it off.

To make it easier to kiss that sensuous mouth?

Probably; there had been no kiss, but that didn't mean one hadn't been planned.

His mouth compressing, he dropped the photographs as though they burned his fingertips. Think possible gold-digger, he advised himself, and find out everything you can about her so you know which strings to pull.

If he had to he'd even buy her off, although it would go against the grain. Still, he'd part with anything if it would save Gillian's marriage; apart from his natural affection for his sister, he owed her more than he could ever repay.

CHAPTER ONE

PETA'S head came up sharply. Hoof-beats coming up the hill? Who the hell could it be? Not Ian, who'd be driving his ute. Her mouth tightened into a straight line. So it had to be Curt Blackwell McIntosh—the owner of Tanekaha Station, hunk, tycoon, and adored brother of Gillian Matheson.

A convulsive jerk beneath her hands switched her attention back to the calf.

'Just stay still,' she told it in her most soothing tone while she eased a rope around it, 'and we'll have you out of this mud in no time—oh, *damn*!' as the dog let out a ferocious fusillade of barks.

'Shut up, Laddie,' she roared, but it was too late; thoroughly spooked, the calf found enough energy to thrash around wildly, spattering her with more smelly mud and water and embedding itself even further in the swamp.

Muttering an oath, she lifted its head so that it could breathe, then snapped a curt order to 'Get in behind' at the chastened dog.

If Curt McIntosh was as big as he looked in photographs, he was just the man to help her drag this calf out!

Her mouth relaxed into a scornful smile. 'Not likely,' she told the calf, now quiescent although its eyes were rolling wildly. 'Far too messy for an international magnate. Still, he might send a minion to help.'

And that would be fine too, provided the minion wasn't Ian.

She squinted against the sun. Like a storm out of the

north, Curt McIntosh and his mount crested the hill and thundered towards her, a single, powerful entity both beautiful and menacing.

An odd chill of apprehension hollowed out her stomach. To quell it, she sniffed, 'Take a good look, Laddie. That's what's known as being born to the saddle!'

But Curt McIntosh hadn't been. He was an Aucklander, and the money that financed his pastoral empire came from the mysterious and inscrutable area of information technology; his firm was a world leader in its field. He might ride like a desert warrior, but his agricultural and pastoral interests were a mere hobby.

Horse and rider changed direction, slowing as they came towards the small patch of swamp. A primitive chill of foreboding shivered across Peta's nerve ends; as well as being a brilliant rider, Curt McIntosh was big. Quelling a crazy urge to abandon the calf and get the hell out of there, she watched the horse ease back into a walk. At least Curt Etc McIntosh and his horse weren't pounding up with a grand flourish that would scare the calf into further suicidal endeavours.

'Of course it's black,' she murmured to the dog bristling with curiosity at her heels. 'Raiders always choose black horses—good for intimidation. Not that he's going to find any loot here, but I bet you an extra dog-biscuit tonight that horse is a stallion.'

She'd heard enough about Curt McIntosh to be very wary; his reputation for ruthlessness had grown along with his fortune, but he'd been ruthless right from the start. Barely out of university, he'd manoeuvred his father out of the family firm in a bitterly fought takeover, dragged the company into profitability, then used its resources to conquer the world.

'The dominant male personified,' she stated beneath her

breath. It hurt her pride to remain kneeling in the mud as though waiting for a big strong man to come and rescue her and the calf, but she didn't dare loosen her grip on its slippery hide to grab the rope.

'Hang on, I'll just tie the horse.' A deep voice, cool, authoritative, completely lord-of-the-manor.

It should have set Peta's teeth on edge; instead, it reached inside her and tied knots in her system. Without looking up she called, 'OK.'

Cool; that's all she had to do—act cool. She had no need to feel guilty; for all McIntosh's toughness and brilliance he couldn't know that his brother-in-law had touched her cheek and looked at her with eyes made hot by unwanted desire and need.

Thank heavens for that pigeon in the puriri tree! Its typically tempestuous interruption had stopped him from doing anything they'd both regret.

Until then she'd had no idea that Ian had crossed the invisible line between friendship and attachment. Shocked and alarmed, since then she'd made darned sure that he hadn't caught her alone.

As though her turbulent thoughts had got through to the calf, it suddenly bawled and tried to lever itself further into the sticky clutches of the mud.

Clutching it, she said, 'Calm down, calm down, I'm trying to help you. And Laddie, if you bark again there'll be no snacks for a month!'

Laddie, barely adult and still not fully trained, tried to restrain himself as Peta struggled with the demented calf. Out of the corner of her eye she saw the tall rider come towards her; Laddie gave up on silence and obedience and let rip with another salvo of defiance. The calf thrashed around, and a lump of smelly goo flew up and hit Peta on the jawbone.

Furious with everyone and everything—most of all with herself—she shouted, 'Quiet!' at the dog, wiped the worst of the mud off onto her shoulder, and bent again to the calf.

Still murmuring in her softest, most reassuring tone, Peta ignored the icy emptiness beneath her ribs. It was, she thought bitterly, utterly typical that the landlord she'd never met should find her spattered in mud and dealing with something no respectable farmer would have allowed happen.

It had to be a McIntosh thing. For all her charm, his sister always managed to make her feel at a total disadvantage too.

Silence echoed around her, while the skin on the back of her neck and between her shoulder blades tightened in a primitive warning. Laddie made a soft growling noise in his throat.

'I'll do that,' a deep voice said.

Although she fiercely resented that uncompromising tone, a bolt of awareness streaked down Peta's spine, setting off alarms through her body. As well as that peremptory command, his voice was textured by power and sexual confidence. It set every prejudice she had buzzing in outrage.

Slowly, deliberately, she turned her head and took in the man behind her with one calm, dismissive survey.

At least that was what it was meant to be. Maddeningly, cold blue eyes snared hers before she'd got any further than his face—handsome, superb bone structure—a face where danger rode shotgun on authority.

Damn, she thought helplessly, he is gorgeous! Her throat closed. And up close he was even bigger than she'd suspected, long-legged and lithe, with shoulders that would be a credit to a rugby player. Clear and hard and ruthless, his gaze summoned an instant, protective antagonism.

Curt McIntosh's formidable toughness hammered home her acute vulnerability. Oh, what she'd have given to be able to get to her feet and look him in the eye!

'Thank you,' she said. 'I almost had her out, and then the dog barked—' Shocked, she stopped the excuse before it had time to shame her.

'Just keep her head above the mud.' He picked up the rope she'd been trying to get under the calf's stomach.

Heart contracting in her chest, Peta ran a swift glance over his clothes. Well-worn the checked shirt and faded jeans might be, but they'd been made for his lean body and long, strongly muscled legs. Of course, his sister patronised the best designers.

It was probably this thought that loosened the links of her self-control. 'You'll get covered in mud,' she pointed out.

His smile narrowed into a thin line. Another shiver—icy this time—scudded down Peta's backbone.

'It wouldn't be the first time,' he said. 'I'm not afraid of a bit of dirt, and you're not strong enough to haul it out by yourself.'

True, and why shouldn't he experience first-hand what rural life could be like? 'It needs know-how, not just brute strength.' She summoned a too-sweet smile, inwardly flinching when his eyes turned into ice crystals. 'Although the brute strength will be very useful.'

The calf chose that moment to kick out in a desperate surge forward. Peta made a swift lunge at it, lost her balance and pitched towards the smelly mud. Just before the point of no return, a hard hand grabbed the waistband of her shorts, another scooped beneath her outstretched arms, and with a strength that overwhelmed her Curt McIntosh yanked her back onto firm land.

Gasping, she struggled to control her legs. For one stark

second she felt the imprint of every muscle in his hard torso on her back, and the strength of his arm across her breasts. Although the heat storming her body robbed her of breath, strength and wits, instinct kicked in. *Move!* it snapped.

'I—thanks,' she muttered. But when he let her go she stumbled, and he caught her again, this time by the shoulders.

'Are you all right?'

The level detachment of his voice humiliated her. 'Yes, thank you,' she said, striving for her usual crispness.

He loosened his grip and she stepped away. With the imprint of his knuckles burning the skin at her waist, she blurted, 'You've got fast reactions for such a big man.'

Oh, God! How was that for truly sophisticated repartee?

His brows rising, he squatted to reach for the calf. Holding its head above the mud he said, 'I hope this isn't one of my calves.'

A spasm of apprehension tightened her nerves another notch. More mildly she said, 'Yes, it's one of yours. If you can lift her enough to get her belly free of the mud, I'll slide the rope under her.'

Be careful, she told herself as he crouched down beside her. Clamp your mouth on any more gauche remarks, and remember to be suitably impressed by his strength and kindness once the calf's out of the swamp.

This man could make her life extremely difficult. Not only did she lease ten vital hectares from him, but her only income this year was the money she'd earn from that contract. As well, sole access to her land was over one of his farm roads.

With two rescuers, one of them impressively powerful and surprisingly deft, freeing the calf turned out to be ridiculously simple. Curt McIntosh moved well, Peta thought reluctantly as they stood up, and he was in full control of those seriously useful muscles. She was no lightweight, and he'd saved her from falling flat on her face in the mud with an ease that seemed effortless, then hauled the calf free without even breathing hard. Clearly he spent hours in the gym—no, he probably paid a personal trainer megabucks to keep him fit.

Ignoring the odd, tugging sensation in the pit of her stomach, she bent to examine the calf, collapsed now on the ground but trying to get to its feet.

'Where do you want her?' Curt asked, astonishing her by picking up the small animal, apparently not concerned at the liberal coating of mud he'd acquired during the rescue.

Infuriatingly, the calf lay still, as though tamed by the overwhelming force of the man's personality.

And if I believe that, Peta thought ironically, I'm an idiot; the poor thing's too exhausted to wriggle even the tip of its tail.

She'd been silent too long; his brows lifted and to her irritation and disgust her heart quickened in involuntary response. The midsummer sun beat down on them, and she wished fervently she'd worn her old jeans instead of the ragged shorts that displayed altogether too much of her long legs.

'On the back of the ute.' She led the way to the elderly, battered vehicle.

He lowered the calf into the calf-cage on the tray of the ute. 'Will she be all right there?'

'I'll drive carefully,' she said. The manners her mother had been so fussy about compelled her to finish with stiff politeness, 'Thank you. If you hadn't helped I'd have taken much longer to get her out.'

He straightened and stepped back, unsparing eyes searching her face with a cool assessment that abraded her already raw composure. 'So we meet at last, Peta Grey,' he said levelly.

Pulses jumping, she could only say, 'Yes. How do you do?' Mortification burned across the long, lovely sweep of her cheekbones. Bullseye, she thought raggedly; yet another supremely sophisticated bit of repartee!

He smiled, and she almost reeled back in shock. Oh, hell, she thought furiously, he could probably soothe rattlesnakes with that smile—female ones, anyway! 'How do you do?' he replied courteously.

Just stop this idiocy now! she ordered herself. Your heart is not really thudding so loud he can hear it.

But perhaps it was, because when she looked up she saw his eyes rest a second on the soft hollow at the base of her throat. Thoughts and emotions jangling around in turbulent disarray, she went on painstakingly, 'And I believe we'll be seeing each other tomorrow night at your sister's barbecue.'

'I'm looking forward to it,' Curt McIntosh said, somehow managing to turn the conventional response into a threat. He looked around at the paddocks that belonged to him. 'Your lease is up for renewal, I believe.'

It wasn't a question; of course he knew it was due for renegotiation. Foreboding brushed her skin like a cold feather. Seriously unnerved, she evaded his gaze and looked past him to his mount. With lowered head, the big black animal was cautiously inspecting Laddie. 'In a month's time.'

'I'll give you fair warning,' he said, still in that pleasant tone, although now she recognised the steel beneath each word.

Defiantly, she lifted her head to meet his eyes. Cold blue had swallowed up the grey rims, and they were too keen.

The hollowness beneath her ribs expanding into a cold vacuum, Peta braced herself. 'Warning of what?'

Instead of answering Curt McIntosh whistled; Laddie frisked across to his frozen owner while the horse—a gelding, Peta noted tensely, not a stallion—paced with measured strides towards the man who'd summoned it.

He swung up into the saddle and gathered the reins in one lean, mud-stained hand, examining her with an unsparing gaze. She took an involuntary step backwards. Horse and rider seemed to blot out the sun.

All trace of emotion gone from his face, from his voice, Curt said, 'I'm in two minds about renewing it.'

Panic kicked her brutally in the stomach. Peta looked him full in his starkly powerful face and tried to hide the thin note of desperation in her voice. 'Why? It would cost you a lot of money to build a bridge across the gully and link it to the rest of the station.'

He didn't tell her that money was the last thing tycoons lacked, but she saw the glint of mockery in the depths of his eyes when he said negligently, 'That's my worry.'

One glance at that formidable face told her that pleas wouldn't work. Swallowing, she said, 'I was informed that it would be all right...'

Her voice tailed away when she realised that he was once more looking at the long line of her throat. Her breath blocked her airways. Then he raised his eyes and she had to stop herself from flinching because dark fire flared for a second in the blue depths.

'Then whoever told you that made promises he knew he might not be able to keep. I have plans for this land.'

Without waiting for an answer, he made a soft, chirruping noise. Obediently the gelding picked up its hooves and turned away.

Motionless, her mind darting after thoughts like a terrier

after rabbits, Peta watched them go. Of course the children of rich parents had advantages, and learning to ride as well as you could walk was just one of them. She'd never learned; her father hadn't seen the necessity.

But then, he hadn't seen the necessity of a lot of things. After he'd died she'd relied on her neighbours' offers of lifts into Kowhai Bay until she'd learned to drive.

And Curt McIntosh was another dominant male who thought he had a God-given right to make decisions and control people.

Slowly, stiffly, she got into the ute, but once in its stuffy interior she sat with hands gripping the wheel while she stared unseeingly ahead.

On the rare occasions they'd met, Gillian Matheson had spoken of her brother—so strong, so clever, so drop-dead stunning that women fell at his feet! But Gillian was a restless, dissatisfied woman, and often her words had seemed to be aimed at her husband; although Peta had listened politely, she hadn't believed in this paragon. After all, extremely powerful magnates were by definition attractive to women—some women, anyway.

She believed Gillian now.

'Up, Laddie!' she called, patting the seat beside her, and waited while the delighted dog jumped in. 'Yes, this is a real treat for you, isn't it? Just don't get used to it; the only reason you get to ride in front is because on the tray you'll spook that calf even more.'

Slotting the key into the ute, she turned it, but something about the engine's note brought her brows together. It was missing again. 'Not now,' she breathed, putting the vehicle into gear.

Instead of working in the garden that evening she'd poke around the motor and see what she could find. And if it wasn't something she could fix it would have to wait, because she couldn't afford any repairs this month.

But during the careful trip down to the calf-shed, she wasn't working out what she could do if the knock in the engine was too much for her basic mechanical skills. Her mind dwelt obsessively on Curt McIntosh, whose touch had sent her hormones on a dizzying circuit of every nerve in her body.

And whose relentless authority and aggressive, arrogant masculinity reminded her so much of her father she had to unclench her jaw and rein in a storm of automatic resentment and anger.

He controlled her future.

If he refused to renew the lease she'd have to get rid of her own stock, the ones she was rearing for sale in two years' time to finance a new tractor. Because Ian's calves—Tanekaha's calves, she corrected hastily—were covered by contract, their needs were paramount. Without the leased acreage she had barely enough land to finish them off and send them back in good condition.

But she desperately needed a new tractor. Hers had to be coaxed along, and six months ago the mechanic told her it wasn't going to last much more than a couple of years—if she was lucky.

She braked and got out to open a gate. Without the income from her stock she'd be in real trouble; extra hours pumping petrol at the local service station wouldn't cover the cost of a new tractor.

Swallowing to ease her dry throat, she got back into the ute and took it through the gate. And there was little chance of more casual work at Kowhai Bay; the little holiday resort sank back into lethargy once the hot Northland sun headed for the equator.

After she'd closed the gate behind the ute, she leaned

against the top bar and looked out over countryside that swept from the boundary to the coast.

Her smallholding was insignificant in that glorious panorama, yet the land she could see was only a small part of Tanekaha Station. Blue hills inland formed the western boundary, and the land stretched far along the coastline of beaches and stark headlands, shimmering golden-green in the bright heat.

Lovely in a wild, rugged fashion, serene under the midsummer sun, it represented power and wealth. If it came to swords at sunrise, Curt McIntosh had every advantage.

Perhaps she should give up the struggle, sell her land for what she could get, and go and find herself a life.

She bit her lip. All she knew was farming.

'And that's what I like doing,' she said belligerently, swinging back into the vehicle and slamming the door behind her.

Once she'd settled the calf undercover in a temporary pen made of hay bales, she glanced at her watch and went inside.

After a shower and a change of clothes, she went across to the bookshelves that bordered the fireplace, taking down her father's Maori dictionary.

'"Tanekaha",' she read out loud, and laughed ironically as a bubbling noise told her the kettle was boiling. 'How very apt!'

Tane was the Maori word for man, *kaha* for strong. Ian Matheson was a strong man, but his brother-in-law was out on his own.

'And whoever chose his first name must have known what sort of baby they were dealing with,' she decided, pouring the water into the pot. 'Curt by name and curt by nature.'

Grimly amused, she returned to the bookshelves and

found another elderly volume. '"English and Scottish Sur-
names",' she murmured as she flipped through it. '"Mc-
Intosh—son of the chieftain"! Somehow I'm not in the
least surprised!'

In the chilly bedroom she'd converted into an office, she
pulled out a file and sank down at the desk, poring over
the lease agreement in search of loopholes.

Curt glanced around his room. The old homestead, now the
head shepherd's house, had been transported to another site
on the station. In its place Gillian had spent the last two
years—and a lot of money—supervising the building of the
new house, and then decorating it. Her innate artistry meant
that each exquisite room breathed good taste, but she'd paid
only lip-service to the homestead's main function as the
administrative head of a substantial pastoral concern.

At least she'd kept the integrity of its rural setting and
hadn't gone for stark minimalism, he thought drily.

He scanned the photograph on the chest of drawers,
taken on the day Gillian married Ian. His sister glowed, so
radiantly happy she seemed incandescent with it, and Ian
was smiling down at her, his expression a betraying mixture
of tenderness and desire.

Almost the same expression with which he'd looked at
Peta Grey in those damned photographs.

What the hell had gone wrong?

It was a rhetorical question. Several things had gone
wrong; an urbanite born and bred and a talented artist,
Gillian had found it difficult to adjust to life in the country
as Ian had worked his way up to managing the biggest
station in what Gillian referred to as 'Curt's collection'.
She'd stopped painting a couple of years previously, about
the time she'd discovered she couldn't have children.

A disappointment Ian clearly shared, Curt thought sternly.

Gillian's suspicions were probably right. In the woman next door, Ian had seen the things his wife lacked—the promise of children and an affinity for the land.

As well, he'd seen something Gillian had missed entirely—a tempting sensuality. Curt swore beneath his breath. Ian's wandering eyes were no longer so startling. Barely concealed beneath the layer of mud and her suspicious antagonism, Peta Grey radiated a vibrant, vital heat that had stirred a dangerous hunger into uncomfortable and reckless life.

It still prowled his body. Not that she was beautiful; *striking* described her exactly. Her skin, fine-grained as the sleekest silk, glowed in the sunlight, its golden tinge echoed by an astonishing golden tracery across her green eyes. Tall and strong, when she walked her lean-limbed, supple grace was like watching music materialise.

Perhaps it was simply her colouring that had got to him; all that gold, he thought with a mocking twist to his smile. Skin, eyes—even the tips of her lashes were gold. Not to forget the golden-brown hair, thick and glossy as a stream of dark honey.

His brain, not normally given to flights of fancy, summoned from some hidden recess a picture of that hair falling across his chest in silken disorder, and his breath quickened.

Hell! He strode across the room to the desk, stopping to flick up the screen of his laptop. While the state-of-the-art equipment purred into life, he sat down and prepared to concentrate on the task ahead.

But work, which usually took precedence over everything else, didn't do the trick today. When he found himself doodling a pair of sultry eyes and remembering the exact texture of her skin beneath his knuckles as he'd hauled her back from the swamp, and the tantalising pressure of her full breasts against his forearm, he swore again, more luridly this time. After putting down the pen with more than normal care, he crumpled the sheet of paper into a ball and lobbed it into the waste-paper basket with barely concealed violence.

Other women had made an impact on him, but none of them had taken up residence in his mind. He resented that sort of power being wielded by a simple country hick on the make, someone he neither knew nor trusted.

He got to his feet. He was, he realised contemptuously, aroused and unable to control it.

The word 'jealousy' floated across his consciousness, only to be instantly dismissed. There had to be some sort of connection for jealousy to happen.

'Accept it,' he said with cool distaste. 'You want Peta Grey—reluctantly—but you're not going to take up Gillian's suggestion and make a play for her.' His main concern was to get her out of his sister's life, and that process had already begun.

Relieved by the summons of his mobile telephone, he caught it up. His frown wasn't reflected in his voice when he answered the query on the other end. 'Working, but you knew that.'

His lover said something teasing, and he laughed. As Anna spoke he noted the long line of dark trees on the northern horizon. They hid, he knew, the small cottage where Peta Grey lived.

Anna's seductive voice seemed to fade; he had to force himself to concentrate on her conversation, and found it difficult to look away from that row of trees.

'...so I'll see you next Friday night?' Anna asked.

'Yes.'

She knew better than to keep him talking; he hung up with a frown.

Time to put an end to their affair. Anna was trying subtly to work her way into his life, and although their relationship was based on more than sex it would be cruel to let her cherish any false illusions. She wasn't in love with him, but in him she probably saw an excellent chance to establish herself.

As Peta no doubt saw Ian.

His expression hardened. It was time Peta Grey learned that actions always had repercussions.

A knock brought his head up. 'Come in.'

Gillian peered around the door, a gallant smile hiding her tension. 'Lunch in fifteen minutes.'

He nodded. 'I'll be there.'

Once she'd closed the door he glanced at his watch before dialling his lawyers in Auckland.

Peta scanned the cloudless sky, then walked back inside. It was going to be a hot, dry summer and autumn; she could feel it in her bones. Each morning she woke to heat and walked across dewless grass that was slowly fading from green to gold. The springs were already failing, the creeks dwindling. The wind stayed serenely in the north-west, pushing humid air from the tropics over the narrow peninsula that was Northland. In the afternoons taunting clouds built in the sky, huge masses of purple-black and grey, only to disappear over the horizon without following through on their promise.

If no rain came she'd need money for supplemental feed for the calves—money she didn't have, and wouldn't get from the bank.

Moving mechanically, she picked up her lunch dishes and washed them. She just had time to shift the older calves into another paddock, then she'd drive to Kowhai Bay for her stint at the petrol station. Once there she'd ask Sandy if she could work longer hours.

That morning the mail had brought a letter from an Auckland firm of solicitors telling her that it was possible the lease would not be renewed. However the contract to raise calves for Tanekaha Station's dairy herds would remain in effect, although if she decided to sell her farm some agreement could be made in which she wouldn't come out the loser.

The cold, impersonal prose removed any lingering hope that Curt Blackwell McIntosh might change his autocratic mind.

Last night she'd sat over the figures until too late, juggling them as she tried—and failed—to find ways of increasing her income.

And when she'd finally gone to bed she couldn't sleep; instead she lay in bed listening to the familiar night sounds and wondered how much her land would be worth if she put it on the market.

In Kowhai Bay's only petrol station, Sandy shook his head when she asked about more work. 'Sorry, Peta, but it's just not there,' he said, dark eyes sympathetic. 'If I give you extra hours, I'll have to sack someone else.'

'It's OK,' she said quickly. 'Don't worry about it.' But her stomach dropped and the flick of fear beneath her heart strengthened into something perilously like panic.

Her shift over, she called into the only real-estate agency in Kowhai Bay, and asked about the value of her land.

'Not much, I'm afraid—although I'd need to come out and check the house and buildings over.' A year or so older than she was, the agent smiled sympathetically at her as she picked up a volume of district maps, flipping the pages until she found the page she wanted.

Pride stung, Peta held her head high.

'It's a difficult one,' the agent said simply. 'No access, that's the biggie—really, you depend on Tanekaha Station's goodwill to get in and out. I wonder what on earth they were thinking of when they let the previous owners cut that block off the station and sell it to your father.'

'There's an access agreement,' Peta told her.

She didn't look convinced. 'Yes, well, there are other problems too—livestock isn't sexy at the moment, and with last month's trade talks failing, beef prices won't rise for at least a couple of years. Anyway, you don't have enough land to make an income from farming. If you planted olives on it, or avocados, you might attract the lifestyle crowd, but it's too far out of town for most of them. They usually prefer to live close to a beach or on the outskirts. And let's face it, Kowhai Bay hasn't yet reached fashionable status.'

'I hope it never does,' Peta said staunchly.

The agent grinned. 'Come on now, Peta, admit that the place could do with a bit of livening up! For a while after Curt McIntosh bought Tanekaha I thought it might happen, but I suppose it's just too far from Auckland—OK if you're rich enough to fly in and out, but not for anyone else.' She looked up. 'If you're thinking of moving, the logical thing to do is ask McIntosh to buy your block.'

CHAPTER TWO

LOOKED at objectively, the land agent's advice was practical—more or less exactly what Peta had been expecting. But how much would Curt pay for her few hectares? As little as possible, she thought, rubbing the back of her neck in frustration; after all, he held all the cards.

'How much do you think it's worth?' she asked, and sucked in her breath as the woman shrugged.

'You'd need to get it valued properly, but off the top of my head and without prejudice, no more than government valuation.'

'I see.' If it sold for government valuation she'd be able to pay off the mortgage she'd inherited from her father. Nothing more; she'd be adrift with no education, and no skills beyond farming.

Peta left the real-estate office so deep in thought that she almost bumped into someone examining the window of Kowhai Bay's sole boutique.

'Peta!'

'Oh—Nadine!' Laughing, they embraced. Peta stepped back and said admiringly, 'Aren't you the fine up-and-coming city lawyer! I guessed you'd be home for Granny Wai's ninetieth birthday.'

'Absolutely. She's so looking forward to it, you can't imagine!'

That night Peta saw for herself. The big hall at the local marae was crowded with people, many of them the matriarch's descendants, mingling with neighbours, local dignitaries, and visitors from points around the world.

Surrounded by flowers and streamers and balloons, relishing the laughter and the gossip and the reunions, Granny held court in an elegant black dress, heirloom greenstone *hei-tiki* pendant gleaming on her breast.

Nadine pushed politely past a couple of elderly men to say with envy, 'That honey-gold colour suits you superbly. Did you make your top?'

'Yes.' Peta enjoyed sewing, and the silky, sleeveless garment had only taken a couple of hours to finish.

'Thought so.' She turned and waved to her great-grandmother. 'Isn't she amazing? You watch—as soon as the band strikes up she'll be on the floor. Pino's threatened to jive with her, and Mum's terrified she'll break her hip, but if Granny wants to jive, Granny will! She's as tough as old boots, bless her.'

A subdued stir by the door caught their attention.

'Uh-oh,' Nadine said beneath her breath. 'Speaking of tough, the Tanekaha Station clan has just arrived.'

Peta opened her mouth then closed it again. Of course the Mathesons and Curt would have been invited.

Her friend sighed elaborately. 'You know, Curt McIntosh is a magnificent, gorgeous man. Pity he's got the soul of a shark.'

'A shark?' Jolted, Peta glanced across the room, in time to see Curt lift Granny's hand to his mouth and kiss it.

The gesture should have looked stagy and incongruous, but he carried it off with a panache that sent heat shafting down her spine. Dragging her gaze back to Nadine's face, she asked, 'A shark as in being dishonest and sleazy?'

'Oh, no, never that! He's got a reputation for absolute fairness; deal well with him, and he'll deal well with you. Just don't expect any loving kindness,' her friend said drily. 'Of course, sharks can't help being the most lethal predators in the sea. It's inborn in them, like being cold-blooded and dangerous.' She peered across the intervening crowd. 'I thought he might bring along the latest very good friend, Anna Lee, but clearly no. This wouldn't be her scene, anyway.'

'Hmm, I deduce that you know her and don't like her.' Peta refused to wonder why discovering that Curt had a lover seared into her composure as painfully as an acid burn.

Her friend rolled her eyes. 'I saw them together a couple of nights ago at her art exhibition. She is very chic. She is very artistic. She does installations. And she thinks lawyers—especially those who haven't yet clawed their way off the bottom rung—are Philistine scum.'

Laughing, Peta shot another glance across the hall, something inside her twisting as her eyes were captured by an enigmatic grey-blue gaze. Curt McIntosh's dark head inclined in a nod that had something regal to it.

Not to be outdone, she responded with an aloof smile before turning back to Nadine. 'Don't tell me you *told* her you didn't like her installations?'

'Of course not!' Nadine primmed her mouth. 'I have much better manners than that. My expression must have given me away. But when I buy an installation it will be more substantial than a collection of found objects depicting the primordial rhythm of creation.'

Peta grinned. 'Urk!'

'Just so,' Nadine said smugly. 'But she's very beautiful, so I don't blame the fabulous Curt for falling for her, even though I'd have expected more from him. He's completely brilliant.' She sighed and added with a smirk, 'It's a pity men are such superficial beings. Yet they've got the gall to claim that *we're* driven by hormones!'

It was almost impossible to imagine Curt at the mercy

of his hormones, Peta decided. He might behave like a shark, but he was fully in control.

On the other hand what did she know about the other sex? Nothing much, just enough to be certain that she was never going to marry a dominant man. Her father's rigid insistence on being head of the family had been enough for her; when—if—she married, she'd choose a kind, decent man who understood that women had needs and brains and the right to have an opinion.

'Evolution has a lot to answer for,' she said brightly, and for the next half-hour or so managed to ignore Curt and the Mathesons.

Later, after several dances and an animated conversation with another school friend who'd come back from Australia for the occasion, she turned around, tossing a laughing remark over her shoulder as she headed off to pay her respects to Granny.

Only to discover a large male blocking her path; she pulled up in mid-stride, stopping far too close to a faultless white shirt and a magnificently tailored suit.

Before she had time to draw breath two strong hands gripped her upper arms. Heat radiated through her in a wild, impulsive flood as Curt murmured in a deep, sardonic voice for her ears only, 'I seem to be making a habit of this.'

He released her, but didn't move away. Around them people talked and laughed and called out, yet she was trapped with him in sizzling silence.

Peta thought headily that the air between them must be glittering in a frenzy of electrons and atoms, or whatever it was made of. She almost looked down to check whether tiny lightning flashes connected them in fierce, strange intimacy.

Pasting a smile onto trembling lips, she mustered her defences and said, 'Be grateful—there's no mud this time.'

Mockery gleamed between his dense black lashes. 'A complete change of appearance,' he agreed with a disturbing intonation that sent more hot little shivers down her spine.

He didn't move; she couldn't. His will and determination bored into her like some psychic energy.

And although she knew it was dangerous, that she should step back, make some light, stupid remark and *get the hell out of there*, she lifted her head and looked him in the face. He was smiling, yet something formidable about his expression reminded her sharply of Nadine's words, although his eyes challenged her description of him as a shark, because sharks were inhumanly cold.

Whereas heat burned in Curt's eyes and touched his smile with a tantalising promise of passionate satisfaction. It enveloped her—a potent, charged aura of sexual charisma hot enough to set sirens clamouring in every cell of her body. Shocked and bewildered, she felt her breasts expand and an odd, drawing sensation tighten their peaks, both disconcerting and intensely pleasurable.

If she didn't get out of there he'd see what was happening. Panicking, she dragged air into her lungs, feeding enough oxygen to her starved brain to prod her instincts into life.

She stepped away and thankfully fell back on the inanities of polite small talk. 'Hello, Curt. Fancy seeing you here.' She hoped that he hadn't heard the feverish inflection in each word.

Fat chance.

His eyes glinted and his smile hardened into mockery. 'Why the surprise?' he drawled.

'It doesn't seem quite your sort of thing.' Desperate to get away, she glanced at her watch. 'I'm just on my way to wish the guest of honour a happy birthday, so if you'll excuse—'

A flourish of chords from the band broke into her words, silencing the chatter; when it died one of Granny's great-grandsons seized the microphone and announced, 'A special request from Granny—an invitation waltz!'

The youngsters groaned, but when Granny chose one of them to dance, the teenager partnered her with expert ease.

'I don't think she's interested in talking to you just now,' Curt said satirically.

'I realise that.' The tension and fear that had ridden her since he'd informed her of his cold-blooded decision to not renew the lease had returned, almost replacing that fierce, perilous awareness. How on earth was she to get away from him without making herself look a fool?

And then the music stopped, and Granny appeared in front of them, her autocratic face alight with humour as she chose Curt.

'Stay there,' she commanded Peta. 'I'll send him back to you when I've finished with him.'

Everyone around laughed, including Peta, although she felt as though her hostess's teasing words had branded her. Once the band started up again, she seized the opportunity to disappear into the crowd, but before she'd taken more than a couple of steps she was claimed by one of Nadine's cousins for the waltz.

They barely had time to catch up on their lives before the young master of ceremonies called out, 'Change again, everyone, for the last time!' and her partner whirled her back to the place he'd found her.

And to Curt.

'Here she is, man,' her partner said, grinning as he relinquished her. 'Apart from Granny she's the best dancer in the room.'

Curt said something Peta didn't catch, but it made Nadine's cousin laugh.

'My dance,' Curt said, and there was nothing humorous in his tone.

Peta stiffened, but she couldn't refuse to dance with him. Heady anticipation battling pride, she let herself be turned into his embrace and swept onto the floor.

Big men were often a little awkward, but not Curt; he moved with a smooth grace that had a strangely weakening effect on her spine and knees. Although the arm around her waist kept her a fraction of an inch away from him, she was sharply, painfully aware of a faint scent, warm and male and sexy, that owed nothing to aftershave.

The melting sensation in the pit of her stomach transmuted into a flood of terrifying response that came too close to hunger. She didn't *do* instant attraction—but then she'd never met another man with this combination of authority and sexual confidence.

'I've met your stunning friend before,' he said. 'In Auckland at an art exhibition.'

'Yes, she told me. You were with the artist.'

Before he could answer an elderly couple strayed into their path. Curt swung her around, pulling her closer as they moved smoothly into a pivot that carried them out of the way of the other dancers.

For a couple of seconds she lay against him, one heavily muscled leg between hers as he turned her, his arm hard across her back. A hot pulse of forbidden pleasure throbbed along her veins and her brain shut down, allowing every tiny stimulus to run riot through her.

And then his arm loosened. For a second she was so dazzled by his closeness that she stayed where she was, until she caught the nearest dancers exchanging knowing smiles.

Abruptly she pulled away. Curt looked down at her, eyes gleaming blue fire beneath his thick lashes. He knew his effect on her.

Sick humiliation ate into her. She stared blindly over his shoulder at the whirling, blurring mass of dancers.

'Anna Lee,' he said.

'What?'

His voice hardened. 'The artist.'

'Oh. Yes, I see.' Pride tightened her sinews, gave her the composure to say evenly, 'Nadine told me that she does installations.'

She was acting like a half-wit, but it was the best reply she could force from a brain that had crumbled into sawdust.

'She does indeed.' The note of irony in his words scraped along her nerves. 'How's the calf?'

Peta marshalled her thoughts into ragged order. 'She seems fine,' she said, trying hard to sound composed and in control.

He swung her around again, and she felt his upper arm flex beneath her fingers. Something hot and feral sizzled through her like fire in dry grass, blazing into swift life.

Surely the music had lasted far longer in this set than any other?

Just then to her intense relief it stopped, and the DJ called out, 'OK, ten minutes for talking, and then we start again!'

Curt McIntosh looked down at her, blue eyes hooded, handsome face impassive. 'Thank you,' he said formally.

Peta produced a smile. 'It was lovely,' she lied. 'Oh, Nadine's waving to me! I'll see what she wants.'

She gave him another smile, a little more genuine this time, and escaped, intent on getting away before her precarious self-possession evaporated entirely.

For the rest of the evening Curt didn't come near her again. On her way home in the small hours she told herself vigorously that she was glad. Dancing with him had been like dancing with temptation...

'And I don't do temptation either,' she told herself as she unlocked her front door.

But before she escaped into the silent house she stooped and picked a gardenia flower from the bush by the steps. Its sweet, sinfully evocative scent floated through her bedroom as she lay awake and fought a treacherous need to retrace every moment she'd spent in Curt's arms.

She stared into the darkness, seeing again the glinting irony in his gaze when he'd realised that her body responded helplessly to the heat and strength of his.

'Stop it,' she commanded herself. 'He was having fun with you, and it wasn't kind. Sharks are predators, and this one wants to take you out of circulation.'

How long was he going to stay at Tanekaha? For a while she toyed with the idea of ringing Gillian Matheson and saying she couldn't come to the barbecue the following night; she could manufacture an emergency easily enough.

But that would be cowardice.

So she'd go. She'd cope because she had to. She wasn't going to give Curt the chance to laugh at her again.

Shaken by a sudden ache of longing for something she didn't understand, she turned over, curled her long body in the bed and wooed sleep with such fervour that eventually she achieved it.

Peta heard the sound of the engine just before breakfast. Frowning, she closed the gate behind her and turned to see the station Land Rover come up the drive. Her heart jumped unexpectedly, only to go cold when Ian's rangy form unfolded from behind the wheel.

'Hello,' she said warily.

'How are you?'

Ever since she'd noticed the worrying change in his attitude she'd braced herself for this meeting. Without moving, she said brightly, 'I'm fine, thanks. What can I do for you?'

'You could make me a cup of coffee,' he suggested with a wry smile.

Ten days ago she wouldn't have thought a thing about it; she'd have made the coffee and they'd have drunk it sitting on the narrow deck while they talked easily about farming matters.

'I'd love to,' she said easily, 'but I'm on my way to feed a calf your brother-in-law helped me drag out of the swamp.'

'I'll come with you.'

After a moment's hesitation she turned and led the way to the calf-shed.

Hiding her wary discomfort with a brisk veneer, she made up the mixture and stayed to make sure the calf drank it. 'She must be feeling better; this time yesterday she didn't want to drink at all.'

Ian observed, 'Curt told us about it.'

'I'd have managed without him,' she said quickly, sad because the friendship and support Ian had offered so unstintingly was shattered. He'd stepped over an invisible boundary and now there was no going back.

He said casually, 'It looks pretty good now.'

'She'll survive.'

Ian's face crinkled into a wry smile. 'Good. What did you think of Curt?'

Peta made a production of her shrug. 'He's more or less as I'd imagined him.'

Ian said, 'And that is?'

'Like any other tycoon,' she said lightly. 'Dominating, formidable, high-handed and more than a bit arrogant.'

He nodded and got to his feet. 'Good-looking too.'

'Yes.' But Curt's handsome face and the impact of his strong bone structure were irrelevant. Like a force of nature, his compelling personality overwhelmed everything else.

Her upwards glance caught an unusual indecision in Ian's face, as though he was trying to make up his mind about something.

Suspecting that it would be better if he never said the words that were in his mind, she said, 'Shouldn't you be on your way home? Gillian will be wondering where you are.'

'Gillian isn't—' The noise of a car engine coming up the drive stopped him in mid-sentence. He turned his head so that he could see through the open end of the shed and in a flat voice said, 'This is her car.'

Peta froze. She hated scenes, and she suspected she was about to be treated to one. Ian moved jerkily out into the sunlight, but she sat there watching the calf drink, ears straining as the engine cut out.

Voices revealed that it was Gillian who'd driven up. And with her, Curt.

Peta's skin tightened as she took in the pattern of sounds, of silences. She should get up and go out; instead, she kept her eyes fixed on the white brush at the end of the calf's tail, watching it swish to and fro as the little animal sucked.

When she heard Gillian's laugh she relaxed a fraction, only to tense up again as the voices approached. Above the calf's noisy, enthusiastic slurps she heard Curt's deep voice, and the foreboding that had been prowling below the surface of her consciousness since the previous night rocketed off the scale.

'Hello, Peta,' Gillian called out. 'Can we come in?'

'Of course.' Still she kept her eyes on the calf, only looking up when it became rude not to acknowledge them.

Clad in casual clothes that proclaimed the imprint of a designer, Gillian looked completely out of place in the calf-shed with its dusty smell of hay and the more earthy scent of young animals. His expression a combination of stubbornness and indecision, Ian walked behind his wife.

In fact, Peta realised, the only person whose self-assurance remained intact and invulnerable was Curt.

Wondering if anything ever put a crack in his self-assurance, Peta greeted them with a brief smile. 'Have you come to examine the patient? As you can see, she's in good heart today.'

Gillian made a soft clucking noise. 'What a pretty little thing,' she cooed, and leaned over to give the curly poll a scratch. 'I thought she'd be covered in mud!'

'No, I brushed her down and dried her yesterday.'

'You didn't explain how she got into the swamp.' Curt's voice, anger running beneath each deliberate word like lava welling through rocks.

The hairs on the back of Peta's neck stood on end in primitive reaction. 'I don't know what spooked her into the swamp, but she was well and truly stuck when I found her.' She smiled wryly. 'And when Curt rode up on his big black horse Laddie's impersonation of a werewolf in hysterics didn't help—the calf bolted even further into the mud.'

Laddie apparently considered the sound of his name to be an invitation and ran towards the calf-pen just as the little animal turned to survey its audience.

'Get in behind!' Peta commanded sternly, leaping up from the hay bale to grab his collar. Her foot slid over a stone and turned her ankle. Although she regained her balance instantly, Ian grabbed her arm.

When Peta said the first thing that came to her mind, it was in a thin voice she hardly recognised. 'Thank you, Ian, but it was just a stone.'

He dropped his hand. 'I thought you were going to end up on your nose!'

Peta prayed no one would recognise the artificial timbre of her laugh. 'That would be twice in twenty-four hours. Curt had to drag me out of the swamp yesterday.'

Curt said, 'Gillian, why don't you go home with Ian? I have something to discuss with Peta. I'll bring your car back, and I won't be more than ten minutes or so.'

The words fell into a silence echoing with repressed emotions. His sister broke it by saying brightly, 'Make sure it's no more than ten minutes; *you* know Mrs Harkness gets very tense when we're late for meals, and *I* know how easily you get sidetracked when business calls.' Her smile at Peta lacked warmth as she linked her arm in her husband's. 'Come on, darling. Take me home.'

His gaze fixed on Curt, Ian said, 'I'll see you when you get back.'

Curt's brows lifted, but he waited until they'd driven away before turning to Peta, still frozen with dismay. She swallowed and met his gaze, hard as flint. Defensively, she folded her arms across her chest and lifted her chin.

In a level voice that didn't conceal the iron in his words, he said, 'If you carry on this thing with Ian you'll regret it.'

He knew. How? Surely that quick grip of Ian's hand hadn't given away his secret? Peta knew she looked guilty and she knew it was unfair—she had done absolutely nothing to precipitate Ian's infatuation.

Without waiting for an answer Curt went on, 'Because cutting off the lease will be only the first step to taking everything you've got away from you.'

Starkly conscious of the ruthless determination in his tone, Peta blurted, 'There is no *thing* with Ian.'

'Don't lie to me.'

'I'm not lying,' she said aggressively, heart thudding crazily beneath her crossed arms. 'And I'm not scared of empty threats. There's no way you can do that.'

'I'll make your life here impossible,' he returned with cold precision. 'To start off with, I'll deny you access over Tanekaha land.'

She stared at him, her swift response drying on her lips. He couldn't do that. Yet one glance from those flat, lethal eyes and Peta knew he would. 'My father had an agreement—'

'It isn't worth the paper it's written on. Any halfway decent lawyer would have it thrown out of court. And if you don't believe me, I'll pay for you to have an independent opinion,' he said contemptuously. He waited for the implications of this to sink in before adding with a brutal lack of emotion, 'Without access your land is valueless— worth only what I'd be prepared to pay for it. And if you run off with Ian that will be peanuts.'

He meant it. Suddenly scared, Peta said harshly, 'I don't plan to run off with him. I don't want—'

'I don't care what *you* want. He wants you—that's obvious. Are you sleeping with him?'

'No!'

Her voice vibrated with outrage, but Curt knew how easy it was to assume that offended tone. One of his lovers had given a very convincing display when he'd told her that he refused to share her sexual favours. He'd had proof then too.

He shrugged. 'Not that it matters. But if you believe that breaking up Ian's marriage will get you a better life, you're wrong. He won't only lose his wife, he'll be out of a job and I'll make sure he never works as anything more than a farmhand for the rest of his life. You might be happy with that; trust me, Ian won't be.'

Green fire mixed with gold flamed in her eyes. Heat radiated from her, enriching the golden lights in her hair and the smooth, warm silk of her skin. Curt resisted the hard pull of lust in his groin.

'I don't want to break up *any* marriage,' she said fiercely, uncrossing her arms to place a hand firmly on each hip. 'Ian means nothing to me.'

So she was just using the poor bastard. Anger gave Curt's words formidable intensity. 'But what do you mean to him?'

Her white teeth bit into her full lower lip. Curt's blood surged through his veins; she managed to invest the most trivial of gestures with an innate sensuality that damned near splintered his self-control.

Face set, she expanded, 'I don't know, and I don't care! He's always been a kind of father figure—for heaven's sake, he must be twenty years older than I am!'

'Twelve. What's that got to do with anything?'

Peta had never disliked anyone so much as she disliked him, a dislike bolstered by a cold, crawling fear. He had every intention of forcing her out of his sister's life—she only had to look at his ruthless face to know that she didn't have a chance of changing his mind.

Panic made her reckless. 'I'm not in the habit of having affairs with men twelve years older than I am!'

One raised brow told her what he thought of that. 'In that case, we might be able to save the situation.'

The calf shuffled about in the hay, the soft noise knotting her nerves.

'What do you mean?' she asked, hating this surrender

even though she wanted nothing more than to get out of this uncomfortable situation.

'It's quite simple.'

She held her breath as he finished, 'All you have to do is make it obvious you don't want anything he's offering.'

She clenched her teeth, but however crude his words were, he'd only put into words the decision she'd already made. 'I'll tell him.'

Curt shook his head. 'You'll show him,' he said succinctly.

Startled, she looked up into a face set in lines as ruthless as any pagan warrior. 'How?'

'You'll transfer your affections to me,' he told her silkily.

His words rang meaninglessly in Peta's ears. 'What?'

CHAPTER THREE

THE colour drained from Peta's skin, leaving her cold and shocked. She couldn't have heard him correctly.

One glance at Curt's implacable face went a long way towards convincing her. He *had* just said, 'You'll transfer your affections to me.'

'No,' she blurted. 'I... You don't have to go that far. I'll just tell him that—that—'

'You'll tell him nothing,' Curt stated imperiously. 'He'll get the message when you start looking sideways at me from beneath your lashes.'

She was shaking. 'No, it's impossible. What about your friend—the artist?'

His face hardened even further. 'Your concern for her welfare does you credit, although I'd believe in it more if you weren't jeopardising my sister's marriage without any apparent qualm.'

'I tell you, I didn't realise—'

He interrupted with a coldly determined, 'I'm not interested in what you knew or realised, or even whether you set a honey trap for Ian. It's not relevant. And neither is my relationship with Anna.'

For some reason this blunt statement cut deeply. Peta flashed, 'Or only in so far as it makes me look like a woman on the make, one who doesn't care who she hurts.'

'Exactly. Concentrate on convincing Ian that you took one look at me and decided to go for the big money.' Curt's smile was a masterpiece of cold cynicism. 'No man likes to be played for a fool by a gold-digger.'

Bewildered, she thought that he shouldn't be able to wound her with such accurate, painful precision. Normally she gave as good as she got; after that insult she had to drag in a painful breath before persisting stubbornly, 'It won't work. I mean—' she gestured at herself '—we don't have anything in common. Ian won't believe it.'

He gave a short, surprised laugh. 'You're not my usual type,' he agreed suavely, 'but Ian's a man, and what you're offering is pretty obvious. He'll be jealous, but he won't be surprised if I take you up on it.'

Enraged, Peta said, 'You—you arrogant bastard!'

'But rich,' he returned with silky derision. 'And for Ian, that's all that's going to matter. As for your clothes, I can fix that.'

Instant suspicion darkened her eyes. 'How?' If he thought she was going into debt at Kowhai Bay's boutique for clothes she'd never wear again, he had another think coming.

'A quick trip to Auckland will provide you with a suitable wardrobe to enhance your not inconsiderable assets.'

Although his deliberate tone chilled her and his hard blue-grey gaze remained fixed on her face, she knew that he'd catalogued every one of those assets. Shamed by a furtive tingle of arousal, she stiffened her shoulders. 'I can't afford a make over.'

'I shall, of course, pay.'

A niggle of pain throbbed in Peta's temple, but she met his eyes without flinching. 'You won't, because I won't do it. The whole idea is impossible—ridiculous.' In her steadiest voice she added the clincher. 'We don't even like each other.'

His brows rose. 'Liking,' he said indifferently, 'has nothing to do with this sort of relationship.'

Peta shook her head. Although she had her pick of scathing observations, spitting any of them out would reveal how much his high-handed attitude hurt her, so she took refuge in silence.

Curt waited, then finished, 'And after seeing us dance together at the marae no one will be surprised.'

Humiliated pride slashed her composure to shreds. Some hidden part of her had been cherishing the memory of that dance with its reckless undercurrent of carnality. Had he been planning this then?

Of course he had, she thought furiously. Nadine was right; he was as cold-blooded as a shark.

Curt waited until it was obvious she wasn't going to answer before finishing, 'So I'll pick you up tonight.'

'Tonight—oh, the barbecue.' Head held high, she met his eyes defiantly. 'I'm not going.'

Although not a muscle in the big, lithe body moved, Peta's senses reacted instantly to an unspoken threat. Adrenalin poured through her and she took an involuntary step backwards. Every sense alert, she forced herself to stand her ground, to meet ice-cold eyes and drag in a deep breath.

The world went still. Into a silence so intense she felt it on her skin like a hammer, he said lethally, 'I don't hurt women.'

'I don't know that.' Her heart pounded as though she'd run a marathon, but beneath the fear burned a bewildering exhilaration. For the first time he was looking at her as a person, not as a woman to be manipulated. And he didn't like her fear.

'You know it now.' His lips barely moved.

Eyes huge in her face, she steeled herself to say, 'I have only your word for it. Why should I believe you when you don't believe me?'

'Believe it.'

She stared at him, then slowly nodded. 'For some strange reason,' she admitted, 'I do. But just in case I'm wrong, you believe that I don't like being threatened.'

Curt shrugged, but colour along his warrior's cheekbones belied his controlled tone. 'You say you don't want Ian to fall in love with you. A relationship between us will kill his affection faster than anything else. Yes, you'll look like a woman on the make. That, surely, is a small price to pay.'

It made cold, hard sense. After all, what did she have to lose? Only her pride. She bit her lip and said resentfully, 'All right. Except that this is a fake relationship.'

'Of course,' he said contemptuously. 'Think of this whole business as a sharp warning to keep your eyes off married men in the future.'

The unfairness of the accusation stung. 'I didn't—'

'I saw a photograph of the two of you together,' he interrupted, his tone scathing. 'Ian's hand was touching your cheek in what was definitely a caress. And you weren't saying no.'

The memory of the pigeon, spooked by something in the plum tree, flashed across Peta's mind. 'Who took it?' she demanded. Surely not Gillian?

'A visiting kid with a new digital camera was trying to get a photograph of the bird. Instead, she got that photo, followed by one of the bird as it flew out of the tree. By then you were both looking at the camera.'

Peta swallowed. 'If she'd waited a second longer she'd have got a photograph of me leaving in haste. And I've made sure I haven't seen him alone since then.'

One black brow lifted in ironic disbelief. 'Until this morning,' he drawled.

Clearly, he was never going to give her even the slightest benefit of the doubt—for him, there was no doubt. He was arrogantly convinced she'd decided to go after Ian and in pursuit of her own advantage, to hell with Gillian's happiness or anything else.

She said desperately, 'Curt, this won't work. It takes more than acting to fool people.'

'Acting?'

Intuition told her what was going to happen next. Run! a despairing inner voice commanded, but an even older instinct locked her muscles so that when he pulled her into his arms she made no attempt to escape the inevitable.

'I don't think we'll need to act,' he said smoothly, and bent his head and kissed her.

It was a blatant act of mastery, possessive and angry, yet when Peta tried to resist, her body refused to accept the commands of her brain. Any other man who crowded her like this would have taken a fist in the solar plexus followed by a knee to his most sensitive region. Instead, treacherous desire and a fierce curiosity kept her prisoner until his kiss worked a barbaric enchantment.

A low sound in her throat startled her; her mouth softened beneath the demanding insistence of his, and an overwhelming tide of passion hit her, so fiercely elemental that it shocked her into surrender.

She had no idea how much later Curt lifted his head. Hugely reluctant, she opened her eyes, flinching when the glitter in his was replaced by a taunt.

'I don't think either of us will have to do much acting,' he said with cool confidence as he let her go.

Mortified, Peta realised she was clutching his shirt. She jerked free of the pressure of his big, aroused body, shivering in the breeze that flowed over acutely sensitised skin.

She'd given him a potent weapon, she realised, infuriated and humiliated by the amused satisfaction in his expression. Rashly, she stated, 'That was assault.'

His eyes gleamed and he gave her a slow, mocking smile. 'Only if you didn't want it.'

Hot-cheeked and indignant, Peta opened her mouth to refute this, but he said brusquely, 'Don't muddy the waters. You wanted it—you couldn't have made it plainer. And you turned to fire when we kissed.'

Throat aching from unspoken tension, she said hoarsely, 'Don't ever do it again.'

He shrugged indolently. 'You're going to have to get used to it, because Ian won't believe in a platonic relationship. If we're going to convince Ian that you've latched on to a better prospect, you'll need to be physically aware of me.'

His brutal bluntness told her how much he despised her. It slashed like a stockwhip across her skin, but she ignored it. He could well be right, she thought wearily. Ian had his pride; he wouldn't want his brother-in-law's leftovers. 'Are you sure this will work?'

'It had better.'

The cold note of menace in his tone tightened every nerve. 'And if it doesn't?'

'Then you'll lose your farm,' he said pleasantly. 'And in case you get any ideas, don't think he'll be able to help you. In New Zealand law, half of what he owns goes to Gillian.'

When she frowned he said in a tone that lifted the hairs on the back of her neck, 'Didn't he tell you that Gillian's money is held in trust for her? If they divorce he'll have nothing; certainly not enough to buy any land.'

Because he was the trustee, she'd bet.

But he had a few good points; he helped her get the calf out of the swamp, and he had to love his sister to be prepared to go slumming for her...

He watched her face, and after a taut few seconds added

deliberately, 'Don't worry, you won't lose financially by joining me in this masquerade.'

Dominating swine, tarring everyone with his own brush! Green-gold eyes glittering, she asked sweetly, 'Does money solve everything for you?'

'Most things,' he said, sounding amused. 'Don't knock it. And if you want to find out how important it is, tell Ian about this.'

With gritty emphasis she said, 'You needn't worry—I'll pretend as well as I can.' She flicked a lock of hair back from her hot face and finished fiercely, 'You're lucky you have a ready-made way to force me into it. What would you have done if you didn't have the power to deny me road access?'

'I'd have offered you more money, of course,' he said coolly. 'I assume you see him as a source of security, and although paying you off goes against the grain, I can provide you with more than he ever could.'

Her lip curled. 'I'm not for sale.'

He laughed beneath his breath and reached for her, linking his fingers at the back of her neck with exquisite gentleness before using his thumbs to force up her chin. 'Everyone's for sale,' he said quietly. 'All a buyer has to do is find the right price.'

'So what would it take to buy you?' she asked in an odd, stifled voice, driven by a strange combination of fury and compassion.

Eyes narrowed into crystalline slivers, he examined her face. 'More than you can pay,' he said with raw intensity. 'More than you could ever pay.'

And he dropped his hands to pull her into him so that he could kiss her again, taking her mouth with urgent hunger in a kiss driven by a dangerous volatility. His mouth devoured hers—and hers met and matched his hunger. Her treacherous body leapt into full life, blazing with a storm of desire made even more intense by the complex turmoil of her emotions.

Every warning bolted from her brain; only when his hand came up to rest on her breast, and she felt the eager centre tighten against his palm did she realise what she had to do.

She yanked herself back; somehow her hair had become loose and when she shook her head a cloud of golden-brown swirled around her stunned face.

Instantly, as though he'd been waiting, Curt let her go and stood staring at her with a black hostility that tightened every quivering nerve into knots.

Attack first. 'You promised that wouldn't happen again,' she accused.

'It won't,' he said harshly. 'I'll see you later.'

He swung on his heel and left her there in the calf-shed with the familiar scents of animals and hay and the milk mixture, and her heart drumming in a dangerous rhythm of anticipation and excitement and anger.

'One day,' she muttered when the car started up outside, 'I hope you fall desperately in love with someone, and I pray she tells you just how bloody-minded and patronising you are and then turns you down *flat*.'

Laddie stretched enthusiastically and yawned, his jaws making a faint clop as they came together.

Peta grimaced and bent to scratch the dog. 'Just as well you're not a guard dog, or I'd be sending you off to the SPCA for dereliction of duty. Why didn't you sink your teeth into his ankle?'

Her voice shook, and as his tail swept from side to side, her attempted smile turned into a trembling contraction of her mouth. She straightened up. 'OK, we'd better do some work and after that I'll work out exactly what I'm wearing to this wretched barbecue.'

In the end she chose a gold shirt she'd made a couple of years previously, combining it with a pair of cuffed trousers the same bronze as her only decent sandals.

So far, so good. She checked herself out in the mirror, frowning when she caught a glimpse of bra through the thin cotton of her shirt. After a moment's thought she opened a drawer and found a camel-coloured T-shirt and put it on under the shirt.

Yes, that was more discreet, although slightly too warm in the humid heat of Northland. Still, after her utter folly in Curt's arms, discretion came first.

In spite of everything, there was a sly satisfaction in looking good. Mouth set in a smile that held more irony than amusement, she tied her hair back with a fine loop of leather and picked up her lipstick. Its warm peachy toning reinforced the lushness of her tender lips.

She was scared. Already in too deep with Curt McIntosh, she vowed that from now on she'd be cool and composed and completely unavailable.

But when Laddie began barking enthusiastically above the low growl of an engine, an aggressive, heady anticipation hollowed out her stomach. For the last time she checked herself in the mirror, and gaped in startled wonder at the difference. She looked alive—skin glowing, mouth full and sensuous, gold sparks lighting up the green depths of her eyes. Even her hair shimmered with new life and vibrancy.

Curt McIntosh should patent his kisses; they'd make him a fortune in the rejuvenation market!

And people were going to notice, she thought uncomfortably.

'Well, that's the point of this whole farcical charade,' she said aloud in a hard voice.

So she wanted Curt McIntosh. Big deal. As long as she didn't make the cardinal mistake of confusing desire with love, she'd be fine. Passion was less complex and infinitely safer. She'd seen first-hand how love could betray. Her mother had given up everything for it—her family and friends, her talent at music, her health. Worn down by hard work and lack of money, she'd struggled through the years because she'd loved her husband.

And in the end it had killed her.

Peta's jaw firmed. No way was she going to surrender to that. Her independence was too precious to jeopardise by losing her heart.

That thought gave her enough calmness to pick up her small bag and open the front door. Tall and autocratic, the sun coaxing blue-black shadows in his dark head, Curt stepped back and lifted his brows, surveying her with open appreciation. Her stupid stomach performed an acrobatic manoeuvre that left her breathless.

Cool, she commanded. Be very, very cool. Right now.

'Quite a transformation.' He bent to pick a bloom from the gardenia by the steps.

'I assume that's a compliment,' she said in a muted voice, overwhelmed by the sight of him in a casual shirt the same grey-blue as his eyes, and sleek black trousers that hugged his hips and made the most of his long legs.

His blue eyes mocked her. 'Of course.' He tucked the gardenia into his top buttonhole and waited while she locked the door.

This time he was driving a Range Rover, a massive thing that combined power with restrained luxury. From his kennel, Laddie watched interestedly as Curt opened the passenger door and closed it behind her.

Already belted in by the time he got in behind the wheel, she linked her hands in her lap and thought, *Cool!* He was far too big, and in the confined space he loomed when he turned to examine her, a frown drawing his brows together.

Hiding her dilating eyes with a quick sweep of her lashes, she stared at the fine-grained olive skin of his throat and demanded, 'What is it?'

A swift hand found the leather tie in her hair and pulled it smoothly down over her ponytail.

'Hey!' she spluttered. Her hair swirled free, settling in a thick topaz cloud across her shoulders; she looked down to see a wave of it sift over his wrist. The westering sun burnished it into a flame of gold and cognac. Her heart began to pound in her ears, a cynical little drum informing her that although her mind and her will might want one thing, her body had its own agenda.

He drawled, 'That's much more grown-up,' and dropped the strip of leather into his pocket as he switched on the engine.

'Agreeing to this doesn't give you the right to manhandle me,' she told him tautly.

He gave her a sardonic smile and backed the vehicle skilfully around. 'I promised not to kiss you. Anything else goes. I'll do whatever needs to be done to save my sister's marriage. And in case you didn't know, what you call man-handling is an indication of attraction.'

Peta opened her mouth to speak, then closed her lips again.

'You were going to say?' he enquired as the vehicle swung out onto the road—his road, she thought bitterly.

'I was going to ask if her marriage was worth saving,' she said.

'That's her decision.' He turned his head to flash a brief, white smile at her. 'So do your best tonight, Peta. No flinching girlishly if I touch you, plenty of smiles and lots of play with those astonishing eyelashes.'

*   *   *

Peta had been to several parties at the homestead before—not the A-list ones, of course, just the neighbourhood affairs. Walking beside a silent Curt through the gardens towards a rear terrace, she thought bleakly that he must love his sister very much to initiate this sham relationship. How had he convinced his lover to agree to it? The thought of Anna Lee, artist and snob, rubbed her already raw nerves painfully.

Curt looked at her. 'Smile.'

She produced a wide, false grin. 'Don't expect me to gaze adoringly into your eyes. No one who knows me would believe it.'

'Didn't you gaze adoringly into the eyes of your previous lovers?'

'No,' she said, clipping the word short. There had been no previous lovers, but that was no business of his.

'I expect you to follow my lead in everything I do,' he said softly, and when her eyes flashed he went on with grim emphasis, 'Or else.'

Actually, he played it perfectly. Inherent sophistication meant he didn't make a show of his supposed interest; he staked his claim far more subtly with glances and smiles, the occasional touch of his hand on her waist or arm, and his possessive air. In an odd way it made her feel protected and safe, and that, she thought warily, was even more dangerous than the flash-fire of sexual hunger she felt whenever he touched her.

If it hadn't been for Ian and Gillian she might have enjoyed the evening, but in their presence she felt as though she were teetering on the edge of a perilous cliff, exposed and vulnerable, waiting for someone to push her over.

Born a hostess, Gillian had done an excellent job with the gardens; from the terrace around the swimming pool parents could sip and watch their children swim, and those who felt energetic worked it off at the tennis courts behind high, vine-covered walls. Any who demanded less strenuous activity tried their hand at *petanque*.

The Mathesons were gracious, as charming as they had ever been, yet an hour later Peta looked around the lovely grounds, the laughing people, and wondered why no one else sensed the strain between their hosts.

'You're doing well,' Curt said, bending as though he were murmuring sweet nothings in her ear.

Painfully aware of Ian's swift glance, she froze.

Curt directed a narrow smile at her. He lifted his hand to her chin and commanded, 'Another smile, Peta.'

The sensual force of his masculinity hit her like a shock wave. She met his half-closed, intent stare with eyes grown dark and her breath barely coming through her lips.

'On second thoughts, that's even better,' he said after a pause, his voice suddenly rough.

You're giving too much away, some distant, despairing remnant of prudence warned. It took a real effort to blink and turn her head.

Across a group of people she met Ian's eyes again, and felt her heart twist at the flash of pain in them. But sorry though she was for him, he had no right to fall in love with her, she thought raggedly.

'I hate this,' she said.

His expression didn't change. 'Then you shouldn't have got yourself into this situation,' he said smoothly, and smiled at her, a slow, sexy movement of his hard, beautiful mouth.

Stifled by his closeness, she glanced up to see him watching the muscles move in her throat as she swallowed. Butterflies tumbled about inside her in dazed confusion; her lips parted and she had to wrench her gaze away.

'Dinner's ready, everyone,' someone—Ian?—called above the heavy thudding of her heart.

'We'd better go and help serve.' Curt took her elbow and steered her towards the table by the pool.

Ordinarily the delectably savoury scents would have coaxed Peta into hunger, but her stomach clenched as she gazed at succulent meat from the spit, fish wrapped in leaves and baked in the coals, and salads that were pictures in green and gold and scarlet.

And Gillian shooed them away. 'Ian and Mrs Harkness and I know what we're doing,' she said, her gaze skimming Peta as she directed a smile at her brother. 'Get something to eat then sit down and enjoy yourselves.'

After filling her plate, Peta allowed Curt to guide her to a table under an immense jacaranda tree. Four other people were already there; they looked up, a little startled when Curt first pulled out a chair for Peta then sat down himself.

Acutely aware of their interest—tomorrow the whole district would be buzzing with gossip, Peta thought mordantly—she tried to appear serenely confident while Curt charmed everyone's initial reserve into open laughter and eager conversation.

A lilac-blue flower drifted down to land on her plate.

'Messy things, jacarandas,' one of the men, the machinery guru on the station, said cheerfully. 'If they're not dripping flowers, it's seedpods or leaves. Don't know why anyone would plant them.'

He grinned unrepentantly at the outcry from the women. His wife accused him of not seeing beauty in anything other than a well-tuned engine, laughing when he admitted it without a jot of shame.

'As for wearing a flower in your buttonhole like Curt,' she said teasingly, 'you'd rather die.'

'I'll bet he didn't pick it,' her husband retorted, winking at his boss.

Curt gave a pirate's grin. 'Mind your own business.'

Without a lie he'd confirmed their suspicions that Peta had picked the gardenia and given it to him, thus clinching their relationship. To these men and their wives, only a man in the throes of desire would have worn it.

It was interesting to see how a master of innuendo worked, Peta thought with raw cynicism.

He leaned towards her. 'Pudding? Gillian's made her special chocolate mousse.'

His eyes were slightly hooded, and although his voice was quiet enough to indicate intimacy, there was a clear warning in his gaze.

Suddenly angry, Peta obeyed an instinct she'd never owned up to before. With slow, subtle deliberation, she held his gaze and let her tongue run the length of her lips. 'I love her mousse,' she said huskily.

His eyes darkened and his lashes drooped further. 'Then you must have some.'

Serves you right, she thought furiously, only to flinch when he took her hand and drew her to her feet.

His fingers locking around hers like manacles, Curt said, 'Who else wants chocolate mousse?'

In a flurry of feminine complaints that they didn't dare eat such wicked indulgences so they'd have to stick to fruit salad, the group rose and went to collect their puddings.

On the way home, Peta broke into a charged silence by saying, 'In the end they all had some of your sister's mousse.'

'It's addictive,' he agreed. He'd just informed her that tomorrow they'd go for a picnic at the beach.

Beneath the vehicle the bars of the cattle stop rattled and headlight beams blazed full onto the house, mercilessly highlighting the need for a new paint job. Laddie sat up and barked, subsiding into silence when Peta got out.

Curt escorted her to the door. Tension spiralled through her and the scent of the gardenia flowers tantalised her nostrils. Each blossom gleamed with a silvery sheen in the soft darkness. In spite of everything, she thought wearily, she'd enjoyed—well, no, that wasn't the right word. Regret ached through her; if only they'd met like ordinary human beings, and this was the end of an ordinary date...

Common sense asserted itself briskly and brutally. He'd never have looked at you, it stated.

At the door when she turned to say good night, Curt said levelly, 'I'll come in.'

Anticipation simmered through her veins. 'What?'

Did he sense it? If he did, his edged smile was calculated to deflate it. 'No one is going to believe that I'll come straight back.'

She clamped down on her instinctive rejection. Compared to the homestead her house was a shack. And if he once walked into it, she might never get rid of his presence.

'No,' he said pleasantly, 'I'm not going to sit in the car. You can make me a cup of coffee and we'll talk like ordinary neighbours over it.'

Ordinary neighbours? He had to be joking. 'I only have instant,' she said inanely.

He shrugged. 'So?' When she still hesitated he said on a note of derision, 'It's all right, Peta, you'll be quite safe.'

'Oh, come in if you must,' she snapped, because she didn't want to be safe.

The Peta who hadn't kissed Curt was a different woman from the one who had; this new Peta had developed a reckless streak a mile wide.

Switching on the lights, she said, 'Sit down, and I'll put on the kettle,' and escaped into the kitchen.

When she brought the coffee in, Curt was standing by the bookshelf examining a volume. She plonked the tray onto a coffee table. 'Black or white?'

Other men almost as tall as he—stock agents, the occasional neighbour—had stood in that room, but none had dwarfed it as he did. And it wasn't just his physical presence; something deeper, more potent than good genes gave him that formidable air of inner strength.

'Black, thanks.' He lowered himself into her father's chair and made it his own.

Sipping her tea, Peta stayed obstinately silent, but when he asked her about the book he'd been looking at she had to answer.

Half an hour later she realised with shock that she was enjoying herself, albeit in a tense, disturbing way. His mind stimulated her and she liked the way he discussed things, with a sharp acuity that kept her on her toes.

And when she disagreed with him, he didn't get angry— surely unusual for a dominant man? Her father's rejection of anyone else's opinions but his own had marred her childhood.

After a quick look at her watch she said, 'I think you should go now.'

Lounging back in the big chair with its faded upholstery, he fixed her with a glinting glance. 'Why?'

'I don't want to get a reputation for being easy,' she said smartly. 'I have to live here.'

There was a short silence while she recalled that she might not be living here for much longer if he decided to close down her access.

With a humourless smile he got to his feet. 'That would never do. My mother drummed into me the importance of not stripping a woman of her good reputation,' he drawled. 'I'll see you tomorrow. Can you be ready by ten?'

'No.' But she wanted to be. She explained, 'I've got calves to feed and move into a new paddock. About eleven-thirty would be better, and I'll have to be back by two-thirty.'

He frowned. 'You work too hard.'

'That's life,' she said flippantly.

She waited until his rear lights had disappeared, then changed and went across to the shed to check the animals. The calf she'd rescued from the swamp was dead.

CHAPTER FOUR

FIGHTING back tears, Peta sat down on a hay bale and blew her nose. She'd believed she was inured to the many different ways animals could die, so why was she crying?

Because it had been a horrible day. Curt had revealed his true colours as a hard-dealing magnate, threatening her with the loss of her livelihood and everything else, and demolishing with brutal contempt her attempts to convince him she wasn't a money-hungry home-wrecker.

She wiped her eyes. And for some reason she wasn't ready to face, his refusal to accept the truth hurt.

That was scary enough, but even more frightening was the physical longing, hot and urgent and uncontrollable, that had engulfed her both times he'd kissed her.

Scariest of all, was the fact that he wanted her too.

The difference was that Curt was in full control of his passions. She wasn't, and if she spent too much time with him desire might deepen into craving.

On the other hand, she thought wearily, surely she had more pride than to choose as her first lover a man who despised her because he thought she was greedy and amoral.

'What else can go wrong?' she said aloud, startled by the thin wobble of her voice in the warm, hay-scented air.

The next morning she was halfway through digging a hole behind the shed when she heard a car come up the drive. Barking importantly, Laddie disappeared, only to fall silent almost immediately.

Someone the dog knew, then. Please, not Ian.

She kept on spading dirt away until Curt asked brusquely, 'What are you doing?'

'Digging a hole.' She concentrated on keeping up a steady rhythm.

'I'll do it.'

She straightened then and gave him a shadowed glance. As she had once before, she said, 'You're not dressed for it. And you might get blisters on your hands.'

He said evenly, 'If you want an undignified wrestling match I'll give you one, but it's only fair to point out that I'm a lot bigger than you are and a lot stronger, and I'll win.'

Peta didn't move.

'So if you make me take the spade off you by force I'll have to conclude that you want to wrestle,' he finished.

A note in his voice warned her that he'd take full advantage of any opportunities she gave him. Muttering something beneath her breath, she slammed the tool into the ground.

'Wise woman,' he said unforgivingly, and picked up the implement. 'The calf, I presume?'

'It was dead when I went to check it last night.'

He nodded and began to dig, his easy movements showing that hard physical labour wasn't new to him. Sensation ambushed her as she watched the smooth flexion of muscles through the material of his shirt and trousers, the effortless power that meant he could do the work in half the time that she could.

Subliminal excitement dilated her eyes, sending exquisite little thrills through her. She had to swallow to ease a suddenly dry throat, and turned blindly towards the shed.

'You look exhausted,' he said abruptly, not even breathing faster. 'Did you get any sleep last night?'

'Not a lot,' she admitted before realising how shaming a confession that was.

Fortunately he took her admission another way. 'How on earth do you expect to farm successfully if the loss of one calf does this to you? Go inside and make yourself a cup of tea.'

She swung around to face him, planting her hands on her hips. 'I've been farming on my own for five years,' she said clearly, 'and I've managed quite well without you. This is *my* farm and *my* loss. I'm not going to be sent off to the house to do housewifely things while some big, strong man does the work.'

Eyes half-closed and speculative, he scanned her face then began to move dirt again. 'Fair enough.'

Astonished, she stared at him.

'We'll bury it together,' he said.

So they did, although he made sure the heaviest work was left to him.

When it was done he helped her move a length of electric fence. Surveying the calves as they frolicked onto the new grass, he asked levelly, 'Why didn't you sell this place when your parents died?'

Peta set off for the house, tossing over her shoulder, 'Why should I?'

'For a better life?' Two long strides caught her up.

'I like farming. And I earn enough to live on.'

'If you did, you wouldn't be working at the local petrol station four hours a day.'

She said stiffly, 'My finances are my concern. The only way you're going to get me out of here is to force me out. But even if I wanted to sell, I have the calf contract to fulfil.'

'A contract that wouldn't stand up in court.'

Although her stride faltered, she walked doggedly on. 'I don't believe you.'

'I don't lie.' When she said nothing he added in a coolly dispassionate tone, 'When Ian drew it up he must have had his mind somewhere else.'

Colour flicked her skin, but she met his hard scrutiny with desperate composure. Her lack of sleep was showing; she couldn't process what he was telling her. 'If that's true—and I'm not accepting it until my lawyer tells me so—what do you plan to do about it?'

His lashes drooped. 'That depends on how co-operative you are,' he drawled.

Assailed by a violent mixture of need and disdain, she sent him a fiery stare.

'What a commonplace mind you've got,' he said pleasantly. 'You're quite safe. I've never had to blackmail a woman into my bed, and I don't plan to start with you.'

'Well, that's a relief.' She hoped the scorn in her voice hid her sudden humiliating disappointment.

His eyes gleamed. 'I wonder if you'd allow yourself to be blackmailed.'

Goaded, she snapped, 'As you've just told me you won't do it, the question is irrelevant.'

He gave her a grin that sizzled through her like honey into pancakes. 'And you've just told me you don't know which way you'd jump.' His amusement died and he was all business. 'I came to tell you that a business call to Japan will probably take most of this afternoon, so the trip to the beach is off. Also, we'll be going to Auckland at the end of this week.'

'We?'

'You and me both.'

How could she dislike him intensely, yet be violently

attracted to him at the same time? Automatically she said, 'I can't just up and leave the farm.'

'I'll send up someone from the station to take care of things.'

Her chin tilted. 'It takes more than a written list of instructions—'

'He can start tomorrow. I'm sure that in three days you can teach him enough to keep the place going.'

Suspicion stirred inside her. She frowned at Laddie, who sat back and regarded her with intelligent interest. 'Why?'

'Why do I want you to go to Auckland? Because it makes the whole scenario much more likely.'

What about Anna Lee? Peta almost blurted the words out, but another glance at Curt's hard, handsome face stopped them before they could escape.

Instead, she evaded the issue. 'I can cope with any social occasion here, but unless you plan to stash me in some motel and ignore me, I haven't got the right clothes to carry off a masquerade in Auckland. And I won't accept them from you.'

When he smiled her heart leapt into her throat. That smile had probably charmed the clothes off more women— worldly women, sophisticated and confident—than she'd reared calves. Its blatant charisma was doing an excellent job of scrambling her brain and melting her willpower and softening her heart, and the fact that he knew exactly what effect it was having on her didn't lessen its impact one bit.

But there was nothing humorous in his tone when he told her, 'You'll accept whatever I decide you need.'

Stubbornly she persisted, 'And even if I did have the right clothes, I don't have the right attitude.'

'I don't plan to hide you away,' he said easily, 'and you have exactly the right attitude. As for clothes—that's easily enough fixed.'

Peta stopped and glared at him. 'I told you, I'm not going to accept anything from you.'

'What a sweetly old-fashioned view,' he drawled.

'It might be, but it's non-negotiable.'

'All right, we'll hire them,' he said with insulting negligence. 'I'll want you to attend a gala evening with me, and neither jeans and a T-shirt nor the fetching outfit you wore to Gillian's barbecue will do the trick. And that is non-negotiable, you prickly little wildcat.'

Little? Undecided whether to be furious or charmed, she set off for the house. He hadn't threatened her openly, but if the contract to rear calves for his dairy operation wouldn't stand up in court Curt could pull the plug on her any time.

He had her exactly where he wanted her—on toast. Helped, of course, by the wistful part of her that would like to go to Auckland, to be with him, to hear him talk and make him laugh…

Taking her silence for assent, he said, 'I'll send a helicopter to pick you up on Friday morning. A farmhand will be here at three this afternoon when you come back from your stint manning the petrol pumps.'

Peta saw salvation. 'I forgot—there's no way I can come. I work at the service station over the weekend.'

'He's already found someone to take your place.'

Outraged, she hid a thread of panicky fear with aggression. 'What did you do—threaten Sandy with the loss of the station account?'

'I didn't have to. No one is indispensable. Of course I'll reimburse you for the loss of your wages.' He waited while she digested this and then finished in a level voice that warned her she'd reached some uncrossable barrier, 'If it makes you feel better, think of yourself as someone on my payroll.'

'Technically, I suppose I already am.' Nevertheless, she felt sleazy and oddly compromised as she finished shortly, 'All right.'

'Good. I'll see you tomorrow.'

By then they'd reached the gravel turning area outside her house. Peta gazed resentfully at the Range Rover and asked, 'Tomorrow? Why?'

He opened the vehicle door and surveyed her with cool intimidation. 'Because I'm supposed to want to.' The cynical note in his voice deepened. 'I'm intrigued by you, remember? Fascinated, in fact; so much so that I can't wait to get you into bed.'

Reaching for her, he pulled her into his arms and bent to kiss her startled gasp from her lips.

It didn't last long, that kiss, but it did a complete demolition job on the few remaining shreds of her composure. When he stepped back she was awash with dizzying and highly suspect pleasure, her mouth slightly parted, lashes drooping over sultry eyes.

The sound of a vehicle coming up the drive scarcely impinged until it stopped a few feet behind the Rover. She turned a dazed, flushed face towards it, barely able to focus on the sign on the door of the utility.

'Tanekaha Station', she read, and the man looking out from it was Ian.

So Curt must have recognised the engine and kissed her to make a point.

Acutely aware that Curt's hand had come to rest on her shoulder, she tried to produce a smile. Her effort was wasted; Ian wasn't looking at her. His gaze was fixed on Curt's face, and instead of his usual expression there was a set weariness in the blunt features.

Curt didn't move; she sensed a waiting, cold patience, the concentrated intensity of a predator watching its prey.

And something else, a primitive possessiveness that said bluntly, *My woman. Keep away.*

'Hello, Ian,' Peta said, nerves quivering at the tension smoking around them.

He glanced at her. 'Everything OK?'

'Yes, although the calf we got out of the swamp died last night.' The words sounded unnaturally stiff, almost formal.

He shrugged. 'It happens. I suppose you've buried it?'

'Curt did,' she said. 'He didn't seem to think I was capable.'

Ian's face eased into a wry half-smile that vanished when Curt said urbanely, 'I'm sure you can do anything you put your mind to. It's just that when I was too young to realise I was being brainwashed, my mother drummed into me that because men are stronger than women they do the heavy work.'

A subtle challenge underpinned the teasing words, and the pressure of his long fingers on her shoulder warned her to follow suit.

Pinning what she hoped was a carefree smile to her lips, she said, 'Whereas my father believed women should be able to look after themselves.'

Ian nodded. 'OK, then, I'll see you around,' he said and put the ute into reverse.

The wheels spun at the weight of a foot incautiously heavy on the accelerator, then gripped and spat out a small spray of stones. When Peta stepped back, Curt's arm settled around her shoulders. She stiffened, but he turned her towards the house and urged her with him.

'That should give him some idea of what's going on,' he said bluntly. 'If he wasn't trying to break my sister's heart I could almost feel sorry for him.'

Peta tried to shrug free of his arm, but he turned her towards him, examining her face with hooded eyes.

'Get used to my touch,' he told her, his survey as dispassionately relentless as the tone of his voice. 'He's still not sure that this is for real; he knows damned well that I'd do anything to save Gillian pain.'

'You're a very noble brother.' She lifted her chin against a betraying surge of painful need.

He dropped his arm and nodded at the door. 'Invite me inside. I deserve a cup of coffee for my exertions on your behalf.'

'Unwanted exertions,' she flashed back, but she opened the door.

Watching her move gracefully about the bleak kitchen, Curt wondered exactly what was going on behind those green, gold-rayed eyes with their dark lashes.

His body stirring in primitive recognition, he thought grimly that keeping a safe distance from her was going to test his willpower. He was no stud, but he was accustomed to having the women he wanted.

What he wasn't accustomed to—and resented—was that with this woman he barely had control over his reactions.

Deciding to use her to cut Ian's little idyll short had been foolhardy, but irresistible. His mouth curved satirically as he acknowledged that if he hadn't wanted her he'd probably have simply made an offer too good for her to resist and bought the farm, making sure she moved as far away from Ian and Gillian as possible.

But no, he'd fallen for her subtle, sensual challenge, and now he was going to have to see the whole thing through.

Dealing with her was rather like taming a tigress—her sleek, lithe beauty hiding latent savagery and open determination. Although she hadn't tried to hide her resentment at his threats, she wasn't afraid of him, and she didn't fawn over him.

And that, he thought cynically, was unusual enough to be a refreshing change.

When she melted in his arms her wild, sweet passion had practically tipped him over some edge he'd never approached with any other woman. Acting or for real? A man's body couldn't lie, but women could and did fool men with mimic desire.

Not that he was going to test her. Although she probably saw Ian as a way out of a life going nowhere, he suspected that she didn't have much experience.

She could even be a virgin. His body reacted to that thought with an elemental appetite that took him completely by surprise. Virginity had never been a requisite in his lovers; in fact, he'd preferred women who knew what to do and what they wanted, but the thought of initiating Peta into the delights of the flesh worked so powerfully on him that he had to sit down.

If she was a virgin, taking her to bed would be unfair.

Just keep that thought in the forefront of your mind, he advised himself sardonically. 'Tell me about your parents.'

Warily, she looked up from pouring boiling water into a mug. 'What do you want to know?'

'Why did they come here?'

She added the milk jug to the tray and picked it up. 'My father should have been born a couple of hundred years ago. He was the last of the pioneers.' She walked across to the coffee table and set the tray down on it. 'He decided that Europe was dying, so when my mother got pregnant with me he moved her here from England.'

'Why Kowhai Bay?'

She handed him the mug of coffee. 'He wanted a warm

climate, which made Northland the logical choice, and this is a good long way from the nearest city.'

'It didn't occur to him that buying land with no legal access was hardly a sensible thing to do?' he suggested.

The corners of her mouth turned down in a brief grimace. 'My father wasn't accustomed to having his decisions questioned.' She pushed a small plate of ginger crunch across. 'Help yourself,' she invited.

Homemade, Curt realised when he'd taken the first bite. And delicious. He watched her pick up her mug, and wondered what her capable, long-fingered hands would feel like on his body. The scent of the gardenia bush at the front door floated in, erotically charging the humid air.

'And your mother agreed to this life?'

Peta studied him above the rim of her mug, green eyes enigmatic. 'She always agreed with him. She thought he was wonderful and perfect in every way. They were ideally suited; he was dominant—in some ways you remind me of him—and she was yielding.' Her full lips twisted. 'But she wasn't strong.'

He suspected that she'd substituted the word dominant for another, more insulting one—domineering? Dominating?

The thought amused him. If he was arrogant, she certainly wasn't as docile as her mother seemed to have been. 'Why didn't you stay on at school?'

'My father believed that book knowledge, as he called it, was no use to anyone in real life. He was convinced that modern civilisation was leading the world to destruction, and that everyone should be able to live off the land.'

'And can you?'

Her shoulders moved in a slight shrug. Curt kept his eyes away from the soft movement of her breasts, but a light tinge of colour stole along her high cheekbones when she answered.

'If I have to.'

He looked at her. 'Did he give you no choice?'

'My mother needed me at home,' she said simply.

Frowning, he recalled the results of the investigation he'd had run on her. 'And then they were killed in a road accident.'

'She was already dying.' Peta turned away so that he couldn't see her face. 'I was glad, in a way. She didn't have to endure much pain, and he didn't have to live without her unstinting love and her conviction that he was always right.'

This, she decided, was far too intimate a conversation. Noticing that he'd finished his ginger crunch, she made a gesture towards the plate. 'There's more.'

He shook his head. 'That was superb. Did you make it?'

Oddly warmed by the compliment, she nodded. 'My father believed that every woman should know how to cook.'

'Very Victorian,' Curt observed, an edge to his voice. 'I'm surprised he didn't settle for a tent, an open fire and a camp oven.'

She laughed a little. 'He was unreasonable,' she conceded, 'but he was passionately committed to his ideas. The kitchen might not be up-to-date but it works. Don't pity me—I'm perfectly happy here.'

He leaned back in the chair and regarded her with half-closed eyes. 'You don't feel any yearning for romance or marriage?'

Peta's father had been a big man, but he'd never had Curt's compelling presence. Last night at the barbecue everyone else had seemed dim and insubstantial, their conversation lacking savour and interest because she'd been so painfully aware of the man with her.

Alarmed by her weakness, she said more crisply than she'd intended, 'At the moment, no, I'm not interested in either.'

His unsparing assessment sent a series of little shivers down her spine. 'In that case you'll be only too eager to help me cut Ian's crush short,' he said pleasantly. 'Are you pumping petrol this morning?'

'Yes.' She glanced at her watch. 'And if I don't get going I'll be late.' She drained her mug and stood up. Awkwardly, she said, 'Thanks for helping me.'

'Even though you didn't need it?' He too got to his feet, his faint smile setting off an unlikely starburst inside her.

'Even then,' she said with a glimmering sideways smile that vanished when she met his eyes.

Coolly measuring, they chilled her through and through.

Working the pumps at the petrol station, she wiped a bead of sweat from her temple and decided that the only thing that made Curt seem at all human was his affection for his sister. Apart from that weakness, as he no doubt saw it, Nadine had got it right. That Peta wanted to kill whatever feelings Ian had developed for her didn't make Curt any less of a cold-blooded user.

Well, not exactly cold-blooded, she decided later as she turned into her drive. He kissed with an expertise that shouted his experience, but was there genuine passion beneath that Ice Man exterior?

Ignoring the consuming she got out of the ute and unlocked the front door. A wave of stuffy air surged out to greet her.

Curt McIntosh was a walking, breathing challenge, and she bet that plenty of women had come to grief picking up the gauntlet of his forbidding self-sufficiency.

Stripping off her petrol-scented clothes, Peta vowed not

to be one of them. What she felt for him had nothing to do with love, and she'd keep a watchful guard on her body because once this charade was over she'd see no more of Curt.

Joe, the elderly odd-job man who arrived a few minutes later, was an old friend. He'd been cowman on the station under the previous owner and he knew how to deal with calves. Briskly she showed him how to use the elderly washing machine to mix the formula.

'You shouldn't be carrying those heavy buckets,' he scolded, forestalling her attempt to pick them up. 'It's not good for you.'

'Joe, I do it twice a day almost all year round!'

'Doesn't make it right,' he said firmly.

And he was so concerned she stood back and let him carry them into the calf-shed, watching as he tipped the liquid into the calf-feeders.

Pitching his voice to rise above the bawl of hungry calves, he said, 'Good-looking girl like you should be looking around for a man to do the heavy work. If I were thirty years younger I'd take you on myself.'

'If you were any younger I'd have snapped you up years ago,' she told him, laughing.

His grin faded as he focused on someone coming up behind them. Peta swung around and met a pair of electric blue eyes. Everything about her went taut; she couldn't breathe, couldn't think, couldn't hear her heart beat.

And then Curt smiled, and life flowed through her again; she heard the contented sound of calves sucking, smelt their clean animal smell and the sweet, summery scent of hay. She even heard a skylark sing in the brilliant blue sky outside.

'Hello, Peta.' His gaze moved to the older man. 'Joe.'

'G'day, Curt.' Respectful but not intimidated, Joe moved on to the next pen and filled the feeder there.

Curt frowned at Peta. 'Did you lift those buckets?'

'Of course.' When his mouth clamped into a hard line she added, 'They're not as heavy as they look.'

Over his shoulder Joe butted in, 'They're every bit as heavy as they look—far too much for a woman to be carrying around!'

His frown deepening, Curt watched the older man walk down to the next pen. 'Why don't you run a hose from the mixer?'

'Because this works perfectly well,' Peta informed him with a thin smile. 'I'm no fragile flower.'

'Possibly not, but you shouldn't be carrying that weight.'

She walked outside into the sunlight and turned to face him, her blood singing through her veins in a wild summons. 'Testosterone clearly muddles male thinking patterns. Relax, Curt. If I couldn't do it easily, I'd have found another way to deal with it. I don't force myself to do things that are too difficult; I'm not stupid.'

'It'll wait,' he said, the magnificent structure of his face more prominent. 'There's been a change of plan,' he said brusquely. 'Can you be ready to leave for Auckland tomorrow morning?'

'No!' she said, incredulous that he should ask her this. 'I can't just drop everything and go. Anyway, it would look too…precipitate! To put it crudely, I'm not that sort of woman, and everyone in the district knows it.'

'All right,' he said after a moment. 'In three days' time. That will give Joe all the information he needs to keep the operation running.'

The tone of his voice told her there'd be no more negotiation. She bit her lip. 'How long do you expect me to stay away?'

'A week should do it,' he said blandly. 'And I come bearing a note from Gillian.'

He took an envelope from the pocket of his shirt and handed it over. Gillian invited her to a casual family dinner that night with a couple of old friends. She glanced up, realising from Curt's expression that she didn't have any choice.

'All right,' she said reluctantly.

'It will be extremely informal,' Curt informed her.

Thoroughly exasperated with Ian for precipitating this situation and Curt for forcing her to bend to his will, she snapped, 'I do know which fork to use.'

'I'd noticed,' he said, deadpan.

For some obscure reason this struck her as funny and she gave a gurgle of laughter.

A flash of blue kindled in his eyes but his voice was level and emotionless. 'That's better. Look on this as your good deed for the month. I'll pick you up around seven.'

He swung on his heel and strode away; unwillingly she admitted that he looked like some—well, some demigod from a young girl's romantic fantasy. And he walked like one too, with a lithe male grace that promised leashed power and uncompromising strength. He was, she thought as she went back into the shed, a man who revealed bone-deep competence in every movement.

It might be another fantasy, but she suspected that he'd be able to deal with any situation that came his way.

She envied that confidence. Her father's views had some-how cut her off from the other children in the district; once she left school she'd seen little of those she'd been friends with. Naturally she'd chafed against his dogmatism and his iron control, but because her mother wasn't well she'd had to go along with it.

Living on the outside had marked her in ways she hadn't realised until she'd grown up.

She and Joe worked together until everything was done. When he left she went inside; instead of working in the vegetable garden for an hour or so she showered, and while her hair dried, hauled clothes out of her wardrobe, trying to decide what clothes would be suitable for dinner at the homestead.

Very informal was so vague as to be meaningless—in Curt's circle it probably indicated that tiaras wouldn't be worn, she thought snidely. The only thing that might suit the occasion were a pair of silk-look capri pants the colour of chocolate. With them she paired a figure-skimming top she'd made in a dark, richly dramatic green.

Once dressed, she looped a tie around her hair, now thankfully dry, then stopped. Would Curt yank it out again? She frowned at her reflection before an idea struck her. Smiling smugly, she picked a hibiscus flower from the bush by the garden shed and tucked it into the knot. Back inside, she surveyed it, her grin widening. The silken petals gleamed in an exotic, almost barbaric blending of crimson and cinnabar.

'I don't think he'll pull the tie off this time,' she said dulcetly to her reflection.

The V-neck of her top needed some sort of necklace, but her mother's silver chain was too delicate for the colours that suited her, so in spite of the rather large expanse of bare golden skin she left it unadorned.

She let out a huff of breath when the Range Rover started up the drive. Her stomach clenched and she stopped, trying to calm her racing pulse with a hand pressed protectively over her heart.

'Oh, don't over-dramatise things,' she muttered furiously and strode to the door, flinging it open with a small crash.

CHAPTER FIVE

'AND I'm delighted to see you too,' Curt said sardonically.

Peta gave a crack of unwilling laughter. How did he do that—make her laugh when she was angry and worried and scared?

Without waiting for an answer, he took her arm and drew her out into the soft light of dusk. Her witless body registered his touch with acute pleasure, and every sense blazed into fierce life as they walked silently through the soft evening, the scent of the gardenias floating around them like a lazy invitation.

At the car he held the door open and said, 'You look superb.'

Stunned, she sent him a swift glance.

Something deep and inscrutable glimmered in the blue depths of his eyes. 'Surely that's not the first time a man's told you that?'

Actually, it was. 'Your sister dresses superbly,' she said with blunt honesty. 'I made this top myself, and the trousers came from a local store.'

'You rise above them,' he said blandly. 'And you know exactly what looks good on you. Forget about where anyone's clothes were bought. You'll fit in.' He closed the door on her.

Flushing, she had to turn her head and pretend to examine the fruit trees down the drive so that he wouldn't see how much pleasure his casual compliment had given her.

When Gillian met them at the door of the homestead,

Peta felt a twinge of humiliation at the instantly concealed surprise in the other woman's eyes. What on earth had Gillian expected—that she'd turn up in jeans and a T-shirt?

Worse was to come when she introduced Peta to her friends—Hunter Radcliffe and his wife, who lived some distance further north. Lucia Radcliffe just happened to have been born princess of a small Mediterranean island.

At least there was no sign of a tiara on her regal head.

It took Peta only one glance to realise that Curt and Hunter Radcliffe were two of a kind—elite, alpha males with more than their fair share of forceful authority.

Like her father...

The following half-hour revealed that the princess was about as different from Peta's mother as anyone could be. Lucia Radcliffe knew her own mind and spoke it, a state of affairs her husband clearly enjoyed.

Strangely enough Peta found herself neither tongue-tied nor awkward. Gillian's manners were perfect and the princess, who insisted on being called plain Lucia, was a charming, warmly interested guest. And while Ian's avoidance of Peta was obvious to her, nobody else gave any indication of noticing.

In spite of the tension sawing at her nerves, she found herself taking part in the conversation as though she'd known them for some time. When she needed it Curt was always there with unobtrusive support. Slowly she relaxed, until a wail from not too far away startled her.

'I'm terribly sorry,' Lucia said, swiftly getting to her feet. She smiled at Peta. 'That is our darling daughter, six months old and hungry! As I'm the source of sustenance I'll deal with it.'

'May I take a peek?' Peta asked.

The princess laughed. 'Of course! We think she's adorable, but then we're a bit biased.'

The baby stopped crying the moment she saw her mother, opening her eyes wide to stare solemnly at Peta before giving a swift, triangular smile.

'Oh—she's gorgeous,' Peta said on a sigh.

The princess picked up the child and held her out. 'Do you want a cuddle? It will have to be quick, because Natalia doesn't like being kept waiting for her dinner.'

'I don't know how to hold babies,' Peta confessed.

Lucia plonked the baby into her embrace, standing back to watch Peta's arms automatically curve around the sweet-smelling bundle.

'I think it's instinctive,' the princess said wisely as Peta smiled into the quizzical little face.

The baby's brows met in a frown, but after a moment she gave a half-smile and turned her head to check out her mother's whereabouts.

'Oh, sweetheart, you are delectable,' Peta breathed, her face lighting up when the baby looked back at her and lifted a chubby, starfish hand to pat her cheek.

Lucia looked past them to the door, her lovely face breaking into a smile. 'Curt, come in. Look, Natalia, here's Curt to see you!'

The baby certainly knew him. Smile turning into a beam, she leaped in Peta's arms, little hands working in excitement.

Curt's gaze rested on Peta's face with a kind of surprise. 'Here,' she said awkwardly, 'you'd better take her.'

He handled the baby with the competence he showed in everything else, his expression softening as he looked down at her. Peta's heart gave an odd wistful jolt; it was the first time she'd seen him lower his defences.

'She is a born coquette,' Lucia said fondly. 'She even flirts with her father.'

Peta watched the tall man laughing at the baby, and for

a couple of heartbeats she couldn't think, couldn't breathe. Occasionally she'd fantasised about life with a kind, gentle man who respected her and listened to her, and in that shadowy dream there were children.

Now, with the impact of a bullet out of darkness, she realised that the only child she wanted was Curt's.

Natalia began to wriggle, and Curt kissed the satiny cheek and handed the baby over to her mother.

Lucia said, 'That's probably the limit of her patience.'

'You and your husband are right—she is adorable,' Peta said, her voice uneven as she headed for the door.

Outside in the hall, something about Curt's steady regard, watchful and deliberate, lifted every tiny hair on her skin.

But when he spoke it was to say, 'You didn't comment on which parent she most resembles.'

Peta steadied her voice before answering, 'She looks like herself, and judging by the set of her chin she's inherited both her father's and mother's share of determination.'

Laughing quietly, he tucked her hand into the crook of his arm. The warmth of his body sent hot shivers roiling across her skin. I'm in real trouble, she thought confusedly. What am I going to do?

Stop fantasising about babies, to start with!

'Lucia can wax eloquent about her strong will,' he said, and sent an enigmatic glance down at her as they walked towards the door of the sitting room. 'Enjoying yourself?'

'Mostly,' she admitted honestly.

He nodded. 'Just remember the whole purpose of this exercise.'

Not exactly a threat, yet his words reminded her brutally that to him she was a pawn, someone to be used for a particular purpose and then discarded. OK, so he liked babies; big deal. Tyrants and dictators liked babies too.

The pain that accompanied her thoughts was bitter medicine, but if it cured her of this feverish desire she'd endure it.

Just outside the door he stopped her with a light touch on her arm, and bent his head. Heart hammering, she looked up—and read cold calculation in his eyes.

He didn't kiss her on the mouth. Instead his lips touched the angle of her jaw, and then his teeth closed for a second on the lobe of her ear, firing a bolt of delicious sensation into the centre of her being.

It was over almost instantly, but the aftermath stayed in her eyes and the delicate colour of her skin. When he opened the door for her and ushered her back into the room, a possessive hand in the small of her back, she saw Ian's face clamp into rigidity.

A needle of pain worked its way through her. It hurt to see Ian suffer, even though she could never return his feelings. Why did things—people—have to change?

When the evening was over she thanked Gillian and Ian civilly and said goodbye to the Radcliffes.

'I hope it's not goodbye,' Lucia said promptly. 'We don't live that far away.'

Not in distance perhaps…

Peta smiled and said something casual and inoffensive.

Halfway home Curt asked, 'Why did you brush off Lucia's invitation?' In spite of his matter-of-fact tone he wanted an answer.

Her face set. 'Because I was there on false pretences,' she returned on a hard note. 'Besides, the princess was only being polite—we won't meet again.'

'Her manners are exquisite,' he agreed, 'but she's learned to protect herself from people she doesn't like. If she hadn't wanted to get to know you better she wouldn't have suggested it.'

'We have nothing in common. Once this charade is over I'll never see her again.'

'You're an inverted snob,' he said coolly.

'I am *not*.' Furious, she flared, 'Except for a relationship with you—a relationship based on blackmail!—what common ground could there possibly be between me and a princess who's married to a millionaire?'

'You seemed to have enough to talk about,' he said neutrally. 'You certainly didn't hold back when it came to discussing the state of the world. And you share a certain forthrightness. Because she spent years having to watch every word she said, Lucia rather enjoys stating her opinions.'

Peta shrugged, but his words echoed in her mind after she'd given him a cup of coffee and tensely waited out the forty-five minutes he insisted on staying.

'More camouflage,' he said laconically.

By the time he finally left her nerves had shredded to rags, but this time he didn't kiss her, although the glitter in his eyes told her that he too felt the swift uprush of hunger, hot and sweet and fiery.

Whenever she smelt the scent of gardenia, she thought wearily as she closed the door behind him, she'd remember his addictive kisses. And wondered if he was deliberately holding back, making her more hungry with each fugitive caress.

No. He might be trying to manipulate her, but not into his bed; he wanted her flushed and eager so that Ian was convinced.

She went back into the sitting room, looking around it with clouded eyes. The contrast between its elderly furnishings, chosen for economy and hard wear, and Gillian's house couldn't have been greater.

About as much contrast as there was between her life and Curt's.

'So stop the sneaky little wish-fulfilment fantasies,' she told herself harshly. 'Curt's baby indeed! You must be mad.'

'First ride in a chopper?' the helicopter pilot enquired, stowing her pack away.

'Yes.'

He grinned and said confidently, 'You'll love it. It's a great day and all Northland's going to be spread out like a map under us.' He took an envelope from his pocket. 'A note from the boss,' he explained, handing it over.

Peta opened it with trembling fingers. It was the first time she'd seen Curt's writing, and for some reason the occasion assumed ridiculous importance.

Like him, his writing breathed bold, aggressive power. He wasn't able to meet her in Auckland; his personal assistant would pick her up.

He signed it simply, 'C'.

Curt by name and curt by nature, she thought, chilled. He was probably making sure he didn't sign any documentation she might be able to use against him.

Well, he didn't need to worry. She knew exactly why she was there. She'd keep her side of the bargain.

The pilot was right; the trip down was fantastic. Peta exclaimed with pleasure as Northland's long peninsula, barely a hundred miles across at its widest part, unrolled beneath them in a glory of gold and green, hemmed by the blue of the Pacific Ocean on the left and the dangerous green waters of the Tasman Sea on the right; estuaries gleamed in the opalescent blues and greens of a paua shell.

'We need rain,' she said, looking down at toast-coloured countryside as they neared Auckland.

'Rain? Have a heart, it's summer,' the pilot expostulated. 'Nobody wants rain in summer.'

And there in a nutshell was the difference between city people and those from the country. She thought of the bag she'd packed so carefully that morning, choosing and discarding clothes, getting more and more stressed until she'd realised that no matter what she took, she couldn't match the exquisite simplicity of the clothes worn by Gillian and Lucia Radcliffe.

With as little taste for humiliation as anyone, she hoped Curt had remembered his promise to hire clothes.

He'd remember. She relaxed as the helicopter began its descent. Overbearing blackmailer he might be, but she'd put down good money on nothing escaping that formidable mind.

Besides, he had an image to sustain, one that home-sewn clothes would wreck. An ironic smile tilted her lips; try as she did, she just couldn't see Curt worrying about his image!

His personal assistant turned out to be a middle-aged woman, elegant and somewhat distant, who nevertheless greeted Peta with a smile and a ready fund of conversation as she drove her to a large house overlooking the harbour in Herne Bay, one of Auckland's marine suburbs.

'Mr McIntosh will be here as soon as he can,' she said, turning into a gateway. 'He's really sorry—an important colleague arrived in Auckland unexpectedly this morning.'

'It's all right,' Peta said easily, trying to convince herself that she wasn't gripped by aching disappointment.

Perhaps some of her feelings showed in her tone, for his assistant gave her a sideways glance. When the engine had died she said, 'In the meantime, he told me that you need additions to your wardrobe. I've organised a woman who dresses people to come along to see you; I think you'll like her.' Her smile relaxed. 'Of course, that might be because she's my daughter.'

Peta tensed, torn between relief and hurt pride. 'I see,' she said woodenly.

'She'll make it as painless as she can. I know how you feel; I hate shopping with a passion and so does my husband. Liz always says that because someone had to do the shopping in our household she was forced to develop a taste for it! Shall we go in?'

Far from resembling the Tanekaha homestead, Curt's house was a gracious relic from the early twentieth century. On the path to the front door, Peta's nostrils quivered at a familiar perfume—a gardenia bush spread its white velvety flowers across the path, their scent filling the air.

Another woman opened the door. How the heck many people did Curt employ?

'Mrs Stable, the housekeeper,' his personal assistant told her quietly.

The housekeeper, a wiry woman in her mid-forties with improbably red hair, showed her to a room that overlooked the harbour. Peta eyed the huge bed, the exquisite furnishings, and the magnificent painting on one wall—and wished herself back home. Damn Curt. How dared he go ahead and organise a shopping spree when she'd specifically told him she wouldn't accept any money from him?

Well, why was she surprised? That was what men like him did—ploughed their way through life, trampling anyone who got in their way.

But she was nothing like her mother. Although she found Curt dangerously desirable, she certainly wasn't in love with him. And even if she had been, pride wouldn't let her follow like a dog at his heel.

And to be fair, the assistant's daughter might have selected clothes from a hire firm...

Peta washed her face, and had just finished storing her pathetically few clothes in the huge wardrobe when someone knocked on the door.

Curt?

Consuming eagerness drove her across the room; she had to take several steadying breaths before she opened the door to a woman whose discreet chicness and resemblance to Curt's PA gave away her identity.

'You must be Liz,' Peta said, masking searing disappointment with a fixed smile.

'I am, indeed. Can I come in?'

'Of course.' She stood back, somewhat startled when the other woman surveyed her with impersonal intensity. 'No offence, but I'm not too happy about this shopping idea,' Peta said, hiding her awkwardness with a brisk overtone.

'It's Curt McIntosh's idea, so we do it.' Liz seemed to come to some decision. 'OK, I can see which designers will be on your wavelength, but can I check the clothes you've brought? Curt said you'd be going to the opening night at a gallery and a dinner party, and spending a day on a yacht. He also said that although the clothes need to be good, they should be useful too, so no wildly impractical stuff. And he said that you've got great colour sense, which is perfectly obvious now I've seen you.'

Pleasure tingled through Peta, temporarily shutting down her indecision.

Liz glanced around, spied clothes through the open door of the walk-in wardrobe, and set off towards them like an elegant bulldozer. Peta opened her mouth.

And then closed it. Feeling alien and abandoned, she stood irresolute.

Liz took down a shirt. 'Did you make this?'

'I—yes.'

'Good finishing.' She directed a quizzical glance at Peta. 'Curt warned me you'd probably object.'

'Did he?' Peta said through gritted teeth. Liz was probably wondering why on earth Curt had allied himself to a country hick. 'Then you can tell him that I didn't, can't you?'

Liz gave a swift, sympathetic grin. 'I've known Curt since Mum went to work for him, and one thing I've learned—well, me and the rest of the world!—is that if you're stupid enough to go hand to hand with him, you'll lose. He fights fair, but he's ruthless and he's utterly determined. How do you think he turned his father's bankrupt business into a worldwide success?'

'I believe he had to dump his father to do it,' Peta said with cutting accusation.

'True, because his father was the problem.' Liz looked at her and seemed to come to some decision. 'I'm not telling you anything everyone doesn't know, so I can say that Mr McIntosh treated the firm like his own personal cash cow. When Curt took it over he turned it on its head and paid off the creditors in an astonishingly short time; he saved the firm and most of the employees' jobs.'

Presumably her mother was one of those employees. 'But to shaft your own father...'

Liz nodded. 'I know. As I said, he's ruthless.'

Peta walked across to the window and stared down past a green lawn, a swimming pool and a fringe of ancient pohutukawa trees. Between their branches the water of the harbour sparkled like gemstone chips.

From behind her Liz said, 'But you know, I'd trust Curt with my life.'

A sound at the door made them both swing around. 'Thank you for that tribute, Liz,' Curt said smoothly. 'Would you like to wait downstairs?'

She'd clapped one hand over her mouth, but she removed it to grin at him. 'Certainly.'

Peta watched with tense awareness as he closed the door. Her heart had kicked into double time and the sensation running riot through her body was undiluted excitement. Three days had only served to hone her involuntary response to his potent male magnetism.

'We made a bargain, you and I,' Curt said pleasantly, but his eyes were grey and cold.

Her jaw angled in defiance. 'I told you I wouldn't let you pay for my clothes. You agreed to hire them.'

'It's not possible.' He lifted his brows when she made an impatient gesture. 'But if it means so much to you, you can pay for them.'

'I can't afford—'

She stopped because he came towards her, and something about his lithe, remorseless advance dried her mouth and stopped her heart.

'If you mean what I think you mean,' she said hoarsely, 'that's disgusting.'

'Disgusting?' He smiled and her blood ran cold. 'What's disgusting about this?' he murmured, and bent his head.

Peta froze as his mouth drifted across one cheekbone. The elusive male scent that was his alone acted like an aphrodisiac on her, switching off her brain to leave her with no protection from the clamouring demands of desire except a basic instinct of self-preservation.

'I am not a prostitute,' she said thickly.

The ugly word hung between them. He laughed softly and said against her ear, 'If you were I wouldn't be doing this…' His mouth moved to the lobe of her ear and he bit gently.

An erotic charge zinged through her, firing every cell into urgent craving.

'...or this,' he finished, and his mouth reached the frantic pulse in the hollow of her throat. He kissed it, and then lifted his mouth a fraction so that his breath blew warm on her sensitised skin. 'And your heart wouldn't be jumping so wildly.'

Tormented delight clamoured through her like a storm. Peta couldn't speak, couldn't tell him to stop using mock tenderness in his subtle, knowledgeable seduction.

She quivered, lost in a rush of desire that burned away the last coherent thought in her brain. Sighing against his lips, she opened her mouth to his.

The other kisses they'd exchanged faded into insignificance; she sensed a difference in him, a darker, deeper hunger beyond the simple desire of man for woman. It fuelled her anticipation into a raging inferno. She shuddered when his hand smoothed up from her waist, coming to rest over the soft mound of her breast. Hot, primeval pleasure burst into life inside her, aching through her body, softening internal pathways, melting her bones...

His touch felt so right, she thought recklessly, linking her arms around his neck and offering him her mouth. She'd been born for this dangerous magic, spent the empty years of her adult life waiting for it.

Eagerly expectant, she held her breath while tension spun between them in the taut, humming silence. Ravished by the pressure of his big, hard body against hers, the powerful strength of his arms, she at last surrendered to her own needs.

His heart thudded against hers, his chest rose and fell, and his arms were hard and demanding around her. Yet he didn't move.

With immense reluctance she forced her heavy lids upwards.

Curt's face was clamped into an expression she didn't

recognise; his eyes glittered and a streak of colour outlined the high, sweeping cheekbones.

Her stomach dropped in endless freefall, and she knew what he was going to say. Humiliated, she tried to turn her face away.

He said something under his breath and his mouth took hers again, hard and fierce and angry, only breaking the kiss to say harshly, 'Not now. Not while Liz is waiting.'

Oh, God, no! She whispered, 'Then what was that about?'

'I'm sorry,' he said, understanding the real question behind the words. He released her and stood with a face like stone, withdrawn to some inner place she could never reach.

She took a jagged indrawn breath, but before she could say anything he spoke again, the raw note banished from his voice.

With a remote deliberation that slammed up impassable barriers, he said, 'I have no excuse; I lost my head. It won't happen again.'

It took all her willpower to step back, to look straight at him. 'Do I have your word on that?'

'Yes.'

Her skin tightened; a heavy weight of loss overwhelmed her. She had to search for a response, and in the end all she could find was a banal, 'Good.'

Curt looked around the bedroom and said with formidable composure, 'An essential part of this masquerade is wearing the right clothes. I'm prepared to pay for them. If you don't agree to that our bargain is over.'

He didn't threaten; he didn't need to. That cold, ruthless tone, his implacable face told her that if she reneged on their deal she'd find herself with no farm, no way of earning her living—nothing.

'Very well,' she said stonily. 'But when I leave here the clothes will stay.'

He shrugged. 'That's entirely up to you. I'll go and tell Liz you'll be ready in ten minutes.'

In the sanctuary of the bathroom, all marble and mirrors and glimmering glass, Peta eyed her reflection. Completely out of place in this cool, sleek sophistication, the woman in the glass blazed with a sensuous earthiness, her mouth kissed red and sultry eyes shooting gold sparks.

Even her hair was wild—she looked as though she'd been plugged into an electric socket.

After fumbling with the taps she ran cold water over her wrists and washed her face, then dragged a comb through her hair and with a vicious twist tightened the tie that dragged it off her face.

Another survey of her reflection convinced her that she'd managed to tone down the telltale sensuality and hunger. Now she just looked…charged, energised, as though she was hurrying eagerly forward to the future.

As though she was in control of her life, she thought hollowly.

At the top of the stairs she heard voices floating up from below; they fell silent when she started down. She swallowed and held her head high, taking each step carefully as Curt watched her with an expression that gave nothing away. Liz followed his gaze, her mobile face registering a moment of comprehension before it too went blank.

Acutely self-conscious, Peta reached the bottom and came towards them.

'You're ready?' Liz said, then gave a short laugh. 'Stupid question. So let's roll.'

'Be back here at five,' Curt said, walking beside Peta towards the open front door. 'Don't let them hack into her hair.'

Shocked, Peta glanced over her shoulder. He was looking at the woman beside her.

'Of course not,' Liz said with a frown. 'It would be a wicked sin. Don't worry, I know what I'm doing.'

Curt transferred his gaze to Peta. 'Have fun.'

Peta's eyes focused somewhere beyond and above his broad shoulder. 'Thank you,' she said on a note of irony, and she and the other woman went out into the summer sunlight.

'Tell me about yourself,' Liz invited as she drove through Auckland's crazy traffic.

'I'm twenty-three,' Peta said, wondering why she needed to do this. 'I work my own farm and I lead a pure and wholesome life.'

Liz laughed. 'Not if you stick with Curt for long,' she warned. 'He's a course in sophistication all on his own. Who's your favourite author?'

'Only one?'

'Run through them, then.'

Peta began with Jane Austen and finished with her latest discovery from the library, adding, 'And I love reading whodunnits and romances.'

'Who doesn't?' Liz said cheerfully. 'OK, so you're a romantic. What do you do for a hobby? What flowers do you have in your garden? Or is it only vegetables?'

The vegetable garden had been her father's domain, one she kept up for economy's sake. Flower gardens, he'd said, were a waste of precious time. 'I have three hibiscus bushes and a gardenia in a pot by the front door. As for hobbies, I sew. Every so often I knit.' When she'd saved enough money to buy the wool.

Liz's brows shot up. 'Interesting. You could be a casual

or a romantic, but my guess is that you're one of the rare people who can wear several looks. We'll see.'

Expertly negotiating a crowded, narrow street, she pulled up outside a shop that had one outrageous dress in the window. 'Let's go,' she said cheerfully.

CHAPTER SIX

WHAT followed was one of the most exhausting afternoons Peta had ever endured. 'And that includes haymaking,' she said wearily over a restorative cup of tea in a small, unfashionable café that made, Liz assured her, the best latte south of the equator. The tea was excellent too.

Liz laughed. 'Admit that you thought all Aucklanders—especially shopaholics—were effete weaklings.'

'I'm not that much of a hayseed,' Peta told her loftily, 'but I had no idea you were going to drag me around a couple of hundred stores and boutiques.'

'Seven,' her companion corrected. 'And now that you've stocked up on caffeine and tannin again, let's get your hair done.'

The stylist took them into a private room. Watching him in the mirror, Peta felt he spent an inordinately long time just letting her hair ripple through his fingers while he frowned at her reflection.

'Good bone structure,' he finally pronounced. 'And I'm not going to mess about with colour—it's perfect as it is. I'll cut it a little shorter and show you a couple of ways to put it up.' He glanced at her hands and shuddered. 'One of the girls will give you a manicure.'

He was a genius with the scissors, but the manicure turned out to be an exercise in sensuous pleasure. On the way home Peta was very aware of the soft gloss of sheen on her nails, and wondered if Curt would like the way they seemed to make her fingers even longer.

No, she thought desperately, what the *hell* are you thinking?

It couldn't be allowed to matter. Unfortunately, it did, and the next few days stretched out before her like an ordeal, one with an infinite possibility of consequences.

All of them bad.

Remember what happened to your mother, she ordered. Unless you're a princess, loving a dominant man leads to misery. The intense, reluctant attraction she felt for Curt was only the first step on the perilous road that had led to her mother sacrificing her individuality, her talent and her freedom to the jealous god of love.

But her mother's tragedy seemed thin and insubstantial, as though Curt's vitality drained life from her memories.

Halfway home, her eye caught the parcels and boxes in the back of Liz's hatchback. While Peta's hair and hands were being groomed, the other woman had collected a range of accessories.

Assailed by an empty feeling of disconnection, Peta stared out at the busy streets.

I don't belong here, she thought sombrely.

Like a girl in a fairytale, carried off across some perilous border between reality and fantasy, she was lost in a world she didn't understand and prey to dangers she barely recognised.

The greatest of which, she thought with a flare of worrying anticipation, was waiting for her in that gracious old house.

Curt had snapped his fingers and people had obeyed, whisking her out of her familiar world and transporting her wherever he ordered them to. She'd obeyed too, because she was afraid of what he could do to her life if she didn't.

And because you don't want Ian to fall in love with you, she reminded herself.

It was too easy to forget that.

'A good afternoon,' Liz said with satisfaction. She drew up on the gravel drive and switched off the engine.

Curt wasn't at home. Peta knew as soon as she walked through the front door; some invisible, intangible force had vanished. Repressing a sinister disappointment, she went with Liz up to her bedroom.

The next hour was spent trying on the carefully chosen clothes, matching them to the accessories Liz had collected. Peta meant to stay aloof and let Liz choose for her, but somehow she found herself offering opinions, falling in love with various garments, wrinkling her nose at others.

'OK, that's fine,' Liz said when the final choices had been packed away in the wardrobe. 'And if I say so myself, we've done a good job. Those clothes not only highlight your good points, they'll take you from breakfast to midnight. It's a pity I can't tell everyone I dressed you—you look stunning. But in my job I have to be the soul of discretion; Curt wouldn't have contacted me if I hadn't been.'

'I know that,' Peta said drily.

Liz nodded. 'You made it a lot easier for me—you've got excellent taste and an inherent understanding of what suits you and doesn't. Now, forget about all this, and just have fun!'

The faintest hint of envy in her tone made Peta wonder just how well she knew Curt, and whether there was perhaps a past attachment between them.

Smiling hard to cover a pang—no, *not* jealousy—Peta waved goodbye, then turned back to the house, feeling more alone than she ever had in her life. After her parents had died she'd at least been in familiar surroundings. Here she knew no one; even Nadine had left her firm of inner-city solicitors for a holiday in Fiji.

After refusing an offer of afternoon tea from the housekeeper, Peta made her way outside and looked around her with wonder and a growing appreciation. For some reason it seemed rude to explore, so she sat in an elegant and extremely comfortable chair on the wide veranda and tried to empty her mind of everything but the way the sun glinted on the harbour.

When the skin tightened between her shoulder blades, she glanced up, and saw Curt walking towards her.

Awkwardly she got up, angry because she'd weakly followed Liz's suggestion to leave on the lion-coloured cotton trousers and the sleeveless T-shirt—made interesting, so Liz had announced, by the mesh overlay.

'They show off those splendid shoulders,' she'd said, slipping a choker of wooden beads in the same golden tones around Peta's throat.

She'd agreed because she felt good in the outfit, but now she could only think that the top exposed far too much skin to Curt's narrowed eyes.

And that's why you left it on, she thought in self-disgust.

She thought of his mouth on her skin, and to her horror her breasts burned and their centres budded in immediate response. He had to notice.

He had noticed; his gaze heated and his mouth curved in the mirthless smile of a hunter sighting prey.

A combustible mixture of satisfaction, distrust and humiliation drove her to ask harshly, 'I hope it's worth the expense.'

His lashes drooped and he stopped and surveyed her at his leisure—for all the world, she thought indignantly, like some pasha checking out the latest slave girl in the harem.

It was her own fault; she'd given him the opportunity to ram home just how much at his disposal she was.

'Absolutely,' he said smoothly. 'Would you like a drink?'

She nodded. 'Something long and cool would be lovely.'

'Wine?' Curt suggested, walking up the steps to the veranda.

She said jerkily, 'Yes, please, but I'd better have some water first. I'm thirsty and I don't want to drink too fast.'

'Wise woman.' He poured a long glass of water from a jug with lemon slices floating on the surface, and handed it over. Surprisingly, he poured another for himself before indicating a recliner. 'Sit down; you look tired. Did Liz wear you out?'

Somehow lying back on the recliner seemed too intimate, as though she was displaying her body for his scrutiny. She chose a nearby chair instead. 'I had no idea trying on clothes could be so exhausting.'

Curt smiled and sat down in another chair. He'd changed from the formal business suit into a pair of light trousers that hugged his narrow hips and muscular thighs. His short-sleeved cotton shirt was open at the neck.

So much untrammelled masculine magnetism took her breath away. Peta took refuge behind her glass and fixed her gaze on the view.

'Liz is a perfectionist,' he observed, 'and like her mother, she's ruthlessly efficient. We're not going out tonight, so you can go to bed early if you want to.'

She took another mouthful of water, letting it slip down her throat. 'I thought the idea was to show ourselves off.'

'Not tonight,' he said.

She stared at him. 'Why?'

'Think, Peta,' he drawled in the tone she had come to hate. 'We haven't seen each other for three days. Why would we want to go out when we can spend the evening alone together?' He invested the final sentence with a mocking tone that didn't hide the underlying purr of sensuality.

'Oh,' she said numbly. Something twisted in the pit of her stomach, a sharp urgency that played havoc with her concentration. She took another sip and swallowed it too quickly.

Curt said, 'I thought you might want to ring and make sure that everything's all right at home.'

'Yes, I'll do that.' She began to stand up.

'Finish your drink first. Joe won't be in yet.'

Slowly she drank down the rest of the water while he spoke of the latest entertainment scandal. From there they moved on to books, discovering that although they liked different authors, they had enough in common to fuel a lively discussion.

Then Curt poured a glass of cool, pale gold wine for her, and somehow they drifted into the perilous field of politics. To Peta's astonishment he listened to her, and even when he disagreed with what she said he didn't resort to ridicule.

It was powerfully stimulating.

Laughing over his caustic summation of one particularly media-hungry member of parliament, she realised incredulously that she was fascinated by more than his male charisma. And this attraction of the mind, she thought warily, was far more dangerous than lust.

He was watching her, his eyes sharply analytical, waiting for her to answer. Dry-mouthed, she said, 'I suppose you have to deal with people like that all the time.'

His brows drew together in a faint frown. 'Most of them are reasonably decent people struggling to juggle a hunger for power with a desire to do some good for the country,' he said, and glanced at his watch. 'Do you want to ring Joe now?'

'Yes, thank you.' The sun was already setting behind the high, forested hills on the western horizon.

He took a sleek mobile phone from his pocket and

handed it over. Their fingers touched, and the awareness that had merely smouldered for the past half-hour burst into flames again.

'You need to put the number in,' Curt said softly.

'Yes.' Start *thinking*, she told herself, and clumsily punched in her number, staring at the harbour through the screen of the trees.

Five minutes later she handed back the telephone, taking care to keep her fingers away from his. 'Everything's fine,' she said lightly, addressing his top shirt button. 'Laddie's decided that as Joe is feeding him, he'd better obey Joe's calls. Which is good going on Joe's part, because a lot of the time Laddie doesn't take any notice of me.'

He asked her about training a cattle dog. Later she thought that he couldn't have any interest in the trials of coaxing an adolescent dog to deal sensibly with calves, but he seemed interested, laughing when she confessed some of the mistakes she and the dog had made.

They ate dinner out on the veranda while the summer evening faded swiftly into a night filled with the sibilant whisper of waves on the beach below, and the fragrance of flowers in the gathering darkness. Fat white candles gleamed in glass cylinders, their steady flames catching the velvety petals of roses in the centre of the table, winking on the silver and the wineglasses.

And picking out with loving fidelity the strong bones and dramatically sensual impact of the man opposite.

The whole scene was straight out of *House and Garden*, Peta thought cynically, trying to protect herself from succumbing to the seductive promise of romantic fantasy.

She managed it, but only just. And only, she admitted once safe in her room, because he didn't touch her at all.

That night she didn't sleep well, waking bleary-eyed and

disoriented to a knock on the door and the shocked realisation that it was almost nine o'clock.

'Coming,' she croaked, and scrambled out of bed.

The housekeeper said with a smile, 'Mr McIntosh suggested I wake you now. He asked me to remind you that
Ms Shaw is collecting you at ten, and that he's meeting
you for lunch at twelve-thirty.'

'I'll be down in twenty minutes,' Peta told her.

Liz took her to a salon, where a woman gave her a facial,
then checked out the cosmetics she used. 'Good choices,
but I think I've got better. Try this lipstick.'

Peta opened her mouth to say she didn't need any more
cosmetics, then closed it again. Being groomed like a prize
cow for showing revolted her, but she'd agreed to it.

And when she left Auckland, once Ian was utterly convinced that she and Curt had had a blazing affair, she'd
leave this whole deal behind and never, ever think of Curt
McIntosh again.

If she could...

Liz dropped her off outside the restaurant. 'Curt's always
on time,' she said with her ready smile. 'He'll be waiting
for you.'

Just how well did she know him? Peta mulled the question over as she walked up the steps, but inside the foyer
she forgot everything else. At the sight of Curt a smile
broke through, soft and tremulous and entirely involuntary.

His brows drew together, accentuating the powerful
framework of his lean face, and then he smiled, and when
she came up to him he took her hand and kissed it.

The unexpected caress jolted her heart until she remembered he'd done the same to Granny Wai.

Eyes fixed on her face, he tucked her hand into his arm
and said in a voice pitched only for her, 'That was brilliant.
Keep it up.'

His observation slashed through her composure with its cynical reminder of the reason she was there. 'I hope I'm not late,' she said, pronouncing each word with care.

'Dead on time.' His smile held a predatory gleam. 'And smelling delicious.'

'The perfume was horribly expensive,' she said crisply. 'I'm glad you think it's worth it.'

He walked her towards the doors of the restaurant. The head waiter appeared as if by magic, frowning at the hostess who'd come forward to deal with them. 'Mr McIntosh, this way, please.'

Walking through the restaurant was purgatory; eyes that gleamed with curiosity scrutinised her, and unknown faces hastily extinguished an avid interest. Several people nodded at Curt. Although he acknowledged them, he didn't stop until the waiter delivered them to a table partially shielded from the rest of the room by a tree in a majestic pot.

With a flourish the waiter produced two menus and re-cited a list of specials, asked if they wanted drinks, and left them to consider their orders.

'If you want wine with your meal their list is particularly good,' Curt told her.

She shook her head. 'Wine in the middle of the day makes me sleepy. But there's no reason why you shouldn't have some.'

'I don't drink in the middle of the day either.'

It was a tiny link between them, one she found herself cherishing for a foolish moment before common sense banished such weakness.

Peta opened the menu and scanned its contents with a sinking heart. 'You're going to have to translate,' she said evenly. 'I can understand some of this, but not much.'

No doubt Anna Lee was able to read any menu, whatever the language.

He shrugged. 'It's no big deal. I know you like seafood, so why not try the fish of the day, which is always superb, and a salad? If you feel like something else after that we can look at the dessert list.'

'I'm not particularly hungry; I've done nothing but be pampered all morning,' she said, closing the menu with relief.

When he didn't say anything she looked across the table. His expression hadn't changed, but in some indiscernible way he'd closed her out.

Tersely she said, 'Isn't it a little pretentious to have a menu in French?'

Her comment called him back from whatever mental region he'd been in, and she felt the impact of his keen attention.

'Possibly,' he said indolently. 'But as the owner is French, we can forgive her for the quirk.'

'Well, yes, of course.' Feeling foolish, she glanced at the tree in its elegant pot, hiding them from most of the restaurant. He'd wanted to show her off as his latest lover, so she was surprised he hadn't chosen a more public table.

As though the question had been written on her face, Curt said, 'This is the table I always have; any other would have looked too obvious. At least two tables have a pretty good view of us, and sitting at one of them is the biggest gossip in New Zealand, who hasn't taken his eyes off us since we came in the door.' He settled back into his chair and surveyed her with a look of pure male authority. 'I think another of those tremulous smiles is in order.'

Peta tried, she really did, but the smile he'd ordered emerged glittering and swift, throwing down a gauntlet that narrowed Curt's eyes.

'On the other hand,' he said levelly, 'perhaps you're right—a dare is much more intriguing.'

He knew what it was about him that attracted women; the genes that had blessed him with a handsome face and eye-catching height. Well-earned cynicism told him that his first million had boosted his appeal, and each subsequent appearance in the Rich List had only added to his standing amongst a certain sort of woman. Although he enjoyed their company, he'd chosen his lovers with discrimination, always being faithful but always making sure they understood the limitations of the affair.

One or two had wanted more; sorry though he'd been to hurt them, he'd cut the connection immediately. He didn't want to leave a trail of broken hearts. The rest had gracefully accepted what he was prepared to give, and when the time came for the affair to die they'd accepted that too.

Until he'd seen Peta covered in mud cradling a terrified calf he'd been arrogantly certain he understood women well enough.

He couldn't understand why she was such a mystery to him. Green, yet not shy, she held her own, challenging him in ways that almost lifted the lid on a streak of recklessness he'd conquered in his high-school years. She was no pushover—except in his arms.

Then she seemed bewildered by her own response. Was she a virgin? Curt moved slightly in his chair, astonished at the sudden clamour in his blood.

Peta said, 'Which one's the gossip?'

'The magnificently primped middle-aged man with the elderly woman.'

Brows climbing, she gave him a swift, mischievous smile that transformed her face for a second. 'Is he a gigolo?' she asked eagerly. 'I've never seen one before.'

He laughed. 'No, he's not; the woman with him is his mother. An hour after he leaves here, it will be all around town that you and I had lunch together, and by tomorrow the North Island will know you're staying with me.'

Snidely she returned, 'Well, those parts of Auckland and the North Island that are interested!'

'True.'

'I'm glad no one knows who I am.'

'They will soon.'

She said in a low voice, 'Then it's no use me trying to appear sophisticated and upmarket. Aren't you worried that once they find out I'm a nothing, nobody's going to believe that you're interested in me?'

'You're considerably more than a nonentity,' he said, his ironic tone at startling variance with the slow appraisal he gave her with half-closed eyes. 'The way you look is what makes this whole thing entirely credible.'

'You're telling me that only tall women need to apply to be your lovers? I hope that's not the only criterion!'

The moment she said it Peta knew she should have bitten her tongue.

Eyes darkening, he leaned forward and said, 'Not at all. I'm surprised you're interested.'

'I'm not,' she returned smartly, lying valiantly.

He picked up her hand and his touch—so light it skimmed her skin—registered in every nerve in her body with shattering impact. 'Look at me, Peta.'

Reluctantly, she obeyed.

'Now smile,' he commanded quietly.

So she did, shivers of bitter pleasure running through her.

Fortunately the waiter returned then, stopping a few steps away from the table and pretending to straighten the silver on a sideboard until Curt let her hand go. Pink-cheeked and breathing fast, Peta held her head high while Curt gave their orders.

Then he set about convincing the entire restaurant—or

those who could see them—that he and Peta were at the start of a red-hot affair.

He did it very well, Peta thought bleakly, smiling like an automaton, trying hard to behave as though she was falling in love with a powerful, incredibly sexy tycoon. Not that he flirted; what was happening was altogether more potent than that light-hearted activity. He simply ignored everyone else in the room, bending his whole attention on her, and it was hugely, headily seductive.

'You were right,' she said, putting her napkin down when she'd eaten all she could. 'That fish was utterly delicious, and so was the salad.'

'Anything else?'

'No, thank you.' She gave a small sigh and forced herself to look at him.

And froze. He was watching her mouth with such absorbed attention that everything around her dimmed and diffused while sensation spun wildly through her body. Stop it, she thought distractedly. Oh, stop it right now!

The pleasant tenor voice from behind her burst into that stillness like a bucket of icy water. 'Curt, dear boy, how are you?'

It was the gossip, beaming benevolently at them both; his mother was nowhere in sight.

Of course Curt recovered—because he'd been faking it, she thought dismally. He got to his feet and the two men shook hands, after which he introduced the intruder. She recovered her composure enough to smile and say his name and then he and Curt exchanged a few pleasantries. Peta was very aware of the keen, not-quite-malicious interest in the eyes of the older man.

'I must go,' he said cheerfully. 'Are we seeing you tonight at the gallery opening?'

Curt nodded. 'We'll be there.'

'Good, good.' He said his goodbyes fussily, and left them.

Would Anna Lee be at the gallery opening? Peta's stomach tightened but she had no right to say no, to turn tail and run.

Outside in the busy street she said, 'You'll have to tell me if the clothes I choose will suit the occasion.'

A large car with tinted windows slid to a halt beside them. Curt nodded to the uniformed driver and opened the back door for her. As she lowered herself into the spacious back seat, he said smoothly, 'I'm sure you'll look stunning—Liz is good at her job.'

'I don't know much about art,' Peta said flatly. Her mother had spoken to her of the great artists, even showing her books that she'd brought home from the library, but only when her father wasn't there.

A sardonic smile curved Curt's mouth. 'Most people there would probably recognise a Monet, and they might know a Colin McCahon because it's got writing on it, but that would be about all.' He looked down at her, and said quietly, 'You'll be fine; I'll be there for you. Moore will take you home now, and I'll be there around six. Put on your safety belt.'

He waited until it was clipped before closing the door. Peta watched him stride down the street as the big car edged out into the traffic, and hugged his words to her heart. *I'll be there for you,* he'd said.

If only, she thought and swift, hard tears ached in her throat.

CHAPTER SEVEN

WINEGLASS in hand, Peta gazed around the art gallery. People chatted, laughed, sipped, eyed each other up—only a few, she noted with faint amusement, were actually bothering to inspect the exhibits.

Her heart contracted into a tight, hard ball when she saw a couple of women frankly ogling Curt. She didn't blame them; he looked magnificent, the male elegance of black and white evening clothes subtly underlining his effortless combination of sexuality and power. Cold panic hit her like a blow, and she felt again that odd sense of disconnection, as though she had stepped off the edge of her world into another where the rules no longer applied.

Then the chattering around them suddenly fell off into what could only be called a subdued hum. People began eyeing them covertly, and while one couple edged back, a few eased closer.

Anna Lee. Peta braced herself and took refuge in an intense scrutiny of her wineglass.

She heard a rich voice say, 'Darling, *there* you are! I wondered if you'd got bored and decided to flee.'

Curt smiled with a trace of irony. 'Hello, Anna. Have you met Peta Grey?'

Her stomach in free fall, Peta turned. The small blonde beside Curt gazed earnestly around and said, 'No, where is he? Should I know him?'

Without a flicker of amusement Curt introduced Peta. At least, she thought as Anna Lee gave a peal of laughter, she wasn't too badly outsmarted in the couture stakes. Not that

her long bronze skirt and silk top had anything like the
sexy panache of the other woman's outfit, a startling purple
bodysuit with an exquisite transparent kimono draped over
it to emphasise her sleek body.

'Why *do* people give their children androgynous names?'
Anna enquired of nobody in particular. She sent Peta a
glance that revealed her mistake had been deliberate. 'Tell
me, Ms Grey, did your parents want a boy?'

'I don't really know,' Peta said, because her father's
heartfelt longing for a son was no business of Anna Lee's.
Skin prickling at the tension in the air, she forced herself
to produce a cool smile.

'Well, at least he got a big strong child,' Anna said dis-
missively, before gazing up at Curt with a confiding smile.
'How was your sojourn in the wilds of Northland? Too
boring, I imagine.'

'On the contrary,' he returned, a thread of steel in the
clipped words. 'I found it fascinating.'

Anna's pout emphasised her lush mouth. 'Amazing,' she
murmured, lengthening the middle syllable. 'I didn't think
gumboots and peasants were your thing.' She turned to Peta
and ladled insolence into her smile. 'What do you think of
the modern trends in New Zealand abstract art?'

Peta said tranquilly, 'I'm afraid I'm an unashamed tra-
ditionalist.'

Anna gave a tinkling little laugh. 'Somehow I'm *not* surprised. Such a pity—you won't find many pretty flowers
here.'

'Well, no,' Peta said every bit as sweetly. 'Some are a
little too derivative of Braque and the Dadaists, but all in
all it's not a bad exhibition.'

'Oh, you've been researching,' Anna cooed, but chagrin
darkened her large eyes. She waved at someone past Peta's

vision and stepped back. 'I'd better circulate. Lovely to see you again, Curt. Ms Grey.'

Curt waited until she'd left before murmuring, 'All right?'

Peta turned glittering green eyes on him. 'You should have warned me that I was being used to break off an affair.'

'It was already over.' His voice warned her not to trespass any further.

'It didn't look like it to me!'

'Stop frowning,' Curt ordered. Behind the narrowed, intimate smile he bestowed on her was an implicit threat.

Although Peta obeyed, she was furious and oddly grieved. Humiliation, she thought stringently, had to be walking into an event where you expected to shine and seeing your ex-lover with another woman, one who was nowhere near so beautiful as you were!

She despised Curt for his effortless handling of the situation. There was something heartless in his self-possession, a dangerous indifference that cut like a knife. Yet his smile sent her blood singing through her veins in a swift rise of desire, darkly intoxicating and perilous.

Being in Curt's power chafed her unbearably, because it meant they weren't equals.

For the next hour she circulated with him, meeting people she recognised from newspaper photographs, people whose faces were familiar from television, several she'd even seen on the big screen. In a tense way she enjoyed it; Curt kept his promise to stay with her, and although everyone seemed curious, they were interesting.

And some of the art was magnificent; she found it intensely stimulating to discuss the pictures with people who understood them.

Eventually Curt said, 'Time to go.'

Outside, she was startled to find that although the sun had set it was still light—the precious few minutes of northern twilight before darkness came down onto the city. As they turned into his drive the first street lamp flicked orange, and the scent of gardenias saturated the sultry air.

'You did well,' Curt said, switching off the car engine as the door of the garage came down behind them.

'Thank you,' she said tonelessly.

She got out before he had time to open the passenger door for her, and waited for him to disarm the security.

Once inside the house he said, 'Dinner will be waiting.'

'I'm afraid I'm not hungry. I'll skip it and go straight up to my room.'

His expression hardened. 'You've eaten nothing.'

The thought of forcing food past her lips nauseated her. 'I don't want anything,' she said abruptly, and ran up the staircase.

Although he didn't answer she fancied she could feel him watch her. Safely in her lovely room she stripped the sleek silk clothes from her body and hung them up, creamed the expensive cosmetics from her face, and showered the last bit of Curt's money off her skin.

Only then, wrapped in her elderly dressing-gown, did she accept that her fury was rooted in jealousy.

Not just jealousy, although that would be bad enough. Disgusted by Curt's action in producing her as the woman in possession—ha! How bitterly ironic that was!—she was more hurt by the aura of connection that still clung around him and Anna Lee.

Restlessly she paced the floor, arms folded across her waist as though to hold herself together.

You've fallen in love with him.

No. To love someone you had to respect him, and she

didn't respect Curt. He'd seen her as someone he could use, and he was deliberately, cold-bloodedly using her.

When had he broken up with Anna?

It could only have been during the three days before she'd come down from Tanekaha, because Nadine had seen them together just before Granny Wai's party.

Even if he had broken off his affair with Anna, taking another woman to the opening tonight was ruthlessness carried to cruel extremes.

On the other hand, he was doing it for his sister.

And perhaps he'd seen a way of killing two birds with one stone—showing Anna that her affair with him was well and truly over, while scotching Ian's guilty affection.

Stop looking for excuses for him, Peta told herself sternly, walking across to the window. Anna might not be the kindest or nicest person in the world, but she didn't deserve humiliation. Nobody did.

A knock on the door startled her. Breath locking in her throat, she froze.

Curt's voice was coldly forceful. 'If you don't open the door, Peta, I'll break it down.'

'Come in, then,' she said, infuriated when her voice quivered in the middle of the defiant challenge.

He'd changed into a T-shirt that showed off his broad shoulders and muscled torso. To her astonishment, he carried a tray. 'Food,' he said. 'Eat it.'

'Or you'll force-feed me?'

'Something like that,' he agreed.

She could imagine him doing just that. 'I'm not hungry,' she said dully.

'Possibly not, but you're upset, and going to bed on an empty stomach won't get you a decent night's sleep. Tomorrow we're going out on a friend's yacht so you'll need to be alert.'

She bit her lip, but her stomach betrayed her, reacting to the delectable scent of food with a beseeching rumble. 'I'll eat it when you've gone.'

'I don't trust you,' he told her.

She stared at him, met implacable blue-grey eyes, and knew she was beaten. With a ramrod spine, and shoulders held so stiffly they ached, she walked across to the small table in the window where he'd set the tray down.

Clearly it hadn't occurred to him that she'd hold out. Well, how could she?

Peta lifted the cover from the plate and stared at a dish of scrambled eggs, smooth and creamy and delicate. 'Did you get your poor housekeeper to do this specially for me?'

'No.' He sounded amused. 'I cooked them.'

'Pull the other leg,' she said without thinking.

He grinned and leaned against the wall. 'I can cook three things,' he said calmly. 'Scrambled eggs is one of them.'

The eggs were as delicious as they looked. After the first mouthful had gone down she asked, 'What are the others?'

'Steak and chips, and Thai red curry,' he told her.

She swallowed another mouthful. 'Why those three in particular?'

'Because I like them.'

Well, yes, of course. Oddly enough the turmoil in her stomach had eased with the arrival of food. Anna's reference to her as a peasant popped into her head; she grimaced.

'Did I get a piece of eggshell in there?' Curt asked.

'No,' she said shortly, glad to be reminded of his perfidy. It astonished her how the simple act of scrambling eggs for her had mellowed her attitude. Clearly she was a pushover.

She said, 'I assume my main function on the yacht is to hang on your arm and gaze adoringly at you?'

'My ego doesn't need stoking quite that badly,' he said

matter-of-factly. 'Besides, I don't want to ruin my reputation for finding both brains and beauty in my lovers.'

Peta had got to her feet and was putting the cover onto the plate. His words startled her into looking up. 'Don't be silly,' she said sharply, because of course she didn't believe him. 'I'm intelligent enough, I suppose, but I'm not beautiful.'

Curt walked across the room towards her. 'The first time I saw you I thought you were the most stunning woman I'd seen for years.'

Hands clenched on either side of the tray, she stared at him. His voice had been unemotional, but as he got closer she realised that his eyes were lit by a blue flame. An answering flame burst into life inside her.

She swallowed to ease her dry throat and croaked, 'I don't believe that for a moment. I was covered in mud.'

'And exceedingly disdainful,' he agreed, removing the tray from her hands and putting it back onto the table. 'I had to stop myself from kissing that sneer from your lovely mouth.'

'You were as arrogant as you could possibly be.'

'As far as I knew, you were my brother-in-law's lover,' he pointed out, and kissed her, his hands tangling in the sleek weight of hair at the nape of her neck.

Shivers of erotic delight leapt from nerve end to nerve end. She'd gone rigid, but his mouth melted her resistance so that she sagged into his arms, lifting her face in mute, open invitation, everything banished from her mind but the sheer physical excitement of his touch.

Rapturously she yielded to the fierce demand of his mouth, the iron power of his arms, the hard support of his body as he cradled her against him—to her own craving, a longing infinitely more complex than simple, straightforward lust.

Something different about the quality of the kiss should
have alerted her to danger, but she was so lost in pleasure
she didn't notice until it was too late to react.

'Sweet and fiery and potent,' he said against her lips, his
voice raw and deep.

Heat scored her skin, but she met his hooded gaze un-
flinchingly, the golden fire that smouldered in the depths
of her eyes matching the blue intensity of his.

Raw need beat up inside her, wild and reckless, and for
the first time in her life Peta understood how the lightning
strike of passion could shatter everything—all common
sense, all the strictures that kept you safe. With Curt she
didn't want to be safe—she wanted to follow this white-
hot primeval hunger to wherever it took her.

Curt touched his lips to the corner of her mouth in a kiss
as soft as it was sensuous, then gently bit the side of her
throat.

Peta's heart filled her body with erotic drumming.

When she gasped his name he said, 'You've got such a
lazy, throaty voice, a summer voice, and then you look at
me and I see storms and a desperation that almost matches
mine.'

His words seemed to come from far away, and she
thrilled to the authentic note of need in them, stark and
carnal and consuming.

Hunger beat up through her, so ferocious she could taste
it in her mouth, feel it stabbing through every cell in her
body.

'I know,' she said, and something in her snapped.

Or perhaps it slotted into place and she knew her mind
for the first time in her life. Even if this was wrong—if
Curt was lying to her—she wanted him. For once she was
going to emerge from the safe blandness of the life she'd

constructed so carefully, and follow her questing heart wherever it led her.

So when his hand slid beneath her robe, she reciprocated with fingers splayed across his shirt. But she could only clench her hand on the thin material because her whole body tensed unbearably while he stroked gently, knowledgeably towards the tightly beaded centre of her breast.

'Are you sure?' His voice was guttural.

'Absolutely.'

Curt forced himself to examine her face, trying not to swear because her tentative caress had shredded his control. She'd said the single word like a vow, her eyes blazing, her head held high and her mouth—oh, God, her *mouth*—firm, for all its lush promise.

He had to fight down the reckless urge to grab her, fling her on the bed and sink into her, lose himself in her sweet fire. Clenching his jaw against stark desire, he let his hand fall. 'I can stop now; soon I won't be able to.'

A savage wanting twisted inside Peta and she shivered. 'Don't even think about it.'

His hard, beautiful mouth compressed, then relaxed into that shark smile. 'Thinking is a real problem right now,' he murmured, a lean hand finding the tie around her waist.

He gave it a rapid, sure tug. The belt dropped free and the front of her gown swung open, revealing that she had nothing on beneath it.

Curt froze, and she looked at his profile, so close, so absorbed, the bold angles and lines clamped into a mask of hunger that should have terrified her.

Instead, her sharp craving exploded into keen torment, fuelled by his closeness and the dark intensity of his gaze on the soft golden curves of her breasts. A rush of pride reinforced her courage; his trademark self-control was shattering in front of her.

He looked into her eyes. Slowly, giving her time to stop him, he pushed the shoulders of the wrap back. The soft material whispered over her skin, licking against it in slow, delicious provocation.

Need savaged her, half pleasure, half pain. Her breath panted between her lips, and it took every scrap of will-power to stand still. At last the gown fell to the floor, and she stood in front of him, tall and slim and naked.

Moving quickly, he hauled the shirt over his head. Lamplight glowed bronze on his big, lithe body, collecting in pools of light and shadow. The unsparing strength of his desire coiled around her, stoking hers to create a conflagration.

'Last chance,' he said harshly.

Peta shook her head.

She expected him to strip off the rest of his clothes, so when he picked her up and carried her across to the bed she gasped.

Muscles coiling, he stooped, hauled the coverlet back and lowered her onto the sheet. Its coolness contrasted with the heat collecting in all the hidden places of her body. Bemused, she ran her hand across the swell of his biceps, letting her fingers loiter sensuously against the fine grain of his skin.

'That's not a good idea,' he said between his teeth.

Humiliation searing through her, she snatched her hand back, but he caught it in mid-air.

'I like to be touched,' he rasped, and kissed her fingers, 'but for this first time, take it slowly.'

He released her and while she lay dazed with excitement because he was planning a future for them, he kicked off his shoes and undid the fastening of his trousers and stepped out of them.

Peta's heart shut down. Sleek-skinned, powerfully made,

he was big everywhere, she thought dazedly—big and experienced—and she had no idea whether she was going to be able to take him. She knew enough about sex to understand that most women could accept most men, and she certainly wanted him, but—

Surprisingly, he understood. 'Don't worry—it will be all right,' he promised in a thick, heated voice, and came down beside her, one arm sliding beneath her neck so that her lips were only a centimetre away from his.

She couldn't control the tension that stiffened her muscles and dried her mouth, but instead of the onslaught she unconsciously feared he kissed the pulse in her throat, and the erotic little caress eased her into pleasure again. She turned her face into his hair, inhaling the subtle, intoxicating scent of his skin.

Enslaved by his kisses, his slow, worshipful caresses, her mind drifted until all she was aware of was the sleek slide of his body against hers and the building excitement inside her—a different kind of tension, one she welcomed because Curt made it so easy.

His mouth and his hands discovered other pleasure points: the sensitive place where her throat joined her shoulder, a certain spot at the back of her neck. Some he kissed, some he nipped, slowly, exquisitely letting her become accustomed to his touch.

At last he said against the upper curve of her breast, 'Not nervous any longer?'

'No,' she said languidly, afloat on a tide of honeyed delight. If she called a halt now she'd never forgive herself.

She lifted a heavy arm and buried her fingers in his hair, warm from his body, black against her skin. If he wanted to pull away she didn't have a hope of holding him, but the pressure of her fingers reiterated her need and her desire and her surrender.

Peta waited, while his breath smoked across her skin, and then he smiled and turned his head slightly and his mouth closed around a pleading nipple.

The first strong tug of suction sent a sexual signal ripping through her; her body arched in astonished response, and a note of wonder broke in the back of her throat.

In one fluid movement Curt slid both arms beneath her back, holding her free of the sheet so that her breasts were offered to him while he resumed the drugging seduction.

Peta had never known such rapture. It swamped everything else, rioting through her in scintillating waves, setting her alight and anchoring her intensely in that bed, in Curt's arms, willing prisoner of his mouth and hands and of the mastery of his lean, aroused body.

When he lifted his head she moaned in dismay, but this time it was to take her mouth, his open hunger displayed for the first time. She responded with ardent agreement, writhing against him, and eventually his hand found the flare of her hips, and delved further into the place that ached for him.

Peta pressed against that seeking hand, gasping when he set up a rhythm, gasping even more when his fingers entered her in a simulation of the intimacy she needed so desperately.

'Please,' she muttered helplessly into his neck. 'Oh, please…'

'You don't need to ask,' he said, his voice abrasive with barely leashed hunger. 'I'm more than willing to please you.'

He positioned himself over her; she looked up into molten eyes and a face drawn into a hard, triumphant mask. For a moment her heart quailed; he filled her vision, blocking out the rest of the world so that all she could see was Curt.

And then he lowered himself and she felt his blunt probe at the passage that waited for him. Peta's eyes widened as he eased slowly in. She swallowed.

The cords in his neck stood out. 'All right?'

'Oh, yes,' she breathed, and hooked her arms around his shoulders and pulled herself up around him, enclosing and enfolding him, offering herself to him in the most basic, most primal way of all.

Blue fire swallowed every shard of grey in his eyes; his powerful shoulders flexed and he thrust hard and deep, taking her in one strong push that cracked Peta's world open and forced her into another dimension.

Colours she had never seen before spun in front of her, unknown sensations ricocheted through her, and she cried out hoarsely and clutched him, fingers digging into his hide as she clenched muscles she hadn't known to exist around the length of him.

'Peta?' he demanded, easing back.

She shuddered at the fierce intensity of his tone. 'Don't you dare stop,' she commanded.

His expression relaxed and he kissed her and began to push again. 'No,' he said against her lips.

Peta learned that making love was like a dance, a smooth meshing of bodies, of rhythm, of movement, of breath and touch and the sounds of their loving—soft murmurings, the relentlessly increasing thud of their hearts. Tender when she wanted tenderness, erotically demanding when she needed that, but always in control, Curt led her along undiscovered pathways of passion until she shuddered and bit his shoulder and moaned deep and long, head flung back in pleasure so keenly sharp it was close to anguish because it wasn't enough…

That was the moment everything changed; a rough, low sound was torn from his throat, and from then on there was nothing deliberate about his movement, nothing controlled or restrained.

Their bodies fought and melded, struggling to reach some unachievable goal in a primitive mating battle that led inexorably to wave after wave of pleasure so extreme she thought she might die of it.

And then a bigger, more dangerous wave caught her and tossed her up into an alternate universe where nothing but ecstasy existed, spreading through her in unbearable delight.

Dimly she heard herself cry out again before she was lost in Curt's possession. Dimly she heard a guttural sound break from him when he too reached that place, and his big body went rigid and they moved together like a single entity.

And then the slow descent into dazed, exhausted peace sucked her into darkness.

She woke to a different darkness and lay in stunned stillness, trying to work out where she was. She was in her usual position, on one side. She was hot—but not with the usual heat of a summer night. This heat came from within her and beat against her.

Subtle sensory clues wove their way between her defences. A different feel to the bed—no movement, but she knew someone was beside her. When she opened her eyes the memories smashed through, and she recalled everything, from her surrender to those final moments when she'd convulsed with unmatched rapture in Curt's arms.

CHAPTER EIGHT

FOR perhaps four heartbeats Peta clamped her eyes shut, longing to take refuge in cowardly sleep, until the practical streak she'd inherited from some unknown ancestor forced her to face the truth. She opened her eyes again.

Enough moonlight seeped through the curtains for her to see the outline of a male torso, and a dark head on the pillow next to hers.

It wasn't an erotic dream; it had really happened. She had made love with Curt McIntosh.

Perhaps some small, involuntary movement from her clued him into awareness, because he turned onto his back as though he'd been waiting for a signal.

'Awake?' he said in a voice that wouldn't have disturbed her if she'd been asleep.

'Yes.' It was a thin thread of sound, and she flinched when he sat up and looked down at her.

The silence had a life of its own, heavy with unspoken thoughts and a sense of impending doom. The contrast between her turbulent emotions and the lazy, sated languor of her body shocked her. Don't be stupid, Peta told herself, adding with scrupulous honesty, or more stupid than you've already been. You knew he was a magnificent lover the first time you saw him.

In a flat, intimidating voice Curt said, 'I'm sorry. I don't usually lose control like that.'

If he'd tried to hurt her he couldn't have made a better job. Perhaps he *had* tried to hurt her. He must be furious with himself for making love to a woman he didn't trust.

An even more stinging thought whipped across her heart. Or perhaps not. He might consider sex the normal way to end an evening spent with a woman—any woman.

'I'm sorry too,' she said brusquely. 'What are you doing in my bed?'

Irony heavy in his voice, he answered, 'Sleeping, until you started making intriguing little noises and tossing about.'

'But you're not asleep now,' she pointed out.

'And you'd like your bed back.'

'It's not mine,' she said foolishly.

He flung the covers back and stood up. Feverish arousal powered through her, short-circuiting her thoughts. Silhouetted against the windows with dim light slipping in muted monotones over his skin, he was a figure from an erotic fantasy, dangerous, disturbing, and powerful.

She sat up, clutched the sheet across her breasts and watched him stride across to a dark heap on the floor that had to be his clothes. As he picked them up she muttered, 'I'm not used to—'

To making love…

Would he think she was trying to make some claim on him? *You took my virginity, now you owe me?* Did he even realise that this had been her first time? She'd felt no pain, and she was almost sure there had been no physical signs to warn him.

Into a silence that tore her composure to shreds, she finished '—to sharing a bed.'

'I gathered that.' His voice was so cold it brought the temperature down to ice-age level. 'We need to talk, but not now. I'll see you at breakfast.'

Silently he walked across the room. Listening to the

shush of the door closing behind him, Peta fought back the tears that thickened in her throat.

What was she going to do?

'Nothing,' Curt said coolly and decisively. 'Last night alters nothing. You stay here until I say you can go.'

Daylight hadn't brought any wise counsel to Peta, who'd spent the rest of the night staring into the darkness and cursing her idiocy. That was, when she wasn't remembering…

She squared her shoulders. 'And when will that be?'

'When Ian is completely convinced that you have no further interest in him.'

She said through her teeth, 'Has it occurred that I could do this, enjoy my little taste of luxury with you, then go back and tell Ian it was all a mistake, that I really loved him all along?'

'Of course it occurred to me,' he told her with a flick of contempt. 'You don't know Ian at all if you think he'll take you back. He believes he's in love with you, and judging by the look on your face in that photograph you gave him enough encouragement to make him feel you reciprocated. He'll see coming to Auckland with me as a betrayal, and he enjoys humiliation as little as the next man.'

'I did *not* encourage him,' she said, knowing it was useless.

'I know guilt when I see it,' he said coolly. 'If his touch was so unexpected, what put that expression on your face?'

Useless it might be, but she decided to try and explain. 'For a couple of months I'd wondered if something was changing, but he's been a good friend to me and I thought—I hoped—I was reading something into his attitude that wasn't there. I did pull away. When he—touched me, I thought that I should have been more definite.'

Curt said satirically, 'Any discouragement must have been so damned subtle as to be unreadable. Not that it matters now; Ian believes that you went after a better prospect in me and dumped him. Whatever story you spin him after this, he won't take you back.'

An ugly suspicion stained her thoughts. Had he deliberately, cold-bloodedly set out to make love to her, to ruin any chance of Ian taking her back? She stared at him, unable to see anything in his face beyond forceful determination.

Yes, this man would do that.

Fighting back the outraged grief of betrayal, she said steadily, 'I hope your sister realises how much she owes you for your efforts on her behalf.'

'Leave her out of this.' His tone set up a wall between them.

A sensible woman wouldn't have let this situation develop to last night's madness. A sensible woman would have guarded her heart carefully, keeping it safe and whole.

A sensible woman wouldn't have fallen fathoms deep in love with a blackmailer.

Crippled by anguish, she had to suck in a breath before she could say, 'How can we leave Gillian out of it? She's the reason I'm here.'

Curt's brows lifted derisively. 'That's a dead end and you know it. If we're allotting blame, Ian and his wandering eyes led to this, but if you'd made it obvious you weren't interested you'd be safely at home. The fact is, against all prudence and common sense last night happened, so we now have to deal with it.'

She turned away, looking around the morning room. Light, airy, angled to catch the morning sun and a view of the Harbour Bridge and the bush-covered slopes of the North Shore, it breathed a sophisticated informality in spite of the magnificent pictures on the walls. Curt's interest in art clearly didn't stop at small, blonde artists.

'*Deal with it* sounds so straightforward,' she said harshly. 'No doubt it is for you. So tell me, just *how* do we deal with it?'

If he said they'd forget about it she'd—she'd do something violent! Their lovemaking had changed her life, even if she wasn't yet ready to accept what that change meant. Literally, she'd never be the same again.

'There's something else to consider,' he said, still in that forbiddingly glacial tone.

Her heart stirred a little. 'What?'

'You were a virgin, weren't you.'

It wasn't a question and his uncompromising expression and tone told her that it would be useless to deny it.

Colour drained from her skin. Dry-mouthed, she looked at her cup and wished she'd chosen coffee; she needed more caffeine than tea could provide. Hell, what she needed was a good slug of some strong spirit. How had he known? Had she been so gauche that anyone would have recognised her complete lack of experience?

He said something under his breath and she flinched. 'You don't need to answer,' he said brusquely.

Silence reverberated around them until Curt said with unexpected gentleness, 'I'm sorry.'

Why? She almost said it, catching the word back in the bare nick of time.

He went on, 'It shouldn't have happened. At least I used protection, so you're not likely to be pregnant.'

Those prosaic words lacerated Peta's emotion. I can't bear this, she thought, desperately struggling to hold on to the disappearing shreds of her confidence.

Always in control, that was Curt—totally, arrogantly self-contained, his love for his sister the only chink in that seamless armour. Even last night he'd had the presence of mind to use protection.

Oh, he'd wanted her, but although he'd apologised for losing his formidable self-control, he hadn't felt anything like the feverish abandon that had loosened her every inhibition.

Bitter pride gave her the strength to say, 'Even if you hadn't, it's highly unlikely—the time's not right.'

'Then don't worry about it.' He glanced at her plate. 'Eat up. I don't recommend sailing on an empty stomach. Which reminds me, if you're likely to be seasick, now is the time to take a pill. I have a supply.'

'I've never been out on a boat,' she told him, 'so I don't know.'

Another silence. When it weighed too heavily to be endured, she glanced up to find him watching her with an arrested expression, as though she'd said something outrageous.

She said stonily, 'We didn't have money for a boat— besides, my father knew nothing about the sea. I'm sure I'm not the only New Zealander who's never sailed.'

Something that might have been anger tightened his lips, but it had gone before she could identify it properly. And when he said, 'Have you ever been sick in a car?' his tone was casual rather than concerned.

'No.'

'Then you'll probably be all right.'

Breakfast turned into a marathon of forcing food into her unwilling mouth, chewing without tasting, and swallowing without pleasure. After another cup of tea Peta fled to the sanctuary of her bedroom.

For this event Liz had suggested a pair of cotton trousers cut with precision to show off good legs, and a sleeveless singlet in a dark tomato red that lent a glow to Peta's tan.

'There's always a wind at sea,' she'd said, adding an unstructured jacket striped in both colours. 'And you need shelter.' She'd plonked a straw hat on Peta's head and held out sunglasses. 'These are seriously good sunglasses, but not the absolute latest. You don't want to look as though everything's brand new.'

Even with her nerves strained tight, Peta had to admit that Liz knew her stuff. Except for one item; the swimsuit. Spare and sleek, it hadn't been cut particularly high or low, but it had revealed every line of her body.

'Of course it does—and you've got the perfect body to wear it,' Liz had said firmly.

Now Peta jutted her jaw and thrust the scrap of material back onto the shelf. Control of her life might have been temporarily taken away from her, but wherever she could assert it, she would.

The only way she'd endure this purgatory was to face facts—she loved Curt and he didn't love her.

She dropped the sunglasses into a straw bag, followed them with a library book she'd brought from home, and clicked the fastening shut, her mind busy as she tried to assemble her thoughts into some sort of order. Perhaps it wasn't love; after all, what did she have to measure her emotions against? This painful fascination, this feeling that Curt was the only real person in a world that had suddenly gone shadowy, could simply mean that she was in lust.

Love meant subjugation, and although Curt had blackmailed her into this situation, he was different from her father. He didn't expect the mental obedience her father had exacted; he didn't, she thought, struggling to put her finger on the difference between the two men, take any difference of opinion personally.

Curt was certainly dominant, but his dominance was based on his knowledge of his own competence and ability, whereas her father—her father, she thought wonderingly, must have been desperately insecure...

Pop psychology—and was she trying to make excuses for Curt's behaviour? She picked up the straw bag and headed for the door.

Only time would tell; if it was lust it would die once she'd regained her freedom. Until then, the only way to keep what few miserable scraps of pride she had left after last night's spectacular extravaganza of emotion and sensation in Curt's arms was to go cold turkey. Making love to him had been magical and addictive, but it wasn't worth the aftermath.

A knock on the door startled her. Curt said through it, 'Are you ready?'

'Yes, I'm ready.' Jaw angled in determination, she opened the door and went out to join him.

Somehow she'd expected the yacht to be some huge, opulent affair with crew and socialites scattered over it and not a sail in sight. Instead she found a long, elegant sloop whose owners and only crew were a pleasant, middle-aged couple, Doug and Mary Anderson, clearly good friends of Curt's. Perhaps he'd decided that she wasn't up to coping with socialites?

Probably. And that hurt too, but at least with these people she could relax—well, as much as possible when Curt sat next to her and dropped a long arm casually around her shoulders. His faint, potent scent mingled with the keen tang of salt to arouse that hidden hunger in every cell of her body.

Peta had never heard of anyone having flashbacks of pleasant occasions, but every time she looked at him some tormenting image from the previous night blazed across her head. When he turned his head to say something to Mary Anderson, she recalled the stark angles of his profile against the pale skin of her breasts. And when Doug offered him the wheel, she saw an echo of the absorbed intentness with which he undressed her, the complete concentration on her pleasure that had wrung such exquisite sensations from her.

Sensations that lingered too close to the surface, she thought savagely. She'd better banish them to some nice dark basement of her mind and lock the door on them before she made a fool of herself.

They motored out of the marina and then Mary took the tiller and Curt and Doug raised sails and heaved on ropes.

When the sails were billowing to everyone's satisfaction, Peta gazed around at a harbour filled with other yachts and made an attempt at small talk. 'This is utterly glorious.'

Mary Anderson laughed. 'You might have a convert here,' she said to Curt. 'But you'd better not take her out on a cold, wet day when the wind's from the south until she's properly hooked.'

No chance of that; by the time winter arrived this farce would be over. The sunlight dimmed, and to Peta's horror tears stung the backs of her eyes.

'I'll go down below and organise some morning tea,' Mary said.

Peta leapt to her feet. 'Can I help?'

'No, it won't take a minute.' Her hostess gave a swift grin, letting her gaze skim Curt's big, lithe body as he lounged in the cockpit. 'Stay up here and enjoy the view.'

Hot-cheeked, Peta let him draw her down beside him. 'I still don't know how yachts sail,' she said quickly, not caring how silly the statement seemed provided it gave her something else to concentrate on.

An indulgent note in Curt's voice grated like a burr; to show him that she did have some brains, she started to ask questions.

'Here, take the wheel,' Doug invited after a few minutes.

'Theory's all very well, but you need to steer a boat to find out what it's all about.'

'I might do something stupid,' she said warily.

Doug grinned. 'Curt won't let you.'

So she got to her feet and put both hands on the wheel, looking askance at the dials in front of her as the yacht's motion transformed into sensation.

'Yes, that's good—hold her steady on the compass reading,' Doug said. 'I'll go and give Mary some help.'

He disappeared down the short flight of stairs that led to the big cabin. Peta sent an imploring glance over her shoulder to Curt, only to discover that he was standing just behind her.

Hugely relieved, she said, 'What do I do now?'

She followed his instructions obediently, fascinated when the yacht leapt beneath her hands like a live creature. 'It responds so easily and quickly,' she said wonderingly, and made the mistake of looking up at the man behind her.

He looked stern and more than a little forbidding, but the gleam in his eyes brought hot colour to her cheeks.

After that, in spite of everything, her spirits began to lift. Partly it was the day—sunlight glinting off the waves, the warm wind flirting with the hair on her neck, the islands like gems scattered across cloth shot with green and gold— but mainly it was Curt's surprising lack of antagonism that cast an intoxicating glamour over her.

Towards lunchtime they were closing in on one of the outer islands when Mary said, 'Time to get lunch ready.'

This time Peta followed her down the three narrow steps that led to the cabin. 'Give me something to do.'

The older woman looked up from the minuscule kitchen—galley, Peta reminded herself—her cheerful smile not entirely hiding her curiosity.

'Not if you don't want to,' she said.

'I'd like to.'

Mary nodded at the makings of a salad. 'You could put that together. Wait for a few minutes, though; once we've gone about to head into Home Bay it will be easier.'

Sure enough, footsteps on the deck above heralded the manoeuvre.

'Ready about,' Doug called, and the yacht made a sharp turn and pitched over onto the other side of the hull.

Peta said, 'This is all totally new to me, but I'm having a great day.'

Her hostess looked at her a little quizzically. 'Most New Zealanders have been on a yacht before they reach your age.'

Peta explained again. 'My parents were into self-sufficiency in a big way, and that makes for hard work with not much time off for pleasure.' Or rest.

Although her answer had clearly roused her hostess's curiosity, she nodded and went back to slicing an impressive bacon and egg pie. 'I see. Well, I'm glad you're enjoying yourself, because Curt is a great sailor.'

How to answer that? Peta said cautiously, 'We haven't known each other long, but I can see he loves it.'

'He's also very good at it—good enough to turn professional.'

Peta gazed at her. 'Really?'

'Yes. He's a natural athlete, but his first love has always been sailing. He was in contention for the Olympics until he realised he was needed in the family firm.'

From which he ousted his father after a bitter battle. Peta picked up the tomatoes she'd sliced and added them to the salad. Something she'd read made her say, 'Is it true he no longer speaks to his father?'

'It's not true,' Mary said abruptly. 'His parents no longer

speak to him.' Her tone warned Peta to ask no more questions.

But as she tore sprigs of basil into pieces, her mind was buzzing. Gillian must have stood by Curt; was she too outcast from the family? It would explain his fierce protectiveness towards his sister.

The yacht slid to a silent halt and the anchor chain rattled down, much louder in the cabin.

'Just in time,' Mary said brightly. 'We decided we'd picnic under the pohutukawas today—it's a lovely little cove, and for a change it doesn't look as though anyone else is here. You go ahead of me up the companionway, and I'll hand the containers to you.'

Once the lunch had been transferred to the cockpit, Doug winked at Peta and teased his wife, 'I know sea air sharpens the appetite, but it looks as though you've organised enough for an orc army on the march. It's going to take a couple of trips to get all that ashore.' He glanced at Curt. 'I'll drop you and Peta off first then come back and collect Mary and the food.'

Once ashore, Curt asked, 'Enjoying yourself?'

'Very much, thank you,' she said politely, squeaking as her bare feet hit dry sand, fiercely hot beneath her soles. She ran barefoot into the shade of the huge trees and pulled herself up onto a low, swooping branch to put on her sandals.

Curt waited, then lifted her from her perch into his arms.

'No!' she said urgently, fighting down instant desire. 'Not here.'

He lifted his brows, that gleam in his eyes turning hard. 'Why do you think Doug brought us ashore first? Relax, I don't consider the more intimate aspects of lovemaking to be a spectator sport.'

The kiss was hard and swift, close to brutal, but only for

a moment. Almost as soon as his lips touched hers they softened, became seducing rather than barbaric. Even as her brain was commanding, *Think jelly! Don't react!* Peta surrendered, and caution and common sense melted like mist on a tropical morning.

They kissed with a kind of desperation, as though starved of each other for years. Lost in the hot clamour of passion, Peta knew she'd never forget the salty air, warm and sensual as the sun's embrace, and the purring whisper of the little waves on the beach, and the long, plaintive screech of some seabird, alien and faintly sinister.

He explored her mouth with finesse that soon transmuted into naked hunger, his arms tightening around her when he brought her hard against his quickening body.

Everything disappeared in the erotic sensation of his wide shoulders flexing beneath her fingers and the taut muscles of his torso hardening against her as he took her mouth in an ever-deepening exploration, a sensual mimicry of the ultimate embrace. Dimly she registered the powerful surge of his heart, the sudden rise of his chest when at last he dragged air into his lungs.

'No,' she muttered, her lips so tender she could barely articulate.

He made a rough sound that could have been regret—or self-derision. 'Any more and the others will find more than they bargained for when they get here,' he agreed, but the abrasive timbre of his words reinforced just how acutely he was aroused.

Not that she needed confirmation; her own body was already ablaze, eagerly preparing for satisfaction.

Frustration tore through her, bitter as winter. She tried to step back and tripped over one of the gnarled roots of the tree. Instantly his arms tightened again.

She saw the moment he reimposed control, shivering when cool blankness transformed the blue of his gaze into icy grey.

'I'm all right,' she said, clenching her teeth to stop them chattering.

He released her, and stooped to pick up the hat that had somehow got pushed off. He set it on her head, then looked down into her face with an intensity that set her heart pounding even harder. His tawny skin was drawn tight over the superb framework of his face, his mouth full and sensuous in the angular strength of his jaw.

Without volition, Peta lifted one hand and traced the outline of his mouth and the flare of one cheekbone, her fingertips lingering against the skin. Fire burned blue in his eyes and he turned his head and kissed the palm of her hand, stepping backwards when the roar of the outboard engine on the dinghy burst in on them.

'Yes, you look well and truly kissed,' he said harshly, turning away as though the sight of her contaminated him.

Rejection burning like acid, Peta said, 'Why is this necessary? I know why you want me seen around with you, but these aren't people who gossip.'

'Why introduce you to my friends?' He shrugged. 'Verisimilitude. If I didn't, Ian would know that this whole elaborate scheme was a set-up.'

It made sense. The Andersons treated Curt like a son, and on the way across the conversation had revealed that Doug, the owner of a newspaper chain, had been a mentor to him.

Peta persisted, 'But why did you kiss me just then?'

His mouth twisted. 'Because I couldn't stop myself,' he said. Not far away the rubber dinghy ran up onto the beach and he turned away, saying abruptly, 'We'd better go along and meet them.'

Desolation, Peta discovered as she put on her sunglasses, was a cold, barren emptiness that echoed through her, shutting out light and laughter and warmth. But helped by the screen of the sunglasses, her wide smile seemed to convince their hosts that she was enjoying herself. They spread a large rug on the wiry grass beneath another tree and unpacked a delicious picnic.

Nibbling a savoury, cheese-flavoured biscuit, Peta thought that it was the sort of picnic featured in the lifestyle sections of expensive magazines; pity everything she ate tasted like dust. The two Andersons sat in low beach chairs, and she and Curt on the large rug; Curt didn't touch her, but no one there could have overlooked his subtly possessive air.

And afterwards he stretched out on his back on the grass like a great cat, utterly relaxed in the sun while they talked of various things. Peta didn't say much, but the conversation had a quiet air of intimacy that encompassed her. She was glad that Curt had found a replacement for parental affection in the Andersons.

'Is Gillian ever going to do anything with her art?' Mary asked forthrightly.

'I doubt it,' Curt told her.

Mary sighed. 'It's a pity; she could be very good if she tried. Interior decorating is all very well, but it's not truly satisfying to someone like Gillian. You know, I think she needs to break her heart.'

'I hope not.' A frosty note in Curt's voice should have warned the older woman off, but it had no effect.

'You don't want to see her hurt, which is fine and noble and brotherly of you,' she said roundly. 'But as long as she considers it to be a hobby she won't value her talent, and she won't ever be happy. She needs to be thrown onto her own resources, forced to find something to make life worth living.'

'My wife,' Doug confided to Peta, 'has a gallery in Auckland. She lives for art, which is why she's so happy to encourage others to sacrifice themselves for it.'

Mary laughed, but defended herself. 'It's wicked to not use a talent. Curt, what did you think of the exhibition the other night?'

The conversation drifted off, and Peta found her eyelids falling. With Curt only a few centimetres away, she should be stiff with tension, but a healing relaxation softened her bones.

When she yawned, Curt looped an arm around her and pulled her down beside him, but this time he left his arm beneath her shoulders. Strangely, she felt protected, as though nothing could hurt her while he was close by.

A chill darkened her mood. Lust? No, this was love, and it had happened before last night, before she'd had any idea of what it would be like to lie in his arms and be taken to ecstasy.

She even knew the moment it had happened; when he'd held Princess Lucia's baby girl, and smiled into her face, and that smile, that tenderness, had stolen Peta's heart.

High on exaltation, she thought fiercely, *Whatever happens, love is a wonderful thing*.

Wonderful and terrifyingly dangerous.

Had this been how her mother felt about her father? Like Gillian, had she believed that it was necessary to sacrifice a talent on love's altar?

'Go to sleep if you want to,' Curt murmured.

Exhaustion and the emotional shock of her revelation must have overwhelmed her, because when she woke the sun had moved westwards and the white heat of midday had mellowed into a golden afternoon.

She froze like an animal caught out in the open, only relaxing once she realised Curt was no longer beside her. Slowly, carefully, she lifted her lashes and peered through them at the swooping patterns of the branches above, the silver backs of the leaves moving like little fishes against the blue sky.

Silently she turned her head and saw the two Andersons, Doug sound asleep, Mary lying on her stomach reading. She looked up and smiled at Peta before returning to her book. Beyond them some hundred metres or so, Curt leaned back against the trunk of another of the big pohutukawa trees and stared out to sea.

For several minutes she allowed herself the secret luxury of gazing at him, embedding his image in her mind. She wanted to be able to recall everything about that moment, from the clean lines and angles that made up his strong profile to the earthy tang of crushed grass and the texture of the rug against her bare legs. Rills of pleasure sang sweetly through her. Last night he'd been all that she'd ever wanted in a lover—masterful and tender by turns, the perfect first lover for any woman.

Tomorrow who knew what might happen, but for today she'd relish every precious moment, hoarding the memories for the days ahead when she'd be alone again.

As though he felt her thoughts, he turned his head. At that distance he wouldn't have been able to see whether or not she was awake, and she hadn't moved, but he held out his hand in a gesture that was both command and offer.

Silently she rose, smiled at Mary and picked up her hat and sunglasses, and went towards him.

Curt waited for her, his eyes unreadable. Without speaking he indicated the beach, and she nodded and set off with him across the sand, damp and cool at first on the soles of her bare feet, then hot and spiky.

'Better keep in the shade,' he said. 'You'll have to excuse the Andersons; they both lead very busy lives, and sailing is usually the only time they get to relax completely.'

'I slept too,' she reminded him. 'Alcohol at lunchtime always makes me sleepy.'

'Half a glass of wine?'

'I'm not a great drinker,' she admitted. 'My father used to make his own beer, but I didn't like it.'

'Had he been drinking before the accident?'

'No. He didn't drink and drive.'

He said unexpectedly, 'It must have been bloody hard on you, losing them when you were so young.'

'It was.' She paused, then added a little less brusquely, 'But death is a fact of life, and after a while you accept it. It brings its own closure.'

Unlike his relationship with his parents. How did he feel about that? Did it hurt him, or had he washed his hands of the father who'd preferred power to the welfare of the people who worked for him?

She'd never know.

He certainly didn't look like a man who held a secret grief in his heart. He didn't look like a man who had a heart.

So why had she tumbled head over heels in love with him?

CHAPTER NINE

PETA'S swift glance took in metallic blue eyes in a hard face. Her heart kicked into helpless longing.

Curt said abruptly, 'I've made a hell of a mess of this. I had no intention of making love with you when I brought you here.'

'It wasn't just you,' she said with difficulty, sidestepping a rock that poked through the sand. From the relative safety of extra distance, she added, 'It takes two.'

'One of us, I suspect, was way out of her depth.'

Shock stopped Peta in her tracks. Did he realise she was in love with him? 'I wanted it,' she said in a brittle voice.

His smile had no trace of humour in it. 'Is that expected to make me feel better?' Then to her astonishment he said, 'Truce?'

'Why?' she asked baldly.

Curt shrugged. 'Because it's too magnificent a day to waste on recriminations?'

Feeling her way with care, she said, 'I don't blame you for what happened last night. You gave me enough opportunities to stop.'

His expression hardened. 'You may not blame me, but I do.'

Of course he did. He couldn't regret it any more than she did—and even as the thought formed in her mind Peta knew it was a lie. Every glorious, abandoned moment had been worth any subsequent pain.

But Curt would know that if by some remote and wilful

trick of mischievous fate she was pregnant, he'd be responsible for the child until it was sixteen.

She'd never be free of him; she knew he wouldn't ignore his child, however much he despised the mother. Part of her rejoiced at that idea; the practical part of her shuddered.

But he wasn't really like her father...

Stop it, she commanded fiercely. Don't dredge up excuses; yes, he has good points, but at bottom he's dominating and high-handed. That's enough.

Yet it was sinfully sweet to walk along the beach beside him in the sunlight and watch the gulls wheeling and swooping over the sea, the sun transforming them into pure, shining expressions of energy and grace.

It felt completely right to be there, and how could that be when it was so wrong? Curt had used a combination of sexual charisma and cold threats to manipulate her into this situation, but if he touched her again she'd be lost in that desperate, bewildering, sensual world where common sense waged a losing battle with treacherous desire and love.

She didn't dare let herself be caught in that trap. A swift upwards glance met level, compelling eyes in a face that revealed no emotion. Bracing herself, she took the hand outstretched to help her up a bank.

Instant fire! His hand turned, tugged, and she went willingly towards him, every thought forgotten in a rising tide of hot anticipation.

And then he dropped her wrist and said abruptly, 'We'd better go back.'

Feeling as though something rare and precious had been snatched from her, she worked hard to convince herself that it was much safer to stay with the Andersons.

While they'd been walking the older couple had taken to the water, swimming with the smooth strokes of people who used a pool every day.

'Do you want to swim? You can change behind the tree.'
Curt indicated a large pohutukawa.

'I didn't bring my togs.'

Brows lifted, he subjected her to another of those measuring glances. 'Can you swim?'

'Of course I can.'

He gave her a long, measuring look, but said nothing and went off to change. Peta sat down on the rug and yanked her library book from her bag, assiduously applying herself to the pages until a movement caught the corner of her eye.

Slowly she turned her head, her breath stopping in her throat. Last night Curt's sheer physical magnetism had stolen her mind away. The same driven need churned inside her now as her gaze roamed his lean, athletic body, polished by the benign sun into burnished bronze.

Making love to Curt, she thought with a stab of panic, had been addictive; one fix and she was already hooked.

She forced her gaze back to the page, but the print danced crazily, and in a few seconds her eyes wandered again. He was swimming across the bay, strong arms cutting through the water as though he had something to prove. Her body tightened, and then loosened in subtle, inviting places. Into her mind there stole the memory of how it had felt to lie in his arms, with the weight of his magnificent body on hers...

Desire swamped her in a yearning, irresistible wave. For the first time in her life she was gripped by a reckless hunger to seize life with both hands and wring all the juice from it, careless of what might follow.

You did that last night, she reminded herself austerely, and now you're afraid you might be pregnant, even though you know it's a hundred-to-one chance. The image of a small child with Curt's splendid bone structure formed in her mind; she recalled the soft, lively feel of Lucia's baby, her sweet scent and charming, triangular smile.

No, she thought, sick with fear at the amount of effort she needed to banish the fancy.

She closed her eyes, forcing herself to face something she'd been resolutely ignoring. From now on, living next door to Tanekaha would be hell. Every time she looked out of her window or gazed across her paddocks she'd remember, and every time she heard his name she'd hurt. Breathing in deeply, she looped her arms around her knees and hid her face in them.

When she got home again, she'd sell the farm to Curt if he wanted it, to whoever would buy it otherwise. Then she'd leave Kowhai Bay—leave Northland, in fact, and make another life.

The decision should have panicked her because she had nothing but her knowledge of farming to offer a prospective employer.

Instead, all she could think of was that breaking every fragile link to Curt would hurt like nothing else she'd ever endured. Setting her jaw, she straightened. She'd coped with her parents' death; she'd deal with this too.

But when she looked out to sea the water glittered so much it hurt her eyes.

Curt came out of the water after the Andersons had joined her on the rug.

'I'll bet he isn't even panting,' Mary observed, eyeing him with an appreciation that held nothing maternal.

Her husband laughed. 'Of course he isn't.'

Peta pretended to flick through her novel while Curt walked up to them, not looking up until he picked up his towel to dry off the surplus water. 'You don't know what you missed,' he said to her.

She swallowed to free her throat of an obstruction and

returned, 'I don't miss twenty minutes of hard swimming, believe me. I like to lie and float, not wear myself out.'

'Piker,' he said evenly, and turned towards the tree.

Peta went rigid. Oh, God, she thought, and then, Oh, hell!

Scored across his back were the imprints of her nails from that final agony of pleasure. Colour burned up through her skin; she didn't dare look at the other couple, but they'd have had to be blind not to see those betraying marks.

When Mary broke the silence with some remark about the wind having changed, she breathed again, but the glory of the day had been dimmed, and for the rest of the afternoon she was on edge.

In a way, it was a relief when they arrived back at Curt's house.

The telephone was ringing as they walked in. 'Leave it,' he said sharply. 'We need to talk.'

But it rang insistently until the answering machine clicked in and a woman's voice said urgently, 'Curt, please answer. It's your mother here and your father's very ill. He wants—oh, Curt, he wants to see you. Please come.'

Curt wrenched the receiver off its cradle and barked into it, 'Where?'

'Oh, Curt, thank God. At home, darling, but please—' Her voice was abruptly silenced as he switched off the answering machine and listened, the skin tightening over the strong bones of his face.

Eventually he said, 'All right, I'll bring her over. Just keep being brave, Mother, until I get there.'

An oddly formal way to address his mother, Peta thought. She said as he hung up, 'I'm so sorry, Curt.'

'You're to come with me,' he said.

Appalled, she met his iron-hard gaze. 'Your mother won't want me at such a time.'

'My father wants to see you.' When she didn't move he reached out and took her by the elbow, guiding her inexorably towards the door. 'I'm not going to deny him anything he wants. His heart is failing.'

His parents lived only ten minutes' drive away in a handsome apartment block that overlooked the Viaduct Basin, a cosmopolitan, vibrant area where the crews and owners of super-yachts mingled with locals to sample the excellent and eclectic selection of cafés and restaurants.

Curt didn't speak until they parked in the visitors' car park. 'My parents and I haven't been on good terms for the past ten years. In fact, this is the first time I'll have spoken to them since I took over the firm. I had to depose him to do it and he never forgave me for it.'

'I'm sorry,' she said, wrenched by sympathy. 'But—why does he want to see me?'

He waited until they were in a lift before saying harshly, 'Probably to find out what sort of woman you are.'

'Why should he think I'm any different from any of your other lovers?' she asked, genuinely puzzled.

'None of them has ever moved in with me.'

'But I haven't—'

'As far as anyone knows, you have.'

The lift stopped and he stepped back to let her out before setting off down an opulently decorated corridor. When he pressed the silent bell on one door, a woman opened it and fell into his arms, clinging to him as she wept.

'Oh, thank God,' she said through her tears. 'Come in, quickly. Gillian and Ian are on their way down.'

Hugh McIntosh was propped up in a bed with a nurse taking his pulse; he looked like an older, exhausted Curt with a self-indulgent twist to his mouth. When they walked in, his eyes opened.

'Leave us alone.' His voice was dry and thin, and his

chest heaved with each word. When the nurse began to object he said, 'I'm dying, damn you. I want some privacy while I do it.'

Manacling Peta's hand, Curt said to his father, 'It's not like you to give up.' He stopped by the bed and looked down at his father, no emotion showing on his face.

A painful smile flickered around his father's lips. 'So this is your latest.'

'No,' Curt said uncompromisingly. 'This is Peta Grey. She lives next to Gillian and Ian, and she has a mind of her own and a nasty tongue.'

The dying man looked at Peta. She said quietly, 'Only when it's necessary.'

His chest heaved again. Panic-stricken, Peta looked around for the nurse, only to realise that he was laughing.

'Good.' Losing interest in her, he transferred his tired gaze to his son. 'Sorry,' he said. 'Stupid of me—never hold grudges, Curt. Cutting off your nose…'

His voice trailed away and he closed his eyes. Mrs McIntosh gave a choked sob and took his hand, clutching it in both of hers as though she could will life into him.

Curt pressed the buzzer, and as the nurse hurried back in he said to Peta, 'You don't need to stay.'

Outside the room she stopped and looked around, wondering what she should do. Go back to Curt's house? Go home to Kowhai Bay? An outsider in a purely family drama, she had no place here.

She found her way into a sitting room overlooking a large garden bright with jacaranda trees and shady walks. A fountain bubbled in the afternoon sun, and several people were playing *petanque* on a white pitch while others watched from the shade of the trees.

Hovering beside the window, she tried to think. She'd left her money in her other bag that morning, so a taxi to

Curt's house was out. Should she walk back? Mentally retracing the route, she thought she'd probably be able to find her way.

But she'd have to interrupt their painful vigil to ask him for the key, and it seemed cowardly to leave him, like running away when he needed her. A painful smile creased her cheeks. Curt didn't need anyone, but she couldn't go.

She sat down on one of the comfortable recliners on the terrace and prepared to wait things out.

When Gillian and Ian arrived a few minutes later she let them in, ignored by Gillian but aware of Ian's strained glance. After that she watched the sun go down and the dusk fall.

The first Peta knew of Hugh McIntosh's death was when she was scooped up by a pair of strong arms. Disoriented, she smiled sleepily at Curt and snuggled into his chest.

His embrace tightened. 'I'll take you home,' he said in a rasping voice that reverberated through her.

'Mmm.' Then she remembered. Stiffening, she looked up into his face.

Lines of tiredness engraved it, and she could have cried for him. She lifted her hand and held it to his cheek, offering mute sympathy. The soft abrasion of his beard tickled when he turned his head and kissed the palm.

'Is she all right?' Ian's voice, carefully neutral.

'She's damp, but she'll be fine.' Curt walked into the room.

'You can put me down,' she said, blinking at the light.

'Why?'

'Because I'm awake now.'

Tear-stained and pale, Gillian said, 'Let him carry you, Peta. He needs to do something.'

But he set her on her feet. When she staggered a little, his arm hooked around her shoulders to support her.

'All right?' he asked.

She looked at him and then at Gillian. 'I'm so sorry,' she said quietly.

Gillian's smile wavered and she choked back a sob. 'Yes,' she said quietly. 'Thank you.'

Curt nodded at his sister and brother-in-law. 'Go to bed, both of you,' he ordered. 'I'll be in touch in the morning.'

Once they were in the lift he leaned back against the wall and closed his eyes. 'I don't know how many times in the last ten years I've asked myself if I could have done anything else, but I couldn't see a way of saving the company that didn't involve getting rid of him. And I knew right from the start that he wouldn't go easily.' Raw anger hardened each word. He straightened up and opened his eyes and looked at her. 'I'd do it again if I had to, even knowing how vindictive he could be. I haven't spoken to my mother all those years—he made her choose between us—and when Gillian lent me her trust money, he banished her too.'

'You slashed his pride to ribbons,' Peta said quietly. 'But I'll bet that as often as you wondered how you could have changed the way you deposed him, he wondered if he could win his family back without humbling himself.'

He gave her a keen glance. The lift sighed to a halt and he ushered her into the foyer. Outside the air was tangy with salt and perfumed by the trees and plants in the front gardens of the ground-floor apartments.

As they reached the car park Curt said, 'What makes you say that?'

'My father was proud too. He thought he knew best and wouldn't accept that my mother was too delicate for his dream. She wasn't tall and strapping like me—I take after him. She was slight and frail and although she did her best she could never quite live up to his expectations. She tried to hide what they both saw as her weaknesses from him, but he demanded such a lot...'

The lights on Curt's car flashed as he pressed the door opener. Once inside, driving slowly through the dark streets, he said, 'Did she hide the symptoms of her illness?'

A long breath shuddered through Peta's lips. 'Yes, until too late. He was utterly devastated, because in spite of everything, he loved her. I'll bet your father loved you too.'

'Two weak men,' Curt said quietly.

She gave him an astonished glance. *Weak?*

Her mouth opened but she closed it again before refuting his remark.

Weak. Of course. How could she not have seen it before? Her father had been unable to deal with reality, so he'd constructed a fantasy world around his family, only to have it shatter into tragedy.

'Yes,' she said on a long sigh as something hard and intransigent inside her melted. 'Yes,' she said again.

How strange that she should owe this insight to Curt.

Back at his house the scent of gardenias floated into her nostrils, sweetly seductive, powerfully erotic.

'Do you want me to carry you in?' he asked.

'No, I'm fine. How—how is your mother?'

'He apologised,' Curt said. 'It made her whole again. She'll grieve, but now she no longer has to tear herself in two she'll be all right.' He unlocked the door. 'At least he tried to make up for what he'd done.'

'Yes.'

He had retreated into some distant region where she couldn't reach him. After he'd bidden her a formal good night and left her at the door of her room, she thought sadly that she'd never reached him except in the most basic way, and he didn't want sex tonight; he wanted comfort. Only Curt wouldn't accept comfort from anyone.

Exhaustion knocked her out before she had time to mull over the events of the night, but when she arrived down to breakfast she'd made a decision.

'I should go home,' she said to Curt once she'd sat down.

He frowned. 'No. It will look odd if you leave now.' His expression hardened. 'People will wonder why my lover isn't by my side comforting me.'

Peta decided that she preferred him withdrawn and grieving. Was he angry with himself for revealing so much to her?

Stiffly, she returned, 'Very well, then, but I'll have to make arrangements for the farm.'

'I'll do that.'

The lingering freshness of a slice of mango turned metallic in her mouth. 'Won't you have other things to do?'

'A few.' He drank some coffee. 'My father had everything organised. He stayed a control freak until the end.'

'Or perhaps he just wanted to make things as easy for your mother as he could,' she said gently.

'Possibly.'

The next three days were forever etched in Peta's mind as the most difficult she'd endured, after those that followed her parents' deaths. Although she couldn't grieve for Hugh McIntosh, she hated the bleak ice of Curt's eyes. He didn't touch her, and the edgy antagonism that had characterised their conversation disappeared behind a shield of aloof reserve.

The huge funeral was nerve-racking; so was the wake afterwards, when she was introduced to a swarm of strangers. At least she felt reasonably confident under the avid eyes and probing little questions, thanks to Curt, who never left her alone, and Liz, who'd come up trumps again with a subdued, superbly cut summer suit.

But eventually it was over. When everyone had gone Curt said abruptly, 'Get into some other clothes and we'll go for a drive. I need fresh air, and I imagine you do too.'

Peta's head came up, but her anger subsided when she saw the weariness in his face. 'Where?'

'Out to Piha.'

She changed into a pair of shorts she'd brought from the farm, and a T-shirt. Neither spoke as they took the road to the west-coast beach, but once she got there she exclaimed out loud.

'Have you never been here before?'

'No,' she said, gazing around. 'It's beautiful.'

'It's dangerous. Look at those waves—they're gentle enough today, but the rip is always waiting. More people die on Piha than any other beach in New Zealand. Let's walk.'

They paced along the beach as the sun went down in a glory of crimson and scarlet around a sombre cloudbank painted deep purple and brooding grey.

After twenty minutes of silence Curt said, 'My father left you half a million dollars.'

Astounded, unable to believe she'd heard correctly, Peta stopped. 'What?'

He smiled with such cynicism it burned into her soul. 'You heard.'

Half a million dollars? What on earth had persuaded the man to do that? Shaking her head, she asked woodenly, 'Why?'

'The family don't intend to contest it.' When she said nothing he added dispassionately, 'It's all yours.'

Her jaw dropped. He watched her with eyes that registered nothing but cold indifference. Peta grabbed for enough control to say something—anything—but in the end could only blurt raggedly, 'I don't understand.'

Curt shrugged as though it didn't matter. 'Do you need to? It will solve all your problems.'

Anger broke through her astonishment, rapidly followed by a chill that seeped up from her bones. They had laughed together, found pleasure in talking together, loved together, and yet he still believed she'd take the money. He hadn't changed his mind about her at all, whereas she—oh, she couldn't bear to look into a future that didn't hold him.

But it had to be done, because Curt would never trust her.

'I don't want it,' she said, heart breaking into shards in her breast.

Curt's brows shot up but he said coolly, 'You don't need to make up your mind so fast. I'm sure you'll see things differently after a few days.'

Wounded in some inner part of her that had never seen the light of day before, she said, 'I won't.'

But she knew it was no use. Hopes she didn't even know she'd been cherishing crumbled into dust, and she gave up on a dream she'd refused to recognise.

Curt gazed out to sea, the final rays of the sun gilding his face so that he looked like some warrior of old, fierce, ruthless, and utterly compelling.

I love him, Peta thought, and his father has just made it impossible for anything to come of it.

No, it wasn't fair to blame Hugh McIntosh. Love, she thought bitterly, was a matter of trust, and Curt didn't trust her. He'd never trust her.

'How long have you known about this?' she asked jaggedly.

'He told us before he died.'

So that was the reason for his withdrawal. What game

had his father been playing? At least her own father had never toyed with strangers' lives. 'I want to go home,' she said quietly. 'Back to Kowhai Bay. Now.'

He nodded. 'All right.'

CHAPTER TEN

PETA threw an armful of yellowing leaves onto the compost heap. The dwarf beans had stopped producing, but she wouldn't be planting anything in their place because tomorrow she'd be gone and the vegetable garden would be Joe's concern.

Dusting dirt from her hands, she set off for the house. The carrier was arriving the next morning to collect her furniture and take it to a storage facility in the nearest sizeable town.

A year ago—even a couple of months ago—she'd have been shattered, but at exactly this time a month ago she'd said goodbye to Curt and left him forever. Since then very little had managed to break through the fog of desolation that cut her off from any other emotion.

Before she'd been carried off by his helicopter, he'd made one request.

'Let me know that you're not pregnant,' he said, and scribbled a number onto a piece of paper and given it to her. 'That will reach me.' He'd paused and looked at her with hard, implacable eyes. 'And if by some remote chance you are pregnant, I want to know that too.'

A couple of weeks later she'd opened a magazine in the supermarket to see a photograph of him at a gala polo match with Anna Lee hanging off his arm, very much the woman in possession.

That was when Peta knew she'd been right to sell her land. Self-defence had driven the decision; every time she looked across Tanekaha's lush paddocks, a rage of grief broke through her apathy.

It had sold fast. The day after she'd put the farm on the market the land agent had rung her, crowing, 'You'll never guess! I've got a firm offer for you—no bargaining, no hassles. You see, I was right to suggest you put a decent price on it instead of letting it go for peanuts.'

'Who wants to buy it?'

'Oh, some entity in Wellington. It must be for investment because they're even prepared to lease the land to you for a peppercorn rental until you finish out your calf-rearing contract. Now, I *was* right, wasn't I, when I told them it would be four months?'

'Yes, you were right.'

Another four months of living next door to Curt's station.

But when she'd rung Ian as a matter of courtesy to let him know the details, he'd suggested that if she wanted to leave straightaway he could send Joe up to take over.

'We could come to some arrangement over the contract,' he said diffidently. 'You've done a good job with those calves—the rest of the contract payment can be a bonus. Moving is always an expensive business.'

Instinctive revulsion at accepting unearned money from Curt led to her stiff answer. 'No, thanks, but if you're happy for Joe to do it, then I'm sure the new owners would transfer the lease.'

And she could take her wounded heart away and never come back. Time fixed everything, so people said; it couldn't happen soon enough for her. She longed for the day when she could say Curt's name without a quiver of emotion.

Ian had said, 'I'll see to it, then.'

He was probably relieved to get rid of her; Gillian certainly would be.

Not as glad as she would be to go. She'd expected grief, but this vast, freezing vacuum turned the days into blanks and each night into an eternity.

A week after she'd signed the sale documents, she'd rung Curt to confirm that she wasn't pregnant. Like her, he'd been cool, noncommittal and aloof, finishing the brief conversation by wishing her the best for the future. Neither had mentioned the letter she'd written to the executor of Hugh McIntosh's estate refusing his bequest.

Of course Curt might not have known about it; the executor was someone from a law firm in Auckland.

Laddie's bark swivelled her head around. Joe had offered to take the dog too, which was a relief; both man and animal would enjoy the change of ownership.

Frowning, she watched Ian's ute come up the hill. A wild hope flared, dashed the moment she recognised Ian behind the wheel. She steeled herself to walk across the lawn and wait at the gate while he pulled up and got out.

'Are you all right? You look tired,' he said, his face shaded by his hat.

Tired, heartbroken—whatever. 'I'm busy packing.' She waited, and when he didn't say anything her brows rose. 'What do you want, Ian?'

'We're moving on, Gillian and I.'

She pretended an interest she didn't feel. 'Where to?'

'We've bought a hill-country station in Poverty Bay.'

With part of Gillian's inheritance, presumably. Peta said steadily, 'I wish you both the very best of luck.'

Looking uncomfortable, he shrugged. 'Thank you. It's a new start in our own place, and Gillian has friends on the East Coast. I—well, I hope your new start is successful too.'

Peta could think of nothing to say so she repeated his answer to her good wishes. 'Thank you.'

'Where are you going?'

Nowhere, into nothing. 'I'm having a short holiday,' she said, 'and after that I'll see about a job.'

'Doing what?'

Of course, he knew about the half-million dollars his father-in-law had willed her. Did he know she'd turned it down? Resentment flared fitfully in her, then died in ashes. It didn't matter; she no longer cared what anyone in the McIntosh family thought of her.

She summoned a bright, meaningless smile. 'Don't worry about me, Ian. I'll be fine.'

'Have you heard from Curt lately?'

The unexpectedness of his question drove the breath from her lungs. It took all her strength to keep her expression under control and her voice steady. 'I was speaking to him a few days ago. Why?'

'I just wondered.' He almost shuffled his feet, but finally held out his hand. 'Good luck, Peta.'

They shook hands and he got back into the ute. As he drove away, she asked herself what on earth all that had been about. Did he harbour some resentment towards her for falling under Curt's spell? Perhaps he'd come to tell her that Curt and Anna were still an item, but hadn't had the courage to do so.

Or perhaps he'd just wanted to say goodbye, she thought drearily, stopping beside the gardenia bush, another thing that reminded her too much of Curt. One solitary blossom lingered amongst the glossy foliage; she picked it, holding it in her cupped fingers. The scent rose in the warm air— heavy, evocative, as disturbingly potent as the memory of ecstasy.

If it hadn't been for Ian she'd probably never have met Curt; certainly never been blackmailed by him.

Never fallen in love with him...

She'd have gone on from day to day, year to year, safe and sheltered from the wilder shores of love.

But surely, she thought, clinging to straws, surely love was never wasted? Eventually the pain must fade, and then she'd be able to live again and be glad that she'd loved him.

Still holding the flower, she went inside and put it into a tumbler of water. Cleaning up the vegetable garden had covered her in grime; sweat ran in rivulets down the back of her neck and between her breasts, and a sharp stabbing at her temple threatened her with a headache. And she still had work to do—the last of the packing, clothes to fling into a suitcase.

But first she'd shower. When she'd left Auckland the clothes Curt had bought for her remained behind; the day after they'd arrived on her doorstep courtesy of a courier van. Determined to own nothing that reminded her of him, nothing to pin hopes to, she'd refused to accept them.

Dry-eyed, she scrubbed the sweat and dirt from her body and washed her hair. She'd just rinsed the shampoo away when she heard Laddie barking again.

Now who? she thought wearily, and scrambled out of the shower, wet hair streaming down her back.

The barks tapered off as she briskly dried herself off. So it was someone she knew; a neighbour, probably. Although she hadn't announced that she was leaving the news had got around, and she'd been moved by the friendly good wishes and injunctions to 'stay in touch' she'd received.

After rubbing the towel over her head she pulled on a cotton shirt and a pair of elderly shorts and opened the front door, pushing the wet mass of hair back from her face.

'Hello,' she said to the figure silhouetted by the brilliant glare of sunlight.

And then her eyes adjusted and she saw who it was. Her mouth dropped open and the world tilted so hideously she had to grab the doorhandle to stop herself from sliding onto the floor.

Curt said something explosive and caught her, his grip calculated to support, not hurt. 'You *are* pregnant!' he accused harshly, carrying her into the sitting room. 'And you're sick with it—you've lost far too much weight!'

'I am not!' Her heart was beating like a snare drum underneath the thin cotton shirt. 'Not pregnant and not sick. I've been busy. Put me down! I'm all right, and I'm dripping all over you.'

He set her on her feet, but retained a firm hold on her shoulders, his expression unguarded and fierce. 'You fainted.'

'No, I just got a shock—I didn't expect to s-see you.' Her tongue fumbled over the words, so she dragged in a deep breath and started again. 'What do you want?'

A perfectly reasonable question, surely, but it seemed to anger him even further. He gave her a small shake before his hands dropped to his sides. With an intensity that scared her, he said between his teeth, 'Don't lie to me, Peta. If you're carrying my child you might as well tell me here and now, because I'll find out—I'm not letting you out of my sight—'

'I told you—I'm *not*.' But oh, how she wished she were...

'I don't trust you,' he said flatly, not giving an inch. 'You're saying that because you know I'd insist on marriage.'

'I wouldn't marry you if you were the last man in the universe,' she snapped, sensation surging through a body that had miraculously, rapturously, sprung to life again. 'Will it convince you if I take a pregnancy test and *prove* there's no baby?'

Hot anger narrowed his eyes in a hooded, dangerous glare. Tension sizzled between them, naked and challenging. Several charged moments later he said more moderately, 'No, you don't have to do that. I believe you. But why have you lost weight? And you did almost faint just then.'

His concern weakened her resolution. Ignoring the first question, she said stonily, 'I've been working in the garden and I—well, I think I must be a bit dehydrated. Also I didn't expect to see you. What do you want?'

'I'll get you something to drink,' he said with another frown.

'I can get it myself—'

He started towards her. 'Peta, just shut up and let me look after you, all right?'

She retreated ahead of him; if he touched her again she'd break into several million fragments. Panicked by his inexorable progress, she finished in a voice she couldn't keep steady, 'Curt, I don't want you here. I don't need you to look after me!'

'Tough,' he said relentlessly, showing his teeth in a smile that sent ice scudding the length of her spine.

By then they'd reached the kitchen. Curt picked up the glass with the gardenia flower in it, tossed the bloom onto the counter and washed the glass out before filling it from the tap. Holding it out to her, he commanded in a tone that brooked no refusal, 'Drink.'

Peta gulped it, mind racing as she tried to work out what was going on. And behind the shock and the turmoil, her heart sang.

Curt said, 'And when you've finished drinking, you can tell me why you're not wearing a bra.'

One hand bunched the material of her shirt over her breasts, hiding them. Her pulse began to pound. 'I've just got out of a shower. I thought you were a neighbour who'd come to say goodbye.'

He came towards her with the lithe, dangerous intensity of a stalking panther. 'I see your furniture's still here.'

'The truck's picking it up tomorrow.' She swallowed and backed up a couple of steps. 'H-how did you know I'd sold?'

'Because I bought the place, of course,' he said indifferently.

'I see.' White-lipped, she stared at him. Idiot! She should have known—that explained the prompt sale, the easy agreement to anything she'd wanted, the whole smooth efficiency of the sale.

He couldn't wait to get rid of her. At that moment she hated him.

'The truck's not coming for your furniture until tomorrow?' He began to undo the buttons of his shirt, long, tanned fingers flicking them open—one, two, three...

Mesmerised, Peta fixed her eyes on the fascinating pattern of dark hair that provided such a subtle tactile contrast to his bronze skin. She licked her lips. 'What—what are you doing?'

His smile was a lazy threat. 'I'm getting ready to make love to you,' he said, and shrugged out of the shirt, letting it drop to the ground.

'No,' she croaked, but her body shouted, Yes!

And he heard it. Triumph lit his face.

Shaking her head doggedly, Peta said, 'You can persuade me, but I don't want it.'

She didn't expect to deter him, but something in her desperate tone must have rung true, because he stopped a pace away from her and examined her in dark, angry frustration.

Finally he swore in a low, self-derisive voice that made her blink, and turned away.

Scanning the powerful male wedge of his shoulders, wondering what was going on behind the hard face, Peta could only think that she had thrown away her last chance to make love with him. And although her body rebelled, she knew she couldn't make any other decision. She wanted much more from him than the quick slaking of an appetite.

She said, 'What about your lover?' The words emerged without conscious thought.

He swung back and stared at her as though she was mad. 'Lover?'

'Anna Lee,' she told him thinly, each word a stab in the heart. 'I saw the photo of you with her at polo. Does she know you're here?'

Coldly precise, he told her, 'That photograph was taken in the five minutes we spent together. Trust doesn't come easily to you, does it? I told you the relationship was off.'

'I learned not to trust from you,' she said sharply, trying to tamp down the relief that warmed her. 'It looked very much *on* in the photograph.'

He strode across to the window as though he couldn't bear to be close to her any more. 'Which just shows,' he said sardonically, 'that you should never trust a photograph.'

'You did.'

'Yes.' Still staring out of the window he said, 'I was wrong.'

Peta swallowed, but when he didn't say anything more she knew she couldn't leave it at that. Her mouth dry, she asked hoarsely, 'Curt, why are you here?'

'I came because I couldn't stay away.' Although he stood with his back to her she could hear every stony word. 'I don't know what the hell you do to me, but it reduces me to an idiot. I came here determined to court you, to show you that I wasn't some blind fool who wanted nothing more from you than mind-blowing sex. And all it took was one look at you, and my control was shot and my brain sank into some Neanderthal craving that won't let me go.'

Her pulse was thudding like a festival drum, and she didn't dare believe he'd actually said those words. Surely they were some figment of a mind that had snapped? Primly, she said into a gathering silence, 'Archaeologists seem to believe that the Neanderthals were actually peaceful people.'

He gave a short, mirthless laugh and at last turned to face her. Bewildered, she saw that the olive skin was stretched over the splendid framework of his face, and his mouth was grim.

'Peta, I've done this all wrong. Can we start over?'

Her heart shuddered to a halt, then began again, banging in her breast so that she couldn't hear her own thoughts. 'Start what?' she asked, still unable to let herself hope.

Curt's smile turned savage, then vanished, leaving his face honed into a predatory alertness. 'When you look at me it's as though you're seeing someone else. Your father?'

She had to swallow before she could say, 'I suppose so. But not always.'

'Did he abuse you?'

'No.' She paused, then added, 'But I've told you—he was a dominant man. Like you.'

And knew with a flash of complete certainty that it no longer mattered. She loved Curt so much that she'd take whatever risk. If he only wanted her for a few months, she'd accept that. If he wanted more—and she didn't dare probe into what 'more' might mean—she was strong enough to cope with his inbuilt authority.

Little beads of moisture forming at her temples, she swallowed. Nothing venture, she thought bravely, nothing win, but it took every ounce of courage she possessed to say, 'It's not important any more.'

'I think it is.' Brows drawing together, he looked around. 'Sit down and I'll make you some tea.'

Automatically she said, 'I'll do it.'

But while she filled the kettle and plugged it into the socket he opened the fridge door and took out milk. She got the tea caddy and teapot from the cupboard and he found the mugs; each of them, she noted as her brain buzzed in useless tumult, being exceedingly careful not to even brush up against each other.

Once seated at the dining table, mugs in front of them, he returned to the attack. 'Tell me about your father. It sounds to me as though he was a man in the grip of an obsession, prepared to sacrifice everything—even those he loved—to it.'

'That describes him fairly accurately,' she agreed, looking down into her teacup. 'The terrible thing is that I think he really did love my mother, yet he didn't seem to realise that his actions doomed her to a kind of half-life. She was a good musician—a violinist until working so hard ruined her hands. He considered it to be just a hobby, and a useless one. She loved art, but he always said that a well-grown vegetable was work of art enough for him. She loved flowers, but he said they took up time that was needed for other things. In a way he starved her of almost everything she loved, yet he couldn't see what he was doing.'

Silence stretched between them, filled with tension and unspoken thoughts. Peta almost jumped when Curt said in a voice so neutral it sounded alien, 'Is that how I seem to you? Totally self-absorbed, so lost in my own private ambitions that I have no interest in anyone else's?'

Thoughts jostled in her mind like chips of ice in a blender. 'I—no,' Peta answered, because every overbearing action of Curt's had been for his sister. Even though he didn't like Ian much, he allowed Gillian her own preferences.

'Surely your mother could have fought for her own interests?'

'She loved him and she wanted him to be happy,' she protested, yearning passionately for the sweet recklessness of desire to swamp her fears. If only he'd sweep her into his arms she'd forget everything but her own rapture.

For a while. She bit her lip. She had to think, and for

once, she had to think without the hangovers from her childhood clouding her logic.

She said, 'I'm not like her, but I think I understand how she felt.'

He said keenly, 'You're afraid, Peta, of something—that's been obvious right from the start. You've called me a dominant man several times, as though that's the worst insult you can hurl at me. But you're certainly not afraid of me; you've stood up against me without quailing.'

'Of course I'm not scared of you,' she retorted. 'It's myself—' She stopped, suddenly wary, unsure of what she'd intended to say. How could she be afraid of herself? Ridiculous!

Determination hardened his face; he wasn't going to let her off easily. 'Is that what scares you? Not fear of being dominated, but fear of falling in love? Because your mother didn't have the strength to stand up for herself—and you—you don't dare let yourself fall in love in case it turns you into a weakling?'

When she didn't answer he smiled with hard irony. 'Look at yourself, my darling! Nobody could ride roughshod over you because you wouldn't let them. I tried, and failed lamentably. You're strong.'

'I don't know what you're talking about,' she muttered.

But a shadow she'd lived under all her life lifted from her. Picking her way through her thoughts, she went on, 'The police said there was no reason for the accident that killed my parents; an onlooker said the car suddenly sped up, then swerved and smashed straight into the concrete power pole.'

He covered her hand with his big one, warming her from the inside. She took in a deep, shuddering breath and went on, 'I think he realised that Mum hadn't mentioned the symptoms of her illness because she was afraid of—oh, of not living up to his standards. And he couldn't bear it. The police said he might have gone to sleep at the wheel, but he never slept in the daytime. I think he drove into that pole deliberately and killed them both so that he didn't have to live with himself.'

Curt swore quietly, but he didn't touch her. 'No wonder you were so damned cautious.' He paused before adding deliberately, 'Do you really believe that love entails surrender and endless sacrifice, the complete subjugation of one person's will to another's?'

'Love?' she whispered, unable to believe that he'd used the word.

He didn't move. 'If what I feel isn't love,' he said in a flat, toneless voice, 'I don't ever want to feel the real thing. Of course I love you! You smashed through my control, turned my life upside down, scrambled my brains so that I made love to you when I knew it was more dangerous than anything I'd ever done. And when you left it ripped my heart from my body and all light from life. My executives think I'm losing it and my poor PA is at her wits' end because she has to remind me about every meeting. My house is haunted by your lovely, challenging ghost. When I smell the gardenias outside you come to me, and I want you so much I can't breathe.'

Peta's eyes burned with unshed tears. 'I know,' she confessed. 'It's like living in a grey limbo.'

More than anything she wanted the inestimable comfort of his arms, the magical euphoria of being held close to him, but he stayed on the other side of the table, linked to her only by his hand tightening around hers.

'So how do you feel about me?' he asked, his voice unnaturally level.

She looked up sharply, and read naked hope in his eyes; incredulously she realised he needed the words too. 'You must know I love you,' she said simply. 'With everything I am, all that I can be.'

And at last he got to his feet and she rose with him and went to him.

'How could you not know?' she asked, trembling as his arms closed around her.

'How could you not?' Tantalising, confident, his mouth touched the corner of hers in a butterfly kiss that sank into the depths of her soul like rain after a long, dry summer.

The soft, purring noise in the back of her throat surprised her; smiling, she lifted her hands and lovingly shaped his face, holding his head still as she looked into burning eyes that promised her everything.

This time his kiss won a passionate response, her mouth parting beneath the hard demand of his, her body exulting in the evidence of his fierce arousal and the wonder of being close to him again, of loving him.

Tremors raked her body when he lifted his head.

'God,' he muttered against her lips. 'I love you so much I'd kill for you. I've spent the last month eating my heart out, lying in bed at night and aching for you, obsessing over the way you look when you smile, when you laugh, when you frown, remembering how sweet and fiery and passionate you were, and how much I enjoy crossing swords with you...'

She closed his mouth with hers, and he lifted her up and swung her into his arms and carried her into the bedroom. As he lowered her to the bed he said, 'I need you so much, my darling heart. So much.'

It was like a vow. She drew his head down to her, and with a smile trembling on her lips said, 'We could probably spend hours discussing who needs who most, but—not now?'

Curt laughed deep in his throat. 'Not now,' he agreed, and came down beside her and slowly, with love and passion and tenderness, they came together.

*   *   *

Much later, when she was lying naked in his arms and he was exploring her body with his fingertips, producing a shivering delight with the lightest touch, he said, 'What's wrong?'

Peta didn't try to gloss it over. 'I can't help wondering what Gillian is going to think of—of us.'

'She'll be too busy patching up her marriage and organising an adoption to worry too much.' When she frowned he said, 'We had a long talk after my father's funeral. I hope I managed to convince her that she owes it to herself to do something with her art. After they got home she had another long discussion with Ian; she thinks everything is going to be all right now. She's decided to stop aiming for the sun and take what she can.'

'That's so sad!' she burst out, because she had aimed for her sun and struck home, and she wanted everyone to be as happy as she was. After all, if it hadn't been for Ian and Gillian, she might never have met Curt...

Curt kissed her forehead. She shivered deliciously at the heated slide of his skin over hers, the sensuous friction rekindling the fires she'd thought sated.

'I may not agree with the way she chooses to live, but it's her decision to make,' he said quietly. 'Besides, my marriage is my own affair. My mother is waiting for us to set a date—what have I said?'

Peta stared into his face, saw a blazing purpose that thrilled her even as it scared her.

He said quietly, 'You are going to marry me, aren't you, Peta?'

Happiness collided with astonishment. 'I didn't think... marriage? Curt, are you sure?'

He bent his head and kissed the pleading tip of one breast. 'I'm not going to settle for anything else, so I'll just have to dazzle you with sex until you finally give in,' he said, his breath playing across the moist skin with unnerving eroticism. 'You're not thinking of my father's unsubtle attempt to manipulate things, are you? It was so bloody typical of him—he had no idea how to deal with people! He guessed, of course, that I was in love with you, and he wanted to make things easier.' He gave an exasperated laugh. 'Or something.'

'No, your father's got nothing to do with it,' she murmured, inwardly shuddering with anticipation so keen it held her on a knife-edge of pleasure. 'I'm not taking the money, anyway.'

His head came up, eyes narrowed to slivers of electric blue. With lips that barely moved, he exclaimed, 'What?'

'Didn't you know?' Astonishment blossomed into joy. 'I sent a letter off as soon as I got back from Auckland, refusing the legacy.'

'No, I didn't know—I've got nothing to do with his estate.'

And then she knew what real happiness was, because he had come for her even though he'd thought she'd taken the money.

Curt said, 'Peta, why? Did you think—?'

Lips trembling, she whispered, 'I'm not capable of thinking anything right now, if you really want to know.'

'Good.' But before he took her back to the enchanted realm of his love, he looked at her with a dangerous smile. 'If you don't want the money we'll form a trust in your name and use it to help people onto their own farms or something. But whatever you decide, I plan to settle more than that on you so that you have the independence you need.'

'No!' she protested, trying to pull away. Eyes enormous and troubled, she stared at his beloved face. 'I don't want it. All I'll ever want, all I'll ever need, is for you to love me.'

'That's a given. Always. But you need freedom,' he said

implacably, adding with a laugh deep in his throat, 'I'll tie you to me every way I can, but money of your own will give you options and choices. You can do anything, be anything you want; all *I* want is for you to be happy.'

'I don't know how to live in your world.'

'You'll cope,' he said confidently. 'And you'll have my mother and me to help you, as well as Lucia Radcliffe.'

Peta surrendered, happiness gilding her eyes, glowing from her skin, curving her lips into a smile that shook him to the core. 'I'll be happy if I have you,' she vowed, and linked her arms around his neck and kissed him with the pent-up ardour of a lifetime.

'Perhaps after fifty years I'll be able to manage to make love to you with some finesse,' he said thickly.

'I don't care,' she said languorously, her eyes sultry and provocative. 'You may have noticed that I'm not much into finesse myself.'

Before the honeyed tide of passion overcame them, she thought that although Curt would always be dominant, he balanced it with compassion and integrity. With him she'd be safe.

And he would be safe with her…

* * * * *

THE BILLION-
DOLLAR BRIDE

by

Kay Thorpe

Kay Thorpe was born in Sheffield. She tried out a variety of jobs after leaving school. Writing began as a hobby, becoming a way of life only after she had her first completed novel accepted for publication in 1968. Since then she's written over fifty, and lives now with her husband, son, German shepherd dog and lucky black cat on the outskirts of Chesterfield in Derbyshire. Her interests include reading, hiking and travel.

CHAPTER ONE

SHE had imagined someone older. Ross Harlow was almost certainly no more than the mid-thirties. The bronzed, hard-boned features were surmounted by thick dark hair crisply styled. Six feet two, she calculated, and well-honed beneath the superbly cut suit.

Grey eyes swept her from head to toe and back again, revealing little in the process. Gina pulled herself together to extend a hand in formal greeting—aware of a warm trickle down her back as long lean fingers closed briefly about hers.

'How is…my grandfather?' she asked.

A muscle contracted along the firm jawline. 'As well as can be expected, I guess.' His glance took in the single leather suitcase on the trolley. 'Is this everything?'

'I wasn't planning on staying long,' she said. 'I might not be here at all if my parents hadn't urged me to come.'

'Good of them.'

Green eyes acquired a spark. 'They're good people.'

His shrug was dismissive. 'I'm sure. I've a car waiting.'

He took the suitcase from the trolley, leaving the latter where it stood in the middle of the arrivals hall as he headed for the exits. Gina had to run to keep up with his lengthy stride. His attitude left a lot to be desired, though she could to a certain extent understand his feelings. She was more of a Harlow than he could ever be.

The limousine parked in the 'no waiting' zone was long and black. A uniformed chauffeur got from the driving seat on their approach, and opened the rear door for her.

Feeling distinctly queen-like, Gina slid onto soft cream leather, feet sinking into the thick carpeting. Not the type of transport she would have imagined a man as essentially masculine as Ross Harlow might favour, but then who was she to judge? This was a different world. A world way outside her experience.

The chauffeur took her suitcase from Ross to put it in the boot, leaving him to slide into the rear seat beside her. He pressed some hidden switch, bringing a glass panel sliding smoothly up from between front and rear seats to cut them off from the driver.

'I gather you're adopted yourself,' Gina said with some deliberation as they pulled out.

The dark head inclined. 'I was fourteen when my mother married Oliver, my sister nine. He gave us both his name.'

'Your natural father didn't object?'

'My mother was widowed.'

'I'm sorry.'

'You don't need to be. Oliver's been a very good husband to her, and an excellent father to Roxanne and me.'

'Better than to his own daughter,' Gina felt moved to state. She shook her head as he made to speak. 'I know she's no longer alive. The letter he sent explained everything. It was his insistence that she gave me up at birth. His wife at the time—my grandmother—died the year after Jenny was killed on the road. He married your mother two years later.'

Ross regarded her for a moment in silence, his expression curious. 'You seem remarkably cool about it all.'

'I don't see any point in crying over something twenty-five years in the past,' she returned. 'My parents are wonderful people. I've had a very good life with them.'

'Assuming you knew you were adopted before receiving

Oliver's letter, you must have wondered about your real parents.'

'Occasionally,' she admitted. 'But never with any intention of looking them up. We moved to England when I was just a few months old, so I'd no memories to disturb me.' She paused, collecting her thoughts. 'The letter said nothing about the man who fathered me.'

Ross lifted his shoulders. 'It seems Jenny would never say who he was.' His regard centred on her face beneath its crown of honey-blonde hair, appraising the deep green eyes, small straight nose and soft full mouth. 'I saw a photograph once. You look very much like her.'

There was no denying the pang that statement elicited. Gina shook off the momentary heartache. It was too late to go down that road. What was done was done. What she had to deal with was the present.

'Did you know she'd once had a child?' she asked.

He shook his head. 'The first I knew was when Oliver told me he'd contacted you.'

'It must have been a real shock.'

'It was all of that,' he agreed drily.

'I'm not here to make any claims, if that's your concern,' she said. 'I'm more than satisfied with what I already have.'

'I understand you own a boutique.'

She turned a deaf ear to suspected disparagement. 'Part own. Hardly on a par with the Harlow empire, but enough to keep me both occupied and solvent. I stayed in one of your hotels once,' she added blandly. 'Very nice.'

Ross's lips twitched. 'We do our best. You'll be staying at the house, of course.'

'Your mother has no objection to that?'

'None that I'm aware of.'

'Do you live there too?' she asked after a moment, and saw the faint smile come and go again.

'I have the penthouse suite in our Beverly Hills concession.'

'Some bachelor pad!'

He gave her a quizzical glance. 'What makes you think I'm unmarried?'

'We spinsters have a sixth sense about such things.'

This time the smile held a genuine if fleeting humour. 'Never met anyone *you* fancied marrying?'

'I prefer independence too,' she returned. 'For now, at any rate.'

They had left the airport environs and were travelling along a multi-lane freeway, with the city spread out in all directions. Los Angeles. Her birthplace. Gina still found it hard to take in.

'Where are we heading for?' she asked.

'Mullholland.' Ross indicated the line of hills ahead. 'Oliver prefers to live above the smog-line.'

'You always call him by his name?'

'It's the way he wanted it. From me, at any rate. Roxanne calls him Dad.'

'How did your sister take the news?'

'Badly,' he said. 'She's accustomed to being the baby of the family.'

Gina did a swift calculation using the figures she'd been given a few minutes ago. Ross had to be thirty-four now, his sister twenty-nine. Some baby!

'Married?' she hazarded.

'Divorced. A hazard in these parts.'

'The reason you haven't tried it yourself yet?'

'Maybe a part of it.' He studied her a moment, an unreadable expression in his eyes. 'You're not what I expected.'

'Is that good news,' she asked, 'or bad?'

His grin was unexpected. 'I'll take a raincheck.'

Gina relaxed a little, glad to have the atmosphere lightened. Meeting her grandfather for the first time, knowing he was dying, wasn't going to be easy, but she'd get through it. All he wanted, he'd said, was to see her before he died—to hear from her own lips that he was forgiven for what he'd done. She could give him that in the circumstances, even if it wasn't entirely true.

The Harlow residence was reached via a winding canyon road affording panoramic views at every bend. Double iron gates, electrically controlled, gave access to a drive and forecourt backed by a house big enough to house a dozen families. White stone walls glowed in the late-afternoon sunlight, outlined against a sky already deepening in hue. A riot of colour met the eyes in every direction.

The chauffeur drove through an archway to bring the car to a stop before a bank of garages built into the hillside. A further archway revealed a wide, bow-fronted terrace affording another superb view over the city, marred only by the smog-line smudging the horizon.

They entered the house via impressive double doors into a vast circular hall floored in marble. A beautifully wrought-iron staircase curved up one wall to an open gallery. The crystal chandelier dropping from a central support high up in the glass-roofed atrium was breathtaking in its size and beauty, the light from above sparking myriad colours.

If the woman who appeared from one of the rooms leading off the hall was Elinor Harlow, she had to be in her mid-fifties at least, Gina reckoned, but it was a very well-preserved mid-fifties. Her dark hair was immaculate, her face beautifully made-up, her figure hourglass in an off-white gown that shouted designer wear.

'It's easy to see you're Jenny's daughter!' she exclaimed. She came forward swiftly to take Gina's hand in hers, her smile warm. 'This means so much to my husband! He bit-terly regrets the way he acted all those years ago. If you can find it in your heart to forgive him...'

'I do,' Gina assured her. 'That's why I'm here.'

'Where is he?' Ross asked.

'Asleep at the moment.' A cloud passed across her face. 'He hasn't been too good at all today.'

'He'll rally.' Ross sounded confident about it. 'He al-ways does. In the meantime, Gina might like to freshen up.'

'I'll show you your room,' Elinor offered. 'Michael will bring your bags up.'

'One bag,' Ross put in. 'Unlike some I could mention, this lady travels light.'

His mother pulled a face at him. 'I believe in covering all eventualities, darling. Who can ever tell what might be needed?'

Gina followed her up the curving staircase, conscious of the grey eyes watching her climb. She was relieved to reach the gallery.

'It's a beautiful house,' she commented. 'And so huge!'

Elinor laughed. 'It's considered on the smaller side by Mullholland standards. You should see the Gregory place further along the road. Now, *that* is really some size! It's said Valentino once owned it.' She opened a door. 'Here you are. I hope you'll be comfortable.'

The bedroom was as large as Gina's whole flat back home, the bed raised on a carpeted platform in the centre and draped in cream silk to match the window dressings, the furnishings exquisite.

'I'm sure I shall,' she said, controlling the urge to express further admiration. This was the way these people lived. Nothing unusual to them.

'Dinner isn't until eight,' Elinor added, 'but I can have something brought up to you if you're hungry.'

'I'm fine,' Gina assured her. 'I ate on the plane. The first time I've travelled first class. I'm not sure I'll ever be able to settle for economy again!' she added jokingly.

'I doubt if you'll ever have to,' the older woman said easily. 'Come on down when you're ready. You'll find us on the top terrace.'

Gina bit her lip, suspecting that the remark might have been misconstrued. She wanted no financial reward for making this trip. She was here to offer some comfort to a dying man, nothing else.

The *en suite* bathroom was a symphony in black and cream, the bath sunken and complete with jacuzzi, the walk-in shower cabinet walled with jets in addition to a vast overhead spray. She came back to the bedroom to find her suitcase laid ready on the stand at the foot of the bed, although she hadn't heard anyone enter the room.

The simple black dress she extracted to hang out was adaptable to any of the eventualities Elinor had mentioned. Not designer wear exactly, but capable of holding its own. Not that she had any desire to compete. She wanted no part of this world of theirs. In fact, the sooner she got back to her own world the better.

Dropped on her right out of the blue, the letter from her grandfather had caused upheaval for both her and her parents. He'd had her traced, he'd said, because he couldn't bear to go to his grave without making some attempt to right the wrong he had done her. She hadn't wanted to come, but the nature of the plea had made it impossible to refuse outright.

It was still only a little gone seven when she made her way downstairs again. With no sign of anyone to ask directions of, she chose one of the doors leading off from the hall, to find herself in what was obviously a formal dining room. The gleaming mahogany table was unset, the heavy silver candlesticks devoid of candles, the whole ambience one of occasional rather than general use.

'Can I help you, ma'am?' asked a voice at her back, and she turned to see a middle-aged man dressed in a conservative grey suit.

'I'm looking for a way out to the upper terrace,' she said. 'I'm...'

'I know who you are, ma'am.' The tone was courteous, his expression neither friendly nor unfriendly. 'If you'll come this way.'

Gina followed him a little uncertainly. The term of address he had used suggested a member of staff rather than family.

'You are?' she asked.

'Alex, ma'am,' he said without turning his head. 'Mr Harlow senior's personal aide.'

He proffered no further information, and she was loath to ask him how her grandfather was. She had the impression that the man no more approved of her presence here than Ross Harlow himself. At least Elinor had extended a welcome.

The house had been deliciously cool. Stepping out onto the wide span of the terrace was like stepping into a furnace, even this early in the year. She was thankful to see the umbrellas shading the tables and loungers set about the paved surface.

Ross Harlow was seated alone at one of the former. He was minus his suit jacket, the sleeves of his cream shirt rolled to reveal tanned forearms. His feet were lifted to rest comfortably against a lower rail of one of the other chairs, one hand about to raise a glass to his lips.

He got up when he saw her, surveying her appearance without comment. 'How's the jet lag?'

'So far, not bad,' Gina acknowledged. 'Surprising, considering it must be close on three in the morning back home.'

'It's always best to try adjusting right away to the time,' he said. 'What would you like to drink?'

'I'll have a Kir, please.'

Ross passed on the request to the man waiting by the wide glass doors through which they'd emerged. Staff demarcation lines didn't appear to be strictly observed, Gina reflected. She took the seat Ross drew out for her, watching him from beneath her lashes as he regained his own seat. Seen in profile, his jawline was firm, a hint of implacability in its set.

'Are you staying for dinner?' she asked.

'I am,' he returned. 'Mother should have told you we only bother dressing for formal occasions. Not that you don't look delightful.'

'Thanks,' she said, refusing to be embarrassed about it. 'As *my* mother would say, when in doubt opt for a compromise. I refrained from putting my hair up.'

Humour briefly lit the grey eyes again. 'You certainly inherited the Harlow quickness of tongue. I've never known Oliver stuck for an answer either.'

'When do I get to see him?' she asked.

'In the morning. He doesn't feel up to it tonight.'

Brows drawn, it was a moment before she could put the question. 'How long does he have?'

The shrug was brief, eyes veiled. 'A few weeks. Maybe more, maybe less. He's a resilient character.' His tone altered a fraction. 'I hope you're not planning on hauling him over the coals when you do see him.'

'Of course not.' She controlled the urge to snap with an

effort. 'I told you before, it's in the past. I'll be on a flight home in a couple of days.'

Ross studied her for a moment or two. 'A hell of a way to come for a couple of days,' he remarked at length.

'I don't see any point in hanging around. As I also told you, I'm not interested in collecting any dues. So far as I'm concerned, you can have it all!'

His jaw tautened abruptly, mouth forming a harder line. 'You think that's all I care about?'

'I think you've probably been groomed to consider yourself the natural successor to all this,' she answered levelly. 'It would only be human nature to resent any possible contender—especially when they're dropped on you the way I've been.'

'It's beyond human nature to do what you're supposedly proposing to do,' came the clipped retort. 'You'd have to be an idiot to take that line, and I reckon you're far from it.'

Gina gazed back at him with a coolness she was far from feeling. 'Idiotic or not, it's the truth.'

'Is this a private fight, or can anyone join in?' asked Elinor Harlow mildly, coming up unnoticed by either of them. 'I must say, for two people who only met a few hours ago, you certainly didn't waste any time getting to grips! Orally, at any rate,' she added with a glimmer of a smile as her son turned a quelling look on her.

She had changed her dress for another in lilac, Gina noted. Not exactly evening wear, but certainly no less dressy than her own. Ross was the odd one out, not her.

Glancing back at him, she caught a derisive gleam in the grey eyes. That he didn't believe a word she'd said was obvious. Well, he'd learn soon enough. Two days maximum, and she was out of here.

He got up to pull out a chair for his mother, sitting down again as drinks arrived borne by a woman in her forties.

'Lydia's our housekeeper,' Elinor said. 'She and Michael take care of everything.'

Michael being the chauffeur, Gina surmised. She smiled at the woman, receiving the briefest acknowledgement. Elinor herself appeared to be the only one ready to offer an unqualified welcome.

'Looking at the two of you, I suppose I should make a bit of an effort,' Ross remarked when Lydia had left. 'Always providing you didn't get round to throwing out my stuff yet?'

Elinor shook her head reprovingly. 'You know perfectly well I haven't.'

'Don't go to any trouble on my account,' Gina told him blandly. 'I've no objection whatsoever to shirtsleeves.'

'I'll bear it in mind.' He drank the rest of his own drink, and pushed back his chair once more. 'See you.'

Elinor eyed Gina shrewdly as her son departed. 'Been getting at you, has he?'

Gina had to smile. 'You could say that. He seems to think I'm lying through my teeth when I say I'm not interested in any financial gain from all this.'

'You have to admit that's an unusual attitude to take,' Elinor commented after a moment. 'Most people in your position would be only too ready to seek compensation.'

'I'm not most people. Naturally, I regret never having known my real mother, but I've had a very good life with two people I love more than anyone in the world. I don't want any compensation.'

'You may have trouble convincing your grandfather of that too,' Elinor said. 'He's full of plans.'

'Then I'm afraid he'll have to unplan.'

The grey eyes, so like her son's, met green for a lengthy

moment, an odd expression in their depths, then she inclined her head. 'You know your own mind.'

'Tell me about yourself,' she went on. 'I know you graduated from university, and you have your own business now, but little else. Is there a man in your life?'

'No one special,' Gina admitted. She adopted a light note. 'I'm what's known as footloose and fancy-free!'

'Not for lack of offers, I'm sure. You're very lovely.'

Gina gave a laugh. 'By Hollywood standards, I'd scarcely make first base!'

'You might be pretty shocked if you saw some Hollywood beauties *au naturel*,' Elinor replied. 'Make-up and lighting can work miracles. You've no need of enhancement.'

'Thanks.' Gina took it all with a pinch of salt. She'd no false vanity about her looks, but Elinor was way over the top. 'Is it always as hot as this?' she asked, more by way of changing the subject than through any need to know.

'This is cool compared to what it will be in a few weeks,' Elinor confirmed. 'We get whatever breeze there is up here, which helps. There's a pool, if you want to cool off any time. It's down on a lower level. You can't see it from here. I swim every morning, if you feel like joining me.'

'I'd like to.' Gina could say that much in all honesty. She liked Elinor Harlow. Better by far than she liked her son.

She closed her mind to the thought that liking had little to do with the responses that individual aroused in her.

They talked desultorily for a while, until Ross joined them again. He was wearing a pair of tailored trousers in dark blue, along with a white shirt. His thick dark hair was still damp from the shower, curling a little at the ends.

'Better?' he asked, with a tilt of an eyebrow in Gina's direction.

'Fine feathers make fine birds,' she responded, adopting the same tone.

'Gina and I were discussing the film industry,' Elinor put in. 'You should take her down to the studio while she's here, Ross. Sam would be only too delighted.'

'According to what she tells me, she isn't going to be here long enough to do any touring,' he said.

'I suppose I could stretch a point,' Gina parried, with absolutely no intention. 'I'm never likely to get the chance to see a film studio again. Of course, if you're too busy...'

He gave a brief shrug. 'I guess I can stretch a point too. I'll make the arrangement. Ready to eat?'

'Well, yes.' She could say that in all honesty. 'Outside or in?'

'Out, but not here. Don't bother bringing your drink,' he added as she made to pick the glass up. 'You can have another.'

'Waste not, want not,' she returned, ignoring the instruction.

Elinor was smiling. 'I think you might have met your match, darling,' she said to her son.

'Don't count on it,' he advised Gina with a challenging glint. 'I'm not on the market.'

'I'm not in the queue,' she returned.

'Let's go and eat,' said Elinor, obviously very entertained by the repartee.

The terrace swept right around the side of the house. Ross saw the two women settled at the table already set out for the meal before taking his own seat. Gina met the grey gaze across the table with an equanimity she was beginning to find a strain to keep up. He disturbed her in more ways than just the one.

The meal was brought out on a heated trolley, from which they all helped themselves. Simply presented though it might be, the food was beautifully prepared. All the same, Gina found herself toying with it, her appetite shrivelled by the tiredness creeping up on her. She'd dozed on the plane, but only fitfully. To all intents and purposes, she'd been up and about for almost twenty-five hours.

'When do I get to meet Roxanne?' she asked at one point, fighting to stay alert.

'When she gets back from Frisco,' Ross supplied. '*If* she gets back before you leave.'

'Stop pushing the girl,' his mother reprimanded. 'She'll leave when she's good and ready to leave.' Her eyes were on Gina's face. 'I think you should go and get a good night's rest. Tomorrow's a new day.'

'You've been reading *Gone with the Wind* again,' commented her son. 'It's time I was off too, if it comes to that. I was due at Pinots an hour ago.'

'I thought the Hollywood scene left you cold,' Elinor remarked.

'Depends who's going to be there.' He was on his feet as he spoke, gaze shifting to Gina. 'I'll let you know about the studio tour.'

'Fine.' She was too tired to conjure any smarter response. 'Goodnight, then.'

'Goodnight.'

She watched him stride across to the house, aware of a spasm deep down inside as she viewed the tapering line from shoulder to hip, the hardness of thigh beneath the fine material of his trousers. It wasn't the first time she'd been physically stirred by a fine male physique, though never quite so strongly, she had to admit.

Forget it, she told herself. The situation was fraught enough without letting sexual attraction in on the act.

'He isn't really as hard as he might appear,' said Elinor,

watching her watching him. 'It's been shock on shock these past weeks.'

'Is there any chance at all for my grandfather?' Gina ventured.

'I'm afraid not. The tumour was inoperable by the time it was diagnosed. You'll find little outward sign of his condition. The medication keeps him pain-free.' Elinor's voice was matter-of-fact, but there was no disguising the pain in her eyes. 'He sent the letter to you before he told us about it. It must have come as a shock for you too.'

'Yes.' The understatement of the year, Gina reflected. 'My parents had no idea of my background.'

'But they didn't object to you coming?'

'Not in the circumstances.' Gina put a hand to her mouth to smother a yawn. 'I'd better call it a day. I can't even think straight right now.'

'Can you find your own way?' Elinor asked. 'Or shall I come with you?'

'I'll be fine.' All Gina wanted at present was to be alone. She gave the older woman a smile. 'See you in the morning, then.'

She went back round the house to enter by the same door from which she'd emerged with Alex a couple of hours or so ago, gaining her room without running into anyone. The bed looked so inviting. She had to force herself to at least remove her make-up before tumbling into it.

Tired though she was, she found sleep hard to come by. Her mind kept endlessly turning. There had never been a shortage of money in the Saxton household. Her father was a company director, her mother the author of two highly acclaimed biographies, their home in Harrow as up-market as any other on the avenue. Far removed from the world these people lived in even so. She may be one of them by birth, but she could never be one of them by choice. Ross was welcome to it all.

CHAPTER TWO

APART from a certain hesitation in his speech, and some restriction in mobility in his left side, there was, as Elinor had said, little to reveal the ravages the brain tumour was wreaking on Oliver Harlow's body. At sixty-five, he still appeared a fine figure of a man.

'You're Jenny's daughter all right,' he said with a catch in his voice. 'I can't tell you how much it means to me to have you here, Gina. To know I'm forgiven for what I did.'

He was taking a lot for granted, but she let it pass.

'I think the best thing we can both of us do now is put it from mind,' she said. She brightened her voice to add, 'You have a stunning home! I'm only just beginning to find my way around. Your wife and I swam together earlier. Not that I'd have thought the pool needed heating in this climate. You could hard boil an egg in there!!'

Oliver laughed. 'Ross would be the first to agree with you. He refuses to use it himself. Elinor insists on a minimum of eighty. She says anything less is too much of a shock on the system.' He paused, his regard centred on her face. 'How did you and Ross get along yesterday?'

Gina kept her expression bland. 'Like a house on fire. He's quite a character.'

'He's all of that.' There was a note of quiet satisfaction in his voice. 'I recognised his potential even at fourteen. Not entirely my doing, of course, but I like to think I played a major part in shaping him.'

They were seated on the terrace beneath one of the wide

umbrellas. Elinor came to join them, looking from one to the other with quizzically lifted brows.

'So, how are things going?'

'I think we can say things are going very well,' her husband answered. 'You'd agree with that, Gina?'

'Of course.' She could scarcely say anything else, she thought.

'Ross rang a minute or two ago,' Elinor went on. 'He's arranged the studio tour we were talking about last night for this afternoon. The studio head, Sam Walker, is an old family friend.'

'Sam knows Jenny had a baby adopted,' Oliver put in. 'One of the few.'

'To be honest, I'm not all that interested in doing this tour,' Gina admitted.

'If Ross has gone to the trouble of arranging it, you'd better pretend to be,' said her grandfather on a humorous note. 'What time will he be here?'

'In half an hour. He's taking you to lunch first,' Elinor added to Gina. 'He said to tell you not to bother dressing up. You'll be far more comfortable in casual wear.'

Gina kept her tone as free of sarcasm as possible. 'Thoughtful of him to worry about my comfort.' She stirred reluctantly. 'I suppose I'd better go and sort something out, then. I think this…' indicating her brief sun top '…might be just a little *too* casual.'

'With a figure like yours, you could wear a sack and still look good,' Oliver commented with a certain complacency. 'The Harlow women have always been well-structured.'

'He's talking about the boobs, darling,' Elinor advised. 'I'd never have made the grade myself if I'd been flat-chested, would I, honey?'

'Not a chance,' he confirmed.

Seeing the look that passed between the two of them,

Gina felt a sudden pang that could only be envy. Her parents aside, she'd never known that depth of feeling for anyone. How Elinor could joke when she was on the verge of losing the man she so obviously loved to distraction was beyond her.

Back in her room, she surveyed her somewhat scant wardrobe, selecting a pair of cotton jeans in off-white, along with a sleeveless beige sweater. The length of her hair caught back in a tortoiseshell slide, she applied no more than a bare sweep of mascara along her lashes, and a dash of pale pink lipstick. If Ross wanted casual, casual was what he would get.

He was waiting for her in the hall when she went down. He was wearing jeans himself, the cut and fit lifting them into a range of their own. Tucked in at the waist, the cotton T-shirt outlined a well-toned midriff.

'Glad to see you took my advice,' he commented. 'You might find sunglasses a help.'

Gina tapped the small white shoulder-bag she was carrying. 'In here—along with my handkerchief.'

The grin came and went. 'Call it a brotherly concern.'

'Strictly speaking,' she said, 'you'd be an uncle, though I'm sure you'd hate me to call you that.'

'You can count on it.'

There was something different about him this morning, Gina reflected as they made their way outdoors. His mood seemed lighter than yesterday. Perhaps because he'd decided to accept her word that she wanted nothing from this relationship. Truth to tell, she didn't think it was the financial aspect that bothered him so much as the possibility that she might lay claim to the business empire he'd been groomed to take over. Well, he could rest easy on both scores.

The open-topped car parked out on the forecourt was

long and low-slung, its dark blue bodywork gleaming in the sunlight, black leather upholstery masculine as it came. Ross saw her into the front passenger seat before going round to slide behind the wheel.

Gina was vibrantly aware of his proximity. The light covering of hair on the arm he extended to fire the ignition was bleached golden by the sun, causing her to wonder if the hair on his chest—assuming he had hair on his chest— was the same.

Not, she assured herself, that it mattered a damn to her anyway. She couldn't afford to let it matter.

Conversation was kept to a minimum on the drive down. Gina wasn't loath to sit back and just admire the scenery. Beverly Hills. Home to so many famous names both past and present. There was a tour, she recalled reading some-where, that was supposed to take in the homes belonging to all the major stars. It must be like living in a goldfish bowl!

'The price to be paid,' Ross remarked when she said as much. 'None of them spend all that much time here, any-way, these days.'

'Do you know any of them?'

'One or two. They're people just like you and me.'

Him, maybe, she thought; she was way outside her nat-ural environment.

Anticipating a city venue for lunch, she was taken by surprise when he turned the car in through a wide gateway, only realising that the long, low building in front of them was a hotel when she saw the discreetly displayed sign.

'Is this where you live?' she queried.

Ross indicated the top left-hand corner of the building. 'Right up there. Easier to eat here than get caught up in the mêlée downtown. The restaurants are second to none.'

'You never fancied a home of your own?'

'Too much of a hassle. I travel a lot.'

He brought the car to a stop at the foot of the broad flight of steps leading up to the entrance, getting out to hand over the keys to a young man in a smart green uniform that matched the overhead canopy. Gina slid from her own seat and went to join him as the valet drove the vehicle away.

'Impressive,' she commented, refusing to be overwhelmed. 'And this is only one of...how many?'

'Twenty-three to date. We don't always build, we acquire and rejuvenate. Which one did you sample?'

'New York. A special deal through a friend in a travel agency. Economy each way, plus two nights in the Harlow. Didn't leave much over for a Fifth Avenue shopping spree, but I managed to pick up a few bargains.'

'Worth the trip?'

'Definitely. Jeans like these cost a bomb back home. I only paid forty dollars.'

The appealing grin lit the lean features once more. 'I meant the accommodation.'

Gina kept a straight face. 'As I already told you, very nice. Of course, we were occupying one of the least expensive rooms, and eating out, so we didn't—'

Dark brows lifted quizzically. 'We?'

'I was with a friend.' Her eyes were on the woman who'd just emerged from the hotel. 'That's Shauna Wallis, isn't it?'

'It is,' Ross confirmed. 'She rents a bungalow in the grounds. The friend male or female?'

'Female.' Her attention was still on the star, who had now been joined by a young man wearing tennis whites. 'She looks rather older than I imagined her to be.'

'Natural daylight can be a killer,' Ross rejoined. 'Dennis is our resident pro. He'll be taking her for a session.'

Gina glanced his way appraisingly, registering the slant to his lips. 'You're a cynic,' she accused.

'A realist,' he said. 'Shauna likes fit young men.'

'And you've no objection to a member of staff providing the service?'

'What he gets up to in his lunch hour is his own business. Talking of which, we'd better get to it ourselves if we're to be at the studio for two. Sam's keeping a slot free for us. He knew Jenny, of course. He's looking forward to meeting you.'

Which was more than she could say, Gina reflected wryly, moving on up the steps along with Ross. Something in her shrank from learning too much about the girl who'd given her life—of creating a tie to the past that she might find difficult to sever.

The hotel was superlative, the vast lobby separated into different sitting areas, some upholstered with tropical-style fabrics, others with leather furniture and plenty of marble. Plant life abounded.

There were people sitting around, groups standing chatting, porters trundling trolleys from the long mahogany desk where three receptionists were hard at work, to the bank of elevators.

'Business seems to be good,' Gina commented.

'It always is.' Ross acknowledged a man in a dark grey suit hovering near by. 'We're eating in the Garden Room.'

'Piers has the table ready for you,' the man replied. His glance flickered Gina's way, the speculation obvious. Far from the boss's usual type, she could almost hear him thinking.

The restaurant just off the lobby was crowded, the buzz of conversation loud. Ross didn't bother waiting for attendance, leading the way through to an outdoor section set beneath a vine-covered loggia. Every table but one was occupied out here too. Gina felt the cynosure of all eyes as they took their seats. At least they weren't the only ones dressed casually, she was glad to note.

The *maître d'* came rushing over, looking distinctly put out. 'Never will you allow me to do my job!' he exclaimed.

Ross gave him a dry smile. 'If you're short of something to do, you can fetch me a Moët.'

'Not for me, thanks,' Gina cut in swiftly. 'I don't like champagne. A kir would be fine.'

'Make that two,' Ross ordered. 'I'm driving.'

'You were driving when you asked for champagne,' she pointed out as the man moved off.

'It was meant for you.' His regard was quizzical. 'The first woman I've ever met who doesn't like champagne!'

Her shrug was light. 'So I'm an oddity.'

'A rarity, for sure. Do I order wine?'

'I'd rather keep a clear head.' She toyed with the stem of a glass, unable to relax under his scrutiny. 'Will you stop looking at me as though I just sprouted a second one?'

'I was actually thinking how refreshing it is to entertain a woman of simple tastes,' he said.

'You mix in the wrong circles,' she retorted, by means deaf to satire.

'Difficult to find any other kind in this town. Most are out for the best deal they can manage for themselves. The reason I find your attitude towards money so hard to accept. Oliver would set you up for life.'

Green eyes met grey, holding fast. 'That's not why I'm here, believe me. If my grandfather was fit and well, I wouldn't have come at all.'

'But you couldn't refuse a dying man's plea.'

Faint though it was, the irony set her teeth on edge. It took a real effort to keep her tongue under control. 'That would have been too cruel.'

The arrival of their drinks cut off whatever reply he'd been about to make. He waited until the waiter had gone before saying levelly, 'Oliver won't let you leave empty-handed.'

'I'm afraid he won't have a choice,' she said. 'I like my life the way it is. I don't want it altering.'

'Your business partner might appreciate an extra influx of capital.'

'Barbara doesn't know anything about all this, and isn't going to know. How many times do I have to say it?'

Ross held up a hand. 'All right, I believe you! I think you're crazy, but I believe you.'

'Good.' She took up the leather-bound menu. 'What would you recommend?'

'Try the Colorado lamb,' he suggested. 'It's a house speciality.'

He wasn't exaggerating. Served with a sweet-pepper lasagne, the dish was mouthwateringly enjoyable. Gina refused dessert, settling for coffee. 'You really didn't have to do any of this, you know,' she said, when Ross glanced at his watch. 'Your time must be at a premium.'

'Not to the extent that I can't take the odd day or two out when necessary. You're doing that yourself.' He paused, regard reflective. 'Where does your partner think you are right now?'

'Spain,' she admitted. 'A quick break. Her turn next month.'

'You don't consider her a close enough friend to know the truth?'

'It's a business relationship. There's no reason for her to know.' She stirred restlessly. 'Shouldn't we be going?'

'Sure.' He pushed back his chair to get to his feet, rounding the table before she could move, to help her to hers. 'No check to wait for,' he said. 'One of the fringe benefits.'

There would, Gina imagined, be many. If she was that way inclined, she could no doubt claim free accommodation in any of the Harlow hotels herself.

No point going down that road, she warned, hardening her resolve. Once she left California, the connection would be finished.

They made the studio lot just before two. Beautifully laid-out gardens fronted the series of white bungalows which were the main offices, with the bulk of a dozen or more sound stages looming beyond.

Small and balding, looking anything but the tycoon Gina had expected, Sam Walker was well into his sixties. He had a meeting in ten minutes, he apologised, but they were welcome to tour the lot.

'Jenny was a lovely girl,' he said. 'A bit of a problem at times, maybe, but no worse than many. I've had three of my own, so I know what it's like. You've got the Harlow bones,' he observed judiciously. 'Look good on the screen. I could set up a test.'

Gina laughed, taking the offer no more seriously than she was sure he intended it to be taken. 'I'm no actress.'

He smiled back. 'Few are, honey.' He shifted his gaze to Ross. 'How's Oliver doing?'

Ross lifted his shoulders, face impassive. 'Holding out. I didn't see him this morning.'

'He seemed fine when I left him on the terrace,' Gina said.

'He'd gone back upstairs when I got there. Said he was feeling tired.'

'Hardly surprising,' Sam commented. 'Only wish there was something to be done. Lucky he can rely on you to keep things under control.' He checked the time on a wall clock opposite. 'Afraid that's it for me. You know your way around, Ross. Feel free. I'll call in to see Oliver first chance I get.'

'Will he?' Gina asked when they were outside again. 'Call, I mean.'

'Like he said, when he can fit it in. He's another who finds it hard to delegate.' Ross took her arm as she made to head for the car park across. 'We'll use one of the run-abouts.'

A studio lot, Gina found, was like a city in miniature. It even had its own fire department. There was a whole lake, a waterfront township, mock-ups of city streets. Somewhat disappointingly, there was no outside filming at present, though several of the sound stages were in use.

They were passing one of the latter, when a personnel door set into one of the large rolling ones opened to emit a whole bunch of people. Ross brought the buggy to a stop as a woman detached herself from the centre of the crowd on sight of them, and came over.

'Running tours as a side-line?' she asked. She flicked a swift assessing glance Gina's way. 'Are you going to introduce us, darling?'

'Given half a chance,' Ross said drily. 'Gina Saxton, Karin Trent.'

The woman's striking face and figure and mane of streaked blonde hair were familiar enough for Gina to have already placed the name before Ross spoke. She might have said as much if the other hadn't so obviously dismissed her as of little importance, her attention returned immediately to Ross.

'You'll be in town for the wrap party next week?'

'Doubtful,' he said.

The pout was too little-girly for a mature woman in Gina's eyes. From the way Ross was acting, the interest was one-sided, but it didn't appear to be getting through to her.

'Call me,' she invited.

She didn't stay for an answer, heading back to where her entourage waited, hips swaying seductively as she walked. Ross put the buggy into motion again, face expressionless.

'I saw her in *Captivation* last year,' Gina commented lightly. 'She was good.'

'She can play a part,' he agreed.

'Do you know her intimately?'

He glanced her way, one dark brow lifted. 'Why the interest?'

'I just thought she may have reason to feel a little proprietorial.'

'On the premise that any woman I sleep with has rights?'

Gina kept her tongue tucked firmly in her cheek. 'More than the ones you don't sleep with. You could do a lot worse, anyway. She's very beautiful.'

'No more than a thousand others.'

'Planning on trying them all out?'

He laughed. 'That much stamina I don't have. You needn't concern yourself over Karin. She's a survivor.'

'You're a bit of a bastard at heart, aren't you?' Gina said coolly.

'Only a bit?' Ross sounded more amused than insulted. 'Why start pulling your punches now?'

'I believe in keeping something in reserve.'

She got out from the buggy as he brought it to a halt at the car park, putting up a hand to reposition the tortoiseshell slide, which had started to slip down.

'Why not let it hang loose?' Ross suggested. 'You have beautiful hair.'

'It's out of the way,' she said, unable to deny a stirring of pleasure at the compliment. 'I'm not out to make an impression.' She dropped her hand again, self-conscious beneath his gaze. 'Are we going back to the house now?'

'I need to call in at the office first,' he said. 'It isn't far from here.'

The American notion of not far differed greatly from her own, Gina had already gathered. She was unsurprised when they took the ramp to the Hollywood Freeway after driving a couple of blocks. The traffic was heavy, with little lane discipline, though it all kept moving at a steady flow.

'Did you talk to your parents yet?' Ross asked.

'This morning,' she acknowledged. 'I told them I'd definitely be back by the weekend.'

'It's Wednesday now,' he said. 'You already booked your return flight?'

'No. But I shouldn't think there'll be much of a problem travelling first class. There were three empty seats on the way out.'

'Not to say it will be the same going east. If you're serious, you'd best get on to it. You can ring the airline from the office.'

'Can't wait to get rid of me?' she mocked.

He looked unmoved. 'You're the one determined to go.'

Which was true enough, she had to admit. It had been almost the first thing she had said to him—repeated several times since.

'I have to. I'm supposedly due back from Spain on Saturday. Barbara's going to be asking questions if I don't turn up at the shop Monday morning.'

'Why a boutique, anyway?' he asked after a moment or two. 'I'd have said you could do a whole lot better.'

'It's no little tinpot affair,' she defended. 'We cater for a pretty high-class clientele.'

'All the same—'

'All the same,' she interposed shortly, 'it's *my* choice, *my* life.'

The shrug signified a loss of interest. Gina stole a glance at the lean, hard profile, wondering what he would have said if she'd admitted to the mistake she'd made in going into the retail business at all. Barbara had carried her along with her enthusiasm, talked her into a partnership she hadn't given nearly enough thought to. Successful enough so far as it went, but not how she wanted to spend years of her life. The trouble now being that Barbara couldn't afford to buy her out, and she didn't have the wherewithal to start over in something new.

She could have, came the sneaking thought, thrust to the back of her mind where it could do least harm.

They left the freeway to cruise down a broad boulevard into the business sector of the city. Gina had anticipated something of an edifice as the headquarters of the Harlow group, but the towering glass structure bearing the insignia took her breath.

The reception lobby was sumptuously furnished, with yards of cream marble underfoot. A large curved desk occupied a central position. The uniformed receptionist on duty greeted Ross with deference as they passed on the way to the lifts.

They took the cage at the end of the row, riding all the way to the eighth floor to emerge on another, smaller, lobby area. The floor here was thickly carpeted, the decor superb in subtle tones of salmon and beige. The paintings around the walls were almost certainly originals.

The woman seated at a central desk was an oil painting herself. A year or two older than Gina, with glossy chestnut hair cut to curve about a set of beautifully balanced features, she stood up to reveal a figure to match in a plain black skirt and white blouse.

'I didn't think you'd be in today, Mr Harlow!' she exclaimed.

'A brief visit,' he assured her. 'I need to check a couple of details.'

Corridors led off to either hand. He chose the right, opening the first door to reveal a huge office with a magnificent view out over the city to the Santa Monica mountains. The desk was a solid block of black mahogany, set at right angles to another holding a communications complex. A group of soft leather club chairs were arranged about a low square coffee-table to form a relaxed conversation area. The same thick cream carpeting was run through here too.

'Have a seat,' Ross invited. 'This won't take long.'

Gina took one of the upright ones set close by the desk as he went behind it to slide into the big leather executive chair. A press of a button brought a computer screen to humming life.

'Everything at the fingertips,' she commented, watching him scroll down a file menu. 'What did we do before computers were invented?'

'Relied even more on a good secretary,' he said. 'Penny's still indispensable.'

'She's very attractive.'

'Isn't she though?' His eyes were still on the screen. 'Happily married, in case you're wondering. And…'

He broke off at the sound of a phone, extracting a mobile from a pocket. 'Harlow,' he announced. 'Oh, hi! What…?' He broke off again, face tautening as he listened. 'We'll be there ASAP.'

Already alerted, Gina came to her feet along with him. 'What is it?'

'Oliver,' he said tersely. 'He had a heart attack. They're on the way to hospital.'

As they battled the late-afternoon traffic build-up, the

journey back across the city was a nightmare. Gina sat through it numbly. She had spent no more than half an hour with her grandfather this morning: there was a very real possibility that it might be the only time she was ever going to have with him.

Ross was silent throughout, but the taut set of his jaw spoke volumes. There was no doubting his feelings for the man who had taken the place of his own father.

They reached the hospital at last, to be directed straight to the coronary unit. They found Elinor seated in a plush waiting room, with a nurse in attendance. The face she raised to her son was tragic.

'He's gone,' she said.

CHAPTER THREE

THE funeral service was attended by what seemed to Gina to be half the city. No more than thirty were invited back to the house afterwards, though several more took it on themselves to make the journey.

Pale but composed, Elinor moved among them, accepting the sympathetic offerings with a word of gratitude, smiling at the anecdotes. Gina admired her fortitude.

It had been taken for granted that she would stay on. Not that she could have brought herself to leave in such circumstances anyway. She'd been forced to tell Barbara the truth, and knew she was going to have some explaining to do when she did get back.

Ross caught her eye, his smile reassuring. He'd been a tower of strength these past few days, making all the arrangements, contacting the necessary people. He'd had trouble locating his sister. Gina had stood in for her when Elinor had so desperately needed another woman to talk to. Not that Roxanne had appreciated it.

Talking animatedly with Sam Walker at present, she showed little sign of grief. The black suit sat her tall, willowy figure beautifully, the whiteness of the silk shirt worn beneath contrasting with the darkness of her hair. She had good looks in abundance, marred only, in Gina's estimation, by a certain hardness about her mouth.

She had made her views clear the moment the two of them met. Not in actual words at the time, but the look in her eyes had left little unsaid. Later, when they were alone, she had left no doubt at all of her feelings. The adoption ruled out any claim on the estate, she declared. Considering her unchanged intentions, Gina hadn't bothered arguing the point.

Ross brought a glass of what looked like whisky across. 'Drink this,' he commanded. 'You look as if you need a stimulant.'

What she needed, she thought, was a good dose of home. Failing that, the whisky would have to do. She took the glass from him and swallowed half the contents in one go, grimacing as the spirit hit the back of her throat.

'Steady,' he warned. 'That's neat Rye.'

'Now he tells me!' Her eyes sought his, knowing she would read nothing there that he didn't want her to see. 'Your mother is bearing up well.'

'She'll make it through. Another half an hour, then I'll start clearing this lot out.' He studied her reflectively. 'Thanks for giving her so much support.'

'No problem,' Gina assured him. 'I only wish there was more I could do. I know how much she loved Oliver.'

'It's going to hit her even harder tonight when it's all over. I'll be staying on.'

'Good.' Gina was relieved to know she wouldn't be facing a lone session with Roxanne should Elinor retire early. 'Tomorrow should be a little easier.'

Ross shook his head. 'Not really. There's the will-reading.'

'Is that absolutely necessary?' she asked. 'I'd have thought it was pretty straightforward.'

'The main part, maybe. But there'll be other bequests. It's a formality that has to be gone through.'

One that could surely wait a while, Gina thought, but what did she know?

'I'd better make some arrangements myself tomorrow,' she said.

Something flickered in the grey eyes. 'Of course. I'll be contacting your parents to thank them for the flowers. That was a nice gesture.'

Sam Walker detached himself from the small group now formed about Roxanne, and came over. He acknowledged Gina with a faint smile and a comforting pat on the arm before turning to Ross.

'Afraid I'll have to get moving,' he said gruffly.

Ross grasped the hand held out to him. 'Thanks for coming, Sam. It can't have been easy.'

The shrug was brief. 'What is? I'll catch your mother on the way out. Keep in touch.'

'He lost his wife last year,' Ross explained as the older man wended his way through the throng. 'As Hollywood marriages go, theirs was one of the rare exceptions.'

'You don't think he'll ever marry again?' Gina murmured.

'Doubtful. Although there are plenty would be more than willing.'

Gina could imagine. The head of a leading studio would be some catch! She felt a sudden wave of self-disgust; she was turning into a real cynic herself. The sooner she was on that plane heading homewards, the better.

'I owe you an apology,' said Ross unexpectedly. 'I was pretty rotten to you when you first arrived.'

Green eyes met grey, striving to conceal her inner emotions. 'Nothing I couldn't handle.'

'So I discovered. I doubt if anything could faze you.'

He didn't know the half of it, she thought. 'I try not to let it,' she returned. 'Shouldn't you be circulating?'

'I've spoken with everyone I need to. Some of them are here uninvited anyway.' He indicated an unoccupied sofa near by. 'Why don't we sit down for a few minutes? It's been a long day.'

Gina couldn't argue with that. She felt bone weary. Ross seized two cups of coffee from the trolley being wheeled around the assembly, depositing them on the low table in front of the sofa to take a seat alongside her.

'Better,' he said.

'Much,' Gina agreed. 'A good thing you decided to hold this inside. The heat out there would have been too much.' She viewed the spacious, luxuriously furnished living room. 'Do you think your mother will stay on here?'

'It's a question I've already asked myself,' he said. 'She'd be better off taking an apartment, where she'd be among people. Whether she'll be ready to do that is something else. She and Oliver spent the whole of their married life together in this house. Not the same one he shared with your grandmother,' he added.

Gina cast an oblique glance at him as he lifted the coffee-cup to his lips, devouring the clean lines of his body in the black suit, the strongly defined contours of his face.

'Does Roxanne always stay here when she's in town?' she asked, needing some distraction.

'When it suits.' There was a sudden harder note to his voice. 'Roxanne does what's best for Roxanne.'

'That doesn't sound very brotherly.'

'Siblings aren't always compatible. We live very different lives. The odds against the two of you getting on were pretty high.'

Gina shot him another glance. 'Why do you say that?'

'Ideals. You have them, Roxanne doesn't. None that I've gleaned, anyway.'

People were beginning to show signs of leaving. He put the cup down and got to his feet again. 'I'd better go and do the honours.'

Gina retired to the terrace until it was over, taking stock of what he'd said about his sister. It had come as something of a shock, she had to admit. Whatever her own opinion of the woman, she would have anticipated a very different attitude from him. It was almost as though he despised her.

Something radical had to have happened between the two of them to cause such a reaction. Not that she was ever likely to find out; she wasn't even sure she'd want to. In a day or two she'd be gone, and could put the whole thing behind her.

It wasn't going to be that easy, she knew. Ross had made too much of an impression to be cast from mind. She'd known the first moment she set eyes on him that it was going to be like that. It happened sometimes; she'd just never expected it to happen to her.

One thing she was pretty certain of: while he'd mellowed towards her on a general front, that was as far as it went for him. No surprise there. She had nothing at all in common with the kind of women he was accustomed to.

Elinor had apparently retired from the fray when she made her way back indoors again, leaving Ross to deal with the remaining stragglers. A glass still in hand, Roxanne viewed her with open contempt.

'There's nothing for you to hang around for now,' she said. 'Why not book yourself a flight home?'

'I intend to,' Gina told her levelly. 'First thing in the morning.'

'What's wrong with tonight?'

'I'm tired.'

'You mean you're hoping my mother is going to beg you to stay on!' The striking face was hard set. 'Don't think I'm blind to the way you've been sucking up to her!'

'I've been doing the job you should have been doing,' Gina retorted bitingly, unable to hold back under the onslaught. 'Trying to offer some comfort.'

'I don't need you to tell me how to act,' came the scathing reply.

'Somebody should.'

'What's going on?' asked Ross, approaching unnoticed by either of them. He looked from one to the other, brows lifted. 'So?'

'I suggested it was time she thought about going home, that's all,' said his sister.

'It's up to Gina to decide for herself,' he stated flatly. 'You could say she's more right to be here than any of us.'

'That's garbage!'

'It's immaterial,' Gina put in firmly before Ross could answer. 'Anyway, I'm going up to change.'

'Good idea,' he said. 'Oliver would probably have disapproved of the black to start with. He always thought the Irish had the right idea when it came to funerals.' He eyed his sister, expression hardening. 'Are you planning on staying?'

'I'm not planning on going anywhere until I know how I stand,' she retorted.

'Now, why would I think otherwise?'

Gina left them to it. Whatever the source of their alienation, it wasn't her business. Gaining the privacy of her room, she stood for a moment or two to collect herself. It was already coming up to six o'clock, which meant they'd been on the go for almost eleven hours. A well-organised eleven hours, perhaps, but no less draining. Elinor must be feeling totally done in.

It was going to be hard leaving her too. They'd become close over the past days. Elinor hadn't said a word against her daughter, though the latter's neglect must have hurt. Roxanne was only interested in what was good for Roxanne, Ross had said. She could believe it.

A needle-like cold shower went some way towards a

physical refreshment. The lounging trousers and matching loose top she donned had been worn before, but her wardrobe had been meant to see her over two or three days at the most, not a week or more. The dress she'd worn that day was the one she'd worn that first evening here, with a silky black jacket concealing the low-cut neckline. She could have bought more clothes, of course, only what would have been the point?

She found Ross on his own downstairs. He'd changed from the black suit into cream trousers and shirt.

'Drink?' he asked.

'Just orange juice, please,' she said.

'Still keeping a clear head?'

'Still recovering from the whisky you gave me,' she countered. 'Is your mother coming down?'

'Shortly.' He brought the glass across. 'Roxanne won't be joining us. She decided there were far more entertaining places to be downtown.'

'Has she always been like that?' Gina asked after a moment.

'Self-centred?' He lifted his shoulders. 'As far back as I can remember. Having Oliver as a father did her no good at all. He was so anxious for her to accept him, he indulged her every whim.'

'Did he indulge you too?'

'He didn't need to. We hit it off from the start. He'd always wanted a son. Maybe if you'd been a boy...' He left it there with another brief shrug. 'We'll never know, will we?'

There was a pause before he spoke again, his regard steady. 'You've been a godsend this last week. Don't think it isn't appreciated.'

'I did nothing special,' she protested.

'You were there for my mother when she needed the

kind of support only another woman can provide. You encouraged her to let it all out instead of bottling it up the way she probably would have done. If Roxanne...' He broke off again, shaking his head. 'What's the point?'

Gina bit back the question trembling on the tip of her tongue. Her involvement with this family was over. It *had* to be over.

She had to keep reminding herself of that throughout the evening. Pale but composed, Elinor accepted her daughter's absence with a wry expression that made Gina seethe at the latter's total lack of filial feeling. None of them ate a great deal, and she was unsurprised when Elinor retired almost immediately after the meal.

'I think I might have an early night myself,' she said into the silence that followed her departure.

'Stay a while,' Ross requested softly. 'I don't feel like being on my own.'

Meeting the grey eyes, Gina subsided back into her seat. 'It must have been hard,' she said, 'to keep up the front all week.'

His smile was faint. 'Pretty hard, yes.'

'I never could understand why men feel they have to keep their emotions under wraps.'

'Childhood conditioning.' There was a pause, a change of tone. 'What was your initial reaction when you got Oliver's letter?'

'Disbelief,' she acknowledged. 'I was sure there must be some mistake.'

'It made no difference to your feelings for the Saxtons?'

'Of course not. There's more to parenthood than just giving birth. They've been wonderful parents.'

'Are they in a position to help you buy your way out of this partnership?'

Brought up short, Gina took a moment or two to gain a

hold on herself. 'What makes you think I want out?' she demanded.

Ross lifted his shoulders. 'Instinct. You're unwilling to talk about the business, and you obviously don't have much of a regard for your partner outside of it.'

'That's very little to go on.'

'But you can't deny it.'

Green eyes flared, the anger overtaken almost immediately by wry acknowledgement as they held the steady grey gaze. 'All right, I can't deny it. And yes, I suppose they would be in a position, if I were willing to ask them. It was my mistake. I'll deal with it.'

'You're a one-off, do you know that?' he said softly. 'In this part of the world, at any rate.'

Gina felt her pulse rate shoot into overdrive as he got to his feet and came over to where she sat. She made no protest when he drew her from the chair, going into his arms without thought of anything beyond this moment.

His mouth was gentle at first, seeking rather than demanding, hardening to passion by slow degrees as the response built in her. It was what she had wanted all week: what she had wanted since the moment she set eyes on him, if she was honest about it. Nothing else mattered right now but the need he was arousing in her, the overwhelming desire to be closer still. He felt the same way, that was obvious. For the moment, at any rate.

She had a brief moment of sanity on the way to her room, but it didn't last. The feel of him at her side, the hand so strong and firm on hers, the subtle masculine scent of him, were enough to drive all other considerations into oblivion.

They undressed each other between kisses, scattering garments behind them as they moved inexorably towards the bed. Ross stood for a moment to view her as she lay nude on the silken cover, eyes travelling the length of her slender curves.

'You're beautiful,' he breathed.

Magnificent, was the adjective that sprang to her mind as she studied him in turn. His body was honed to a peak of fitness, chest broad and deep, narrowing down to waist and hip, the muscle ribbed across his stomach. The wiry curls of hair covering his chest were marginally lighter in colour than those enclosing the essence of his manhood.

He lay down at her side on the bed, propping himself on an elbow to watch her face as he drifted a fingertip down between her breasts and over the fluttering plane of her stomach with exquisite sensitivity. Gina felt the spasms start deep, her thighs parting of their own accord to allow him free access to the moist centre he sought.

She was ready for him now, but he was in no hurry to seek release for himself, making her writhe and arch in a mixture of agony and ecstasy—drawing moan after moan from her throat as he took all control away from her.

'Enough!' she heard herself pleading. 'No more!'

Ross gave a low laugh. 'We didn't even get started yet!'

He lowered his head to take one peaking, aching nipple between lips and teeth in a combination of nibbling and sucking that drove her wild. She ran her fingers into the thick dark hair, relishing the clean crisp feel of it—holding him close even as she begged him to stop.

By the time he finally moved on top of her, she was almost over the top herself. The sensation when he slid inside her was like nothing she had ever known. Even then, he kept control of himself, his movements measured, deepening the penetration by slow degrees until he reached a point where he couldn't hold out any longer himself.

It was some time before either of them could find the

strength to move so much as a limb. Gina had never felt so totally enervated in her life.

'Well worth waiting for,' Ross murmured against her shoulder.

'Waiting for?' she queried hazily.

'I could have done that the very first night you were here,' he said.

Gina was silent for a moment or two, absorbing the claim. 'You didn't give that impression,' she said at length.

He gave the same low laugh, putting his lips to the side of her neck just below her ear. 'I didn't intend to.'

'Because you believed I was only here for what I could get?'

'Something like that. There's a hell of a difference between lust and trust.'

'But you trust me now?'

'After the way you've acted these past few days, I can't do anything else,' he said softly. 'Mother would have gone to pieces without you.'

'She'd have had you.'

'I couldn't have provided the kind of support you provided. I already told you that.'

He kissed her again, on the lips this time, bringing her back to life. Gina thrust the thoughts hovering on the edge of her mind aside as desire rose in her once more. Whatever the consequences, she was way past saying no to this.

The sun was well up in the sky when she woke from a sleep that had held a quality of exhaustion. Ross was gone from her side, of course. She would have expected nothing else.

Last night had been a serious mistake; she'd known it even while it was happening. Leaving was going to be so much harder.

Not that it would make a great deal of difference to Ross, she was sure. He'd needed a woman last night, and she had been available. He'd even been prepared, she recalled, which suggested forward planning. The pleasure he'd so obviously gained from making love to her would be no more than he was accustomed to gaining from any woman for certain.

Neither Ross nor his sister were about when she went down. She settled for coffee and toast for breakfast, then took the opportunity to make a phone call before going to look for Elinor. She found her laid out on the pool deck.

'Why not join me?' the other invited. 'It's going to rain later.'

'I have to pack,' Gina told her. 'I rang the airport. I'm on a flight at ten-fifteen tonight.'

Elinor sat up abruptly. 'You can't go yet. There's Oliver's will to be read. I told you he'd made plans.'

Gina sank to a seat on a nearby lounger. It had been inevitable from the start, she supposed. 'I really wish he hadn't,' she said. 'It wasn't why I came.'

'I know that. I told Oliver how you felt.' Elinor shook her head. 'It made no difference. I didn't really expect it to. The will was redrawn to include you before you got here. He didn't tell me exactly what he intended, but I'm sure you'll find yourself well able to travel first class from now on. If you try turning it down,' she added, 'it will be like kicking him in the face.'

Gina bit her lip. 'That puts me in a cleft stick.'

'So, accept it.' Elinor gave a faint smile. 'Is money such an evil thing?'

'No,' Gina was bound to admit. 'I just didn't…'

'Didn't want any of us seeing you as a gold-digger,' Elinor finished for her as her voice petered out. 'Oliver made sure you were a worthy bearer of the Harlow bloodline before he wrote you that letter, believe me. The fact that you looked for nothing from him only served to prove he'd made no mistake about you. Ross had his doubts to begin with, but you've even managed to win him over.'

'But not Roxanne,' Gina said, shying away from thinking about Ross right now.

Elinor gave a sigh. 'I'm afraid Roxanne sees you as a threat to the size of her own inheritance. Not that Oliver will have left her anything but well provided for. Ross will be taking control of the company, of course. Oliver always intended he should. The reason he insisted on a legal adoption, so that the name at least would be continued. I was unable to have any more children myself,' she went on, sensing the unspoken question. 'Oliver knew that when he married me. What he did to Jenny and you was wrong—no one can ever deny that—but he was a good man in so many other ways.'

'I'm sure of it.' Gina's voice was gentle. 'He obviously loved you a great deal.'

Tears glistened momentarily in the older woman's eyes. 'I loved him a great deal too. Which is why I'd move heaven and earth to see his wishes fulfilled.'

Leaving her with very little choice, Gina acknowledged. 'All right,' she said resignedly. 'What time will the reading be?'

'Two o'clock.'

'Then there's no reason why I can't make that flight.'

'I'd really appreciate it if you could stay a little longer,' Elinor entreated. 'You're the only one I can talk to. Your partner can surely handle the business for a few more days?'

Another cleft stick, Gina thought unhappily. If she insisted on leaving, she let Elinor down, yet if she stayed on, Ross might take it that she'd read more into last night than he'd ever intended. Her acceptance of whatever her grand-father had left her was going to prove embarrassing enough after all her protestations, without that.

'I imagine so,' she said, without allowing herself any more time to think about it. 'I'll give her a call.'

She left Elinor to resume her sunbathing, and went back indoors. There was a telephone in her room, but she couldn't summon the energy to go all the way up there. It would be well into the afternoon back home, she calculated, though Barbara should still be at the shop.

She was. What she wasn't was delighted to hear what her partner had to say.

'It's already been more than a week,' she complained. 'How *much* longer?'

'Two or three days,' Gina hazarded. 'I'm sure you're managing just fine without me. Anyway, I'll be in touch as soon as I have a return date.'

Roxanne was standing a few feet away when she turned from the hall phone. From the way she was dressed, Gina could only deduce that she'd only just returned from last night's outing.

'Had a good time?' she asked before the other could speak.

'Very, if it's any concern of yours,' came the taut reply. 'If you think you're staying on here, you can think again!'

'Would that really be any concern of *yours*?' Gina returned levelly. 'I was under the impression that this is your mother's house.'

Eyes glittering, Roxanne looked ready to spit. Gina left her standing there. Not for the first time, she wished none of this had ever happened; that her grandfather had just let the past ride. His attack of conscience had turned her life upside down in more ways than just the one.

She made no mention of the will when she phoned her

parents later. There was little point until she knew what she would be dealing with. They did their best to empathise with Elinor's needs in the circumstances, but it was apparent that they were none too happy. It couldn't be easy for them, Gina reflected wryly.

The morning wore on. Neither brother nor sister put in an appearance for lunch.

'Ross went in to the office,' Elinor said. 'Roxanne is probably still sleeping off last night's excesses.' She sighed and shook her head. 'I really don't know how she got to be the way she is these days. She's my daughter, and I love her, of course, but there are times when I really don't like her very much.'

She said no more, looking as though she regretted having said as much as she had. Gina wished she could offer some reassurance, but she'd have to lie through her teeth to do it. Roxanne was a spoilt bitch; there were no other words for her.

Ross arrived some minutes after the lawyer who was to perform the will-reading, joining the gathering in the library with apologies for keeping them all waiting. Gina kept her eyes fixed firmly to the front as he took a seat close by, but she was conscious of his gaze. So much for all the denials, she could sense him thinking.

The lawyer dealt first of all with the more minor bequests, including the staff. They were then asked to leave the room while the rest of the will was read. Listening to the seemingly endless list of charities and organisations deemed worthy of benefit, Gina could only assume that the sums being tossed around were of little overall importance.

She heard Roxanne mutter, 'About time too!' when they finally came to the main bequests.

'To my adopted daughter, Roxanne,' the lawyer read out,

'I leave the sum of one million dollars, invested to provide an income for life. To my beloved wife, Elinor, I leave—'

'A lousy million!' Roxanne was on her feet, eyes blazing. 'He can't do this to me!'

'Shut up, and sit down!' said Ross forcefully. 'Be thankful he didn't cut you out altogether. One more word, and you're out of here,' he threatened as she opened her mouth to loose another tirade.

'To my beloved wife, Elinor,' the lawyer repeated as Roxanne subsided reluctantly, 'I leave all my worldly goods and personal finances.'

He paused, as if gathering himself, not lifting his eyes from the page in front of him. 'My company holdings I leave to be equally divided between my adopted son, Ross Harlow, and my granddaughter, Virginia Saxton, on condition that the two of them marry. Should they fail to comply with said condition, the shares to be thrown open to the rest of the board.'

CHAPTER FOUR

THE silence that reigned after that final announcement seemed to last for ever. Gina felt as if she'd been hit over the head with a brick.

Roxanne was the first to recover the power of speech. 'There's no way I'm standing for this!' she jerked out. 'I get a lousy million while *she* gets half the company! Ross, don't just sit there!'

'What would you have me do?' he asked on what Gina considered an astonishingly calm note.

'We can contest it. He wasn't in his right mind!'

'Don't you dare say that!' Elinor flared. 'Oliver knew what he was doing. Gina has Harlow blood in her veins. She has a right to inherit!'

Gina found her voice with an effort, forcing herself to look directly at Ross. 'I'd no idea this was going to happen. I didn't even know I was in the will at all until your mother told me this morning.'

'That was all I knew myself,' Elinor declared. 'Oliver didn't tell me what his intentions were. Not that I find it so unreasonable,' she added staunchly.

Roxanne gazed at her incredulously. 'Are *you* mad too?'

'Don't speak to her like that!' Ross clipped. 'It's obvious that Oliver was going to make provision for his granddaughter. Admittedly, I didn't anticipate he'd go quite this far, but I'm sure we can sort something out.'

Such as what? Gina wondered, still too dazed to think straight. How could her grandfather have done this to the

man he'd groomed to take over from him? How could he
have done it to her, if it came to that?

Ross looked across at her, his expression controlled. 'I
think we need to talk. Not here. Alone.'

A part of her wanted to say here and now that there was
no point in discussing something that wasn't going to happen, but some instinct kept the words from forming. She
got to her feet like an automaton to accompany him from
the room. Raised once more in bitter complaint, Roxanne's
voice was a chain-saw in her ears.

Ross took her to what had been her grandfather's study,
inviting her to a seat. He didn't sit down himself, leaning
against the desk edge with hands thrust deep into trouser
pockets. Looking at him now, Gina found it hard to believe
that last night had ever happened.

'I don't…' she began, breaking off as Ross shook his
head.

'You don't have to convince me. You were as shocked
as any of us back there. I've no quarrel with Oliver's sen-
timents, only with his manner of expressing them. I think
the tumour must have affected his reasoning. Otherwise,
he'd have seen how impossible a situation he was creating.
However, what's done is done. Short of contesting the will
in court—which I've no intention of doing—we're left with
two options.'

He held up a staying hand as she made to speak. 'Hear
me out. I have a fifteen-per-cent holding, Oliver had sixty,
with the other twenty-five spread across the board. If we
don't comply with the condition he set down, we'll be giving certain members the opportunity to acquire enough
stock to take over control of the company. I've no intention
of allowing that to happen either.' The pause was brief.
'Which reduces the options to just the one.'

Gina gazed at him in silence for several moments,

searching the lean features for some sign of the man she'd spent the night with. There was no softening of expression as he gazed back at her—no penetrating the grey eyes. He was a totally unknown quantity again.

'In your view, perhaps,' she got out. 'Not in mine! You really think I'd marry a man I don't even know just to...' She broke off as he tilted an ironic eyebrow, feeling the warmth rising under her skin. 'Just to satisfy his lust for power!' she finished on a hardened edge.

'It won't be just to my advantage,' he returned imperturbably. 'You'll be worth millions in your own right. Can you honestly say that means nothing at all to you?'

She could say it, Gina acknowledged wryly, but it wouldn't be true. Who could possibly be unaffected by the idea of being worth millions?

'No, I can't,' she admitted. 'But money isn't the be-all and end-all. There's such a thing as integrity.'

'You think Oliver was lacking it in making the condition to start with?'

'I think you were right about his judgement being affected,' she said carefully.

Ross studied her for a lengthy moment or two, still giving little away. When he spoke again it was with a certain calculation.

'It won't be a long-term marriage. There's nothing to stop us divorcing after everything is settled. In the meantime, we both live our own lives. I'd continue to run the company, of course. You needn't be involved. All I'd ask is that you sell me enough shares to make up the fifty-one per cent for overall control.'

The anger flooding her had all the force of a rip tide. Last night had meant nothing to him because she meant nothing to him. She'd known that, of course, but having it rammed down her throat this way was too much! The urge to get back at him overrode all other considerations, bringing unstudied words to her lips.

'I might not have your business acumen, but if I go along with this I'll be taking my place on the board—both before and after the divorce.'

'Don't be ridiculous!' Ross's jaw was hard set. 'You've about as much idea of running a company as I have of stocking a boutique!'

'So, you'll just have to show me the ropes. You'll still be the major stock-holder.'

The grey eyes were like granite. 'I thought I had you figured. Seems I was wrong.'

'All the way,' she retorted, still carried along on the same furious wave. 'I won't pretend last night wasn't enjoyable, but don't run away with the idea that it affects here and now in any way. As your mother pointed out, I'm the only real Harlow. Not that I object to you having top billing. My grandfather regarded you highly.'

The curl of his lip had the same impact as a slap in the face, jolting her to her senses for a moment. But only for a moment. She'd chosen her path, she told herself doggedly; she wasn't going to detour from it now. What kind of an idiot would she be to turn her back on millions?

'I guess the boutique's no longer an issue,' he said.

Gina lifted her shoulders. 'Barbara can have it and be welcome.'

'And your parents? How are they likely to react?'

Up until this moment, she hadn't given a thought to that aspect. But she'd gone too far now to turn back.

'They'll cope,' she said, shocked by how callous she sounded. 'They'd want what's best for me.'

Ross gave a brief, grim smile. 'Fair enough. We'll start in the morning. There's a board meeting scheduled at ten.'

It was going too fast. Far too fast! Yet something in her

refused to let go. 'I'll look forward to it,' she said. 'Shall we be going in together?'

'Michael will bring you in. I shan't be here in the morning.'

'Someone else scheduled for tonight?' she asked sweetly. 'Karin Trent, maybe? She certainly seemed eager enough.'

Ross didn't rise to it. 'We'd better go and tell the others what's happening. You'll find Roxanne a lot harder to deal with than my mother, but don't look to me for help.'

'I shan't need any help,' she declared with more spirit than conviction. 'Your sister's claws aren't *that* sharp.'

One dark brow lifted sardonically. 'I wouldn't count on it.'

Gina got to her feet, not in the least surprised to feel her legs give. She stiffened as he moved instinctively to slide a steadying hand beneath her elbow, jerking away from him. 'I'm fine!'

Ross made no answer. He looked totally in command of himself again. She hardened her resolve, refusing to listen to the small inner voice warning of heartache to come from all this.

They found Elinor and Roxanne in the living room. His job done for now, the lawyer had departed.

'If you think I'm settling for a lousy million, you're mistaken!' Roxanne burst out the moment they appeared. 'I want what's due to me!'

'You're getting a great deal more than you merit,' her brother answered shortly. 'If it had been up to me, you'd have got nothing.'

'You're so damned self-righteous!' she flung at him. 'There are two sides to every tale!'

'I've heard your side,' he said. 'Countless times! Anyway, it isn't you we're here to discuss.' He shifted his glance to his mother. 'We're going through with it.'

Totally disregarding the circumstances, Elinor looked frankly delighted. She came over to give Gina a hug. 'There's no one I'd rather have for a daughter-in-law!'

Gina swallowed thickly, wondering if she'd be quite so enthusiastic if she knew how short a duration the relationship would have. The deeper she got into this charade, the worse it became. It wasn't too late to back out, of course. All she had to do was say the word.

'I assume you'll want the wedding as soon as possible,' Elinor said, addressing her son. 'We might just about manage it in a month with the right people organising.'

'Don't get carried away,' he returned drily. 'A civil ceremony will be quite adequate.'

'You can't do that!' She sounded horrified. 'Not for *this* family in *this* town! It has to be the full works!'

'I don't think so.'

'I do.' Gina said it with deliberation, anger at his summary dismissal overruling any wavering. 'Your mother's right. It will be expected.'

Ross slanted a lip. 'If you fancy being the centre of a media circus, by all means go ahead. Just don't complain when your whole life story is put under the microscope!'

'It's all going to come out anyway,' Elinor declared. 'A quiet wedding isn't going to stop the circus. The best way of handling it all is to carry on regardless.'

She turned her attention back to Gina, her smile reassuring. 'You'll stay here for the time being, of course. Michael can drive you around until you get a car. Or there's Oliver's Cadillac in the garage still. I know he'd have wanted you to have it.'

'I think I'd as soon wait until I know my way around a little better,' Gina responded, feeling everything starting to spin out of control again. 'It's such a huge city.'

'Afraid of getting lost?' Roxanne sneered.

Gina didn't turn her head. 'I think that's what I just said, yes. I'll study a map before I venture out on my own.'

'I need a drink,' Ross said brusquely. 'Anyone else?'

'Too early for me,' declared Elinor.

It was still only a little gone three, Gina realised with a sense of shock, glancing at her watch.

'I'll have a gin and tonic, please,' she said, in need of a rod to stiffen her backbone.

Roxanne stalked across to the door, her face set in hard, ugly lines. It will stay like that if the wind changes, Gina was tempted to comment, refraining on the grounds that it was scarcely an adult way to behave. Roxanne had been her enemy since the moment they'd met. Understandably, she was even further from mellowing now.

It was impossible to restrain her curiosity over what she could have done to turn her brother so much against her. Oliver too, if the comparatively paltry sum he had left her was anything to go by. From the way the will had been worded, she wouldn't even be able to get her hands on the capital.

Not her concern, anyway. She was going to have enough on her plate living up to the role she had landed herself in.

She watched Ross as he poured the drinks, unable to conquer the quivering deep down in the pit of her stomach at the images impressed on her mind's eye of that leanly muscled masculine body devoid of all clothing. When it came to performance in bed, he knew it all. Born of experience, of course. He'd probably lost count of the number of women he'd had.

Married, they'd each live their own lives, he'd said in the study. That meant they'd both of them be free to do whatever they wanted to do. For him, that would definitely include seeing other women.

There was no mistaking the emotion running through her

at the thought. While he might not be quite the man she had thought him to be, he still had the same hold on her. A major part of the reason she had agreed to comply with the condition, if she was honest about it—for what good it would do her. He'd wanted her last night, and might well want her again if she showed willing, but it wouldn't mean anything. This was to be a marriage of convenience, nothing more.

She steeled herself to meet his eyes when she took the glass from him, to thank him for it levelly. As usual, she had no idea what was going on in his mind.

'You're going to need to extend your wardrobe, of course,' Elinor announced. 'I can meet you downtown for lunch tomorrow, then show you the best places to go.'

'She might prefer to have her own things sent over,' Ross observed.

'I'm talking about now,' his mother returned. She looked animated, her eyes sparkling the way they hadn't done in days. 'You'll be expected to attend all kinds of functions, Gina. There's a big charity event coming up. You'll need something really special for that.'

'You'll scare the girl to death,' Ross commented drily.

If Gina had been beginning to feel a bit overwhelmed, the ''girl'' gave her the impetus to rise above it. 'On the contrary,' she said coolly, 'I can't wait to get started. It's a great idea, Elinor. The clothes I have back home wouldn't be suitable anyway.'

Ross shrugged. 'Fine. I'll make sure you have the backing. It's going to take a day or two to get accounts opened for you.'

'I can cover my own expenses!' Gina flashed, evoking another of the sardonic smiles.

'The places my mother will have in mind, I'd doubt it.'

'He's right,' Elinor agreed. 'A dress suitable for the

event I'm talking about will cost several thousand dollars alone, to say nothing of the rest. In the circles you'll be moving in, the clothes say it all.'

Gina bit her lip, only just beginning to realise what she had let herself in for. 'It seems I don't have much choice, then,' she said.

'Wonderful! We'll go to Harry's Bar for lunch, then hit Rodeo. The little cream suit you had on the other day will be quite suitable.' She gave a laugh. 'No pun intended!'

It was worth a great deal to see her mood so much lightened, Gina reflected, smiling with her. She sobered again inwardly on remembering that while Elinor could hardly imagine the marriage was an ideal love match, she had no notion that it would only be a temporary one. Now wasn't the time to disillusion her though.

Ross left half an hour later without attempting any further one-to-one commune. Gina had a feeling he was relying on tomorrow's meeting to show her just how ridiculous her aims in that direction at least were. In truth, she had to agree with him, but she wasn't prepared to let him push her aside. What she didn't know, she could learn.

Elinor filled in a little more detail about the company for her. Oliver had handed over the presidential reins to Ross when he was diagnosed. Including herself, the board now totalled nine. Four members, led by a man called Warren Boxhall, were keen to see the company floated on the open market. A move Oliver had rejected out of hand, as had Ross.

'As there's no chance now of Warren buying up enough stock to gain control, he'll try to persuade you into seeing things his way,' Elinor warned. 'With your thirty per cent alongside, they could force the issue.'

'So far as I'm concerned, the company is totally safe,' Gina assured her.

Elinor smiled. 'I'm sure of it. You're a Harlow through and through.' She hesitated before adding. 'I know this marriage is being forced on you, but it will work out. I sense the two of you already have feelings for each other. Right?'

Outright denial was a waste of time and breath, Gina acknowledged. Elinor was no fool.

'Of a kind,' she said.

'That's where it all starts, honey. The rest will follow. You're what Ross needs in a wife. Someone capable of standing up to him—bringing him down a peg or two.' She laughed at the expression on Gina's face. 'I'm under no illusion about my son. He's very strong-willed. To the point of arrogance at times.'

'I'd noticed,' Gina murmured.

'On the good side, he's steadfast and true to those who gain his friendship. Wives and husbands should be friends as well as lovers. Oliver was certainly mine.'

Guilt-ridden, Gina had to bite her tongue to stop herself from coming clean. Bringing Elinor down to earth with regard to this marriage would not only be cruel in the circumstances, but would also achieve nothing. Planning the wedding would give her a new lease of life these coming weeks. At least let her have that.

Roxanne failed to appear again the rest of the afternoon. Believing she had probably gone out, Gina had a shock on going up to her room to change for the evening, to find the other already there waiting for her. A very different Roxanne, smiling and apologetic.

'I've treated you badly,' she said frankly. 'I guess I was suffering from jealousy. Dad and I were always so close. I looked on him as my real father. I didn't even know about you until I got here the other day. Can you imagine the shock it was?'

'It must have been.' Gina was cautious, not at all sure where this was going. 'I felt the same when I got Grandfather's letter. I'd never had any idea what my background was.'

'Of course you didn't. It must be terrible never to have known your mother—your real mother, I mean.'

'It would have been nice to meet her,' Gina agreed, 'but there's no point fretting about it. At least I had the chance to meet my grandfather, even if it was only for a little while. And I'm sorry for the way things have worked out,' she felt bound to add. 'It never occurred to me that he'd do what he did.'

The expression that crossed the other face was come and gone too quickly for analysis. 'You must be wondering why he left me so little.'

'It isn't my business,' Gina refuted.

'He didn't like some of my friends,' Roxanne went on as if she hadn't spoken. 'He believed they were only interested in me because I'm a Harlow. This was his way of proving it.'

Gina kept her tone level. 'He thought they'd desert you once they realised you were only worth a million?'

'Exactly.' Roxanne sighed. 'Whether they do or not, I'm stuffed!'

'You owe money?' Gina hazarded.

'Afraid so. I invested in a project I thought was sound, but it fell through. The people I borrowed the money from are pressing for repayment.'

'Surely they can wait until your inheritance is through,' Gina said uncertainly.

Roxanne gave a brittle laugh. 'I only get the income, remember. I can't touch the capital.'

It was obvious now where this was going, Gina thought wryly. So much for the apparent change of heart.

'How much do you owe?' she asked.

The pause was brief. 'Three hundred.'

'That doesn't sound very bad.'

A hint of a sneer touched Roxanne's lips. 'Three hundred thousand.'

Gina gazed at her in stupefaction. The idea of borrowing that much money was crazy enough, losing it a nightmare! She hardly knew what to say.

'You're asking *me* for help?' she got out.

Roxanne spread her hands in an appealing gesture. 'I've no one else to turn to.'

'There's your mother, or Ross.'

The smile acquired a harder edge. 'I'd rather keep them out of it.'

That at least should be no surprise, Gina reflected. She lifted her shoulders in semi-apology. 'I don't see what I can do. I don't have access to any money myself until the will is proved.'

'You will have once Ross gets accounts opened for you.' Roxanne was all eagerness again, sensing victory. 'I'd be eternally grateful!'

Until the next time she found herself in financial trouble, Gina told herself. Even if she found herself in a position to come across with that amount of money, all she would be doing was giving Roxanne the idea that she was a soft touch.

'I'm sorry,' she said.

The anticipatory expression vanished, replaced by a hatred intense enough to make her take a step back. 'You'll regret this!' Roxanne spat. 'I'll make sure of it!'

If Gina had felt any sympathy at all, it was wiped out by the sheer vehemence in that statement. Roxanne didn't linger any longer, slamming the door as she left the room.

Legs shaky, Gina sank to a seat. She felt all churned up

inside. The adopted Harlows were two of a kind beneath the skin. They cared nothing for anyone but themselves.

Ross was going to learn she was no pushover too, she vowed, hardening her attitude again. She'd give him something to think about tomorrow!

The drive downtown next day was accomplished in near silence. Gina had left the screen between front and rear seats of the limousine open, but Michael seemed disinclined to converse.

She had spent a rough night, one minute tempted to throw in the towel and head for home, the next resolved to see things through to the bitter end. Money might not be the be-all and end-all, but it certainly had its uses: millions of them in this particular case.

She was nervous about the coming meeting, but determined too, deliberately lingering until there was little chance of reaching the offices in time to be in the boardroom by ten. Making an entrance, it was called.

It was already five minutes past the hour when Michael brought the car to a halt before the imposing entrance to the block. Wearing the cream suit along with high-heeled beige shoes, she felt confident enough in her appearance to swan into the reception hall as though she owned the place.

The receptionist had obviously been warned of her coming. The smile with which he directed her to a small, separate lift round a corner from the general run was dazzling. When Ross's secretary came forward to greet her when the doors opened again, Gina thought for a moment that she'd come to the wrong floor. The reception area certainly looked very similar.

'Penny, isn't it?' she said.

The other woman smiled and nodded. 'That's right. Penny Loxley. It's nice to meet you again, Miss Saxton.'

Gina returned the smile. 'My name's Virginia. Gina for short. I'd rather you called me that.'

'I'd be glad to.' Penny indicated double doors across the wide expanse of carpet. 'They're all here.'

Gina gave a laugh. 'And I'm late, on my very first morning!'

'Your privilege.' Penny wasn't attempting to hide her amusement, recognising the ploy for what it was. 'I'll take you in.'

Crossing the floor in her wake, Gina nerved herself for the coming ordeal. There were six men and two women seated at the gleaming mahogany table that stretched almost the length of the panelled room. Heads turned in unison at the opening of the door, differing expressions on every face.

The men came to their feet as Penny made what Gina considered a totally unnecessary announcement. Mentally girding her loins, she waved an airy hand.

'Please, do sit down, everyone. There's no need for formality.'

Ross viewed her expressionlessly as she made her way towards the head of the table, where he still stood. Wearing a suit similar in cut and colour to the one in which he'd greeted her at the airport, he looked the executive from head to toe. At least, she assumed so, being unable to see his feet as yet.

'You're late,' he said.

'I know.' Reaching the head of the table, she gave the occupants of it a wide smile. 'Dreadful of me to keep you all waiting. I just couldn't make up my mind what to wear!' She turned the smile full power on Ross. 'Where shall I sit?'

A dangerous glint in his eyes, he indicated the empty leather chair on his right. 'Where else would you sit?'

'Terrific!' She took the seat, looking round the assembly with overt interest. Of them all, only one face registered anything approaching benevolence. The two women, both of whom were in their fifties, wore expressions fit to turn the milk sour. Gina wondered how they'd look if she gave way to mad impulse and stuck her tongue out at the pair of them.

Ross began an introduction, going clockwise around the table. Warren Boxhall turned out to be the assumedly friendly one. Some ten years older than Ross, he was still a very attractive man. The other names all ran together in her mind. Matching them to the right faces would prove a problem for a while.

'Why don't you just carry on as though I wasn't here?' she suggested blithely when the introductions were over. 'Listen and learn is my motto! Mind you, I don't know about anyone else, but coffee would be very welcome.'

'It will be here shortly,' said Ross, sounding unruffled. 'In the meantime, we'll do as you say and carry on.'

Gina marshalled her forces over the following minutes, bent on absorbing as much as she could of the proceedings. Running an organisation the size of Harlows was certainly no sinecure.

Coffee arrived and was drunk on the hoof, as the saying went, discussion continuing apace. Gina was engrossed. This was business with a capital B! It made the boutique seem like a child's plaything.

She needed to put Barbara in the picture, came the distracting thought. She certainly wasn't going to need an income from the boutique. As the driving force behind the whole enterprise, it was only fair that her partner should benefit.

Telling her parents about the will was going to be the most difficult. The money angle they could no doubt handle, the marriage was another matter—although in their case, the impermanency would probably come as some relief.

She came back to her present surroundings to hear Ross closing the meeting. Chairs were pushed back, legs stretched, mouths exercised in low conversation as the other directors made their way from the room. It was ten to one that she was the main topic, Gina reflected.

'Just what were you playing at back there?' Ross asked on a curious note.

She gathered herself, returning his gaze with a bland expression. 'Playing at?'

'You know what I'm talking about.' He still hadn't raised his voice. 'Turning up late, acting the dumb blonde.'

'Isn't that what you take me for?' she asked.

The grey eyes took on a new expression as he studied her, his mouth slanting. 'If that's the impression I gave you the other night, I'm losing my touch. I took you to bed because it was what both of us wanted. What both of us want still, if we're honest about it. This marriage doesn't have to be a totally celibate one.'

'So far as I'm concerned, it does,' Gina retorted. 'I'm sure you'll have no difficulty in satisfying your needs outside of it. As I will myself,' she added with purpose.

There was a pause while he continued to regard her with that same enigmatic expression, then he inclined his head. 'I guess we can run with that. I'm due to take a trip to Vancouver. You'd better come too.'

'Why?' she asked, mind whirling again.

'I'd have thought it obvious. If you're going to take a responsible role in the company, you need to have some insight into the business. The Vancouver Harlow is our most recent addition. Built to order. I haven't seen it myself yet.'

'Would the company head normally do an inspection?'

'A company head does whatever he—or she—feels like doing,' he said. 'One of the perks of the job, you might say. We'll be here for the charity ball, though, so you'll still need that dress.'

Gina only heard the one word. 'You'll be going too?'

'I was going anyway.' Ross glanced at his watch. 'You'd better get moving. My mother should be here any minute, ready and eager. She never could resist a shopping spree.' His tone softened just a fraction. 'She thinks a lot of you, Gina.'

'I think a lot of her too,' she said truthfully. 'Which makes it doubly hard allowing her to think the marriage might be for real.'

'She knows it's no love match.' He made an abrupt movement. 'I'll come down with you. I've a luncheon appointment myself.'

No doubt with a woman, she thought.

Penny had been in the room throughout the meeting, taking down the minutes, her presence unobtrusive. She'd departed with the others, but was still at her desk in the outer lobby.

'Are you going to be in this afternoon,' she asked Ross, 'or shall I reschedule your three o'clock?'

'I'll be in.' He viewed her quizzically. 'There's something different about you this morning.'

'I know.' Her smile was radiant. 'I'm pregnant!'

'That's great!' Ross sounded genuinely delighted. 'You take care, now.'

'She had a miscarriage last year,' he advised in the lift. 'Let's hope to God she keeps this one!'

'You're very fond of her, aren't you?' Gina remarked. She shook her head in negation as he shot her a sharp glance. 'I'm not suggesting anything beyond that.'

'Good. Penny's a lovely woman any man would fancy, but even if she weren't crazy about her husband, office affairs are strictly no go.'

'For you personally, or the company as a whole?'

'Both, for preference, although keeping tabs on all our employees would prove pretty difficult. So long as it's discreet, and doesn't interfere with work, it's easier to turn a blind eye.'

'Is this luncheon date business or pleasure?' she asked, trying to sound casual about it.

'Considering you're calling it a date rather than an appointment, I'd say you already made up your mind,' he returned drily. 'I *am* meeting a woman, as it happens. Isabel Dantry. She's one of the city's top investment bankers.'

They had reached the ground floor. Gina exited ahead of him, waving a hand to Elinor just coming through the main doors. What he'd said a few minutes ago about the marriage not necessarily being a celibate one still loomed large in her mind. Drawn to him the way she still was despite everything, was it such a bad idea? Who was to say that deeper feelings might not develop between them, given the incentive?

CHAPTER FIVE

FINE feathers made fine birds indeed, Gina thought, gazing at her reflection in the cheval mirror. The pale green silk gown skimmed her body from asymmetrical neckline to ankle, outlining every curve without clinging. The sandals that went with it were mere wisps of kid leather, totteringly high yet so beautifully balanced they felt quite secure.

Her hair had been cut and styled only that morning, falling now in smooth golden abundance to her shoulders. One arm was bare, adorned only by a diamond bracelet, the other covered from shoulder to wrist. Her only other jewellery was a pair of diamond drop earrings.

For what it had all cost, she certainly should look good though! Elinor didn't know the meaning of frugality. These weren't the only things they'd purchased the other afternoon. Nor, if Elinor had anything to do with it, would they be the last. As a Harlow, she had an image to live up to.

She had seen comparatively little of Ross over the last few days. An office had been arranged for her, and a secretary allocated, but so far all she'd done was plough through reams of paperwork relating to the company. Not that she could visualise a time when she'd be capable of doing all that much else, for all her posturing.

Warren Boxhall had waited no more than a day to make the approach Elinor had anticipated. While his charm hadn't evaporated when she turned down his suggestion that they combine forces, Gina suspected that he hadn't by any means given up on the notion. If the company was

69

floated on the market, he stood to make millions more from his shares than he could ever draw in dividends.

Ross was due any minute. They were using the limousine to take them to the charity do, along with Michael's services. It wouldn't do, Gina had gathered from Elinor, to arrive at a function like this in anything other. She was nervous, she had to admit. This was her first time out in public, so to speak. She wondered who Ross would have been taking if he weren't taking her. He would have had a wide choice for certain.

Bracing herself, she took a final glance in the mirror, then swept up the filmy stole and slim evening purse, and made for the door.

Ross had already arrived. Stomach tensing in the stark black and white, he watched her descend the stairs, eyes scanning her from top to toe with an expression she found encouraging.

'You look stunning!' he said.

'Doesn't she!' echoed Elinor with some self-congratulation, watching from a doorway.

Ross took the stole from her, hands lingering for a heartbeat as he slid it about her shoulders. Gina could feel the firm warmth of them through the fine material, stirring memories of the way they'd felt on her bare skin less than a week ago. He had to be aware of the tremor running through her.

If he was, he gave no sign of it. Elinor saw the pair of them off with satisfaction oozing from every pore. Looking rather less po-faced than usual, Michael saw them into the car before getting behind the wheel.

'Do you have to wait around to bring us back?' Gina queried when they were moving.

'Yes, ma'am,' he said.

'Not tonight,' Ross told him easily. 'We'll take a cab when we're ready.'

'That's very good of you, sir.' Michael sounded a little taken-aback. 'Lydia will be pleased.'

Ross put the screen up, indicating an end to the conversation: a move Gina found a little embarrassing.

'Don't you chat with staff?' she asked pointedly.

'Not when I have other things on my mind,' he said. 'You realise you're going to be the centre of a great deal of attention tonight? And not just for the way you look.'

'Meaning word got around about the will?' she asked after a moment.

'Meaning word got around. It's caused a stir, to say the least. You've had no media approach yet?'

'No.' Gina was alarmed. 'Am I likely to have?'

'Very much so. It's a big story. Somebody might even fancy making a film of it.'

'You're joking!'

The smile was fleeting. 'Stranger things have happened. You said you'd maybe missed your true vocation. You could play yourself.'

It was Gina's turn to smile. 'I'll pass, thanks.' She hesitated before tagging on diffidently, 'If you were planning on coming to this thing before all this happened, you must have had a partner already in mind.'

'True,' he confirmed.

'She must feel very…disgruntled about it. About it all, in fact.'

Amusement crinkled his eyes. 'That's one way of putting it.'

'But you'll have told her the marriage is only temporary, of course.'

'I see no reason to tell anyone,' he said. 'It's strictly between the two of us.'

'You really don't give a damn, do you?' Gina accused.

Leaning comfortably into the corner of his seat, Ross regarded her with ironically lifted brows. 'Why the surprise? You had me down for a bastard less than twenty-four hours after we met.'

'Sound judgement,' she returned caustically. 'Women are obviously just cannon fodder to you!'

His mouth curved again. 'You certainly have a way with words! I wouldn't say I'd sown any more wild oats than other men my age.'

'But marriage never figured on the agenda.'

'In this town, it's a path to disaster.'

'Your mother and Oliver lasted pretty well,' she pointed out.

'The exception, not the rule.' There was a pause, a subtle change of tone. 'How did your folks take the news?'

More a desire for a change of subject than any real interest, Gina conjectured. 'I didn't tell them yet,' she admitted reluctantly.

Dark brows drew together. 'Why not?'

'I'm still having difficulty accepting it all myself.' That was certainly no lie. 'I'm planning to ring them tomorrow.'

'Your partner too—assuming you haven't told her either?'

'Barbara too.'

'You still intend handing over the business to her wholesale?'

'Of course,' she said. 'I'm hardly going to need the income.'

'True enough. All the same, it's a gesture many wouldn't be prepared to make. I hope she appreciates it.'

Right now, Gina had other concerns on her mind. Another few minutes, and she would be facing a world she'd hitherto only seen on screen: the centre of attention, Ross had warned. It was going to take every ounce of self-confidence she could muster to get her through the coming hours—to say nothing of the days and weeks following. Why, oh, why had she agreed to this fiasco?

The event was being held at the downtown Harlow. Flashbulbs started popping the moment they alighted from the car, while a host of clamouring journalists pressed in around them. Ross handled it all with aplomb, whisking her straight through to the hotel foyer.

Gina hadn't been in the place before this, and was impressed with its size and dignified splendour. Ross was greeted from all sides as they mingled with the crowd already occupying the spacious lobby, fielding the comments with an insouciance Gina wished she could emulate. She lost count of names and faces, although she recognised several stars of film and television. She felt totally overwhelmed. Never in a million years could she fit in to this environment, she thought depressedly.

But then, she wasn't going to need to, was she? Not for long, at any rate.

Two television crews were filming the arrivals. Ross avoided one presenter making a beeline for them by steering her into a lift about to close its doors. He left his hand where it was under her elbow as they rose to the top floor. The heels she was wearing brought her eyes on a level with his jawline. She could see the smooth, firm line on the periphery of her vision, catch the faint scent of his aftershave. The tension inside her at the moment had nothing to do with nerves.

Lit by glittering chandeliers, the huge room scintillated with crystal and silver, the carpet underfoot so thick, Gina could feel her heels sinking half an inch into it. Their table was way up at the front on the edge of the dance floor, with yet another gauntlet to run by way of the people already seated there. The smile on her face felt permanently etched.

Two of the other couples were mere acquaintances, she gathered. Both in their thirties, Meryl and Jack Thornton were old friends, involved in real estate. They put her at ease immediately, whatever curiosity they might feel kept under bounds.

Gina found the sumptuous five-course meal more than a little incongruous considering the purpose for which the event was being held. There was dancing between courses. Held close in Ross's arms, the hard muscularity of his thighs against hers, she felt the tension mounting. She could tell herself he was an out-and-out swine until the cows came home, but it made absolutely no difference to the effect he was having on her. She wanted him desperately.

The brush of his lips against her cheek almost finished her. 'Keep feeling the same way,' he murmured against her skin. 'The evening won't last for ever.'

She should tell him to get lost, she knew, but she couldn't summon the necessary strength of mind. That he could still find her desirable in a room containing so much feminine beauty was a stimulus in itself. Why not make the most of what time they had together? she asked herself. Cliché it might be, but half a loaf was still better than none.

It was coming up to midnight before the main purpose of the evening was brought to the fore. The charity was for children in need. Gina wasn't all that surprised to hear Harlows announced as one of the main sponsors. The devastation came when she was asked up along with Ross to front the appeal for further donations from those present.

'Bear with it,' he murmured as they made their way forward.

She did, though only just. Keeping a smile on her face, knowing speculation was rife throughout the whole assembly, was one of the most arduous things she'd ever done. She envied the ease with which Ross launched into a brief spiel about the aims of the charity, only too thankful that she wasn't called on to say anything herself.

Both cheques and cash were deposited in the baskets that were circulated among the guests with a readiness she found admirable. The people here were all of them mon-eyed, but that didn't necessarily foster philanthropy.

'I keep trying to persuade Ross to invest in a property,' Meryl declared when the two of them visited the powder room together a little later, 'but he won't play. Not that I can blame him too much, considering his place. Terrific, isn't it?'

'I haven't seen it yet,' Gina admitted.

'You haven't?' Meryl sounded surprised. 'I'd have thought…' She broke off, shaking her head in self-recrimination. 'Forget it.'

Gina took the bull by the horns. 'You don't have to keep treading lightly round the subject. It has to be a pretty general topic at the moment.'

Meryl laughed, obviously relieved. 'You could say that! It's been a bit of a shock, I have to admit. Even more so for Ross, I imagine. He's managed to steer well clear of marriage up to now. Not for want of trying by at least one person I could mention.'

Gina concentrated on applying lipstick. 'No one here to-night?'

'I guess she would have been if you hadn't come into the picture. She'll be fuming. No man puts Dione Richards aside—even for a future wife!'

Gina felt her stomach turn over. '*The* Dione Richards?' she asked.

'The one and only. You've seen her films?'

'A couple of them.'

'Hardly the world's greatest actress, but good box office. One look into those big baby blues and men turn to mush! Jack no exception,' she added drily. She viewed Gina appraisingly through the mirror. 'You aren't at the back of the line when it comes to looks yourself. Terrific figure too! Lucky Ross. He could have been stuck with a real plain Jane.'

For what difference it made, Gina reflected on the way back to the table. Dione Richards had been voted the most beautiful woman in the world only last year. Who could compete with that?

The intimate little smile Ross gave her on her return to the table was a boost nevertheless. Dione might have the edge on looks, but she didn't have the man. Not tonight, at any rate. She was probably being all kinds of a fool in contemplating what she was contemplating, but she couldn't help herself. She wanted him. Right now, that was all she could think about.

People were already beginning to leave. Gina was more than half expecting the suggestion that they call it a day themselves. From the look in Meryl's eyes when they took their leave, the other woman was well aware of where they were heading. She schooled herself not to care. She was doing what a whole lot of others did for once, and seizing the moment.

There was a cab already waiting. Gina made no demur when Ross told the driver to take them to the Beverly Hills Harlow. She held nothing back when he drew her to him to kiss her.

'I've been wanting to do that all evening,' he said against her hair.

'So why didn't you?' she murmured. 'Plenty of others were kissing.'

His laugh was low-pitched. 'I don't believe in starting something I can't finish.'

The champagne she had consumed was making her head swim; the movement of the car wasn't helping. She made an effort to focus her mind on other things.

'Neither do I,' she said.

He kissed her again, teasing her lips apart with the tip of his tongue and bringing the blood hammering into her ears. The silky probing of the soft inner flesh was electrifying. She felt a dampness between her thighs, a spasming in her groin: sensations that for the present overrode everything else.

It was only when she got out of the car at the hotel that the nausea began to make itself felt. She did her best to tamp the queasiness down. It would pass, she assured herself. She hadn't had all that much.

There were few people in the lobby. Even so, Gina was aware of eyes following the pair of them as they made their way to a small, obviously private lift off the main concourse. The motion as they rose was of no assistance whatsoever. She could only hope and pray that she wouldn't throw up.

She had only the vaguest impression of her surroundings when Ross opened the door. He'd made no attempt at conversation in the lift, nor did he say anything now. He took her arm and steered her to another door leading off the entrance hall, opening it to reveal a bathroom. Right then, Gina had but the one thought in mind. She made it just in time.

It seemed an age before the retching stopped. Even then, her head wouldn't stop whirling. How could she have been so stupid? she thought miserably. She'd told Ross she didn't like champagne, when what she should have said was that it generally didn't like her. Ignoring that danger simply because everyone else was drinking the stuff and she needed the boost was ridiculous.

Well, she was paying for it now. She must be the first woman he had ever brought back here who'd finished up with her head stuck down a toilet bowl! The mere thought of facing him after this was enough to stir nausea again.

It had to be done, of course. She could hardly stay in here all night. A face and mouth rinse went some small way towards refreshing her, but there was no denying the unsteadiness still in her limbs when she finally emerged from the bathroom.

Waiting in the hallway, Ross viewed her with apparently solicitous enquiry. 'Better?' he asked.

Gina nodded, not trusting her voice, wishing she hadn't as pain spliced through her head.

'Obviously not,' he said, seeing her wince. 'Feeling dizzy?'

There was no point denying it when every step she took betrayed the fact. 'I'm sorry about this,' she got out.

His shrug was dismissive. 'It happens. I should have remembered what you said about not liking champagne.'

'I didn't have to drink it,' she responded. 'If you'll call a cab, I—'

'You can't go anywhere like that,' he cut in decisively. 'You'd better use the spare room for tonight, and we'll see how you feel in the morning.'

'I can't...' she began, desisting abruptly as her stomach contracted again. There was no way she dared get in a car feeling this way. 'I'm sorry,' she repeated. 'I know you were expecting...'

There was irony in the smile that touched his lips as she let the words trail away. 'I'll get over it. Think you can make it to the bedroom—or shall I carry you?'

'I'm a bit dizzy, not paralytic!' she said, seeking refuge

in humour, however weak. 'What about your mother? Won't she be concerned if I don't turn up?'

'I doubt it.' The irony was there in his voice this time.

Meaning Elinor would probably have taken it for granted that the two of them would be spending the night together, Gina assumed. And why not? They were both adults. The fact that right now she felt anything but was another story.

The bedroom he took her to was large and beautifully furnished, the two beds queen sized. There was an *en suite*, Ross pointed out.

'Can you cope OK?' he asked from the doorway.

Gina forced herself to look at him directly. He had taken off both jacket and tie while she'd been in the bathroom, and loosened the collar of his pristine white dress shirt. Hair ruffled as though from the passage of a hand through it, he looked like a man who'd undergone, and was probably still undergoing, severe frustration. Hardly to be wondered at considering the way she'd been in the car.

'I'll be fine,' she said, wishing she could believe it. 'Goodnight, Ross. And…thanks.'

'No problem.'

He closed the door softly between them, leaving her standing there biting her lip. She'd made a total fool of herself, and for what? Ross wasn't going to develop any deeper feelings than he'd already shown for her. There was every possibility that after tonight, he wouldn't want to know anyway.

She awoke to the faint sound of music. Memory brought a swift return of last night's depression, forcibly overcome. There was nothing to be gained from wallowing in it.

Lifting her head cautiously from the pillows, she was relieved to feel no more than a faint tightness behind her eyes. She might deserve to suffer a hangover, but it would have been more than she could cope with.

Surprisingly, it was only a little gone eight o'clock. The dress she'd taken off last night was slung over a chair: the thought of putting it on again was anathema to her, but she didn't have much choice.

She'd slept nude. Taking up the scanty lace bra and matching panties, she went through to the *en suite*, regarding her bleary-eyed appearance in wry distaste. Her hair didn't look too bad, and would look even better with a brush through, but all she had in her purse was a lipstick. Not that Ross was likely to give a damn how she looked this morning.

She took a shower, and donned her underwear. The long white towelling bathrobe hung on the door was just about her size. Obviously kept ready for female visitors using the spare bathroom, Gina thought, and took it. It went against the grain to wear something others had worn before her—even if it did smell freshly laundered—but at least it saved her from putting on the dress again right away.

The music was still playing when she left the bedroom. Double doors gave access to a living area the size of a football field, with floor-to-ceiling windows providing a superb view out to the mountains.

Wearing a silk robe over what appeared to be black pyjama trousers, Ross was seated at a table on the balcony that ran the whole width of the room. He looked up from his newspaper as she emerged, the lift of his eyebrow asking the question.

'I'm OK,' she said, reluctant to look at him directly. 'Is that coffee I can smell?'

He took up the pot without answering, and poured another cup, pushing it across to her as she took a seat.

'You look like a well-scrubbed schoolgirl,' he observed.

'I feel like a thoroughly chastised one,' she returned. 'I should have had more sense!'

'If wishes were horses,' he quoted. 'I've over-indulged too many times in the past myself to come the heavy.'

'But not to the same extent, I'll bet.'

'I was lucky enough to finish up with just a bad head. You don't have to flay yourself. You're not the first, you won't be the last.'

She glanced at him from beneath her lashes, every sense alive to the impact of the lean-featured, freshly shaved face. The robe revealed a glimpse of sun-kissed bare chest. She touched the tip of her tongue to dry lips.

'Hungry?' he asked, jerking her head up. She met his eyes in some confusion, sure he must know exactly what was going through her mind.

If he did, he was keeping it to himself. His expression was devoid of irony.

'A bit,' she admitted. 'Do you have a kitchen?'

'There's a service area behind the screen over there,' indicating the far side of the room. 'I make my own coffee and toast, or even occasionally produce a full breakfast, but I use Room Service for everything else when I'm in. What do you fancy?'

'Toast sounds good. I can make it myself,' she added quickly.

The smile was brief. 'I've no intention of stopping you. You can do me a couple of slices while you're at it.'

She went back inside to cross to the screened area, finding time on the way to appraise the light, modern decor. The furnishings were Scandinavian, she guessed, the quality outstanding. But then, what else would she expect?

As anticipated, the kitchen—or service area, as Ross preferred to call it—was well-equipped with both storage and appliances, including a typical American refrigerator-freezer big enough to house a whole family's food for a year. Gina took a peep inside while she was waiting for the toast to cook, finding it somewhat sparsely stocked. No point in keeping a lot of food around, she supposed, if Ross didn't do much cooking for himself.

There had been no butter on the table out there, from what she could recall. She put a dish of the small individual packs on a tray along with a selection of preserves and the rack of toast, added cutlery and bore the whole lot outside.

'Very domesticated,' Ross commented, eyeing the spread.

Gina found a laugh, determined to carry this through with nonchalance—no matter how spurious. 'The product of my upbringing.'

He took a piece of the toast and spread butter on it, ignoring the preserves. 'Maybe something to be said for it after all.'

'I hardly see you settling for a domesticated lifestyle,' she said lightly.

'There could be advantages.'

'Like having a woman available at all times?'

The tilt of a lip brought sudden warmth to her cheeks. She hadn't meant to say that, it had just slipped out.

'Not that you've ever had any difficulty in that direction, of course,' she added, digging herself an even deeper hole.

'I did last night,' he observed. He watched her colour rise with a certain relish. 'You still owe me.'

'I owe you nothing!' she retorted, resenting the implication. 'I'm sorry if you were frustrated, but like you said a while ago, it happens!'

The grey eyes mocked her anger. 'Calm down. I'm not claiming immediate reparation. In fact, I'll be taking you back to Buena Vista shortly. We're leaving for Vancouver this afternoon.'

Gina gazed at him in stunned silence for a moment, the wind taken completely from her sails. She'd forgotten completely about the proposed trip. Even if she'd remembered, she wouldn't have expected it to be quite this soon.

'We'll be taking one of the company jets, so there's no hard and fast timetable,' Ross continued. 'You'll need enough for two or three days. You might want to stick a swimsuit in too. The Vancouver Harlow has three pools.'

Gina found her voice with an effort. 'I really can't see the point in my coming with you.'

'Experience,' he said. 'If you're serious about staying on board after the divorce, you need all you can get.'

'If that's meant to remind me that the marriage will only be temporary, it isn't necessary!' she flashed. 'I wouldn't try denying the physical attraction, but that's as far as it goes for me too.'

'Then we've neither of us anything to worry about,' he returned, unmoved. 'Better eat your toast, before it goes completely cold.'

Gina forbore from further comment. Refusing out of hand to accompany him on this trip would call for reasons she wasn't prepared to give. For all his talk of owing him, she doubted if he meant it. Seeing her drunk and incapable last night, and scrubbed clean like a schoolgirl this morning—as he'd so delicately put it—was enough to put any man off for life.

She finished the toast with little appetite. There was a canopy over the part of the balcony they were occupying, affording shade from the full glare of the sun, but the heat was steadily rising. Green and verdant, the mountains looked cool and inviting.

'You can go up there another day,' Ross said, following

the direction of her gaze. He pushed back his chair and got to his feet, not bothering to catch the belt of his robe as the two ends slid silkily apart. 'I'll go and get dressed. See you in ten.'

Gina stayed right where she was. It was hardly going to take her any time at all to throw on the only garment available to her. The glimpse she'd just had of that well-toned body had set every nerve-end tingling again. She needed a moment or two to bring her pulse rate down.

The way she felt at present, a flight home was a more sensible course than the trip to Vancouver. Except that sense didn't come into it. She'd committed herself by accepting the condition in the first place. The future of the company was at stake too. Warren couldn't be allowed to gain control.

She had to force herself to move in the end. The door to what she assumed was Ross's bedroom was partly ajar when she went out into the hall. From the sound of it, he was on the phone, his tone lightly placatory.

'Naturally I would. It was unavoidable in the circumstances. I'm going to be out of town for a few days, but I'll give you a call as soon as I get back.'

Gina continued on her way feeling even more disconsolate. That was Dione Richards he was talking to, for certain. She filled in the unspoken part of the first overheard sentence, 'Naturally I would rather have been with you.' He almost certainly wouldn't have suffered the frustration she had inflicted on him.

He was ready and waiting in jeans and a T-shirt when she emerged wearing the green dress.

'Is there a back way out?' she asked. 'If I have to cross the lobby in this, everyone will know I spent the night here.'

'The staff will know anyway. Hotel grapevines are second to none.' Ross sounded unconcerned. 'There is a back way, but I can't guarantee a clear run. Hold your head up and look them straight in the eye. It's nobody's business but ours.'

All very well for him to talk, she thought sourly.

They descended to the ground floor without speaking, emerging round the corner from the main concourse and heading down a long corridor lined with doors. Expecting one of them to open any minute, Gina drew a breath of relief when they turned another corner to traverse a narrower corridor, with windows overlooking the rear of the hotel. Ross pushed a pair of fire doors open to afford an exit onto a large paved area backed by a line of huge bins.

'Stay here, if you're still feeling sensitive, and I'll fetch the cab I ordered round for you,' he said.

'Cab?' she queried.

The glance he gave her was impatient. 'I left my car up at the house. If I take another, that's going to be stuck there too.'

'Of course.' She summoned a smile. 'You're right, I'm being ridiculous. I'll come with you.'

It took a few minutes to walk round to the front of the place. Her bravado went into swift decline when she saw all the comings and goings, revived by sheer force of will. Head up, she stalked to the waiting cab, ignoring the glances cast her way.

Like cabbies the world over, the driver showed no reaction to her appearance, but simply put the vehicle into motion. If she'd been on her own, Gina could have relaxed a little; with Ross seated beside her, there was no chance. The effect he had on her was unchanged by last night's fiasco. The merest brush of his bare arm against hers sent a surge like an electric shock through her body. She wished she'd never slept with him at all. What wasn't known couldn't be missed.

CHAPTER SIX

IT WAS almost ten when they reached the house. Ross declined to come indoors with her.

'I've things to see to before we go,' he said. 'I'll pick you up at two. Wear something—'

'Comfortable,' Gina finished for him. 'Yes, I know.'

She didn't wait to see him drive off. There was no one around when she went inside. She made her bedroom in double-quick time, closing the door in some small relief.

The dress left ready to be taken for cleaning, she slid into a pair of jeans and pulled a T-shirt over her head, before turning her attention to the question of packing. Two or three days, Ross had said. A pretty lengthy tour of inspection.

The only suitcase she had available was the one she'd brought with her just two weeks ago. She chose clothes at random from the selection now in the wardrobes, picking out a lightweight trouser suit to wear on the plane. This was a business trip, nothing else. From now on, she concentrated all her attention in that direction.

It was still only eleven. Leaving her face bare of make-up for the present, she made her way back downstairs to seek Elinor.

The latter was under an umbrella down on the pool deck. She looked up from her book with a welcoming smile.

'Hi! How long have you been back?'

'About an hour.' Gina sank to a seat on a nearby lounger, eyeing the older woman with some reserve. 'Aren't you going to ask what happened?'

Elinor laughed. 'Honey, the way you looked last night, I don't need to ask! I knew the two of you were made for each other the first time I saw you together. Maybe it isn't exactly the ideal way to start a marriage, but you'll make a go of it. You're off to a good start already.'

Torn by guilt again, Gina opted for some light relief. 'I wouldn't be too sure about that. I drank too much champagne and made myself ill. I spent the night in Ross's guest room.'

'Poor Ross!' Elinor's eyes were sparkling. 'He must be feeling really deprived! Not that you need worry. Starvation only increases the appetite. Are you packed yet?'

Gina looked at her blankly. 'You knew about this afternoon?'

'Only since last night. Ross told me while we were waiting for you to come down. He's planning to spend the weekend on Vancouver Island after you get through vetting the new place apparently. It will be good for the two of you to have a couple of days on your own together.

'I'm going to start needing your help with the wedding plans when you get back,' she added. 'The organisers have everything in hand with regard to the church and reception, but we have to get your dress chosen. There isn't going to be time to have it made, but we'll find something suitable. What about bridesmaids?'

Gina shook her head, hardly knowing what to say.

'I've a cousin with twin daughters your age, if you've no one else in mind. They'd be thrilled to do it!'

'That would be great.'

The wedding was the last thing Gina wanted to talk about—the last thing she wanted to think about right now. If Ross hadn't already aborted the Vancouver Island idea, he could forget it. A celibate relationship offered far fewer pitfalls.

Clad casually himself in trousers and open-necked shirt, with a light linen jacket, he arrived at five minutes to the hour.

'Glad to see you took me at my word,' he commented, approving the suit. He glanced down at the smallish suitcase she'd handed him. 'Is this it?'

'You said two or three days,' she returned.

'And you believe in travelling light. I should have remembered.' He looked at his mother. 'I'll call tonight. Are you going to be OK?'

A bit late to be thinking of that, Gina thought, although Elinor didn't seem concerned.

'I'll be fine,' she assured him. 'I'm out to dinner tonight, meeting a group for lunch tomorrow, and attending a charity affair in the afternoon, so I'll be pretty busy. I'll look forward to hearing all about it when you get back,' she added to Gina.

On impulse, Gina went over and kissed her on the cheek. 'I'll keep a daily diary,' she promised.

Ross glanced at his watch. 'I know I said time wasn't pressing, but I'd like to at least get in the air before dark!'

'Patience,' admonished his mother, 'is a virtue!'

'The beggar's virtue.' He opened the front passenger door of the waiting car. 'Ready?'

Gina slid into the seat feeling anything but, pulses dancing the usual fandango as the scent of his aftershave tantalised her nostrils. No backsliding, she told herself resolutely. She couldn't afford to become any more involved than she already was.

Seating eight, the sleek private jet was all soft leather and walnut inside. Apart from a slight detour to avoid a storm front building over the Sierra Nevada range, they made good time, landing at Vancouver at six-thirty.

There was a limousine waiting to take them directly to the hotel. Impressive enough from the outside, the latter was even more so inside, the lobby alone a symphony in glass and sumptuous carpeting. Unlike the general chains, every Harlow was designed differently to suit its intended clientele: an individuality that had helped make the company name what it was. Gina very much approved of those differences herself. She'd stayed in hotels where even the pictures on the bedroom walls were obviously out of a job lot spread around the chain.

They were greeted with deference by the general manager himself, and efficiently roomed in adjoining suites. There were connecting doors between the two, Gina noted, securely locked at present.

Ross had elected to have dinner in one of the four restaurants. Dressing for it in a simple linen tunic that had cost enough to have kept her for a month back home, she went back over the flight in her mind's eye.

Conversation had proved surprisingly easy. Ross had even refrained from ironic comment when she'd asked the hostess looking after them for an orange juice instead of champagne. It seemed pretty obvious that he'd lost interest in persuing the physical side of their relationship, for which she could hardly blame him. What she needed to do was foster the same attitude.

One look at him when he called for her, tall, dark and devastating in a silver-grey suit, and she was forced to acknowledge herself a lost cause. She would just have to live with it, she thought resignedly.

'Nice outfit,' he commented.

'I try,' she said, wondering how she could sound so collected when every part of her yearned for contact with that hard, masculine body. 'I imagine word will have gone round by now that you're in the building.'

'That *we're* in the building,' he corrected. 'Having the general manager check us in will have set the ball in motion. I'd have preferred him to keep it low-key.'

'So that you could see how the place was being run without people knowing who you are?' she hazarded, eliciting a brief smile.

'The departmental heads are hand-picked. Poached from other hotels in some cases. For what they're being paid, I think they can be trusted to keep things running smoothly, whether we're here or not. I haven't noted a single thing to complain about as yet. The way it should be.' His voice briskened. 'If you're ready.'

The chosen restaurant was on the first floor—second here, Gina reminded herself—and already well populated. While he addressed them both by name, the *maître d'* refrained from making any deferential show as he saw them seated. Their table was in an alcove affording privacy from their immediate neighbours. A prior arrangement on Ross's part, Gina fancied.

Pristine white damask cloths set with sparkling crystal and silverware made an excellent impression. An arrangement of seasonal flowers occupied central position: renewed every day, judging from their unblemished appearance. The lighting was designed to cast a soft glow over every table: enough to see what was being eaten, but immensely flattering to the skin.

'It's all so beautifully done,' Gina commented. She gave a laugh, determined to keep her end up. 'If you'd told me even a month ago that I'd be living it up on this level, I'd never have believed it!'

Ross regarded her with tolerant expression. 'You'll get accustomed to it. A few more months, and you'll be taking it all for granted.'

'The way you do?' she said, shying away from thoughts of that future.

'It's been a part of my life for the last twenty years. The first fourteen weren't exactly on the breadline either. My father was a banker. A bit of a womaniser too, unfortunately. And if you say, like father, like son, I'll put you across my knee,' he threatened.

'What, here?' she asked. 'That would be a new kind of floor show!'

He laughed. 'Are you ever stuck fast for an answer?'

'Only when I'm drunk.' She pulled a wry face. 'I felt a total wreck this morning!'

'You looked remarkably far from it,' he said. 'Few women can get away with a bare face in bright sunlight—especially after spending half the night throwing up.'

'It wasn't half the night,' she said in mock indignation, trying not to read too much into the compliment. 'It just felt like it.'

'Forget it,' he advised. 'I'm going to.'

The arrival of the wine waiter took his attention. Not about to take any risks, Gina asked for a kir. Ross ordered a bottle of some wine she didn't recognise by name for himself.

She watched him as he spoke to the waiter, unable to conquer the inner turmoil. His mouth was so sensual; she could feel it on hers, nibbling, teasing; tongue flickering delicately between her lips, enticing her to respond in kind. She'd always hated French kissing, but with Ross it was so different, so utterly alluring. She ached to be with him again, nude in his arms, his hands exploring her body.

She came down to earth to find him watching her curiously, the waiter departed. 'I asked you if you'd decided what you'd like to eat yet,' he said.

Gina was grateful once more for the subdued lighting.

'Sorry, I was miles away. I'll have the melon and the salmon,' she added, plumping for the first dishes that sprang to mind.

She kept a firmer grip on herself during the meal, turning the conversation to the company. Ross answered all her questions readily enough.

'Did you call your parents?' he asked over coffee.

'I didn't have time,' she said.

'You had at least a couple of hours after I dropped you at the house,' he pointed out. 'Don't you think it time you put them in the picture?'

Gina made a helpless little gesture. 'It's going to be such a shock for them.'

'It's going to be that whatever time you call.' He paused, adding when she failed to reply, 'Do you want me to do it for you?'

'That would be even worse! I'll do it tomorrow.'

'What are you going to tell them?'

'No more than I have to. Like your mother, they'd be devastated to know what the plan really is. You do realise she's taking it for granted the...arrangement will be permanent?'

'I'd rather gained that impression, yes.'

'Are you willing to tell her the truth?'

'No,' he admitted. 'Not yet, at any rate. It's helping her through a bad time. Best you let your parents assume the same for now.'

He was so matter-of-fact about it all, Gina thought hollowly.

'We should have had the quick civil ceremony you wanted,' she said. 'The whole thing is getting out of hand.'

'Too late now,' Ross observed. 'You'll just have to put up with it. Me too, unfortunately.'

'Are there likely to be a lot of guests?' she asked after a moment.

'With my mother compiling the list, at least a couple of hundred.'

'Some from the film world too?'

'From all sources. Excluding Karin Trent, if that's who you've got in mind,' he added drily.

It wasn't Karin she was thinking of, but she let it pass. If it was true that Dione Richards had designs on Ross herself, it was unlikely that she'd be attending either. Not that the wedding would necessarily put a stop to their association. For all she knew, Ross had already told the woman he'd soon be free again.

It was only a little after ten, but she had had enough. 'I think I'm going to turn in,' she said. 'I didn't get all that much sleep last night.'

'Sure.' Ross came to his feet along with her. 'An early night will do us both good.'

Her heart rate increased, dropping again as she met the dispassionate grey eyes. Whatever attraction she'd had for him, it was so obviously dead and gone.

There were plenty of people still milling around the lobby. They took an interior lift rather than the glass one that climbed the outside of the building, losing people at each floor to arrive at their own as sole occupants.

The suite Gina was occupying was first in line. She fished the keycard from her purse with unsteady hands, dropping it on the carpet. Ross picked it up and inserted it in the slot, pushing open one of the double doors to allow her access.

'See you at breakfast,' he said, and moved on. leaving her standing there feeling thoroughly depressed. It made better sense to keep things on a purely businesslike level, she knew, but the way Ross made her feel, the coming weeks were going to be hell to live through.

Breakfast was delivered to the suite with speed and efficiency. Gina took it on trust that the regular guests would receive the same service. A hotel of this calibre couldn't afford any less.

Ross would be planning a tour of the place today, she assumed. She'd accompany him because it would be expected of her, and do her best to act the part she'd been allocated. She was, after all, a major stock-holder. Or would be, once the marriage licence was signed.

She was finishing her coffee when Ross arrived at nine. He was wearing the same suit he'd worn last night, though with a different shirt and tie, and looked ready for business.

'The GM is taking us on a tour of the place,' he said. 'I'd as soon do it without him, but the suggestion might not go down very well.'

'You're the big boss,' Gina returned with deliberated flippancy. 'Your word is surely his command!'

'Not if we want to keep him.' The emphasis on the 'we' was slight. 'Conroy was persuaded to put off retirement for a couple of years to take the job on. I'm told he can be touchy.'

He took in the table bearing the remnants of her breakfast. 'I see you had Room Service too. How did you find it?'

'Excellent. Not that I'd have expected anything less.' She briskened her voice to add, 'You don't really need me on the tour. I'd probably just get in the way. I thought I might take a look at the shopping arcade down on mezzanine. From the glimpse I got of it last night, it's certainly worth visiting.'

'You can shop any time,' he said decisively. 'Conroy would take it as a personal insult.'

Mr Conroy could go run up a shutter! she thought, but refrained from voicing the sentiment. 'That definitely wouldn't do,' she said instead, keeping the sarcasm low-key. 'Still, I don't suppose it's going to take all day?'

'I'd doubt it.' Ross studied her, a glimmer of what could have been derision deep down in the grey eyes. 'I have to go out myself later this afternoon. You'll have plenty of time to look round the arcade then.'

'Business?' she asked before she could stop herself, and saw the glimmer become a definite gleam.

'Of a kind. I'll be back in good time for dinner.'

Which you'll be eating alone, she felt like telling him. That he would be seeing some woman, she didn't doubt. Like a sailor, he probably had one stashed in every port!

The tour took her mind off her personal problems for a while. For the first time, she began to realise just how much went into the running of a large hotel. Ross found no major fault in any department, much to James Conroy's gratification.

They had lunch in his private quarters, along with the assistant general manager. Tall and fair-haired, Neil Baxter was in his mid-thirties. Young for his position, Gina gathered, though obviously more than capable. She found him perhaps a bit too much on the serious side, but pleasant enough.

Ross left the hotel at three, still without saying where he was going. Not that she had any right to know, Gina conceded hollowly. They were both of them free agents.

Try as she might to stop it, her imagination went into overdrive over the next hour. If it was a woman he was seeing, they would almost certainly be in bed by now. She could visualise the scene: the clothing scattered across the floor; the writhing naked bodies. She'd no right to the jealousy sweeping her, but it was all-consuming.

Holding several top-class shops, the arcade provided some slight distraction. The prices in the boutique still appeared pretty exorbitant to her, though it seemed churlish not to buy anything, with the assistants so eager to see her suited. She settled for a skirt and long-sleeved top in her favourite cream, leaving them to be delivered to her suite.

Neil Baxter was passing as she emerged from the shop. 'We serve English tea in the Empress lounge,' he said, on realising she was on her own. 'I often take advantage myself. Perhaps you'd join me?'

Glad of any company at present, Gina was only too ready to take him up on the invitation.

The lounge was already well occupied. Tea was served to individual tables on silver trays in finest china, with a tempting selection of sandwiches and cakes. Judging from the snippets of conversation filtering across, it wasn't just English clientele who availed themselves of the service.

'We get all nationalities,' Neil confirmed. 'Even those who'd never normally drink the stuff. It's the ambience they like. There's something very civilised about afternoon tea.'

He accepted the cup Gina had poured for him, making an appreciative face as he took a sip. 'Excellent!'

'Just like back home,' Gina concurred.

There was a pause. When Neil spoke again it was a little tentatively. 'Is it true that you and Mr Harlow are just business partners?'

She should tell him it was none of *his* business, Gina knew, but she was sick of the pretence. 'True enough,' she said. 'A marriage of convenience, it's called.'

She regretted it the moment the words left her lips, but it was too late for retraction. Not that it mattered a deal, she defended. The only one with any illusions about the marriage was too far away for the grapevine to reach. Anyway, even Elinor would have to know some time.

'So I can ask you out to dinner without crossing any demarcation lines,' Neil confirmed.

Caught on the hop, Gina sought refuge in humour. 'You Canadians certainly don't waste any time!'

'Nothing ventured, nothing gained,' he returned.

In no way blind to the fact that her position was probably the main draw, her first inclination was to refuse. On the other hand, she thought, why not take advantage of the opportunity to show Ross *she* wasn't stuck fast for companionship either? Why should she be expected to hang around until he deigned to put in an appearance?

'Nice idea,' she said before she could change her mind. 'But not here.'

'Of course.' Neil sounded agreeable to anything. 'I know just the place. What time would you like to eat?'

'Let's make it early,' she suggested. 'Seven?'

'Fine by me. I'll have a cab waiting at ten before. It's only a short drive away.'

She was doing this for all the wrong reasons, Gina thought ruefully, but she couldn't back out now. Anyway, it was doubtful if Neil had anything but his own business interests in mind.

There was no sound from the adjoining suite when she finally went up at six—even with her ear pressed against the communicating door. She thought of pushing a note under the door, abandoning the idea on the grounds that she owed Ross no explanation. For all she knew, he'd be out all night.

Being so much further north, it was a great deal cooler here than in LA. She donned the skirt and top already delivered, topping them with a short beige jacket she'd brought with her and sliding her feet into high-heeled leather sandals. She'd already acquired a touch of Los Angeles gloss, she acknowledged, studying her smooth, shining hair and flawless make-up in the mirror. All down to Elinor's efforts.

Neil was waiting for her in the lobby at a quarter to the hour. He viewed her with open appreciation as she crossed the wide expanse to join him, seemingly oblivious to the glances drawn their way from the duty staff. Gina had the distinct feeling that she was something of a trophy.

As he'd said, the restaurant he'd chosen was only a short distance away. It was small, intimate and very up-market, and its menus bore no prices. She agreed without much interest when he suggested they share the Châteaubriand, not really in the mood for eating at all.

Stilted at first, conversation eased a little over the course of the meal. Gina avoided any personal probing into her own background by encouraging him to talk about himself, which he wasn't all that loath to do.

'A couple of years, and I'll be ready to take over from James when he finally retires,' he said, after filling her in on his progress since leaving university. 'Not that I invited you out in the hope of advancing my career,' he added hastily.

'It hadn't occurred to me,' Gina assured him, lying through her teeth. 'I'm sure you'll make a fine GM.'

They were on to the coffee stage when the call came through. Neil pulled a wry face as he slipped the mobile back into his pocket. 'Afraid I'm needed. Some kind of problem with one of the convention groups.'

'Duty comes first,' she said, grateful for a reason to end the evening.

It was still only a little after nine when they reached the hotel. Neil went immediately to deal with whatever had blown up, leaving Gina to make her way to her suite. If

Ross had returned, he would probably be at dinner in one or other of the restaurants. If he hadn't yet come back, it was likely that he'd be spending the night out.

Not that she could care less what he did from now on, she told herself unconvincingly.

The maid who had turned down her bed last night had left lamps lit throughout the suite. Gina came to an abrupt stop on seeing Ross lounging in a chair.

'The wanderer returns!' he observed.

Gina recovered her voice, and something of her wits. 'How did you get in here?'

'I had the communicating doors opened up.' He viewed her from head to foot and back again, gaze coming to rest on her face with an expression she found disquieting. 'I said I'd be back for dinner.'

'Did you? I must have forgotten.' She kept her tone inconsequential. 'Afraid I already ate. Neil Baxter invited me out.'

'So I understand.'

'He was called back in to take care of some problem,' she added. 'I'd have thought someone else could have handled it.'

'Depends on the nature of the problem. It's his job to be available when needed—especially with Conroy out of town for the night. You realise he has an eye to the main chance, of course?'

Green eyes sparked. 'Meaning, he asked me out with a view to feathering his own nest? He's in no need of any backing from me. He's already in line for the GM's job when James Conroy decides he's had enough.'

'It isn't a foregone conclusion, by any means. He'll be well aware of that. A word from the top at the right time could swing it for him.'

It was what she had thought herself, but she wasn't about

to admit it. Ross hadn't moved from the chair, his whole attitude a spur to the anger building inside her.

'If you've finished, I'd like some privacy,' she said. 'You've no right to be here in *my* suite to start with!'

'I'll go when I'm good and ready,' he rejoined. 'One or two points we need to get straight. When I said we'd each live our own lives, I meant with some discretion. Swanning around with a member of staff can hardly be called that! The whole place was buzzing when I got back.'

'So what?' she demanded. 'Everyone knows the marriage is just a means to an end.'

'I don't give a damn what everyone knows!' Ross wasn't lounging any more, a dangerous spark in his eyes. 'Just take note.'

'Your precious pride suffering?' she asked scathingly. 'Means so much to a man, doesn't it? At least I didn't spend the whole afternoon...'

Ross hoisted a sardonic eyebrow as she broke off, biting her lip. 'Where exactly do you think I've been all afternoon?'

'Ten to one, with a woman,' she said, not about to back down again. 'Two nights' deprivation takes some making up for.'

Anger turned suddenly to amusement. 'Spoken with feeling! And there I was thinking I was being the true gallant giving you chance to catch up on your sleep last night.'

The wind taken completely out of her sails, Gina sought some pungent response. 'Don't flatter yourself!' was the best she could come up with, serving only to increase the amusement.

'Why try denying something that's so patently obvious? You were as ready as I was the other night, before the champagne caught up with you. As ready as you are now, in fact.'

'Of all the arrogant...' She caught herself up, realising how hackneyed she sounded, fury mounting as she met the grey eyes. 'I've no intention of providing you with entertainment of *any* kind from here-on-in!'

'Oh, I think you could be persuaded.'

Gina stood her ground as he came slowly, almost lazily to his feet, heart hammering against her ribcage, stomach muscles tensed. 'I'm telling you no!' she fired at him.

She may as well have held her tongue for all the notice he took. She struggled slightly as he slid his arms about her, but her heart wasn't in it. No part of her was in it.

His mouth was passionate. She found herself answering in the same vein, lips moving beneath his, parting to allow him access to the inner softness, her body moulding to his shape with abandonment.

She made no protest when he lifted her in his arms and bore her across to the bedroom, wanting him too desperately to care what she might reveal. There were lamps lit in here too, the beds already turned back by the maid. Ross laid her down on the nearest, stripping off his shirt before coming down alongside her to kiss her with mounting urgency.

She sought the buckle of his belt, easing the leather through the slot and sliding the zip to find him, while he removed her brief undergarment. They joined together in a frenzy, fired by the same surging, irresistible need.

It was some time before either of them could summon the energy to move after the tumultuous climax. Gina floated on a sea of satisfaction, mind blanked of everything outside of this moment.

'That went a whole lot faster than intended,' Ross murmured. He raised his head to look at her, scanning her face feature by feature, his smile slow. 'You're a hell of a woman, Gina Saxton!'

She was a hell of an idiot, letting this happen again, she thought wryly as reality intruded. She made a supreme effort to adopt the same easy, semi-teasing attitude, sliding a finger end across the firm lips.

'Must be the Harlow in me!'

Laughter sparkled his eyes. 'One thing you're certainly not is boring!'

'I do my best.' She stiffened in sudden realisation. 'You didn't use anything!'

'Didn't have time to think about it,' he admitted. His expression altered as he looked at her. 'I take it you're protected?'

Gina choked back the instinctive denial, closing heart and mind to the possible consequences. 'Of course.'

'That's OK, then.' He dropped a swift kiss on her lips, then rolled away from her to sit up. 'I'll be back. We've all night to come yet. The next couple of days, too, for that matter. We're going across to the island tomorrow. I've rented a house for the weekend.'

He was taking it for granted that she was as ready as he obviously was to take whatever pleasure was to be had from the affair, but she was past the point of no return. Whatever the eventual cost, it would be worth it, she told herself.

CHAPTER SEVEN

IT WAS raining when they left the mainland, a warm, soft gentle rain that petered out as they passed beneath Lion's Gate Bridge. Mountains reared to either side of the Straight, white-capped and breathtaking. As they neared the island, the coastline broke into coves and inlets, and stretches of beach. Above and beyond lay the dark mass of forest.

They docked at Nanaimo, heading out onto the Island Highway running up the east coast in the car Ross had commandeered from the hotel. The scenery was magnificent, a wilderness barely touched by man.

'Have you been here before?' Gina asked, taking it all in.

'Once,' Ross acknowledged. 'Years ago.'

'Alone?'

'No.' His tone was easy. 'With a couple of college friends. We lived rough, camping out, fishing and hunting for food. Male bonding, it's called these days. Back then, it was just three guys with a yen to experience life in the raw for a while. Always meant to come back some time. Just never got round to it.'

Gina glanced his way, appraising the hard-edged profile outlined against the backcloth of forest; trying to visualise the younger image. She wished she could have known him then—except that she would have been about ten at the time he was speaking of.

The house he'd rented lay in a small private bay reached by a narrow dirt road. Built like an oversized log cabin, it overlooked the Straight, with superb views from the wide rear veranda to the mainland mountain ranges. Inside lay three *en suite* bedrooms, along with huge lounging and dining areas and a kitchen fitted with every aid to modern living.

'I left it to the agency to arrange a delivery,' said Ross when Gina opened the refrigerator door to discover it packed with food. 'They'll have tried to cover all tastes. There's a hot tub out back. Be a good place to share a nightcap, don't you think?'

'Can't think of a better,' she said, closing out any dissenting voices. 'Did you arrange all this yesterday?'

'Among other things.' He drew her to him, leaning his back against a work surface as he used both hands to smooth the hair back from her face, scrutinising every feature in much the same way he'd done the night before. The look in his eyes sent her pulse rate soaring. 'You're beautiful!'

'Hardly on a par with some I could mention,' she returned lightly, trying to stay on top of her emotions.

'If you're talking about the general LA line-up, you're streets ahead of most,' he said. 'You don't need to pile on the make-up to look good.'

His kiss was no let-down. She put everything she knew into answering it. They made love lying on a bearskin rug in front of a flaming log fire—both fakes, but realistic enough to add atmosphere. Confident in their isolation, Gina relinquished all inhibitions, answering every call made on her with a passion to match.

'Whoever it was that said all English women were frigid obviously chose the wrong samples,' Ross observed at one point, taking a moment or two to recover.

'Either that, or he was useless at it himself,' she returned, not really caring either way. 'That's something you'll never need to worry about.'

He laughed softly. 'Not this side of seventy, at any rate, I hope!'

'Only seventy?' she teased. 'Charlie Chaplin was still fathering babies in *his* seventies.'

She'd managed to forget about last night's neglect until now. The reminder of what it might possibly have achieved sent her spirits suddenly plunging. What she would do if it did happen, she couldn't begin to think.

Best not to go down that road at all unless forced, she told herself resolutely. It *was* only a chance.

Ross had made no reply to the sally. It was only when she turned her head to look at him that she realised he'd actually dozed off. She lay quietly studying the incisive features, feeling the warm, possessive weight of his hand at her breast. A month ago she hadn't even known he existed. From that to this was difficult to believe.

She was in love with him, she finally admitted. She'd fallen hook, line and sinker that very first week. Walking away then would have been hard, but nowhere near as hard as it was going to be when the time eventually came. The old saying about making one's bed and lying in it was more than apt.

But that wasn't now. Giving way to the need coursing through her again, she ran feather-light fingers down the arm stretched across her, and on down the length of his body, feeling muscle ripple beneath the taut, bronzed skin. His eyes opened as she found him, his response instant, the slow smile a stimulant in itself. Not that she needed any stimulation.

The afternoon was drawing to a close when they reluctantly decided enough was enough for the present. They took showers, then cooked steaks on the barbecue outside.

Gina made a salad and opened a bottle of wine, vowing to keep her own consumption to the one glass. She wanted to be in full awareness of every minute of this weekend together. For Ross it might just be sex; for her it was everything she had ever imagined lovemaking could be with the right person.

Apart from the occasional vessel passing through the Straight, there were few lights to be seen. Vancouver could be a million miles away. The night air was cool, but the hot tub more than compensated. Head back against the side-cushion, limbs relaxed in the delicious, bubbling warmth, memory on a back burner for the moment, Gina felt at peace with the world.

'I could stay here for ever,' she murmured dreamily.

'I know the feeling,' Ross rejoined. 'Life can be a bit too demanding at times.'

'It's what you wanted, though, isn't it?' she said. 'The company, I mean.'

'Sure,' he agreed. 'But it isn't everything. Oliver recognised that much himself—especially in the last few years. He took time out to be with my mother whenever he could. They did a lot of travelling together. Buena Vista isn't their only home. There are other properties in Barbados, and the Bahamas. I don't imagine she'll want to keep them on now though.'

'You wouldn't consider taking them over yourself?' Gina ventured.

'I might the Barbados one, if she has no objection. I had a hand in designing the place. You'd enjoy Barbados,' he added. 'It's a very laid-back island. Beautiful too. We could honeymoon there, if you like.'

She gave a brittle laugh. 'Oh, sure!'

'Why not?' he said. 'Don't you fancy a couple of weeks of this kind of thing?'

She looked at him in startled realisation. 'You're serious, aren't you?'

'Never more. We're going to need some rest and recuperation after the wedding, believe me. Not that I'd anticipate too much resting,' he added on a note that set the fires burning all over again.

Making love in a hot tub was an experience outside anything she could ever have imagined, though she doubted if it was new to Ross. Wrapped in the thick towelling robe he fetched from the house afterwards, wine glass in hand, his arm about her shoulders, she felt the closest she'd ever been to heaven. If only it could be like this for real, she thought yearningly.

'Have you seen anything of Roxanne since the will-reading?' she asked, bringing herself down to earth again.

'No,' he said. 'She's done a disappearing act.'

'Aren't you worried about her?'

Broad shoulders lifted. 'She can take care of herself.'

'What did she do to turn you against her?' Gina queried tentatively. 'Was it to do with money?'

Ross looked down at her, gaze sharpened. 'Has she approached you for any?'

'Yes,' she admitted. 'She needed to repay a loan.'

'You didn't give it to her?'

'The will had only just been read. I didn't have it *to* give. In any case...'

'In any case?' he prompted as she let the words trail away.

'It was rather a large amount.'

'*How* large?'

'Three hundred thousand.'

He said something harsh under his breath. 'I should have known!'

Gina would have happily left the whole subject alone at that point, but if Roxanne was to become her sister-in-law, for however short a time, it needed to be aired.

'Known what?' she asked.

'That she was still up to the same old tricks. She drove Gary into bankruptcy before leaving him. Ruined his life, *and* his health. I tried to warn him what she was like before he married her, but he wouldn't listen. He worshipped her.'

'Where is he now?' Gina ventured.

'Dead.' The tone was hard. 'He got into difficulties while swimming in the sea apparently. His body was never recovered.'

She drew in a breath. 'You don't think…'

'Who knows? Whichever way, he's gone. We were at Yale together.'

'He was here with you on that camping trip?'

'Yes.' Ross removed the arm from her shoulders, putting his glass down on the table. 'You called your parents yesterday, I take it?'

She shook her head, seeing impatience spring suddenly in his eyes.

'What are you waiting for?' he demanded.

'Courage,' she admitted. 'They're going to be badly hurt. Especially my mother. She's already feeling pushed out.'

'There's no reason why she should. Anyway, they have to know some time. It's Sunday tomorrow. A good day to find them both at home.'

He was right, of course. It was more than time she let them know what was going on. 'I'll do it first thing,' she promised.

'I'll make sure of it this time,' he said hardly. 'You're not backing out on me, Gina. There's too much at stake.'

'I've no intention of backing out,' she retorted, resenting his tone. 'Do you really think I'd turn down millions?'

Cynicism overtook impatience as he surveyed her. 'No, I guess not. Let's get to bed.'

It was on the tip of her tongue to tell him he'd be spending the night on his own, but that would be as much deprivation to her as to him. She was turning into the kind of person she would have decried not so very long ago, she acknowledged wryly.

She made the phone call straight after breakfast. Her father, it turned out, was playing golf, but her mother made no secret of their disappointment in her for leaving it so long to get in touch.

She received the news about the will badly enough. The wedding plans left her too disturbed to speak at all for several seconds.

'How can you possibly marry someone you only met such a short time ago?' she got out. 'You can't even have got to know him properly!'

She'd certainly got to know him improperly over the last twenty-four hours, Gina reflected.

'I really do know what I'm doing, Mom,' she said, feeling a total fraud.

Ross took the receiver from her, startling her because she hadn't realised he was that close.

'Hello, Mrs Saxton,' he said. 'I can understand how you must be feeling, but I can assure you Gina is going to be well taken care of. You've done a wonderful job bringing her up. She's a credit to you. I'm looking forward to meeting you and your husband. My mother too. She'll be speaking to you herself shortly, to make arrangements.' He listened for a moment or two, expression unrevealing. 'That really wouldn't be practical, I'm afraid.'

He handed the instrument back to Gina. 'She wants to speak to you again.'

'I was saying that if you're going to be married at all, it should be here,' her mother said. 'What did he mean by it not being practical?'

Gina sought some diplomatic explanation. 'Just that

there'd be far too many people who wouldn't be able to make it,' she managed. 'A whole lot easier for you to come over here. You *will* come, won't you?' she added anxiously.

'As if we'd think of refusing.' Jean Saxton sounded resigned, though far from happy about it. 'It's going to be a shock for your father.'

'I know.' It was all Gina could say. 'I'll ring you again tomorrow.'

She replaced the receiver, hating herself. Hating Ross too at present.

'That's the rottenest thing I've ever done!' she burst out.

Ross slid his hands about her slender waist, drawing her closer to put his lips first to her temple then slowly down her cheek to probe the very tip of his tongue into the hollow just behind her earlobe, sending shivers chasing the length of her spine.

'Come on back to bed,' he said softly.

'Is sex all you can think about?' she accused, drawing a smile as he shifted his gaze from her flushed bare face under the tousled blonde hair down to the soft swelling curves revealed by the robe that had slipped back over her shoulders.

'Right now, yes,' he said.

They landed back in LA early on the Monday afternoon, driving straight to Buena Vista. Elinor welcomed them eagerly.

'The formal announcement went in on Saturday,' she said when they were seated on the terrace with drinks to hand. 'The media are already vying for exclusives.'

'No exclusives,' Ross declared with finality. 'Have you heard from Roxanne at all?'

'Not a word,' she confirmed. 'I've called the apartment

several times, but she's never in. Not that it's unusual, of course.'

'I'll take a run over and check,' he said. 'I've got the number of those friends of hers in Frisco somewhere, too. I can give them a try.'

'Any particular reason why you're so keen to get hold of her?' his mother asked.

'She wanted Gina to give her three hundred thousand to pay off a loan. I want to know who the debtor is.'

'I should never have mentioned it,' Gina said unhappily.

He shook his head. 'I'm glad you did. There's no way she could get her hands on that amount in a lump sum, so the debt must still be outstanding. Always providing she was telling you the truth to start with. She may just have been trying you out for a future soft touch.'

He got up again, leaving his drink untouched. 'I'll leave you two to talk weddings for now.'

Gina studied the glass in her hand as he headed back to the house, looking up to meet Elinor's smile.

'I'd say the weekend went well,' she observed.

'Apart from breaking the news to my parents.'

'I was wondering when you were going to get round to it.' Elinor was hesitant, obviously only too aware of the difficulties. 'How did they take it?'

'Not very well,' Gina admitted. 'Although I've only spoken to my mother up to now.'

'It stands to reason it would be a shock for her, but I'm sure she'll come round. Perhaps I could call her myself?'

'Ross already spoke to her. I'm not sure whether it helped all that much, but they will be coming for the wedding.'

Elinor looked relieved. 'I'll speak to them later, then. They'll be staying here, of course. What about your partner?'

Gina had totally forgotten about Barbara until this moment. Another phone call she still had to make. 'She'll be too busy with the shop,' she said.

'Of course. Especially now she'll be running it on her own. Ross told me you were making over your share of the business to her.'

'I'm hardly going to be in need of it.' Gina gave a short laugh. 'I sometimes feel I'm living in fantasy land!'

'You'll adjust,' Elinor assured her. 'A year from now, you'll wonder how you lived any other kind of life.'

A year from now she may not even be here, Gina reflected. She didn't really see herself hanging around after the divorce went through. It was a hollow thought.

'I'm sorry for letting on about Roxanne wanting money,' she said, looking for a change of subject.

Elinor sighed and shrugged. 'It's nothing new, believe me. She probably borrowed on the strength of her expectations. I should have warned her that Oliver lost faith in her after Gary died. Gary was her husband.'

'I know. Ross told me.' Gina hesitated, not sure she should say any more than that. On the other hand, having it all in the open could save a lot of bitten lips. 'I suppose it was even harder for him to accept, Gary being such an old and close friend.'

'The only son of one of Oliver's oldest and closest friends too. Oliver blamed himself for giving her too much. She grew up expecting everything to be handed to her on a platter. Gary did his best to satisfy her, but it was never enough. She wouldn't even contemplate a baby. Not that she'd have been anything of a mother, I'm afraid.'

Elinor made a dismissive gesture reminiscent of her son's mannerism, briskening her tone. 'Enough of that. You and I have a lot to get through. Tomorrow, we go dress-hunting. I've already seen one or two I'd personally consider suitable, but you're the one who'll be wearing it. The invitations are ready to go out too. I thought you might like to look through the list.'

Gina shook her head. 'There's really no point. I shan't know anyone.'

'Ross must see to it that you meet some of them beforehand, then. Now, about the reception. I thought burgundy, cream and lemon would be a bit different for the colour scheme. Of course, you might have your own ideas?'

Gina shook her head, happy to just go along. If nothing else, the wedding had given Elinor something to occupy her mind at a time when she so badly needed it. The fact that it was all of it meaningless was something she herself just had to live with.

The media circus got under way without delay. PRINCE CHARMING TO WED HIS CINDERELLA blared one trite headline, HARLOW MAGNATES TO SEAL PARTNERSHIP FOR LIFE another. Gina grew rapidly weary of turning down the requests for interviews, for TV appearances; of dodging cameras wherever they went; of the sheer pressure of being in the public eye.

'Why are they making so much of it?' she asked Ross one morning after running a whole gauntlet of photographers outside the house. 'I know the Harlow name has a lot of standing, but they've the whole of Hollywood to go at for copy of the kind they're after, for heaven's sake!'

'As I told you before, the storyline *is* pure Hollywood,' he said. 'It will blow over. In the meantime, I'm afraid you'll just have to grin and bear it.'

They were in his office. Gina had called in on her way to attend a charity luncheon her future mother-in-law had arranged. Shirtsleeves rolled, he was leafing through a whole sheaf of literature concerning a South American property they were considering. Viewing the dark head, the hairline crisp against bronzed skin, she felt the familiar constriction in the pit of her stomach.

Drawn into the welter of wedding arrangements, she hadn't been able to spend much time here herself, and she'd seen little enough of him the past couple of weeks. They'd attended one or two functions, and she'd met a lot of people, but they hadn't spent a solitary night together since Vancouver.

Not that he'd have spent all his alone, she was certain.

'My parents arrive tomorrow,' she said. 'Are you going to be free to come with me to the airport?'

'Should be,' he agreed without looking up. 'I've a lunch appointment with Isabel, but nothing after that. Isabel Dantry,' he added, sensing the unspoken question. 'The investment banker? You'll be needing advice yourself once everything's settled. I'll have to introduce you.'

'I may not want to invest,' she said. 'We're not all into the must-have-more syndrome. The whole point of having money is to enjoy it, not just sit watching it grow!'

That did get a result. Ross studied her speculatively, taking in the spots of high colour on her cheekbones. 'Your genuine opinion, or just bloody-mindedness?'

'What would I have to be bloody-minded about?' she asked.

'You tell me,' he invited. 'You're obviously here for a purpose.'

'I came to ask you about the airport.'

'You could have done that on the phone.'

'So maybe I'm just sick and tired of this whole fiasco!' she burst out, giving way to the emotions that had been eating into her for days. 'Maybe I'm regretting ever agreeing to it in the first place!'

'Too late.' His tone was deceptively mild. 'You burned your bridges when you gave the go-ahead.'

She'd burned a whole lot more in allowing herself to fall for him, she thought bitterly. All she was to him was a means to an end.

'Bear up,' he said. 'In four days we'll be in Barbados with it all behind us. The house has its own private beach. We can swim in the nude, make love under the stars. Sound good?'

'Idyllic.' She looked at her watch. 'I'd better be on my way.'

'How's my mother getting there?' he asked as she rose to her feet.

'Michael is driving her in. I'm using the Cadillac.' She kept her tone level. 'Time I got to grips with the system.'

'Sure.' His attention was already drifting back to the file still in his hand. 'I'll see you tomorrow, then.'

Penny had been missing when Gina had arrived, but she was at her desk now. She looked up with a smile.

'Hi! How's it all going?'

Gina forced a smile in return. 'Swimmingly! How are you?'

'Wonderful! Just coming up to the twelfth week!'

Until this moment, Gina had totally forgotten the other woman was pregnant. She made an appropriate response, unable to deny a certain envy. Penny had a real marriage, a good marriage—the kind she'd always imagined for herself.

The fear that *she* might be pregnant had proved groundless, for which she could only be thankful. She was on the Pill now, though it wasn't going to be necessary because she wouldn't be sleeping with Ross again under any circumstances. She'd had enough of being used.

CHAPTER EIGHT

THE Saxtons arrived on an early-evening flight from Heathrow looking typically travel-weary after the long haul. They greeted Ross with reservation.

'I have to say, it's not the way we'd have preferred,' Leslie Saxton declared, 'but Gina is old enough to make her own decisions. All we ask is that you take care of her. She's very precious to us.'

'She's very precious to me too,' Ross assured him.

True enough, considering what he stood to lose without her, the she in question thought hardly.

'Will you stop talking about me as if I'm not here!' she exclaimed, summoning a laugh. 'We'd better get out to the car before Michael gets moved on.'

'Michael?' her mother queried.

'Elinor's chauffeur. She's really eager to see you both.'

The two of them were quiet on the journey. Gina had a very good idea how they were feeling. She'd been more than a bit overwhelmed by it all herself on arrival. She was still in many ways.

She cast a swift glance at the man occupying the other pull-down seat, pulses quickening as always to the impact of his dark good looks. There was no turning off the phys-ical attraction, but her resolution remained strong. He was in for a rude awakening.

Elinor was warm and welcoming without gushing. She left it to Gina to show the newcomers to the bedroom they'd be occupying for the length of their stay, inviting them back down for a light supper when they'd sorted themselves out a little.

'I can see why you wouldn't want to give all this up,' Jean Saxton observed on the way to the room. 'It's a whole different world. But why rush into marriage the way you're doing?'

Gina had only told them she'd been left the shares, not the rest, but they were going to find out sooner or later.

'Oliver made it a condition that Ross and I married,' she said, bracing herself for the inevitable reaction.

Jean stopped in mid-step, her pleasantly featured face expressing a multitude of emotions. 'You mean you don't even have any feelings for him?'

'I didn't say that.' Gina did her best to sound positive. 'It's simply happening sooner than it might have done in normal circumstances.'

'But it isn't exactly a love match?'

'Not in the accepted sense, perhaps.'

'What other sense is there?' Jean sounded disturbed. 'You've changed since you came here, Gina. There's a hardness in you that was never there before.'

'It's called self-confidence,' she returned lightly. 'Something you have to develop to survive in this neck of the woods. You don't have to worry about me, Mom. I really do know what I'm doing.'

'You said that before, and I didn't believe it then,' Jean rejoined. 'I know you're not our own flesh and blood, but we love you, Gina. Of course we're going to worry!'

'I think we'd better move on,' Leslie put in diplomatically. 'We can talk later.'

Gina saw them to the bedroom, closing the door on them feeling thoroughly ashamed. She was still deceiving them. Elinor too.

Ross was seated out on the terrace alone. He regarded her shrewdly as she joined him. 'Trouble?'

'I told them about the condition,' she said. 'They're far from over the moon about it.'

'Maybe you should have left them in happy ignorance, then.'

'And have someone else fill them in? Not that they were happy about it anyway.'

Ross surveyed her for a moment, brows drawn. 'And how do you feel?'

'Oh, ecstatic!' She made no attempt to downplay the irony. 'I'm going to be a millionairess. What could be better than that?'

'If you're thinking about backing out again, you can forget it,' he said on a harder note. 'We've come this far, we'll go the rest. What brought this mood on anyway? You were fine about it until yesterday.'

She'd been fine until he left her to stew for two weeks, she could have told him, but that would be giving too much away.

'I'd convinced myself that money made up for everything else we're missing,' she lied. 'I was wrong.'

'I wouldn't say we're missing all that much,' he rejoined.

'You mean the sex?' She lifted her shoulders, fighting to maintain control. 'You can get that anywhere. So can I, if it comes to that. Oh, I'll go through with it, don't worry. I've got too used to the good life to turn it down on a point of principle. Did you manage to trace Roxanne?'

He accepted the sudden switch without comment, face expressionless. 'She's in Phoenix. Been there some weeks apparently, with some man she met in Frisco.'

'She'll be at the wedding?'

'I didn't get to speak to her. The man she's living with said she was resting and didn't want to be disturbed. He's to pass on the message. What she does about it is entirely up to her.'

He got to his feet as her parents emerged from the house along with his mother, tone easy again. 'How about a drink before we eat? I always find it a good way to wind down after a long flight.'

The evening was long, conversation stilted. Gina couldn't blame her parents for feeling the way they did. She should have told them everything from the beginning, she acknowledged ruefully. It would at least have given them time to come to some kind of terms.

Elinor made every effort to keep things going, but it was a losing battle. Jean broke the party up at ten, claiming she could hardly keep her eyes open.

'I think I'll have an early night myself,' Elinor said when the Saxtons had departed. 'There are things I have to catch up on.'

'Do you need any help?' Gina offered, reluctant to be left alone with Ross.

The other shook her head. 'Nothing to do with the wedding. That's all in hand now. Don't make a noise when you leave,' she told her son. 'You know how sound carries at night up here. We've a full programme planned for tomorrow.'

'I'll watch it,' he promised. 'I shan't be long, anyway. I've a heavy day tomorrow too.'

Gina picked up her wine glass and drained it as Elinor departed, putting it down again with a thud. 'I think I'll do the same,' she said.

'Not yet.' Ross spoke quietly but with purpose. 'We need to talk.'

'I said all I needed to say earlier,' she returned. 'Wrong time, wrong place, if it's sex you've got in mind.'

The spark that sprang in the grey eyes was pulse-jerking.

'If it was, we wouldn't be sitting here. Sorry if I haven't been dancing attendance as much as you'd like this past week or two. I've been pretty tied up.'

She didn't doubt it. The question was, with whom?

'Just how long will we have to stay married?' she asked, keeping a tight rein on her tongue.

The expression that crossed the lean features was come and gone too fast for analysis. 'A few months, maybe.'

'It's *that* easy to get divorced over here?'

'It can be, providing both parties are in agreement.'

'Maybe you should have me sign a pre-nuptial agreement,' she said. 'After all, you'll still be worth a lot more than I will.'

His lips twisted. 'If you're going to keep this up, I'll leave you to that early night.'

Gina got up with him, steeling herself not to weaken. 'Will you be here tomorrow?'

'My best man's due in from Vegas at five,' he said. 'We might make it for dinner. Otherwise, I'll see you in church.'

He made no attempt to kiss her, unsurprisingly, just turned and went. Gina stood for several minutes where he'd left her, wishing her grandfather had left well alone. Discounting the mistake she'd made over the business, she'd been happy enough in her old life. She'd certainly have been a whole lot better off never knowing Ross existed.

While never fully relaxing her guard, Jean loosened up a little over the course of a day spent touring the city. She and Leslie had been living and working in Bakersfield at the time of the adoption, so LA wasn't exactly new territory, though they found it strange after twenty-five years in a totally different environment.

Back at the house by four, Gina took advantage of the

afternoon sun to chill out for an hour down at the pool, needing to be alone for a while.

This time tomorrow she would be on her way to the church. One of the city's grandest, naturally. Every bride was supposed to dream of her big day, where she'd be the centre of attention, but not every bride was called on to face the degree of attention she was going to be undergoing tomorrow. And for what? A marriage already scheduled to end. She could make Ross pay dearly by refusing to agree to the divorce, of course, but what was the use?

Elinor came to join her, looking a little concerned. 'You've been so quiet all day,' she said. 'Are you OK?'

'Just a bit tired,' Gina claimed. 'I didn't get much sleep last night.'

'You'll probably get even less tonight,' Elinor observed. 'I didn't sleep at all the night before I married Oliver. I'm so glad he found you again. Not just for his sake, but for mine and Ross's too. I'm gaining a daughter, Ross the kind of wife I always hoped he'd have some day. Apart from having Oliver here with us, I couldn't be happier than I am right now.'

Gina murmured some response, feeling lower than ever. Elinor might be living in cloud cuckoo land where the marriage was concerned, but she was such a genuine person. She deserved so much better than this.

She went up to shower and dress for the evening at six, coming down to find Ross had arrived with his best man, Brady Leeson. She already knew Brady had been the third man on the Vancouver Island venture. Ruggedly attractive beneath a shock of bright copper hair, he greeted her with frank admiration.

'The description didn't do you justice,' he said.

He would know the reason for the marriage, Gina assumed, wondering just what the description had been.

Whether Ross would have told him all of it was open to doubt. She avoided looking at the latter directly, though she could feel his gaze on her. He was still angry with her; she could feel that too. He was going to be angrier still tomorrow night—for what good it would do him.

The two of them left again soon after dinner. Not to take advantage of an early night, Gina suspected. She went up herself at ten, leaving her parents to Elinor.

She expected to be awake half the night worrying about all she had to face the next day, but she slept right through till seven. Mental exhaustion, she reckoned. The morning passed with excruciating slowness. She ate lunch only because both her mother and Elinor insisted she have something on her stomach to see her through until the reception. Five o'clock in the afternoon seemed a strange time to hold a wedding, but it was quite the done thing here.

She'd already met the twins who were to be her bridesmaids. They arrived at one, along with the hairdresser and beautician. Outnumbered, Leslie made himself scarce until it was time to don his own wedding outfit.

Elinor, Jean and the bridesmaids left the house at four in a white stretch limousine. Gina and her father were to travel in a vintage Rolls-Royce, which would also carry her and Ross to the reception.

Watching her descend the stairs in the lovely, classically styled white gown, Leslie blinked hard on the moisture gathering in the corners of his eyes. 'You look so beautiful,' he said. 'We're going to miss you!'

'I'm going to miss you too,' she said truthfully, despising herself for doing this to them. 'But it isn't as if we're never going to see one another again. I'll come over as often as I can.'

If Leslie noticed that she said 'I' rather than 'we', he didn't comment on it.

The Rolls drew a lot of attention on the journey downtown. Gina had anticipated some media attention, but was totally unprepared for the crowds of watchers gathered behind rope barriers outside the church, for the banks of cameras, the television crews. Flash bulbs almost blinded her as she traversed the red carpet spread across the pavement. It took everything she had to keep a smile on her face. The bride must at least *look* blissful.

It was something of a relief to gain the shelter of the church entrance, where the twins in their garnet dresses awaited her, but it was only the start. Packed rows of faces all turned her way as they started down the aisle to the strains of the 'Canon in D' by Johann Pachelbel.

Standing at the aisle end of the third row from the front, sapphire eyes glittering beneath her wide-brimmed cream hat, Dione Richards was only too recognisable. Gina doubted if Elinor would have added her name to the guest list, considering recent associations, which meant Ross must have. But then, why not? The congregation was probably peppered with his conquests.

Looking superb in a dark blue tuxedo, he awaited her coming at the foot of the red-carpeted steps leading to the altar proper. Gina felt her throat contract as she met his eyes, her chest go tight as a drum.

'I see you put your hair up,' he murmured with an ironic tilt to his lips as she took her place by his side.

'I thought the occasion warranted it this time,' she said.

Time moved in a series of impressions after that: the solemnity of the service; signing the register; walking back down the aisle on the arm of the man now her husband, narrowly suppressing the urge to blow a kiss to Dione; facing the mêlée outside again.

'Thank God that's over!' Ross exclaimed in the car taking the two of them on to the reception. He studied her face, making no attempt to touch her. 'You look wonderful!'

'I feel like an exhibit,' she said. Conscious of the lack of a screen between them and the chauffeur, she made an effort to lighten both tone and expression. 'I didn't expect quite so many people out there.'

'Weddings are a draw any day of the week,' Ross returned. 'We still have the reception to get through, so don't start relaxing yet.' The pause was meaningful. 'We'll have plenty of time for that this next couple of weeks. I cleared the decks as far as possible, so there shouldn't be any problem.'

Only the one he'd still to learn of, she thought. They were due to spend tonight at the apartment, flying out to Barbados in the morning. She looked forward to seeing his expression when he realised the honeymoon he'd cleared the decks for was going to be a non-event.

It wasn't far to the hotel. Yet another phalanx of photographers awaited their arrival. Elinor and her parents, along with the best man and bridesmaids, had already formed the welcoming line-up in readiness for the guests even now beginning to arrive. Taking her place at Ross's side, Gina geared herself up for yet another ordeal.

It took an age. Her hand felt crushed from all the shaking, her face stiff from keeping the smile going brightly. She'd met some of them already, but hadn't retained any names. She felt like throwing her arms round Meryl Thornton in sheer relief.

'We must get together again,' Meryl said. 'I'll give you a call when you get back.'

'Do,' Gina urged.

Her enthusiasm faded as the next in line moved into view. The beautiful, superbly dressed brunette wore a smile that left her eyes devoid of any hint of warmth.

'Congratulations,' Dione said in a silky purr, not bothering to extend a hand. She turned her attention immediately to Ross, the smile altering in character. 'You're a lucky man. She's really quite lovely!'

'Isn't she?' he agreed. 'Glad you could make it, Dione.'

'As if I could possibly miss *such* an occasion!' she said with deliberated extravagance.

She went on her way, trailing the man she was with, leaving Gina gritting her teeth. The knowledge that Ross had slept with the woman—and was more than likely sleeping with her still—was impossible to just ignore.

'Bear up,' he murmured. 'It's almost the end of the line.'

From the superb ice carvings decorating each and every table, through an equally superb five-course meal to the accompaniment of music played by a top-line quartet, the reception was exquisitely presented. Both bridegroom and best man did their duty with speeches that drew laughter and applause, while Leslie produced a short but well-thought-out piece that made Gina want to cry.

There was dancing after they finished eating, started off by the bridal pair themselves in accordance with tradition.

'Another half an hour, and we'll leave them to it,' Ross said on the floor. He kissed her, smiling drily at the applause that greeted the gesture. 'I think we can be said to have given it our best shot.'

Gina made no reply. Unprepared for it—although she should have been—the kiss had disturbed her carefully nurtured objectivity. The feel of him, lean and hard against her, undermined her even further.

'I notice Roxanne didn't bother to turn up,' she said, desperate for something to take her mind off bodily urges she couldn't control. 'Haven't you even heard from her?'

'Not a word.'

He sounded indifferent, but he had to feel *something*, she

thought. No matter what she'd done, Roxanne was his only sibling. He couldn't just disown her altogether.

'Your mother must be hurt,' she said.

'She's been that too many times to expect much else.'

'Surely if you talked to her. Really talked to her, I mean.'

'Unless it's attached to an offer of money, talking's useless. I'd have thought you'd recognised that much for yourself.'

The slow movement of the body so close to hers was robbing her of the ability to think clearly about anything but just that. She ached in every fibre with the need to be closer still, to be part of him again. It was going to take every ounce of will-power she had to do what she planned on doing.

So don't, whispered a small voice at the back of her mind.

A man she couldn't for the life of her remember receiving earlier tapped Ross on the shoulder. 'Time you gave the rest of us poor slobs a chance,' he grinned.

Laughing, Ross relinquished her into the other arms. 'Just don't take any advantages,' he warned.

Gina pasted the smile back on her face as the newcomer swung her into motion again, aware of the watching eyes. So much for getting away!

Others joined in, crowding the dance floor to the extent that it was impossible to do little more than sway in time to the music. Someone else claimed her, then someone else again. She did her best to keep up a light conversation with them all. It was all part and parcel of the occasion. Something she just had to bear with. Inwardly, she was still grappling with the temptation to abandon everything and just go with the flow.

It took the glimpse through the crowd of Dione in Ross's arms to bring the battle to an abrupt end. They looked what they were: two people on intimate terms with each other. The fury sweeping through her was all-consuming. He could at least have left the damned woman alone on this of all occasions—if only for the look of it!

She put up a pretence of enjoying herself far too much to leave when he did come to find her some half an hour later.

'Have another glass of champagne!' she invited, fishing a bottle from the ice bucket by the table where she was sitting with the Thorntons and others. 'The night is still young!'

Ross eyed her quizzically. 'How many have you had?'

With no intention of allowing alcohol to ruin her plan of attack, she'd stuck to the bare minimum, but she wasn't about to admit it. 'I lost count,' she said airily. 'Does it matter? I'm not driving.'

'We've a five-hour flight in the morning,' he returned. 'You're going to be tired.'

One of the men at the table said something low-toned to his neighbour, drawing a grin. Ross ignored the pair of them. 'It's midnight already.'

'The witching hour!' she exclaimed. 'That surely calls for another drink! A last dance, then,' as he shook his head. 'Listen, they're playing our song!'

There was a deep-down spark in the grey eyes, though his expression remained easy. He put out a hand. 'So they are.'

The quartet were playing a number she didn't even recognise. Ross drew her close, his hands hard at her waist. Her eyes were on a level with his mouth; she could feel his breath on her cheek, cool and fresh.

'Game still on, then,' he said softly.

'If that's what you want to call it,' she rejoined. 'Smile,

darling, we're under surveillance! You wouldn't want to give the media the wrong impression, would you?'

'The media weren't admitted,' he said. 'What was it you said once about a floor show?'

She gave a laugh. 'Bridegroom arrested for wife-beating at wedding reception. That would definitely make the head-lines!'

His jaw tautened. 'Cut it out!'

'Sure.' She used the word with deliberation. 'My lips are sealed!'

'Why?' he asked after a moment.

'You know why,' she said, abandoning the act. 'What's the point in making out this is anything but a means to get our hands on the shares my grandfather left? I'll live with you because I don't want the Harlow name made a total mockery of, but I won't sleep with you again.'

The hands at her back had hardened still further. 'Is that a fact?'

'You can bet on it,' she said. 'I'll be occupying the guest room tonight.'

He held her a little away from him to look into her vibrant face beneath the sparkling diamond tiara Elinor had talked her into having, mouth dangerously set. 'I wouldn't count on it.'

'Oh, I doubt if you'd resort to force!'

'I don't intend to,' he said. 'You're no ice maiden, Gina. We already proved that.'

'Things can change.' There was a hard knot in her throat, another in her chest, but she wasn't about to go under. 'You don't need me to prove your virility. There's a more than adequate supply of willing partners out there. In here too, if it comes to that. Dione Richards, for instance. The two of you looked very cosy!'

There was derision in his eyes now. 'Cosy is the last

word I'd apply to Dione. She doesn't have any bearing on the situation anyway. We've some sorting out to do.'

It had to come eventually, Gina acknowledged. They may as well get it over with.

'I'm ready when you are,' she said.

She drew her first deep breath as he led her off the floor again, aware of the weakness in her limbs. She'd amazed herself these last few minutes; she'd certainly given Ross a shock. He wasn't going to get through her guard, whatever pressure he brought to bear. It was time he realised that she had a will just as strong as his when it came to the test.

It was only when taking her leave of her parents that she realised she wouldn't be seeing them again. They were flying home the day after tomorrow—no, actually tomorrow, considering it was already gone twelve.

'I'll call you from Barbados,' she promised, wondering what she would tell them. She could always fall back on describing the scenery and the weather, she supposed. They'd hardly expect any more intimate details.

Elinor gave both her and Ross warm hugs. 'See you when you get back,' she said.

Gina avoided looking at her mother, knowing how she must feel hearing that. She loved both the Saxtons very much, and always would, but there was no denying that things could never be quite the same.

Michael was waiting to drive the three of them back to the house. Ross had ordered a cab. It was coming up to two by the time they reached the Beverly Harlow.

He'd said nothing in the cab, and said nothing on the way up to the apartment. Waiting while he unlocked the outer door, Gina was totally unprepared for his sudden move to sweep her up and carry her over the threshold.

'That's one tradition out of the way,' he said tautly. 'One more to go!'

She struggled as he bore her through to the main bedroom, but it made no impression on him. He dropped her on the Empire-sized bed, keeping her down with a hand on her shoulder. Her dress fastened down the front with tiny pearl buttons to waist-level. Gina caught at his hand as he began to unfasten them.

'Don't you damn well dare!' she said through her teeth. 'I told you it's no go!'

He gave a short laugh. 'We'll see, shall we?'

She twisted her head away as he came down over her, but she couldn't escape his mouth. If the kiss had been forceful she could have held on to the fury driving her, but his lips were almost gentle, brushing, teasing, playing with the soft fullness, his tongue a silky caress.

She could do nothing to curb the heat and hunger spreading through her. Her lips parted, allowing him access, her body abandoning one kind of tension to gain another. Her hands lifted to the dark head, fingers plunging into the crisp thickness of his hair, the past days wiped from mind by the emotional storm consuming her.

The buttons popped with a faint pinging sound as he ran a hand down behind the bodice of the dress. Gina didn't care about the ruination, didn't care about anything but making up for the deprivation she'd suffered. Ross reached behind her to lower the long zip, easing the whole dress down over her hips to drop it in a silken pile on the floor.

She was wearing little beneath, her stockings garter-topped, her panties and bra mere wisps of white lace. He left the stockings on, coming down again to put his lips to each peaking, tingling nipple in turn, dragging moans from her aching throat at the exquisite sensation.

He moved on slowly, tantalising her quivering flesh with

tiny kisses, nuzzling her waist, her hipbone, lingering for eternity on the fluttering skin just above the triangle of blonde hair before sliding lower still to penetrate the very centre of her being. Back arched, lips parted on a silent scream, Gina was lost to everything but that flickering flame, shudder after shudder running through her as she climaxed.

She made a soft sound of protest when he lifted himself away from her, but it was only to rid himself of his own clothing. She needed no further stimulus, and he offered none, each powerful thrust of his loins a token of his mastery, carrying her through to an overwhelming finale.

It took him a moment or two to recover enough strength to lift himself away from her. Gina lay motionless as he got up. He'd made his point. She was incapable of saying no to him and meaning it.

She watched him as he headed for the bathroom, even now feeling a stirring inside at the mere sight of the leanly muscled back and firm masculine behind. Where they went from here she wasn't sure. She'd goaded him into what had just happened; she might also have called time on whatever feelings he did have for her.

She'd pulled herself together enough to have got up and donned a negligee by the time Ross emerged from the bathroom. He was wearing a towelling robe similar to the one in the guest suite. From the look of his hair, he'd stuck his head under the shower. To cool off, she imagined.

'We need to talk,' he said before she could open her mouth. Not that she had any idea what to say anyway. 'Properly, I mean. No more point-scoring.' His regard was dispassionate. 'Agreed?'

'Agreed,' she said low-toned.

'We both of us knew what we were getting into when this started,' he continued. 'The physical attraction was a bonus. It can be still if you stop trying to make me out to be the bad guy.'

'You mean accept you the way you are, or do the other thing,' she retorted.

'There you go again!' Exasperation drew a line between his brows. 'I mean we should take advantage of the situation and get the most out of the relationship. We're good together. I'd say we just proved that.'

'What we just proved,' she said wryly, 'is that I'm weak in the won't department.'

A smile touched his lips. 'You think I'd have forced you if you hadn't given in?'

She shook her head. 'You wouldn't demean yourself.'

'Glad you realise it.' He waited a moment in anticipation of some further comment from her. 'So?'

'So, I think you're right, and we should make the best of things,' she said, smothering her deeper emotions.

'Apology accepted.' He laughed as her eyes sparked. 'I guess I asked for it to a great extent.'

There was a pause. Once again Ross was the one to break it. 'How do you feel about cementing the pact in time-honoured fashion?'

'I thought we just did,' she said.

'Call it a preliminary bout. Main event still to come.'

With her insides already melting, Gina let go of the last remnants of self-preservation, rewarded by the flare in his eyes as she let the negligee fall to the ground. At least he still wanted her.

CHAPTER NINE

BARBADOS was a dream island, the villa a delight. Open-plan for the most part, with acres of coolly tiled floor, the decor was pure Caribbean. Gina loved it on sight.

The maid service she would happily have done without, though Ross appeared to have no objection. They spent the first couple of days on the private beach, swimming when they felt like it, sunbathing with proper caution and generally chilling out. Lovemaking was left for the moonlit, star-spangled nights.

They toured the island in one of the open-sided, soft-topped Jeeps, passing through fields of swaying sugar cane where workers paused in their toil to wave a cheerful greeting. Gina much enjoyed the Barbadian dialect, although finding it difficult sometimes to derive a meaning. The phrase 'I ain't no bride', overheard spoken by one man to another, left her totally baffled until Ross explained it simply meant the speaker was no model of good behaviour, and had nothing whatsoever to do with the marital state.

The first ripple in the sea came when they had lunch at one of the island's top hotels one day. Gina had noted the way a woman seated alone at a table on the far side of the restaurant kept eyeing them, but didn't expect to return from a visit to the bathroom to find the attractive redhead now seated at their table in conversation with Ross.

'Hi there!' she greeted, still laughing over some remark he'd apparently just made. 'I'm Samantha Barton. Ross tells me you're on your honeymoon. I wouldn't have come over if I'd known that.'

133

'Sam lives here,' Ross explained. 'She has a design studio on Broad Street. I didn't see her when we came in.'

'I moved here to escape the LA rat race a couple of years ago,' Samantha tagged on. 'Never looked back. What do you think of the island?'

'It's beautiful,' Gina acknowledged, putting on a sociable front. 'I could live here myself.'

'Especially in the Harlow villa! I had the use of it for a few weeks until I got myself sorted out.'

'You're a friend of the family, then?' Gina hazarded.

'More an acquaintance. I've done some design work at Buena Vista. Ross arranged for me to use the villa.' She turned her attention back his way, her smile a little too intimate for Gina's comfort. 'I was very grateful.'

Gina made a mental note to check whether Ross had visited the island himself a couple of years ago, pulling herself up sharply on the realisation that she was falling into the same old trap. Judging from the woman's looks and air of familiarity, it was on the cards that there had been some interaction between the two of them in the past, but even if the marriage had been real, his life prior to their own meeting would have been his affair, not hers.

Samantha was here at the hotel to advise on the restaurant redecoration, it appeared. She had a house up the west coast near Speightstown.

'I'm having a bit of a soirée tonight,' she said casually on preparing to leave at last. 'I'd love the two of you to come.'

'We'll be there,' Ross promised before Gina could think up an adequate reason why not.

'Great! Eight onwards, then.' She gave Gina a look that held just a hint of triumph. 'Look forward to seeing you.'

'You don't seem too enthused,' Ross observed in the silence that followed her departure.

Gina summoned a smile, a light rejoinder. 'I'm not all that bothered about meeting a load of people we're never likely to see again.'

'We've had a week on our own,' he said. 'I'd have thought you'd be ready for some company.'

'Meaning, you are?' she asked.

'I guess I am, yes,' he said. 'For a few hours, at any rate.'

She kept the smile going. 'That's fine, then.'

The subject wasn't mentioned for the rest of the afternoon. They took a boat out and spent an enjoyable three hours touring the coastline. Gina had meant it when she'd said she could live there herself. Compared with LA, the island was an oasis of peace and laid-back tranquillity.

It was late when they got back to the villa. There was just time to grab a bite to eat before dressing for the evening affair. With Samantha close to Ross in age, Gina chose to emphasise her comparative youth with a bias-cut dress designed to show off her figure to its best advantage. Fitted to mid-thigh from a wide, boat-shaped neckline that left her shoulders almost bare and offered a tantalising glimpse of softer flesh, it flared just enough to draw attention to the length of leg left exposed. A pair of spindle-heeled sandals made the latter look even longer.

Not bad, she thought critically, viewing her reflection. On impulse, she swept her hair up, leaving little tendrils to curl into her nape and about her face. Smoothed with just a hint of shadow, lashes darkened by mascara, her eyes were vivid against her tanned skin.

Emerging from the *en suite* bathroom, the briefest of towels slung about lean hips, Ross gave a low whistle. 'That,' he exclaimed, 'is a sight to perk any man up!'

'I didn't realise you needed perking up,' she said.

He laughed. 'A figure of speech, I think you'd call it. You look fantastic, anyway!'

There was a moment when he seemed about to make some other observation, then he moved to the bed, where his clothes for the evening were ready laid out, and began to dress.

Gina had hoped he was going to suggest they stayed home instead of going to this party. She would willingly have sacrificed all the effort she'd put into her appearance. As it obviously wasn't to be, she just had to make the best of it.

Striking himself in dark brown trousers and shirt, along with a cream jacket, Ross kept a casual conversation going as they headed along the coast. Gina made every effort to respond in the same vein, hauling herself over the coals for allowing herself to be dragged down again. So what if he and Samantha had had something going in the past? It wasn't to say he still harboured a desire for her.

She was clutching at straws, and she knew it. The way the two of them had been looking at one another when she first saw them together, there was certainly something there.

The house at the romantically named Cobblers Cove was about the same size as the Harlow residence. Built to a similar, open-plan design, and superbly furnished, it was already teeming with people when they got there. So much for the 'bit of a soirée', Gina thought drily.

Eye-catching in gold, Samantha greeted the pair of them like guests of honour. It was obvious from the start that most people there knew who they were. Obvious, too, that it was a moneyed crowd. Samantha must be doing very well indeed to move in such circles, Gina reflected.

She certainly lost little time in separating the two of them, leaving her in the company of an older, distinguished-looking man called Adrian, while she dragged

Ross off to meet someone who was in the hotel business there on the island, and looking to sell. Gina could have claimed that it was as much of interest to her to meet this person, considering her shares in the company, but Ross made no attempt to say it, and she wasn't about to kick him in the teeth in front of everyone.

'I'm surprised Ross would be willing to share you, looking the way you do,' Adrian declared. 'I certainly wouldn't!'

'Have you known Samantha long?' Gina asked, taking the gambit no more seriously than it was meant.

'Just over a year,' he said. 'We live together.' He read the unspoken question in her swift glance, his smile untroubled. 'I'm forty-six. Not that much more than the difference between you and your husband, I'd say. What's in a few years, anyway?'

What indeed? she thought, relieved that Samantha had a man of her own in tow. A ridiculous reaction, she had to admit.

'Is the house yours?' she asked.

'It is. Had it built last year. The interior decor's all down to Sam though. She's a clever lady.' The pause was brief. 'She tells me she and your husband are old friends. I sense a bit more than that.'

Gina steeled herself to show no emotion. 'Would you be bothered if there had been more?'

His shrug was philosophical. 'What happened before we met isn't important. All I ask is faithfulness while we're together. I dare say you feel the same way.'

She might feel it, she could have told him, there was a fat chance of it happening. 'I hadn't really thought about it,' she prevaricated. 'I suppose I just take it for granted.'

'Take nothing for granted,' he warned. 'There is a lot of temptation out there. I'm not immune to it myself—espe-

cially right now.' The last with a smile that robbed the
words of any ulterior motive. 'You're a very lovely young
woman, Gina. A man would have to be insensible not to
be aware of it.

'Having said that, it's maybe the wrong moment to ask
if you'd like to see the gardens,' he added on a humorous
note. 'I'm in need of a breath of fresh air after all this
conditioned stuff.'

There was no sign of Ross and Samantha in the immediate vicinity. Gina forced herself to concentrate on the man
in front of her. 'I'd love to see the gardens. I could do with
a breather myself.'

People had already spilled out onto the spacious stone-
paved patio, some dancing on an oval floor which appeared
to be covering a pool below, music provided by a trio. Gina
caught a glimpse of the sea through the trees backing the
patio, shining silver in the moonlight.

The gardens lay to either side and the front of the house.
Subtly lit, they were the best Gina had ever seen. Myriad
scents assailed her nostrils.

'It's wonderful,' she told Adrian with sincerity. 'I'd love
a garden like this, only we have an apartment.'

'So move to a house,' he said, as if it were the simplest
thing in the world. 'Or have one built to your own speci-
fication. An apartment's no place to have children.
Assuming you plan to have children.'

'Of course.' Gina kept the smile going with an effort.
'Not just yet though. I'm still getting used to being married.'

'I wouldn't wait too long,' he advised. 'My wife and I
might still be together if we'd started a family.'

If a marriage had to rely on children to keep it going, it
wasn't worth much to start with, she thought.

They returned to the patio via a path that brought them

out to the rear, just in time to see Samantha and Ross emerge from another path leading into the trees.

There was nothing to be read from either face. Samantha was the first to speak, her tone blithe.

'I've been showing Ross the new boat. He thinks he may go for one himself if he decides to keep the house on. Where did you two get to?'

'I've been showing Gina the gardens.' Adrian sounded easy enough on the surface, though Gina thought she detected a certain wariness. The two of them had been missing nearly an hour. Time enough for anything.

'How did the meeting go?' she asked with some deliberation. 'Is the hotel a viable proposition?'

'Not for Harlows,' Ross answered smoothly. 'Why don't we have a dance as we're out here?'

A curt refusal trembled on her lips, bitten back with some difficulty. She accompanied him onto the floor in silence, unable to stop herself from stiffening when he put his arms about her.

'Something bothering you?' he asked.

'What makes you think anything is bothering me?' she countered.

'Because I may as well be holding a stick of celery. I realise you weren't too keen on coming, but you looked happy enough a few minutes ago with Adrian.'

'I was,' she said. 'He's a very nice man. Attractive too, for his age. Samantha's done well for herself.'

'Yes, she has. So has he. They make a good pair.'

'Better than the two of you did?' The words were out before she could stop them this time, instantly regretted.

It was a moment or two before Ross answered. When he did speak it was with measured tones. 'Is this what I can expect every time you meet a woman I'm already acquainted with?'

'No, of course not.' She did her best to achieve the right note. 'We're *both* of us completely free agents. So, are you really considering keeping the villa on?'

An indefinable expression crossed the lean features. 'Maybe. I haven't decided yet.' He drew her closer, nuzzling his lips to her cheek. 'I want you!'

A need initiated by another woman, she thought.

'It's early yet,' she said lightly. 'And we haven't danced together for at least a week!'

His laugh was low. 'Not vertically, at any rate.'

'You have a one-track mind,' she accused, adopting the same bantering note.

'So you keep telling me. I think we'll call it a night all the same. Here, at any rate.'

Gina was by no means loath to leave the place. She at least had the satisfaction of seeing Samantha look a little put out when they announced their departure, although the other covered it swiftly with a smile, and a hope to see them again before they returned to LA. Adrian was cordial in his farewells, but made no attempt to echo the sentiment, leaving Gina with the feeling that he might harbour some doubts of his own about that missing hour.

The drive back down the coast in the scented night was pleasurable. She was going to miss all this when they went back, Gina acknowledged. It was doubtful if they'd be visiting the island again. She'd be well able to visit it herself in time to come, of course, but she probably wouldn't. There were plenty of other places to go. Places with no memories to plague her.

Elinor greeted the pair of them with unbridled happiness when they showed up there the day after landing back. She'd so missed having her around, she told Gina. The house had felt so empty.

'I think I might look for something a little smaller, and closer to town,' she said when the three of them were ensconced, as usual, on the terrace. 'An apartment, maybe.'

'I've got a better idea,' Ross put in. 'Why don't you move into the apartment, and we'll take over here? You'll have Room Service on tap when you want it. Maid Service too.'

His mother looked far from turned off by the suggestion, though a little tentative when she glanced Gina's way. 'How would you feel about it?'

Perplexed, she could have told her. Why Ross would want a house the size of this one, she couldn't begin to imagine.

'I'd love it,' she said, unable to see any other possible reply in the circumstances.

'That's settled, then,' Ross declared. 'I'll get things started first thing Monday. I guess you'll want a complete make-over before you move in,' he added to Elinor. 'You never did care for the decor.'

'True enough. I'll get my designer to look at it.' She sounded really enthused. 'You'll want to change things here, too, Gina.'

'I like it exactly the way it is,' Gina answered truthfully, still reeling at the swiftness with which the whole matter was being arranged. 'We have very similar tastes. Are you quite sure about it all?' she felt bound to ask. 'I mean, I know the apartment is big, but it doesn't begin to compare with what you have here. What about the pool, for instance? You swim every morning.'

'The Beverly Harlow has two pools. I'll just make sure I get down there before breakfast.' Elinor obviously had no doubts in mind. She got to her feet. 'I'll go and give Maurice a call. He'll be snowed under as usual, but he'll just have to squeeze me in somehow.'

The pause stretched for several seconds after she'd gone. Ross was the first to speak. 'Any objections?'

'Why would I object?' Gina asked shortly. 'I'd just have appreciated some prior warning.'

'The idea only came to me when my mother mentioned moving,' he said. 'I'd rather keep the place in the family. It will get Meryl and Jack off my back too. They've been on at me to move into the property market for years. I'm sure you'll enjoy living up here better than the apartment.'

She was forced to concede that much. Big as it was, the apartment still felt constrictive in comparison. Probably because the balcony was its only private outside space.

'You really believe your mother will be happy there?' she asked.

'If she already had apartment-living in mind, then yes,' he said. 'She'll transform it anyway. Or Maurice will. She'll have meant what she said about this place too. She won't mind if you want to change things.'

Gina kept her tone steady. 'I don't see much point, considering I'll only be here a few months, at the most.'

The pause was lengthy. When he spoke again it was without particular expression. 'Are you still planning on staying with the company after we finish? Taking an active part, I mean.'

'I doubt it,' she admitted. 'I might go back home to England. Either way, you can have the fifty-one per cent.'

If he was gratified by the offer, it wasn't noticeable. 'What would you do back in England?'

She shrugged. 'Anything that took my fancy, I suppose. I might even travel. Apart from Spain and Italy, and here, of course, I haven't been all that far. I always fancied taking the Trans-Siberian across Russia. Then there's the Great Wall of China, the Taj Mahal, the Valley of Kings.'

'Sounds like a full world tour,' Ross commented drily. 'On your own?'

'The best way to do it,' she said. 'Only myself to please. Anyway, it's just a pipedream at present.'

'It won't be after tomorrow. All we have to do is complete the paperwork. If you're serious about selling me the shares, I'll need another six per cent. We can arrange that at the same time. You'll still retain twenty-four per cent, with a right to draw dividends on it twice a year, whatever you decide to do with your life.'

'Fine.' Gina didn't want to think about it. She'd been talking through her hat with all that guff about touring the world on her own. What kind of pleasure would there be in seeing the sights she had mentioned with no one to share the experience?

The housekeeper came out bearing a round of drinks and some light refreshments on a tray. Her attitude was a little more congenial than it had been in the early days, but Gina still found her difficult to get along with.

'What about staff?' she asked when the woman had gone. 'You'll hardly have need of a chauffeur for a start, and Lydia has never been all that enamoured of me.'

Ross lifted his shoulders. 'Michael does other jobs, and Lydia keeps everything running smoothly. Unless you fancy taking it on yourself?'

She cast a glance at him, disconcerted by his somewhat brusque tone. 'I just thought—'

'It's your choice,' he interposed. 'If you want new people in, have them—if you can find any available. Good, trustworthy staff are like gold here. They can pick and choose jobs.'

Implying that they were fortunate to have the pair at all, Gina took it. There was a possibility that they might decide a change was called for themselves, once it was realised what was to happen—maybe even taking the daily cleaning staff with them. If she didn't want to be left without any help at all, she'd perhaps better start putting some effort into cultivating the relationship.

It took that thought to bring home to her just how far she'd come from the person she'd been two months ago. She'd sworn not to become blasé about her new lifestyle, but she was starting to take certain aspects of it for granted. That stopped right here!

Ross extracted his mobile from a pocket, the expression crossing his face when he glanced at the display unreadable. He must have the set on vibration signal only, Gina thought as he put the instrument to his ear. She preferred an audible tone herself.

'Hi,' he said. 'How are you?' He listened for a moment, then added briefly, 'Afraid I'm tied up right now. I'll ring you later.'

If it hadn't been for the familiar greeting, Gina might have taken it that the call was from a business associate. Suspicion reared its head when he slid the phone back into his pocket without comment, though she did her best to smother it.

Elinor returned looking a little uncertain. Maurice, it seemed, would only agree to tackle the apartment if work could begin right away.

'No problem,' Ross assured her. 'We can move up tomorrow, and leave a clear field. Considering we don't have any furnishings to transport, it shouldn't be too difficult a job. Most of our personal stuff will go in the cars.'

'I can send Michael down with the limo,' his mother offered, carried away by enthusiasm again. 'It's good to know the house will be staying in the family! Oliver would like it too.' She caught herself up as if in sudden recollection, her glance shifting to Gina. 'Sorry, darling, I'm running away with it all. If you need more time…?'

Gina shook her head smilingly, determined not to go for Ross in front of his mother. 'The decision's made. Why wait? We can use my old room for the time being.'

'Oh, no, you'll have the master suite, of course! I'll have Lydia make a start right away.'

Grey eyes met green, the latter smouldering. Ross lifted a quizzical eyebrow, whether genuinely unaware of the reason for her anger, or simply playing dumb, Gina wasn't sure. If she was honest about it, being sidelined again was only a contributory factor. She was almost certain that the phone call had been from some woman.

By the time they left the house at five, everything was arranged. The move would be made the next day, after they'd seen the lawyers.

'So, let's have it,' Ross said when they were on the road. 'I can feel the heat here!'

'I don't like being railroaded!' she said tautly. 'First the house, now the move! This might be a temporary affair, but while we *are* married I expect a say in things!'

There was a dangerous slant to his lips. 'I'll make whatever decisions I think fit, whenever I think fit. As you said a while ago, you'll only be around a few more months.'

It was true, of course, but it still hurt. Damn him! she thought fiercely. Damn this whole farce of a marriage!

The silence was heavy. He reached out and switched on the radio. Gina stole a glance at him, taking in the set of his jaw. That he was good and angry there was no doubt. Well, so was she!

About what exactly, though? came the question. The presumption might spark a certain umbrage, but it wasn't worth getting in a rage about. Neither should she be judging him on the evidence of one phone call she couldn't even be sure was from a woman at all.

He went straight in for a shower when they got to the apartment. Gathering the outer clothing he'd discarded, Gina felt the shape of his mobile in a trouser pocket. Unable to resist the urge, she dialled up the last call received.

The name that appeared above the number displayed was only too familiar: Dione. She put the phone back where she'd found it, chest tight. He'd said he would call back later. To make arrangements to meet, she assumed. She should have left well alone. What the heart didn't know it couldn't grieve over.

As it was to be their last night in the hotel, they had dinner in the Barlborough restaurant. Told of their coming departure, the *maître d'* expressed his regrets, along with his hope that they would continue to dine there occasionally. The senior Mrs Harlow would be well taken care of by everyone, he assured them.

'She'll make sure of that for herself,' Ross observed as the man departed. 'She may come across as easy-going, but heaven help anybody who falls down on a job they're paid to do!'

'I still think she may be making a mistake,' Gina said, finding no reason to hold her opinion when it came to someone she thought a lot of. 'It's so different from what she's been used to.'

'She needs a different environment. The house has too many memories just now.' Ross studied her across the lamplit table. 'Maybe for you too.'

She shook her head. 'I didn't have long enough with Grandfather to develop any. I'll always regret that.'

'His fault, not yours. At least he died knowing he'd done his best to put things right.'

'Yes.' Gina took up her glass, wondering whether the action they were taking to get round his edict would have crossed his mind. It was very possible that Ross was right in saying the tumour must have affected his reason.

'You told me you'd once seen a photograph of my mother,' she said. 'Do you know where it might be now?'

Ross shook his head. 'It was several years ago. I was using the computer in the study, and was looking for more paper for the printer. The photograph was in a drawer. It isn't there now,' he added, anticipating the question. 'I've looked for it. My mother doesn't know what happened to it either, I'm afraid. You do look like her though. Even more so these days.'

'Since I was made over to LA standards, you mean?'

He made a small, impatient gesture. 'I didn't mean it like that, but if it's the way you want to see it…'

Gina bit her lip. They'd only just got back on reasonable terms, now here she was throwing a spanner in the works again. All down to that phone call. So far he'd had little opportunity to make the return call, but there was no doubt in her mind that he would be making it.

She made an effort to put the other woman to the back of her mind. There was nothing to be gained from agonising over her.

The move to Buena Vista went smoothly. Apart from personal items, there was little to transport. By late afternoon they were more or less settled into their new home.

The master suite was the last word in luxury. The sitting room adjoining the bedroom opened via French doors onto a balcony overlooking the fantastic view. From up here, the sea looked closer, reminding Gina that she'd only been out that far once in two whole months. It would take years to become as familiar with the city as Ross himself was. Years she just wasn't going to have.

Elinor had basic plans for the apartment already drawn up. The work was due to start the next day, with completion in four days. Ross reckoned there was no reason why the paperwork dealing with the transaction shouldn't be completed by then.

'The Petersons have agreed to stay on, by the way,' he said that night. 'Although Lydia had some reservations. She seems to think you don't like her.'

'I barely know her,' Gina protested. 'She isn't easy to get to know. I had the feeling from the beginning that she thought I'd no right to be here at all.'

'Are you sure you weren't being a little over-sensitive?' he asked.

Eyeing his reflection through the dressing-table mirror as he lay nude on the bed, she was in no mood for argument. 'Probably so,' she said. 'You do realise it's that time of the month?'

'I didn't, but I guess I do now.' He sounded more amused than disappointed. 'I dare say I can cope.'

More than adequately, she found when she joined him in bed. Lovemaking didn't necessarily have to involve penetration, he said when she reminded him again. He took her to the heights with just lips and tongue, inciting her to respond in kind. Held in his arms later, listening to his steady breathing, she knew she was never going to find another man who could fulfil her the way Ross could. It was a bleak thought.

CHAPTER TEN

THAT first week went by swiftly. There was a board meeting on the Friday, at which Gina was content to sit back and simply imbibe.

'Things seem to be going well between you and Ross,' Warren Boxhall remarked afterwards, having called in to her office before taking his departure.

'Why wouldn't they be?' she returned. 'We're hardly going to be at loggerheads after three weeks.'

'It's been known,' he said. '*My* marriage went down the pan on honeymoon!'

'Which one?' she asked blandly, drawing a laugh.

'The last one. Last time I venture down the marital road,' he added. 'Too costly.'

'Only when it breaks down. You've obviously never met the right person.'

'I have,' he rejoined, with a mock sigh, 'but just too late.'

Gina was unable to contain a laugh of her own. 'If that's supposed to soften me up, you're way off track. I'm happy with things the way they are.'

'You and Ross might be OK, but we're not all in the same bracket,' he said. 'I've three lots of alimony to find!'

'Be thankful you didn't have children with any of them,' she rejoined, refusing to sympathise.

His sigh this time was genuine. 'You're a hard woman, but I don't give up easily. I'll win you round yet!'

Not in a lifetime, she thought, but she didn't bother saying it.

Ross was lunching with Isabel Dantry again. He hadn't

suggested she tagged along, and she wasn't going to suggest it. With capital from the shares she'd let Ross have, she was in a position to start making investments on her own account. What she'd said to Ross about not being interested in increasing her fortune had been baloney, but she certainly didn't see much sense in actioning it until she knew where she was eventually going to finish up.

Eager to show her what had been done to the apartment to date, Elinor had suggested she come over for lunch. Gina hardly recognised the place when they viewed it after eating in the restaurant. The Scandinavian furnishings were gone, the neutral walls in the living room painted a deep green, the stripped-pine floor covered in thickly piled, off-white carpeting. Figured gold drapes had replaced the blinds at the windows.

'I wasn't sure about the colour at first, but Maurice says it will show off my art collection to much greater effect,' Elinor said. 'He's going to position them tomorrow. Sorry to leave so many gaps at the house,' she added, 'but they were all presents from Oliver.'

'They're about the only things you *have* taken,' Gina chided. 'Surely some of the furnishings would fit here too?'

'Not according to Maurice. He demands a free hand throughout.'

'We met someone in Barbados who once did some design work for you at the house,' Gina said casually. 'Samantha Barton?'

Elinor's brow wrinkled for a moment, then cleared. 'Oh, yes! About three years ago. I used her just the once when Maurice was out of the country. She made over two of the bedrooms. Good, though not up to Maurice. Was she there on vacation?'

'She's in business there. Doing very well too, it seems.'

'That's nice.'

It was obvious Elinor had no inkling that anything had occurred between the woman and her son, nor any interest in pursuing the subject. Time she forgot about it herself, Gina acknowledged. Samantha wasn't the problem.

It was gone three when the two of them left the hotel. Too late to bother going back to the office, Gina decided. Not that she'd be missed. Her usefulness to the company was nil at present. She sometimes doubted if it would ever be anything but.

She had a swim with Elinor back at the house, then spent an hour or so basking in the late-afternoon sun. Ross still wasn't home when she went up to shower at six.

He arrived some twenty minutes later, coming straight upstairs.

'Traffic was murderous tonight,' he said, peeling off his jacket. 'Two accidents on Hollywood. How about you? Had a good afternoon?'

'Pleasant,' she acknowledged. 'The apartment's looking very different.'

He laughed. 'I imagine it is.'

'I'm surprised,' Gina remarked, 'that *you* don't want the house restyled.'

'What suits one place doesn't suit another. I've no quarrel with the decor here. As I've said before, there's nothing to stop you from altering it if you want to though.'

'As I've said before, I don't. Apart from a few pictures to cover the holes left by your mother's, it's perfect the way it is.'

'As wives go, you have to be one on your own,' Ross observed drily, already on his way to the bathroom.

As wives anywhere went, she was, she thought acidly. She was wearing a semi-sheer black peignoir over the briefest of black underwear, but he didn't appear to have even noticed. More important things on his mind, she took it.

She was fully dressed when he emerged from the bathroom. He took fresh boxer shorts from a drawer, dropping the towel wrapping his hips to pull them on. Muscle rippled beneath the tanned skin of his upper arms and shoulders in tune with his movements. Gina had an urge to go to him, to slide her arms about his lean waist and press her lips to the smoothly tapering back. A week ago she might have given way. Tonight, she let the momentum pass.

Ross slid his trouser zip, and buckled the leather belt, eyeing her across the width of the room. 'New dress?'

She held back on the sarcasm, settling for a shake of her head.

'Looks good on you, anyway,' he commented. 'But then, you look good in anything. That black item you were wearing when I came in almost stopped me in my tracks!'

'It wasn't noticeable,' she said before she could stop herself, and saw his mouth widen.

'I'd been an hour held up on the freeway. One call outweighed the other at the time. Maybe you could wear it again later.'

'I'm not dressing up just to entice you,' she declared coolly. 'I may not even feel like it later.'

The glint in his eyes became a gleam, not wholly of amusement. 'I always did like a challenge.'

'That wasn't…' Gina broke off, holding her hands up in mock surrender. She should know better by now than to take him on in a battle of wills. He only had to touch her to melt any resistance, and he knew it.

Unless he was seeing her in the day, he'd had no opportunity since they moved up here to meet with Dione. They'd been out to dinner one evening, the others they'd spent here with Elinor, as they were doing tonight. She was moving into the apartment tomorrow. There would be no need for Ross to continue acting the dutiful husband. No reason why he shouldn't stay out all night if he wanted to.

That wasn't the only reason she was going to miss her mother-in-law. They'd become close friends. Elinor was bent on involving her in the charity work she took such interest in herself. Gina was already drawn to it. More, she had to admit, than she was drawn to the world of big business: especially taking her limited time here into consideration. She could at least do some good while she *was* here.

She put the proposition over at dinner, drawing a delighted response from Elinor. Ross's reaction was less easy to define. If it was what she wanted, he said. Obviously, as a major shareholder, she'd still be expected to attend board meetings. Gina could see no real reason for that either, as she was hardly going to be making any useful contribution, but it was only once a month.

'If I'm not going to be here, there's little point getting to grips with the job,' she said later when Ross queried the decision.

'Your choice,' he rejoined expressionlessly. 'Before I forget to mention it again, we're at a première next week. Dione Richards' new film. You'll be needing something special. They're big occasions.'

Gina kept a tight rein on herself. 'Don't worry, I won't let you down.'

It wasn't what he'd meant, as she was very well aware. Unlike most men caught in similar traps, he made no attempt to correct the impression, simply shrugged and left it.

There had been a time when the mere idea of attending a film première would have had her over the moon, she thought as he turned away. If it had been any other film, she might still feel the same, but if it had been any other film, they probably wouldn't be going. Ross wasn't into that kind of function on a regular basis, she was pretty certain.

She'd go, of course. She wouldn't give the other woman the satisfaction of a refusal. But it would take every scrap of self-control she could muster to get her through the event.

Elinor gave no outward indication of finding it a wrench to leave the house she'd shared with her husband for so many years, but Gina wasn't wholly deceived.

'I feel as though we've driven her out,' she said to Ross that evening.

'It was her suggestion that she move in the first place,' he returned. 'The rest made obvious sense.'

'It's all so cut and dried to you, isn't it?' she responded after a moment. 'No room for sentiment.'

'No room for over-emotionalism, for certain.' The glance he turned her way held a hint of impatience. 'I think I can claim to know my mother rather better than you do. If she hadn't wanted to go, she wouldn't have gone. It's as simple as that.'

They'd eaten dinner indoors due to an unexpected late-afternoon shower that had soaked the chair cushions before they could be covered, and were now seated in the living room, neither of them watching the television playing with sound muted. Ross had been out most of the day playing golf, arriving home at six looking out of sorts. Lousy game, he'd said shortly when she asked.

Gina had never played golf herself, and considered losing a game a totally inadequate reason for ill-humour. *If* that was the reason. Lugging around a set of clubs was no proof of a game actually played. Although why would an afternoon spent with Dione put him in a bad mood? she asked herself.

'I suppose we should think about having some people to dinner ourselves now we're on our own,' she said, abandoning the previous subject. 'Maybe eight, counting the two of us. Do you reckon Lydia would cope?'

'She's done it before. My mother entertained on a regular basis before Oliver was diagnosed.' Ross sounded far from interested. 'Who did you have in mind?'

'The Thorntons for certain. They've already had us over there. The others, I'm not too sure. Maybe you should choose.'

He shook his head. 'It's your idea, *your* baby. Just don't make it a birthday party. I'm a mite past blowing out candles.'

'I didn't even know you'd a birthday coming up,' she said. 'Which is it?'

'I'll be thirty-five in a couple of weeks.' His smile was faint. 'Getting on a bit, as they say. When's your birthday?'

'October,' she acknowledged. 'Three more months.'

'I can count.' The irony was heavy. 'If you're thinking we'll be divorced by then, you'd better think again. I'm given to understand that the only way we'll get it through that fast is to go to Reno. Even then, it may not be valid outside the country.'

Gina gazed at him in silence, her mind in a spin. 'How long *will* we have to wait, then?' she got out at length.

The grey eyes held steady. 'The year out, at least.'

'A year!'

His regard sharpened into mockery. 'Afraid you'll just have to accept it. It could be worse.'

Not from where she was sitting, she thought dispiritedly. It was bad enough now living with a man whose only feeling for her was physically orientated. How would it be after a whole year? To say nothing of Dione Richards and her like!

'It doesn't mean *I* have to stay that long though,' she said, grasping at any straw she could find. 'Your mother is the only one likely to be upset by the break-up, but she'd have time to come to terms with it if we started having problems, and decided to take some time apart.'

Ross inclined his head, face impassive. 'Maybe. Let's see how it goes, shall we?'

He shifted his gaze to the open terrace doors. 'It stopped raining. How about a moonlit swim?'

The sudden change of subject left her floundering for a moment. 'It's barely an hour since we ate,' she said at length.

'More than long enough. Especially in water as warm as that out there. I've never used it at night before.'

It would be one way of calming down after the shock he'd just given her, Gina acknowledged.

'I'll fetch suits and towels down,' she said.

'We don't need suits, and there are plenty of towels in the locker down there.' He was already on his feet, extending an inviting hand.

The Petersons had all day Saturday off. Gina knew they'd gone to a concert tonight, and wouldn't be back until late. The thought of sliding into the water unhampered by clothing of any kind was too tempting to resist.

The atmosphere was sultry after the rain. Heated by the sun alone this time of year, the water felt like warm silk on the skin. Gina swam a length underwater, coming to rest on the broad steps leading out from the shallow end. Spread far and wide, the city below was a wonderland of sparkling, multicoloured lights.

'It has its own special beauty, doesn't it?' she said as Ross surfaced beside her.

'So do you,' he returned softly.

He put his hands about her hips, drawing her down into

the water again and pinning her against the side to kiss her with fast rising passion. She allowed her legs to float buoyantly upwards, wrapping them about his waist as he drove to the very centre of her being. His lips burned like fire trailing down the taut line of her throat to find the pulse fluttering in the vulnerable hollow.

She climaxed in shuddering ecstasy, the cry torn from her mingling with his deeper, rougher tone. He made no immediate move to withdraw, cupping her buttocks in both hands to hold her in position, the grey eyes almost black as he looked down into hers. He moved her gently against him, smile deepening as he felt the tremors run through her.

'I always did envy the female recovery rate.'

'You're not doing so badly yourself,' she said unsteadily.

'With the right incentive.'

He kissed her again, more gently than before. His skin was slick beneath her fingers, the muscle dormant for the moment. Gina slid her arms tighter about him as he came slowly back to full, pulsing life.

Later, lying in bed, she went back over the whole evening, trying to work out what she was going to do. The man who'd made love to her in the pool down there had been somehow different—almost tender at times. Maybe there was a chance of deepening the passion he had for her into something worthwhile after all. Maybe...

Her thoughts broke off as Ross turned over in his sleep, his hand seeking her breast. The name he murmured was indistinct, but it certainly wasn't hers.

She chose Versace for the première. Pale gold in colour, it was designed in Roman style, the silver bands wrapping her midriff emphasising both the firm thrust of her breasts and the taut slenderness of her waist. Her hair caught up in a cascade of curls, her make-up flawless, she knew she'd never looked better.

Ross approved the effect wholeheartedly. 'Oliver would have been proud of you,' he said. He took a blue velvet box from his bedside drawer. 'This seems to have been a lucky choice.'

The box contained a necklet of beaten silver, along with matching drop earrings.

'Sheer luck, or a word in your ear from a certain person?' Gina asked as he fastened the necklet for her.

He laughed. 'I might have had a little help.'

'It's perfect anyway.' She turned to slide her arms about his neck and kiss him, eyes emerald-bright. 'You're *so* good to me, Ross!'

If he was aware of the irony, he wasn't rising to it. 'We'd better get going,' he said. 'Mustn't mess up your hair.'

The state of her hair was the last thing on Gina's mind right now, but she had to concede he had a point. While not part of the film world itself, they were still camera fodder by reason of both the Harlow name and the story behind their marriage.

Michael drove them down in the limousine Elinor had decided she no longer needed. He would also be waiting to drive them on to the party after the showing, then later home again. Gina would have happily taken a cab for the latter journey, but Ross didn't suggest it this time.

It was brought home to her just how much interest their story still generated when they alighted from the car at the cinema to recognition from the crowds outside the barriers. Gina doubted if she could have made that walk along the red carpet with any degree of aplomb two months ago; even now, she felt the smile plastered to her face must look utterly phoney. At least she didn't have to pause and wave every few paces, as the stars of the silver screen were doing.

The evening-gowned woman presenter drawing aside some of the arrivals to speak on camera homed in on them as they drew level, refusing to acknowledge any lack of enthusiasm.

'And here we have the couple whose romance set the whole city alight just a few weeks ago!' she announced into the microphone. 'And very well you both look on it! That's a lovely dress, Gina!' She didn't wait for any response—had it been forthcoming—turning her attention to Ross. 'Handsome as any other hero here tonight! Did you ever fancy becoming a film star yourself, Ross?'

'Not since I was seven,' he answered easily, drawing a laugh from the crowd. 'Have a nice evening, Sue.'

Gina stole a glance at him as they moved on into the foyer. 'She's right, you know. You'd make a great cowboy! White hat, naturally.'

'They don't make goody-versus-baddy Westerns any more,' he said. 'And that's enough from you, gal!'

She pulled a face at him, sighing resignedly as flash bulbs popped once more. She had to remember that every gesture, every expression was being captured on camera for public display. There was every chance that some journalist with nothing better to write about would use the grimace as a sign that the marriage was already beginning to break down. Not that it might be such a bad thing at that, came the thought. The rift had to start somewhere.

Sam Walker greeted the pair of them with the familiarity of an old friend. Dione hadn't arrived yet, he said, but they were welcome to go straight through and take their seats if they preferred to escape the TV crews all vying for position.

They did so, to find many rows already well occupied.

Ross chose seats on the end of a row about halfway down the auditorium, welcomed by a couple Gina hadn't met before. Ross introduced them as Anna and Carl Sinden, both part of the production team.

Dione arrived trailing a whole retinue, traversing the aisle issuing extravagant greetings right and left. She looked magnificent in the scarlet gown, Gina had to admit. The glance bestowed on her as the woman passed by was cool, the smile reserved for Ross and Ross alone. He showed no visible reaction, but something tautened ominously in the pit of her stomach.

She sat through the two-hour showing with little idea of the storyline. As Meryl Thornton had once said, Dione wasn't the finest screen actress, but she had a presence that commanded attention. The applause when the credits rolled was loud and prolonged.

'Another box-office hit!' Carl proclaimed with satisfaction. 'Mark was good too, of course, but it's still Dione's vehicle. What do you think, Gina?'

So far as Gina was concerned, Mark Lester was way above Dione's class in the acting stakes, but that wasn't the question being asked. 'Oh, definitely,' she said. 'She's really something!'

Ross gave her a sharpened glance, as if he had caught some discordant note in her voice, but made no comment. Watch the innuendo, Gina warned herself.

The celebration was being held at the studio head's home. A grand old relic from the early twenties, what the house lacked in architectural beauty it made up for in character. The staircase rising from the grand central hall was straight from *Gone with the Wind*, the vast living areas furnished in an eclectic mix of old and new that somehow worked.

There was space and to spare inside, even more of it

outside on the spreading patios. Fringed with palm trees, the free-form pool was a real temptation in the sultry heat: a temptation some of the younger element lost little time in giving way to, with scant respect for the garments they were wearing.

'What can't be salvaged can always be replaced,' Ross commented when Gina remarked on the probable ruination of several designer dresses. 'Those kids have never had to work for what they've got.'

The 'kids' he was referring to were in their late teens, early twenties, but maturity was light-years away, Gina had to agree, if their behaviour was taken into account. Not that anyone else seemed to find the scene reprehensible.

There was dancing both indoors and out, with a regular banquet laid out in a side-room for people to help themselves to. Drawn into a small crowd, along with Anna and Carl, Gina did her best to keep up with a conversation centred on the mechanics of film-making.

Ross had gone to replenish their glasses. Twenty minutes ago, according to her watch. He'd probably got waylaid by someone. She clamped down on the thought that jumped into mind. He wouldn't dare. Not here!

Another ten minutes went by before she finally gave way to the urge beginning to consume her. She made some excuse, and left the people she was with to go back into the house, wandering from room to room in search of her missing husband.

There was no sign of him. Nor was Dione in evidence. There was no closing out the suspicion gnawing at her. The smile Dione had given Ross back at the première had been one of complacency, as if in knowledge of her power to stir him. If they were together now...

Throat tight, Gina forced a smile for the benefit of people around her. Short of searching all the bedrooms, she was left with little choice but to wait for Ross to put in an appearance. Sam Walker collared her, introducing her to the people he was with at the moment. Faced with more film talk, she had difficulty keeping her end up.

She jerked involuntarily when Ross slid his hands about her waist from behind.

'I've been looking everywhere for you!' he said, nodding a greeting to the others in the group. 'I left you outside.'

'About forty minutes ago,' she answered with a lightness purely for effect. 'What happened to the drink you were supposed to be fetching me?'

'I kept getting cornered. I put the glasses down somewhere. Anyway, I see you've been taken good care of.'

'You're a lucky man,' observed one of the older men in the group with somewhat heavy gallantry.

'I know.' Ross removed one hand from her waist, but left the other where it was, urging her gently into movement. 'More than I deserve!'

'You can say that again,' Gina murmured under her breath, and received a querying glance.

'What did you say?'

'I was beginning to think you'd gone home,' she improvised. 'You disappeared so completely.'

'Easy enough to do in this mêlée. Have you had enough yet, or do we stay to the bitter end?'

Gina made no immediate answer, her eyes on the woman who had just come through the double doors from the hall. Dione looked like a cat satiated with cream; she could almost hear the purr. There wasn't a hair on the beautiful dark head out of place, but there would have been time to fix it.

'Oh, definitely stay,' she heard herself saying. 'It's such an experience!'

Ross studied her for a moment, then he shrugged. 'No problem.'

It might be for Michael, waiting with the car, it occurred to her, but she couldn't face being alone with Ross in the back of it right now for fear she'd start throwing accusations in his face. The evidence was purely circumstantial, of course, just as it had been with Samantha, but she was as certain as she could be that he'd been with Dione.

Bored half out of her mind by the endless film talk, she stuck it out till the general exodus got under way around one. Hollywood parties didn't tend to run too far into the small hours: studio days started early. Ross had made no further suggestion to leave, though she'd sensed a growing irritation.

Michael was asleep in the driving seat when they finally got out to the car. Conscience-stricken, Gina was moved to apologise for keeping him waiting so long.

'It isn't at all necessary, ma'am,' he said, looking uncomfortable.

'You embarrassed the man,' Ross said shortly in the car.

'Isn't it the done thing to say sorry to a servant?' she asked, equally shortly.

There was cynicism in his glance. 'He's well paid for what he does. He won't have been sitting there all the time. All the drivers will have been fed and watered round the back.'

'I wasn't to know that,' she defended. 'It just seemed so cavalier.'

'Maybe you should have considered that earlier.' There was a pause, a change of tone. 'Why the sudden yen to stay on anyway? You weren't enjoying it.'

'Into mind-reading now, are you?'

'I can read body language. You've been on edge all

night.' He paused again, eyes on her face. 'Want to try again?'

'Not particularly.' She leaned her head back against the rest, closing her eyes. 'Wake me when we arrive.'

Ross said something short and sharp beneath his breath. He wasn't touching her in any way, but she could feel the anger radiating from him. He could simmer all he liked, she told herself hardily. He could also forget about any lovemaking where she was concerned. And this time she really did mean it!

He was silent for the rest of the journey. Gina thrust open the door and slid from her seat the moment the car came to a stop, heading indoors and straight upstairs without a backward glance. She was tense as a coiled wire when she got to the suite, but single-minded in intent.

She'd expected Ross to follow her, but he didn't. She was in bed when he finally came up more than half an hour later. Wide awake, she lay motionless as he undressed. He used the bathroom, emerging again to come across and slide between the sheets. She could feel his body heat, catch the emotive male scent of his skin.

The silence stretching between them was almost tangible. Gina found herself holding her breath, waiting for something—anything—to happen.

'Go to sleep,' he said brusquely. 'I'm not in the mood either.'

It should have been a relief, but it wasn't. Despite everything, she still wanted him, she acknowledged achingly.

CHAPTER ELEVEN

THE dinner party proved a successful event. Lydia excelled herself in the catering department, producing four courses *par excellence*, as one guest was moved to remark.

'If you and your husband ever feel like a change, just let me know!' she said shamelessly to Lydia when coffee was brought out to where they sat on the terrace. 'There's a house in the grounds goes with the job.'

'We've always been very comfortable here,' the house-keeper returned. 'But I'll bear it in mind.'

If the latter remark was for her benefit, it made little impact, Gina could have told her. She'd done her level best to get on friendly terms with the woman, but there was still a barrier there.

The men were holding a group discussion on their own. The topic appeared to be golf. Gina wondered how they'd react if she told them to get their asses over here and join the rest of the party.

'You don't golf yourself?' Anna Sinden asked, watching her watching them.

'Never even tried,' Gina acknowledged. 'I realise that makes me something of an oddity here.'

Anna laughed. 'If you are, I am too. Carl plays whenever he possibly can. A good thing we share work, or I wouldn't see much of him. I hadn't realised Ross was an enthusiast too,' she added. 'They must play different courses.'

Or even different games, Gina thought.

'I've given Peter an ultimatum,' declared the woman

who had offered Lydia a job. 'Either I get a bigger share of his time, or I find myself a lover.'

'Has it worked?' asked Meryl.

'Well, we're off on a lengthy cruise the end of the month. The new Queen M. You and Ross should join us, Gina. There were a couple more staterooms still available when we booked last week.'

Peter Rossiter was head of a countrywide store chain, providing June with a multimillion-dollar lifestyle she took entirely for granted. Gina found her likeable enough, but couldn't visualise spending any real length of time in her company. Not that it was likely.

'Nice thought, but I'm planning on taking a trip back to England at the end of the month,' she parried. 'It seems ages since I was there.'

'On your own?' Meryl asked.

The trip had been merely an excuse, though she could hardly admit it in June's hearing. 'I'd think so,' she said. 'Ross has far too much on. Anyone want more coffee?'

Thunder was rolling in the distance when the party broke up around midnight, with occasional electrical flashes lighting up the southern horizon.

'Looks like San Diego's getting it tonight,' Ross observed as the last car pulled away. 'Hopefully, it will keep on moving south.'

He turned back to the house, glancing her way as she fell into step. 'It seemed to go well enough.'

'I think so, yes.'

Gina could think of nothing to add. The past two days had been fraught. For her, at any rate. Ross had made no approach since the other night, but otherwise appeared untouched by the conflict. She'd gathered the impression that any move to restore marital intimacy would have to come from her.

There was a good possibility that she had jumped to the wrong conclusion, she'd been forced to admit. Apart from the phone call Dione had made, she had no concrete evidence that they were in contact at all. One thing she did know: things couldn't go on like this.

'Can we put the other night down to PMS?' she asked, trying to inject a little humour.

Ross lifted a quizzical eyebrow. 'I thought that was only supposed to come just before a period?'

'It is, but I don't have any other excuse for acting up the way I did,' she said. 'I don't know what got into me.'

A hint of a smile flickered across his mouth. 'I know what didn't. I felt decidedly unlover-like that night. Do I take it we're back on good terms again?'

'If you want to be,' she said.

'I think that goes without saying.'

He slid an arm across her shoulders, turning her towards him, face lit by the security light on the wall behind him. Gina met his lips in some relief, resolved to keep her possessiveness in check from now on. They were both free agents. If she wanted to be with him at all, she had to accept it.

Meryl rang after breakfast to say thanks for a great evening.

'Thought I'd catch you before you left,' she said. 'Assuming you're downtown today?'

'Actually, I've backed out.' Gina kept her tone neutral. 'I know the company history from the bottom up, but it doesn't make me of all that much use when it comes to the running of. I've joined Elinor on her charity committee.'

'You know your own mind.' Meryl hesitated. 'About this trip back to England… There's nothing wrong, is there? With you and Ross, I mean. I know the marriage was more or less forced on you both, but you seemed to be making a real go of it.'

Now was the time to admit that the trip had never been a serious proposition, Gina acknowledged, but it was going to sound so anti-June.

'It seems such a long time since I saw my parents,' she said, thinking that was true enough at least.

'Well, don't stay away too long, will you?'

Was there a warning in that last? Gina wondered, replacing the receiver. Did Meryl know something she wasn't prepared to say up front?

She cut the speculation right there before it could expand into something she'd vowed to leave well alone.

Ross had gone back upstairs to get his briefcase. 'What's on your agenda today?' he asked when he came down again.

'Nothing,' she said. 'I might laze around.'

'Why not?' There was no censure in his voice, but no particular interest either, his mind obviously on other matters. 'We've a reservation at Spago's tonight. Seven-thirty. I'll give you a call if I'm going to be late, and you can meet me down there.'

Gina steered clear of the question of what might hold him up, concentrating instead on the fact that he'd made the reservation before they'd made up their differences last night. A small comfort, but a comfort nevertheless.

His parting kiss left her yearning. Not just for more of the same; she'd have been happy to settle for his company alone.

Left to her own devices, she took a book down to the pool deck, discarding it after reading a few paragraphs. Shaded by the wide spread of the umbrella, with a light breeze playing over her body, she had to acknowledge that most people would give a great deal to be doing what she was doing right now. She would be able to do very much whatever she wanted to do for the rest of her life once this was all over. There were other men in the world. Somewhere out there she would find one to take Ross's place, however long she had to wait.

She must have dozed off, waking with a start when someone said her name. Roxanne regarded her with open contempt.

'Enjoying the life you stole from me?'

'Hardly stole from you,' Gina rejoined, gathering her resources. 'You lost it.' She sat up, regarding her sister-in-law with unthrilled eyes. 'Are you alone?'

'If you mean, did I bring the man I was shacked up with, the answer is no,' she said. 'I ditched him a week ago. Where's my mother?'

She obviously didn't know about the switch. It was, thought Gina wryly, going to be another bad shock for her.

'You'll find her down at the Beverly Harlow,' she said. 'We swapped homes.'

'You did *what*?' Roxanne looked stunned.

'Your mother's idea—well, Ross's to start with, but she was all for it.'

'This place, for an *apartment*!'

'With appropriate financial adjustment, of course.' In actual fact, Gina had no idea what adjustment, if any, had been made, but she wasn't about to let Roxanne know that. 'She's had the whole place revamped, of course. You won't recognise it.'

'You scheming...' Roxanne broke off, teeth clenching. 'You think you've got it made, don't you?' she bit out. 'All this, and Ross too! Just don't imagine you've got him hogtied in *every* direction!'

'I don't imagine anything.' Gina was having great difficulty hanging on to her temper. 'I think you'd better leave.'

'Oh, don't worry, I'm going.' The tone was scathing now. 'Ross would do whatever was necessary to secure the damned company, but you're no match for Dione, believe me!'

She didn't wait for any response, turning about to head for the steps leading back to the upper levels. Not that Gina had a response ready anyway.

She got up from the lounger and plunged into the pool, swimming end to end half a dozen times in an effort to blank out her sister-in-law's vitriol. It didn't work, of course. All Roxanne had done was underline what she already knew.

The day wore on. Elinor rang mid-afternoon to say Roxanne had paid her a visit.

'It wasn't exactly a mother-daughter love-in,' she observed ruefully. 'How did I manage to bring two such disparate children into the world? I understand she called on you first. I hope she didn't upset you.'

'Not to any degree.' Gina kept her tone level. 'Did she say where she's living at the moment?'

'She still has her apartment in Glendale. Oliver bought it for her when she left Gary. At least, she's no longer with the man Ross spoke to. I asked her about the money she's supposed to owe. She said it was taken care of.'

By her, or by Ross? Gina wondered. If there had ever been any truth in the story to start with.

'I'm glad she's at least back in touch,' she said. 'You must have worried about her.'

'Something I can't help doing, even when it's unappreciated. I'm just thankful not to have the same concerns over Ross.' Elinor briskened her voice. 'How about lunch after tomorrow's committee meeting?'

'Love to.' Gina could at least say that in all honesty.

'See you down here at half after nine, then.'

There was no call from Ross to say he'd be running extra late. She was out of the shower and ready dressed for the evening when he arrived at six-thirty.

'Why didn't you tell me you were planning to go back to England?' he asked without preamble. 'Why leave me to hear about it from someone else?'

'It was just a spur-of-the-moment idea to stop June from going on about joining them on this cruise they're taking,' Gina protested.

'If that was true, you'd have put Meryl right this morning when she called you.'

Green eyes sparked. 'She had no right to call *you* about it!'

'She's concerned. She thinks things might not be all that good between us.'

'I'm sure you reassured her on that point. Assuming you still don't want anyone else to know what we've got planned.'

'It's no one else's business,' he said brusquely. 'I've no objection to you taking a trip back home, just to you not discussing it with me first. I'll make the arrangements.'

Gina swallowed on the sudden hard lump in her throat. Talk about hoist with one's own petard! 'I might think about it in a week or two,' she said, 'but there's too much coming up right now.'

'Fine. Just let me know when you *are* ready.'

So he could plan his own itinerary, she thought as he turned away to start undressing. With her out of the way for a while, he'd be left with a clear field. He might even bring Dione back here.

He'd booked Spago Beverly Hills, not the Sunset Boulevard arm. Gina hadn't been before. For star-gazing, it was reputably among the best in the city. She spotted at least three familiar faces on the way to their table.

It was only after they were seated that she saw Dione across the room. Ross had his back to her, but Gina was sure he was aware of her presence. Though she doubted if it had been a deliberate arrangement, the chances of the woman being here had to be pretty high. Her co-star, Mark Lester, was with her.

She shifted her gaze as the other woman looked across, studying the menu handed to her without taking in a word. She was more than half prepared for the arrival of the *maître d'* at Ross's elbow with an invitation for the two of them to join Miss Richards and Mr Lester at their table, feeling her heart miss a beat when he politely declined without so much as a glance in Dione's direction.

Could she possibly be wrong after all? she wondered. Would he really treat a woman he had feelings for in such a cavalier fashion?

Unless she'd done something to displease him. Dining with Mark Lester, for instance—maybe sleeping with him too. Snubbing her in public the way he just had was the biggest insult he could offer a star of her magnitude. It could mean the affair was over.

Even if it did, it made no difference to his feelings for her, Gina warned herself, but her spirits lifted regardless.

'I'll have the salad to start,' she said on an upbeat note. 'Then the *rhindsgulasch mit spatzle*, whatever that is.'

'Austrian beef stew on pasta.' Ross regarded her speculatively. 'You sound very animated!'

'Hunger,' she claimed. 'I only had fruit at lunch.'

'Not dieting, I hope?' he said. 'You don't need to.'

'Not dieting,' she confirmed. 'I just didn't feel like anything more at the time.'

She wasn't lying about the hunger. Still choked up from

Roxanne's visit, she hadn't actually eaten anything at all at lunch. Buoyed up the way she was at present, she felt she could tackle anything put in front of her.

Dione was still at table when they left the restaurant. Gina couldn't resist glancing her way, to be met by a gaze that fairly glittered with malice. Not that she gave a damn. Ross couldn't be making his indifference clearer. That was what mattered. Right now, it was all that mattered.

He took the surprise birthday party she arranged in good part when it came to the crunch. The beautifully restored E-type Jaguar she had had delivered on the morning drew covetous comment from the men.

'You might try having a word with my wife,' one said to her. 'The best she ever came up with was a bucking-bronco ride for the gym. Nearly broke my back first time I tried it out!'

Ross had received the present with a pleasure allied to some other emotion she'd been unable to deduce. He maybe thought it a bit over-the-top, considering their situation, but she refused to regret the gesture.

He waited until the last guest had left before springing the news on her.

'It's lucky I was here for this. I'm off to New York first thing in the morning. Union problems.'

'Do you have to handle it yourself?' she asked with constraint.

'I'll be taking a couple of people with me, but there are times when it's necessary to bring in the big guns before things blow up out of all proportion.'

'How long do you think you'll be gone?'

'As long as it takes to come to some agreement. A couple of days, maybe more.'

I could come with you, it was on the tip of her tongue

to suggest. She beat the impulse down with difficulty. Even if he'd proved amenable, which was doubtful, she had commitments of her own.

'Why don't you spend a couple of nights down at the apartment?' Ross suggested. 'I know Mother would love to have you.'

'I'll be fine here,' she said, determined not to have him think she couldn't manage without him for a few days.

He took an eight o'clock flight, due in at Kennedy at four-thirty New York time. Allowing him a generous couple of hours to get to the hotel, Gina hoped for a call mid-afternoon—if only to say he'd arrived safely.

It hadn't come when Elinor called at six to suggest she came down to dinner rather than spend the evening on her own. She'd be damned if she'd hang around waiting any longer, she thought irately. He could reach her on her mobile if and when he got round to it.

'A man all over!' her mother-in-law observed, on learning of the omission. 'Oliver was just the same. I remember one time he was gone two whole days before he got round to calling. Could never understand what all the fuss was about.'

They were eating out on the apartment balcony, surrounded by aromatic candles to keep any flying stock at bay. Gina sought a change of subject.

'Do you ever have regrets about leaving Buena Vista? You must miss the view from up there at times, if nothing else.'

Elinor smiled. 'The view from here isn't bad either. This place suits me wonderfully. Big enough to entertain in, and easy to maintain. Needless to say, I rarely use the kitchen. In fact, Maurice has persuaded me to have it taken out and the whole area opened up.

'You should use him yourself when you do get round to making some changes,' she added. 'He's the best there is!'

The most expensive, for certain, Gina reflected. She hardly need concern herself with costs, it was true, but it was a difficult habit to break. In any case, there was no point in making changes to a house she wasn't going to be in for all that much longer.

They'd finished the meal and were relaxing over coffee when her mobile finally rang. Ross came through loud and clear.

'I tried the house. Where are you?'

'With your mother,' she said. 'It must be late there.'

'Eleven-forty,' he confirmed. 'I've been tied up since I arrived.'

Gina caught back the first words that rose to her lips. 'So, how's it going?' she substituted.

'None too good so far. It's going to take a lot of talking to find a meeting point. Are you staying down there after all, then?'

'No.' Gina paused, listening. 'What's the noise I can hear in the background? It sounds like someone laughing.'

'It is. The GM's wife came to dinner with us. We're having a nightcap before turning in. I take it you'll be home if I call again in the morning, then?'

'Yes. Just remember the time difference though. I don't fancy being woken at the crack of dawn.'

'I'll make every effort,' he said drily.

He'd rung off before she could say anything else. Not that there was anything else *to* say. Elinor looked at her expectantly as she put the set down again.

'Bad news?'

'They're having difficulties,' Gina told her.

'Problems, problems, always problems!' Elinor sounded sympathetic. 'Like Oliver, he has to be there in the thick of it. You'll have to start putting your foot down. There's absolutely no need for him to handle everything personally.'

'I can imagine his reaction if I tried it,' Gina commented, eliciting a chuckle.

'I said start. It took me years to make any real impression.'

Years she wasn't going to have, Gina thought, descending into depression again.

She made the lengthy drive back to the house without incident. The caller display showed just the one call received at eight thirty-five, minus any message. Ross had called her mobile number at eight-forty——eleven-forty, as he'd said, New York time—and he'd been on line less than five minutes. It had taken him more than five hours to find a slot in which to make those calls.

But then, he'd had far more important things to do with his time.

It was the first night she'd spent alone since the wedding. She slept fitfully, waking at seven feeling far from refreshed. There was a luncheon in aid of the Cystic Fibrosis Association today. She didn't feel like going, but, having taken all this on, she wasn't going to start crying off.

Due to leave the house by ten, at nine forty-five, with no call as yet from Ross, she could no longer hold out. The hotel number was on file. She asked to be put through to Mr Harlow's suite.

There was a lengthy pause before the man came back on line. 'I'm sorry, Mrs Harlow,' he said courteously,' Mr Harlow isn't in the hotel at present. Do you wish to leave a message?'

Gina declined and rang off, angry with herself for having given way in the first place. It was evident that Ross hadn't given *her* a thought since last night.

The luncheon went off smoothly, raising a substantial sum. Gina had left her mobile switched off during the meal. Switching it on again afterwards, she saw there was a message on her answer phone. Ross sounded remote:

'I tried to reach you at home earlier, but you'd already left. I'll try to speak to you later.'

'Something wrong?' Elinor asked, seeing her expression.

Gina donned a smile. 'Nothing at all. How about doing Rodeo while we're in the area?'

It was gone seven when she finally got home. Michael had fetched the mail in from the box, leaving it stacked on a hall table. Gina went through it swiftly. Most of it was for Ross, but there was one envelope addressed to her for personal attention. Delivered by courier, it appeared.

The single sheet inside proved to be a photostatted copy of a New York newspaper gossip column, with one item marked:

A little bird tells me a certain recently married but still hot-as-they-come hotelier was in town with a starry old flame last night. Can it be that the spark has reignited—or did it never go out?

How long Gina stood there gazing at the cutting, she couldn't have said. It was referring to Ross and Dione, of course. It had to be! The woman she'd heard laughing last night hadn't been the GM's wife at all. Ross had made the call on his mobile, not the hotel landline, as might have been expected. He could have been anywhere.

Whatever his reason for giving Dione the elbow in Spago that night, he'd obviously got over it. Whether she'd discovered he was going to be in New York, and gone there with a view to making up, or had been in the city already, there was no way of knowing. It might even have been arranged, the union meeting a blind. However it had happened, the rift was obviously healed.

With New York over three thousand miles away, she would have known nothing about it if someone hadn't seen fit to send this through. It must have been faxed to a courier office as soon as the paper was published, then brought straight out. The three-hour time difference allowed for it.

The anger sweeping through her allowed no consideration. Enough was enough!

A call to the airport secured her a seat on a flight to La Guardia at nine-fifteen that evening, arriving five-twenty in the morning. She left the house again with just the handbag she'd carried all day, intent on only one thing—confrontation. What happened after that, she neither knew nor cared at present.

Despite the heavy traffic, she was left with almost an hour to wait at the airport until boarding time. She hadn't stopped to change from the lime-green suit she'd attended the luncheon in, standing out by virtue of it amidst the generally more casually clad throng. Catching a glimpse of herself in a mirrored stand, Gina wondered how she could look so outwardly cool and composed when she was such a mess inside.

The flight was long, but uneventful. Cocooned in the reclined first-class seat, she even managed to sleep a little. She spent twenty minutes tidying herself up in the bathroom before they started the descent, shunning all thoughts of retreat. Ross might have no feeling for her other than the physical attraction, but he owed her better than this. If she hadn't agreed to the marriage, he could all too easily have lost the power he set so much store by.

They landed ten minutes early to an overcast day in keeping with her mood. It was still barely six when she emerged into the arrivals hall. A newsstand provided a pre-

vious day's copy of the newspaper named on the fax. There
had been no trickery: the item was there right enough. Not
a column Ross was likely to have perused himself, so he'd
be unprepared.

All to the good, she thought. There was every chance of
finding the two of them together. What she would do if she
did, she had no clear idea as yet.

The hotel reception had several early check-outs already
lined up when she arrived after a cab journey that had
seemed to take for ever. Unwilling to wait, she told a hovering under-manager who she was.

From the expression that swiftly crossed the man's face,
she suspected that if he hadn't actually seen yesterday's
news item, he knew about it. As probably did the whole of
the staff. She kept her head high. Speculation could run riot
for all she cared.

In possession of a keycard to the suite, she ascended to
the tenth floor. She'd altered her watch to New York time
on the plane. It was exactly seven twenty-five when she let
herself into the suite.

The door she took to be to the bedroom stood open, but
there was no sound of movement from within. Little light
either. She went through without hesitation, striding straight
to the window to fling open the heavy drapes.

Jerked awake, Ross rolled over and sat up, shielding his
eyes against the flood of light. Looking at him, Gina felt
the turmoil of the last hours drain suddenly from her as
reason returned. She'd come all this way to face him with
a snippet of gossip that named no names, and may even
have been a plant by her beloved sister-in-law, for all she
knew. Why hadn't she considered that before letting emotion overcome her?

Ross gazed at her blankly for a moment, coming wide

awake as realisation dawned. 'What happened?' he asked urgently.

Throat dry as a bone, she looked for some way out of the situation that didn't involve the truth.

'Nothing happened,' she said. 'I have a couple of days free, so I thought I'd come and join you. Maybe do some shopping.'

'Via the red-eye!'

'It was a spur-of-the-moment decision.' She attempted a laugh. 'Crazy, I know!'

'Crazy isn't the word!' Ross turned his head to look at the bedside clock. 'I ordered a seven o'clock call.'

'Looks like somebody slipped up.' Gina fought to maintain an insouciant note. 'Heads will roll!'

'It's very possible,' he said. 'Who brought you up?'

'No one. I got the key from Reception.'

'Just for the asking?'

'They knew who I was.'

He threw back the sheet and got to his feet, naked as he usually was in bed. 'I need a cold shower. You'd better call Room Service and order breakfast for us both.'

'I already ate on the plane,' she said.

'Then order some for me.'

Gina tried to bring some order to a mind going off at tangents as the door closed behind him. The fact that Dione wasn't with him here in the bed was no actual proof that the item was a plant. On the other hand, he certainly hadn't looked like a man caught out. Thrown off balance for a minute or two, yes.

Shelving the problem for the moment, she went back to the living room, taking off her jacket and slinging it over a chair before picking up the phone to call Room Service. She ordered the full English for Ross, and toast for herself, having lied about eating breakfast on the plane. She could sense the unspoken question from below. Word of her arrival obviously hadn't filtered through to the kitchens yet, though it soon would. Hotel grapevines were second to none, Ross had said once. It seemed a long, long time ago now.

He was wearing suit trousers and a crisp white shirt when he emerged from the bedroom, the pale-grey silk tie slung beneath the collar not yet knotted. Gina had made coffee using the facilities provided. She poured him a cup without bothering to ask, meeting his eyes with a faint shrug, still not certain how to play things.

'You don't need to say it. I shouldn't be here. It was a mad impulse.'

The smile was brief. 'I could think of worse ones. You look remarkably good for someone who travelled all night.'

'An advantage women have in being able to cover the ravages with make-up,' she said. 'Anyway, travelling first class isn't that much of a strain. I ordered full English for you. You can always leave what you don't want.'

'You've changed your tune,' Ross observed ironically. 'Waste not, want not—wasn't that what you told me the night you arrived?'

'You have too good a memory,' she returned. 'Anyway, I was just fighting my corner.'

A knock on the outer door heralded the arrival of Room Service. Gina sat in silence while the trolley was wheeled in and unloaded onto the table in the dining area, meeting the waiter's frankly curious glance with a nod and a smile.

'I suppose he must wonder what I'm doing here,' she murmured after he departed.

'I'm still not all that sure myself,' Ross admitted. 'But as you are, better make the most of it. I'm due at a union meeting at nine, so you'll be doing it on your own. It's likely to be a long process.'

The confirmation that there really was a union problem made an arranged assignation even less likely, she conceded wryly. He mustn't know what had really brought her haring out here. Jealousy was too revealing an emotion.

She took a seat at the table, buttering herself a piece of toast while Ross helped himself to one or two items from the covered hot dishes. He had such wonderful hands, she thought yearningly, watching their movements.

'I don't see any bag,' he remarked, glancing round the room.

'I didn't bring one.' She forced a laugh as his gaze returned to her. 'As I said, a sudden mad impulse! I can buy everything I need.'

Ross shook his head, as if abandoning all attempts at rationalisation. 'Does my mother know about this?'

'No,' she admitted. Neither did the Petersons, she could have added. They would in all probability take it that she'd spent the night at the apartment with her mother-in-law. If she didn't go straight back today, they would need to be given some explanation for her disappearance. After spending most of the day with her, Elinor herself was going to be taken aback, to say the least, by her sudden decision.

'I think you'd better give her a call before she calls out the feds to report a kidnapping,' he said. He studied her, looked on the verge of saying something else, then apparently changed his mind, pushing back his chair to get to his feet. 'We'll talk later.'

'About what?' Gina heard herself ask.

'This whole situation.' He sounded suddenly weary.

He'd left his briefcase on the chair where she'd deposited her handbag on first entering the suite. She watched him as he went to get it, numbly aware that she'd precipitated what could be the beginning of the end. He'd had enough, that was obvious. So had she, if it came to that. The sooner they parted, the sooner she got her life together again.

Her handbag toppled off the chair as he took up the briefcase, falling upside down and spilling its contents on the carpet. Ross went down on a knee to gather them up. Fatalistically, Gina saw him straighten the crumpled fax page she had shoved in the bag last night; saw him come to an abrupt halt as the marked item caught his eye. She steeled herself to face him as he straightened.

'Where did *this* come from?' he demanded.

'It was sent to the house some time yesterday,' she said tonelessly. 'I'm not sure by whom.'

'I've a very good idea,' he said, 'but that can wait. You took it as proof that I'd arranged to meet Dione here?'

Gina made a resigned gesture. 'Yes.'

'How long have you suspected I was still seeing her?'

She looked at him uncertainly, struck by something in both tone and expression that didn't jell with what she was expecting. 'I suppose, all the time.'

'It didn't occur to you to ask me outright?'

'We were each to live our own lives,' she reminded him. 'You'd have told me it was none of my business.'

'Maybe in the beginning. I thought we were past that stage.'

'Are you saying you haven't been seeing her?' she asked after a lengthy moment.

'Yes. Not since the wedding, at any rate.'

Gina felt a cautious unfurling begin deep inside. 'Why?' she whispered.

His lips slanted. 'I'd have thought the answer to that obvious. I lost interest in her when I fell in love with my wife.' He shook his head as she made to speak. 'It's all right. I know you don't feel the same way.'

Gina hardly knew whether to laugh or cry. 'I fell in love

with you long before that,' she said. 'I've been eaten up with jealousy over Dione.' Her voice was husky. 'It's no confidence booster competing with a woman voted the most beautiful in the world.'

'Dione's the product of an industry,' Ross said softly. 'When it comes to natural beauty, there's no comparison.'

Gina went into the arms held out to her, meeting his lips with relief singing through her veins. No more heartache, no more dreading the day they eventually parted. The marriage was real at last.

'You're going to be dreadfully late for your meeting,' she murmured a long time later.

Ross put his lips to her temple where the hair clung damply. 'It can wait. They can all wait! I've far more important matters to attend to right now.'

He looked down at her as she lay beneath him, searching her face feature by feature as though to commit it to memory. 'It never occurred to me that someone with your looks could feel threatened by other women.'

'So little you men know,' she said.

'So it appears.' He was silent a moment just watching her, the look in his eyes a joy to see. 'Whoever sent that fax did us both a favour unbeknowingly. It smacks of Dione's touch, though I wouldn't be surprised if my sister had a hand in it too. They've a lot in common. The reason they get on together.'

'She certainly hates me,' Gina acknowledged wryly.

'You inherited what she thinks should have been hers. She's borne a grudge against me since the day I told her she was responsible for Gary's death.'

'You wouldn't turn your back on her completely though?'

'I wouldn't see her in trouble, no. But she'll be in it up

to her treacherous little neck if she tries any more tricks. She hasn't, has she?' he added, catching the flicker in her eyes.

Gina shook her head, seeing nothing to be gained from telling him about the afternoon Roxanne had caught her by the pool. 'I can deal with anything now,' she said. 'Anything at all!'

He laughed. 'I know the feeling! There were times these past few weeks when I've despaired of it ever coming to this. Especially when you looked so shattered at the thought of a year before we could think about divorce. It wasn't true, anyway. I've no actual idea how long it has to be. I just wanted the breathing space.'

He put his lips to hers again, the tenderness more telling than any passion. '*We* are going to have a long and happy marriage, Mrs Harlow! No more mistrust. I've never loved a woman before. Not in any real sense. Believe me.'

'I do,' she said huskily. 'I feel the same way about you. Dione shot her bolt, and she lost. So did Roxanne. Can we put it all behind us?'

'We already did,' he said.

HOW TO MARRY A
BILLIONAIRE

by

Ally Blake

Having once been a professional cheerleader, **Ally
Blake**'s motto is "Smile and the world smiles with
you". One way to make Ally smile is by sending her
on holidays, especially to locations which inspire her
writing. New York and Italy are by far her favourite
destinations. Other things that make her smile are
the gracious city of Melbourne, the gritty Colling-
wood football team, and her gorgeous husband
Mark.

Reading romance novels was a smile-worthy pursuit
from long back, so with such valuable preparation
already behind her, she wrote and sold her first
book. Her career as a writer also gives her a perfectly reasonable excuse to indulge in her stationery
addiction. That alone is enough to keep her grinning every day!

Ally would love for you to visit her at her website
www.allyblake.com

CHAPTER ONE

IT WAS love at first sight.

'I have never seen anything more beautiful,' Cara said as she stared through the window of the stylish Chapel Street shoe store.

'You simply have to have them,' Gracie agreed, her nose pressed up against the window-pane.

'They're frivolous. Certainly not a necessity.'

'So be frivolous, while you're still young enough for it to be charming.'

'But they're Kate Madden Designs!' Cara pointed out, hoping that at least would be argument enough to stop her from making such a rash purchase.

'So?'

'So, they cost more than my father used to earn in a week!'

Gracie turned to her. 'Now that's the strangest reason I have ever heard for not spending one's own hard-earned money. Even from Cara, the Queen of Thrift.'

Cara decided it was best to keep focussing on the shoes.

'And how much do *you* earn a week?' Gracie asked as though talking to a two-year-old.

'More than my father,' Cara admitted.

'So there you go!' Gracie grabbed Cara by the upper arms and turned her so they were face to face, the shoes glistening on the periphery of their vision. 'You have no choice. This is the big time. This is *not* mucking about with styling mousse and safety pins in converted warehouses, styling emaciated models for magazines. This is *not* getting kudos for finding designer clothes at bargain-basement prices. This is gold credit cards. This is limousines. This is television!' Gracie spread her hands before her as though indicating the way of the future. 'You want to make an impression and these are the shoes that will do it.'

Cara's gaze was irresistibly drawn back to the stunning creations sitting atop their own black velvet stand. The shoes were elegant, they were red, they were embroidered satin, and they had heels one could use as a lethal weapon if ever one found the need. In a word, they were unforgettable.

'And just think,' Gracie said, leaning her head on Cara's shoulder as she returned to her vigil before the coolest shoes ever made, 'if you don't get the job, at least you'll have a killer pair of shoes to console you.'

Cara nodded. The thing was, she had to get the job. She would be twenty-seven in a couple of months, the same age her father was the first time he filed for bankruptcy, and if her serious plans to have the St Kilda Storeys apartment building paid off by that time were to come to fruition, bar winning the Lotto, this was the only way it would be done.

And it *would* be done. There were no two ways about it. The property would be hers. Every brick. Every roof tile. Every grain of dirt. Only then would she be free of the constant feeling that one of those bricks resided in her chest.

Gracie was right. The fact that Cara was infamous for scouting out vintage pieces at charity shop prices would not hold her in much stead in the new crowd in which she would be moving. Television was about being cutting edge, not thrifty. And if she was going to land the high-paying job styling the star of the biggest television show ever to hit Australian screens, she would have to be unforgettable or bust.

*   *   *

'You have to be kidding me!' Adam said, his voice a mix of shock and laughter.

'Nope,' Chris returned with a big sunny grin. 'I'm going to be on TV as the main attraction in my very own dating programme.'

Adam's laughter dried up the moment he realised this was no laughing matter. Though his friend and business partner was practically a genius when it came to creating cutting-edge telecommunications innovations, he was not a practical joker.

'The contract was signed, sealed and delivered as of this morning,' Chris said.

Adam shot from his chair and paced up and down the room. 'I wish you had told me you were considering doing this, Chris. You really should have consulted me first.'

'Ah, no, I shouldn't have.'

Adam stopped pacing and glared at his friend. But Chris, who usually gave in to Adam's will, stared right back. This would take some care. 'You're the one who put me in charge of the public face of this company, and, as such, if you plan on doing anything that might alter Revolution Wireless's image in any way, you must consult me first.'

'This is not about the company,' Chris said. 'This is about me. Thus it is officially none of your business as Head of Marketing for Revolution Wireless. But as my friend, I wanted you to know.'

'Fine. Now, as your *friend*, I'm telling you it is the most ridiculous thing I have ever heard. A television dating show? Come on! If you're looking for a girl, I'll take you out and find you one. I know plenty of women who would be happy to escort one of Australia's most eligible bachelors.'

When Chris didn't budge, Adam grabbed him by the arm

and made to tug him out the door. 'There's literally millions of them out there in the real world. I can find you one on any street corner right now!'

Chris shrugged out of Adam's grasp, his fists clenched at his side. 'I don't want some escort girl I can pick up on any old street corner.'

Seeing how upset Chris was becoming, Adam took a moment to rein in his concern, which was fast running out of control. 'That's not what I meant and you know it.'

'I want a woman with whom to spend my quiet moments,' Chris explained. 'I want a wife. I certainly don't want one of your cast-offs. The women you date are the complete antithesis of what any sane man would want in a wife. Any man apart from your father, of course. While we're talking about relationships, let's talk about yours.'

Adam decided to ignore that final jab and focussed on the bits *he* wanted to focus on. 'This is about you, mate, not me, and my point is you could have anyone you want. Where has this all come from all of a sudden? Why now?'

Chris shrugged and softened a very little, his palms flattening out until they hung straight by his side. 'It's time. I work too much to go the regular route of dating by numbers. The years have slipped away without my even knowing it. I'm turning thirty-five this year.'

'I'm thirty-five already.'

That earned Adam two raised eyebrows.

'Chris, by the way you're acting anyone would think that was middle-aged. We're still young men, with our whole lives in front of us.'

'Exactly my point. While I am still a young man, I want someone with whom to share as much of that remaining time as possible.'

Adam felt himself running out of arguments and it bothered him to see Chris so certain. Sunny, cheery Chris, always glued to his laptop, creating brilliant business solutions for their hip, rising-star telecommunications company, was suddenly searching beyond the limits of his clever mind for satisfaction. The world outside had finally beckoned.

And despite his protestations about the effects Chris's plans would have on the image of the company, that wasn't really what had Adam spooked. He was perfectly aware that the big bad world could swallow a good-natured guy like Chris whole.

'OK, then,' Adam said, rallying his forces, focussing every lick of attention on his foolish friend, 'please explain to me why you think you need to go on a TV dating show to find a wife?'

'Because it's the only way I can meet women who have no idea who I am.'

Adam shook his head. 'Run that by me again.'

'The producers have gone to incredible trouble to pick out thirty women from all over Australia. Thirty attractive, accomplished, interesting women who have been given extensive compatibility tests. Thirty women who have no clue who owns Revolution Wireless, and thus have no idea how much I am worth. They will get to know me just for me. Chris, everyday Aussie bloke. Not Chris Geyer, richest single Australian man under forty.'

And *that* Adam understood. As two of the young owners of the Revolution Wireless telecommunications giant, one of Australia's fastest expanding business empires, he and Chris were considered prime pickings by the women in their regular social circles who knew *exactly* what they were worth.

Chris's earlier comments slammed into his thoughts. So what if he dated women dripping in diamonds and lofty aspirations, just like the ones who had taken his father to the cleaners over and over again? That way at least he had no chance of ever mistaking his feelings for any of them and therefore would never succumb to the same fate. And he had no intention of allowing his kind-hearted, naive friend to fall into that trap either. Especially with some buck-toothed ignoramus chosen by a TV exec with nothing on his mind bar ratings.

'I'm on my way to the television station now. Are you coming with me? I could do with some moral support, if that's on offer,' Chris said as he swung his jacket over his shoulder and headed for the door.

'Oh, I'm coming,' Adam said. 'But only so that on the drive over there I can do everything in my power to talk you out of it.'

'OK, but you're not coming into the meeting with me,' Chris said. 'You're too bloody good-looking. They'll forget about me in a heartbeat and do everything they can to snap you up instead.'

'Don't panic, mate,' Adam drawled. 'I wouldn't be in your shoes for the world.'

Cara checked her lip gloss in her compact mirror for the third time on the cab drive over.

She had dressed conservatively, as she figured that was how they would want her to dress their guy. She wore a vintage black jersey crossover dress and simple silver antique jewellery. Her short curly bob was pulled away from her face and anchored with a large red hibiscus, and her make-up was subtle, all so that nothing could take away from her new red satin Kate Madden Designs shoes, which were expensive enough to make that month's mortgage payments a squeeze.

The feeling of a brick in her chest grew heavier at the recollection of the price she had paid for them. But if she got the job it wouldn't matter—she would be free and clear. And that was the goal she had to keep dangling in front of herself like a carrot in front of a mule.

She closed the compact, smacked her lips together once more and found the taxi driver watching her in the rear-view mirror. She sent him a self-conscious smile.

'Big date?' he asked.

Cara shook her head. 'Job interview.'

'At the TV station? What sort of job? Are you a news-reader or something?'

'No, nothing like that. I'm hoping to land a job on one of those new dating shows. I don't even know the title or anything. It's all pretty hush-hush, actually.'

She jolted forward lightly in her seat as he unexpectedly pumped the brakes.

'Really?' the driver said. 'Are you going to be one of those girls in bikinis who sit in a hot tub all day?'

'Gosh, no!' she declared. 'I'm a behind-the-scenes type. I'm going for the job of styling the male lead in the show.'

'Oh,' the driver said before focussing more fully on the road ahead. Obviously hot tubs and bikinis were much more his scene.

He soon pulled up outside the old concrete building that housed the television studios. Cara hopped out and handed the cash through the driver's side window.

'Good luck,' the driver said. 'And I'll look out for you on the small screen.'

He gave her the once-over and Cara knew he didn't be-lieve her for a second and was happily measuring her up for a bikini. Knowing she looked more like a ballet dancer than a *Baywatch* babe didn't stop her from blushing in hu-miliation as he gave a little shrug as if to say he'd seen better.

Cara tugged at her born-again dress, patted down her curls, took a deep breath, and headed inside.

Adam sat upstairs in the top-floor foyer of the television station, cracking his knuckles.

He could have waited in the car. He could have browsed in the shop windows near the television station. He could have taken advantage of the heretofore unheard-of spare time and chosen to stop and smell the flowers in the park nearby. But he hadn't. He wanted to be where Chris was. And since Chris had been taken into a closed-door meeting, the foyer was as close as he was going to get.

After a good hour spent counting tiles on the ceiling of the open-plan waiting room Adam was itching to leave. And to take Chris with him. If there was even the slightest hint that Chris might change his mind, Adam wanted to be there to snap him up and take him back to the real world of stock prices and innovative technologies. A quantifiable world that never pretended to be anything other than what it was.

So Adam waited close to the source, his knuckles cracking, his eyes seeking out any movement that passed his way.

Cara checked her reflection in the lift doors.

She lifted a hand to pat down her hair. She was pleased to see the new caramel highlights in her curly chestnut bob gave her the exact hint of sophistication she was after. The huge red flower that held her hair back was securely fastened but still she dug it in deeper. It would be just like her to have the thing fall out of her hair and dangle at an illogical angle down her back for the whole day without her knowing, her intelligence and talent and new caramel highlights becoming blurred behind her often clumsy exterior.

Her best friends called her 'classy Cara' because she was always so put together, but it was also half a joke since they knew what it took for her to be that way.

She looked down at her unforgettable shoes for moral support. It took almost all of her concentration to remain upright, they were so high and delicate. And she was someone who had to lift her feet so as not to trip even when walking in bare feet.

The lift grumbled to a halt on the top floor and her stomach dropped away. At the last minute she closed her eyes, tapped the heels of her red shoes together and made a wish to whichever good fairies might have been listening.

'Let me have this job and I will never want anything else again.'

The lift doors opened, as did her eyes, and she stepped ahead, unforgettable red shoes leading the way.

Adam looked up at the whir of the lift.

A woman exited, walking like a ballerina: head held high, shoulders back, deliberate, as if she had a book on her head and had no intention of letting that book fall.

This woman had enough going for her that Adam stopped cracking his knuckles and let his hands drift to rest casually across the back of the couch.

She stopped outside the lift and checked the staff listings, bending slightly from the waist and affording Adam a nice view of…a very nice view. Seeming satisfied she was in the right place, she walked his way.

Only when she came closer did he notice evidence of nerves. She swallowed too many times, her eyes flitting about the place as if she was cataloguing everything in the room, and her knuckles showed white against the sleek black portfolio she clutched in her hands like a lifeline.

Finally her fluttery gaze cut his way.

She managed half a smile, her smooth full lips kicking up at one side, highlighting the sexiest little smile line along one pale cheek.

'Excuse me,' she said in a charmingly husky voice, 'but is this the place to wait for the guys from…?' She paused, her mouth closing in an adorable little pout as she found the words she was looking for. 'I don't even know what it's called. The new TV dating show?' A concerned crease appeared above her dainty nose as she awaited his answer.

'This is the place,' he said, drawing his eyes from the crease to her blinking eyes. Green, they were, and magnetic. Like a cat's eyes.

'Oh, thank goodness,' she said, a slim hand moving to her chest while her cat's eyes went back to their dazzled flickering. 'I've had one heck of a time finding where to go. Seems it's all so secretive most of the staff in the building knew nothing about it. But after my bumbling efforts I'm sure the whole place knows by now.'

She took a seat on the opposite couch, sitting upright, with her portfolio still clutched in her hands.

'Are you here to be interviewed?' he asked.

'That I am. And I can't believe how nervous I feel. I've never done anything like this before.'

Ready to ask, *Like what exactly?* Adam suddenly realised that this woman could be one of Chris's dates. And his first uncensored thought was that Chris was a lucky guy. Adam shifted in his seat, suddenly feeling a mite uncomfortable in the woman's sparkling presence.

Then he also remembered that none of the women was to know whom they were going to be meeting on the show. Just some guy, some poor slob hankering for a woman. Not his friend Chris; sweet guy and a billionaire.

But the funny thing was this woman seemed like a sweet

girl too. A sweet girl with eyes that deserved a double take and a mouth that begged to be kissed.

Adam shook his head to clear the muddy thoughts. What did it matter that she was seriously attractive? He was only finding himself so quickly riveted by her because of any possible harm she might bring to Chris.

It was a defence mechanism. That was all.

Chris was too nice to know what was best for him and it was Adam's job to look out for the guy. He owed him that much. If not everything.

The door to the offices beyond opened, and a young, hip television-exec type, with unironed clothes and too much gel in his hair, popped his head out.

'Cara Marlowe?'

Adam's lady friend stood up.

'That's me.'

'Great,' the guy said with an encouraging smile. 'Come on through.'

The woman shot Adam a parting grin that included the sexy smile line once more. 'Wish me luck.'

Luck meant that within days this fresh-faced, sweet and seriously compelling woman could be dating his best friend. And he found that all he could say was, 'Go get 'em.'

Cara followed the young guy, whose name was Jeff, through a maze of corridors and cubicles to his office within the bowels of the top floor of the television station.

'Take a seat,' he ordered.

She did.

'Coffee?'

'Ah, no, thanks.' With caffeine in her veins she'd be bouncing off the walls in no time.

'I'm not so good as you,' Jeff said, waving his empty mug at her. 'I'll be back in a sec.'

Cara sat upright on the plain simple chair as she waited for Jeff to return. She stared down at her red shoes, which glistened prettily back at her. And she winced. Jeff had walked ahead of her the whole time and she was sure he had not even glanced at her feet once.

But the guy in the foyer had. She was sure of that. In fact she was sure he had compiled an internal data file of every inch of her, so intense had been his gaze. It was all she had been able to do to keep her footing. New shoes or no new shoes. A guy like that would make any rational woman's knees go weak without even trying.

He had dark wavy hair, intense blue eyes, a solid build, hands that looked as though they could play the piano and change a light bulb. He was a hunk and a half. She wondered briefly what he was doing there, waiting in the foyer where those involved with the new secret show had been told to wait.

What if he was the single guy? The one she might have to style? She pictured him in his immaculate suit with his glossy shoes and his expensive haircut. If he was the one, her job would be redundant. She would have nothing more to do than straighten his tie and run her hands through his hair just before the cameras rolled.

The thought of getting so up close and personal with that particular gentleman made her suddenly uncomfortable. She shifted in her seat, then gave a little laugh out loud. What need would a guy like that have to go on a dating show? He was gorgeous. The strong, silent type. She imagined a wave of horror rolling across those deep blue eyes at the mere suggestion.

An alarm went off somewhere in the building and Cara clicked back to the present and remembered she was meant to be preparing for the most important job interview of her life. That was what she should have been focussed on, not daydreaming about the exact shade of some stranger's blue eyes. But of course she was only thinking about him so much because of the possible boost he could provide her financial status.

It was a survival mechanism. That was all.

Her focus cleared and she saw her red shoes still gleaming up at her. She had more important things to think about then and there than some chance acquaintance with Mr Handsome out there. She had to make a grand impression on Jeff.

She crossed her legs one way but the shoes were still hidden, so she crossed them the other way instead.

She hadn't even heard Jeff return so as she swung her right leg over her left she connected fully with the poor guy's upper thigh. His coffee-cup did a triple back somersault over his desk, trailing steaming milky coffee over everything in its path. The accompanying 'Oof' that sprang from Jeff's mouth told her that the connection had not been a light one. She leapt to her feet, disentangling herself as she went.

'Jeff, I am so sorry! Here, sit down, please.'

She manoeuvred Jeff into her chair, then reached over to place his tilted empty cup upright, as though it made any difference.

'Are you OK?' she asked, her attention zeroing in on the guy who held her financial stability in his hands. Hands which were currently stuffed between his legs.

'Did I hurt you a great deal? What can I do to help?'

He took a few moments to gather his breath before he finally said, 'When can you start?'

'Start what?' she asked, suddenly worried what she might be called upon to do to *help*.

'The job. The gig. The show.'

'I'm hired?' Cara asked, her squeaky voice showcasing her scepticism.

'That you are,' Jeff promised, his breathing returning to normal.

'Don't you want to see my portfolio?'

'No need. We've seen what you can do and you come highly recommended by those who've worked with you, including Maya Rampling of *Fresh* magazine, who seems to think you are, and I quote, "a gift from the heavens", and whose help we will certainly need for marketing the show later on. And that's enough for us.'

Cara spun about on the spot but had to right herself against the table when her dainty shoes threatened to give way beneath her.

'So, are you ours for the having?'

'I am all yours, Jeff. You can have me now.'

The young guy glanced up at her with the beginnings of a smile on his face. Cara snapped her mouth shut and waited for the perfectly reasonable response to her unfortunate phrasing, but instead his kind glance hit the floor once more. He shook his head.

'Those are some shoes you're wearing there, Ms Marlowe. And it pains me to imagine what they might have done to me had we not given you the job.'

CHAPTER TWO

'ADAM TYLER, right?' a husky voice called from behind Adam.

Adam turned to find the lovely lady he had met half an hour before. He blinked. It was a delaying tactic. It gave him a moment to size up the opposition or the problem before he spoke. But whereas before the woman was all elegant nerves, now she was all big smiles and gorgeous dimples. And those were qualities in a woman that he had never seen as a problem.

'That's right,' he said, many years of practice masking everything but nonchalance in his laconic voice.

'Well, now, you see I got the job.' She gave him a little curtsy before continuing. 'And I was told that you were the man I needed to see.'

'Excuse me?'

'To get the dirt on our man of the hour.'

He stood up straight, his hands clasped behind his back, and watched as she shifted from one foot to the other, all but dancing on those high red shoes of hers. Then all of a sudden she stopped fidgeting, piercing him with a stare so sharp he couldn't move. He couldn't even blink. He just stood there and waited for the acute green gaze to give him a reprieve.

'Adam Tyler,' she repeated, her bright eyes flashing as the unexpectedly sharp mind behind them whirred to life. 'Head of Marketing for Revolution Wireless?'

He watched her carefully as the cogs and wheels clicked in her mind. Revolution Wireless. Billionaire. Chris. She would have the whole deal figured out in no time. So much for them recruiting ignoramuses.

It slammed into his mind that nobody was meant to know anything about Chris. That was the whole point, the beauty of the idea, that Chris would be an unknown, just a guy meeting a girl. But suddenly that was all disintegrating before him.

And disintegration was just what Adam wanted.

Her gaze drifted away from him as, like a good girl, she put two and two together. 'Chris Geyer. The name was familiar but I couldn't place it before. He's one of your partners, right?'

He decided to keep his mouth shut. Maybe the fates had put her here just for him. Maybe he didn't need to convince Chris. She could be the spanner in the works all on her own.

'So it's not a joke,' she said. '*The Billionaire Bachelor* is not some hook to get a bunch of poor girls all excited only to have the fake Persian rug whipped out from under them. *The Billionaire Bachelor* is the real deal.'

Adam cringed on the inside. If that was to be the title of the show, Chris was dead meat.

But instead of venting his infuriation with internal screams behind closed eyes, Adam paid close attention to the woman before him, anticipating the inevitable moment when those eyes of hers would skitter back his way, lit all the brighter by the glitter of dollar signs. He braced himself, willing her to get it over with. Willing her to show herself as nothing special, as one of the countless many.

Her glance landed upon him, their eyes clashed, and he took in a short anticipatory breath as he looked for the sly smile that would no doubt touch at the corner of that luscious mouth. The tension inside him grew by the second as he waited for her to feed his disenchantment with womankind.

But the moment never came. Instead of a sly smile, there was a furrowed brow and what he guessed were teeth biting at her inner cheek. She wasn't looking at him as the answer to all her hopes and dreams, she was looking at him as though she felt sorry for him. And where he had been prepared to be disenchanted, instead he was stunned.

She finally collected herself and smiled, but her expression was infinitesimally cooler than when she had first burst from the inner room, all coltish legs and curtsies.

'So, anyway,' she said, her tone pleasant but no longer perky, almost as though she preferred to pretend the past two minutes hadn't existed. 'I have been told that the TV station has an account at a lovely little bistro around the corner and I was hoping that I could take you there for lunch.'

'I'm sorry,' Adam said, gathering his wits after being befuddled by her strange response, 'but I don't think that's in the rules of the game.'

Her confusion was evident. She took in a short breath as though ready to question his comment, before she obviously figured it out for herself, her eyes brightening again with the realisation.

'Please! I am not a contestant! The *last* thing I want or need is some brazen, bawdy billionaire breathing down my neck. Funny, though. You're the second man today to think that. What is it about me that screams bikinis and hot tubs, I wonder?' She said it more to herself than to him, but he still took a brief moment to consider the image.

Her conservative outfit did little to hide the long, lean curves and those unbelievable red shoes did things to her legs and her posture that made his mind turn easily to bikinis and hot tubs.

She moved over to the couch and sat down, patting the seat beside her, beckoning him to join her.

If she wasn't a possible love interest for Chris, then who was she? His interest stirred, he did as he was told, sidling over and sitting beside her, one leg hooking up to cross on top of the other and his arms reaching out to lie across the back of the long leather couch.

'I should have done this better,' she said, holding out a slim ringless hand. 'I'm Cara Marlowe.'

He shook her hand, taking a moment to enjoy the crisp, cool contact. But he waited for her to talk. He found that another good tactic. Most people could not leave silence well alone and they were more likely to fill it with interesting information than if they were questioned directly.

'I am going to be Chris's stylist for the duration of the shoot. It will be my job to dress him.'

'Dress him?'

'Choose his outfits,' she explained. She then reached out and touched his knee, her voice affecting the tones of a New York gossip show host. 'Honey, if I had to actually dress the guy, I'd be asking for a lot more money!'

Adam glanced at her slim hand resting on his knee. It felt nice until it recoiled as though scorched, then moved to slap across her unruly mouth.

'Sorry,' she said. 'I'm a tad overexcited right now. First I get the job of a lifetime and then I meet a real live Australian Businessman of the Year. I would love to talk to you about that some time. Sorry. There I go again. Taking liberties with a practical stranger. My tongue tends to have a mind of its own when my adrenalin is off and running.'

He gave her a slight nod, though he was again quietly stunned. She knew about his award too? And she was obviously a heck of a lot more impressed with that than with his bank balance. In Adam's long experience with women, this one was proving to be more unusual with every word that came from her lovely mouth.

She was an enigma wrapped in a very enticing dress. A girl with a good head on her shoulders, and a seriously charming face to boot. A woman with such a sexy, husky kick to her voice it could lure sailors to dash their ships upon mountains of rock, whose words spoke, not of the expected sly seduction, but of exuberant enthusiasm for her job.

No matter whom Chris was destined to date on the show, it seemed he would have at least one socially aware woman on set with whom to shoot the breeze. Struck curiously dumb by the thought, Adam once more decided it best to let her do the talking.

And she did.

'So, since they will have your friend Chris tied up for the next couple of hours, let's get out of here and have a natter.'

Even despite becoming lost in those expressive eyes, he somehow managed to pick out the pertinent information. A couple of hours until he saw Chris again? If he had to sit in the dull room for a second longer he would explode even if he was in the company of such an engaging woman.

Secondly, Adam knew when a golden opportunity landed in his lap. He couldn't hide the smile that began to warm him from the inside out. She was to be Chris's stylist. Thoughts of Chris in bizarre golfing outfits or excessive amounts of tartan wove their way through his devious mind. If he couldn't convince Chris he was doing the wrong thing, here was the perfect opportunity to interrupt the process from an entirely unrelated angle.

'It seems that you and I are destined to have a lunch date.'

'Excellent,' she said.

Adam stood, holding out an elbow in invitation. 'Well, then, Ms Marlowe, shall we?'

'Only if you call me Cara,' she said, standing, placing a hand lightly in the crook of his offered arm. Her beguiling smile giving him a third reason to accept the lunch offer with increasing pleasure.

Cara watched Adam from the corner of her eye as she perused the large menu in the lovely little bistro around the corner.

I am having lunch with Adam Tyler, she thought, knowing she would rather be picking his brains about his business practices than about his friend.

As a connoisseur of stories about locals made good, she knew the highlights of his career as reported inside and outside of the business pages. Inside were tales of a marketing guru, part-owner of the fastest growing company in Australia. Awards and plaudits followed in his wake like tin cans clattering along behind a wedding car. Outside the business pages he was more well known for being a playboy-billionaire type, not quite hip enough to make it onto the cover of any of the supermarket gossip magazines, but certainly fascinating enough to grace their social pages time and again.

No wonder too. In the flesh he was pretty darned gorgeous. He oozed manliness, from the woodsy scent of his aftershave, to the easy way he wore his suits. From the practised nonchalance of every effortless movement, to the fact that that very nonchalance could not cover up the fact that his mind did not miss a beat behind those fierce, hooded eyes. Beneath the cool exterior beat the pulse of a brilliant, shrewd, powerful man to whom success on every front would have come all too easily.

And all she'd been able to do was go goo-goo and paw him and talk about bikinis and hot tubs. It was not exactly the impression she would have hoped to make on someone whose business acumen she greatly admired.

She found him looking her way, his eyes faintly questioning, and she knew she had been caught staring. She shot him a big cheesy grin, then went back to flicking through the menu.

The last thing she wanted was to be turning all gooey over some guy with money. And a billionaire? That was entirely out of the question. Money meant power. Money meant control. And Cara was not about to give any of her hard-earned power and control away.

Especially to one who, above and beyond the whole gorgeous, blue-eyed, strapping, silent man thing, was so obviously involved in *The Billionaire Bachelor* project against his will. He was trouble in a three-piece suit. No doubt about it.

'You made up your mind?' Adam asked.

'You bet I have,' she said, her voice deep with determination.

Then after a few seconds of ensuing silence she looked up to find the waiter smiling blandly at her. She quickly picked the first thing that came into focus to cover up the fact that she'd had no idea Adam had been asking about the meal.

'So how does this all work?' Adam asked once they had settled and begun their starters.

Cara opened her mouth to answer but then Jeff's smiling face popped into her mind. 'Tell a soul a thing and you will be out on your backside,' he had said. 'Great recommendations or not.'

'Sorry,' Cara said, 'I'm not sure what I can really tell you. My contract has confidentiality clauses up the wazoo.'

'You've already given away the title of the show.'

Her hands flew to cover her warming cheeks. 'Oh, heavens, I have, haven't I? I'm going to blow this before it even starts. You have permission to stuff a napkin in my mouth if I let it run away from me again.'

'Thank you,' Adam said, 'that's always worth knowing.' He eyed her warily over his herb bread. 'Anyway, I don't mean about the show itself. I know more than I would like to about all that. I was wondering about specifics. For example, will Chris be at work tomorrow?'

'Well, I guess I can tell you that it will take about two weeks. By tomorrow morning at the latest, all of those involved will be sequestered in the Ivy Hotel in the city. And nobody will be able to come and go unless authorised by the producers.'

She watched for Adam's reaction to this news. When Jeff had told her she had all but freaked out, her mind running over with everything she would have to do that night to get her regular life up to date before she disappeared from the face of the earth. But this guy merely nodded and blinked and she had no idea if he was happy or sad or freaking out behind those dark blue eyes.

'Why will you be sequestered, do you think?' he asked.

'To keep any of us from blabbing to the press.'

'About what?'

'The juicy details. The name of the show...'

Adam smiled and it was all Cara could do to go on, the charming appeal it brought to his strong face was so unexpected.

'The star of the show,' she continued. 'The fact there even is a show. When word gets out, the producers want to control the spin. I've worked in the fashion biz for a number of years now and what it boils down to is the fact that sex sells. Television is sexy. Secrets are sexy. There is nothing sexier to eighteen-to-thirty-five-year-old women than a man so in tune with himself that he is openly looking for love. And the producers of the show want to reap the benefits.'

She finished her statement with a deep intake of breath. Now she was certain of it. The way he was watching her, weighing her words so carefully—this guy had ulterior motive written all over him. He smiled easily enough, and his body language certainly showed that he was open to anything she had to offer. *Any conversation topic,* she thought, giving herself a mental slap. But if for some reason he wanted this all to go away, she was pretty sure he would have his way. And it made her so nervous her chest hurt.

It sure didn't help her nerves that he continued to be just as unreservedly attractive as he was when she first laid eyes on him. It would have been more helpful for her jitters if he slouched, or fixed his hair an inordinate number of times, or if he professed a predilection for polka music.

She took a sip of water to stem the urge to babble and her mind whizzed back, hoping desperately she had not said anything idiotic or anything she shouldn't have. She was pretty sure she had done well. 'That's all I'm prepared to tell,' she said. 'Sorry.'

He shrugged. A movement so slight she didn't know if he'd really shrugged at all or if she'd just caught his essential indifference.

'OK, then, back to the reason why we're here,' Cara said, deciding it was about time she took control of the conversation if she was to get anything useful out of him. 'Tell me about Chris.'

'What would you like to know?' Adam asked.

'What does he look like, for starters?' Though Adam was

recognisable to her, she could not have picked the other owners of Revolution Wireless out of a line-up if her job depended on it.

Adam blinked. She had already pegged the fact that he did that when he was biding his time. Cara bit her bottom lip. Time-biding was not on her list of most favourite things.

'Does he look anything like you, for instance?'

'In some ways, yes. In other ways not at all.'

'I see,' she said. 'And what does he do for fun?'

This time the blink was different. It was loaded with thought. But she knew not what about.

'He creates telecommunications innovations,' Adam finally said.

Her lip-biting increased to a calorie-burning rate.

'OK. So how do you two know each other? Just from work? What rings his bells? What sort of woman do you think he is trying to land?'

Give me anything, please!

'We know each other from school.'

She waited for more but…nothing came.

'Fantastic,' she said, her patience finally running down. Sure, she had the job, but the last thing she needed was for it to work out so badly that she never worked again. Even with a mortgage paid off, a girl had city council rates and amenities to keep her working ad infinitum. And this guy had nothing to offer her but a bit of a crush.

'Well, that's all I needed,' she said, refolding her napkin and making ready to leave. 'Now I know he looks exactly yet nothing like you, he invents stuff for a living and he once went to school, I'm all set. With those specifics in mind I can now make sure he doesn't look like a complete dud for the millions of people who will watch him eagle-eyed every week.'

'Wait,' Adam said, his hand landing atop hers.

Cara let out a nervous breath, seriously glad her bluff had worked. She sat down slowly and shot him her best blasé expression, but she knew already she was up against a professional in that department.

This time she waited for him to talk. If she was sitting with the best she might as well learn from him. And after a few seconds of duelling silence she realised that his hand was still atop hers.

Her gaze flittered down. His hand captured her attention once again. It was big and broad and tanned, especially lying on top of her own, which was small and pale. As she stared the silence changed. It became thick and noisy with unuttered complications.

Slowly she slipped her hand away and he didn't stop her. She bit her lip to bring herself back to the present, then looked him straight in the eye and said, 'Adam, please tell me about your friend so I can make this as easy for him as I can.'

Adam had been ready to convince the girl to have Chris decked out with spats and a walking stick if that was what it would take to have his friend give up the game. But with her looking at him like that, beseeching, pleading, he found himself wilting. He told himself it was only because she made a good point.

It was in her power to make Chris look like an idiot. And when she had asked what Chris did for fun, Adam had baulked because he knew that Chris did nothing. Chris had worked tirelessly for years to achieve their joint goal, and now he was simply asking for some 'him' time. Didn't he deserve at least that much?

'So you really don't know what he looks like?' Adam asked.

She shook her head, slowly, as though if she went any

faster he would not be able to keep up. 'Nope. Not a bit. I have no idea if he's old, young, thin, fat, balding or has a glorious head of hair.'

It was fair enough that she didn't. Come to think of it, he was the only one who seemed to end up in any of those other types of magazines, the ones that the guys at work liked to snip out and stick on the corkboard in the kitchenette.

Cara blinked at him, her lashes sweeping down onto her cheeks in a look that spoke of pure and simple time-biding. And it took him a second to recover. He had to remind himself of the good-head-behind-the-pretty-face theory he had stumbled onto earlier.

Adam shifted in his seat, unused to being on the receiving end of his own tricks. This woman was a quick learner and he knew then and there he would have to stay on his toes. If this was to go smoothly for Chris, and thus work out to Revolution Wireless's best advantage, he would have to keep a close eye on this one.

'OK, then,' Adam began, 'first things first, Chris ain't anywhere near brazen, so wipe that idea out right now. Picture a man…'

Cara leant forward, resting her chin on the heel of her palms as the guy across the table gave a rundown of the life and times of Chris Geyer. Stories of childhood antics, of bad dates, of a love of education, of a twenty-year friendship ran thick and fast. Cara listened with half an ear, smiling in all the right places, building up the idea of a friendly teddy-bear type whom she was more and more looking forward to meeting.

But the other half of her mind was focussed on the man telling the story. All efforts at nonchalance put aside, he became a charismatic, vibrant story-teller. Her nerves dissolved with every captivating word and she couldn't take her eyes off him.

She could tell that he usually hid behind his laconic attitude so that he could measure the world without it measuring him. But behind the attitude lurked the guy who ran one of the most successful marketing campaigns the country had ever seen. This was the guy who could sell cookies to Girl Guides, he was just that compelling.

As she often did when she met new people, Cara pictured how she would light him. If ever, one day, she had the chance to do so, it would be all about shadows, taking advantage of those fantastic cheekbones and that straight nose. She would brush his hair back a tad further, knowing that he would only curl up more inside himself and make himself that much more intriguing. The carefully constructed remoteness, the seriously attractive mystery, the gorgeous depths of those navy-blue eyes...

'Don't you need to take any notes?' Adam asked, his hands stopping mid-demonstration of how a mobile phone was built.

Cara snapped back to the present with such a jolt, her elbow slipped off the table and she had to catch herself before her chin followed in its wake.

'Are you OK?' he asked, lifting from his seat, reaching for her, his expression bright with surprise.

Bad. Bad Cara. What on earth had she been doing, daydreaming like that? Her attention had become wrapped in the words of some strapping stranger when her focus for the next two weeks should be blissfully caught up in the ins and outs of the most challenging and significant job of her life.

'Yes, I'm fine,' she said. 'And no as well. I don't need to take notes. Really.' She jabbed furiously at her temple. 'All stored up here.'

'So are you a Cary Grant fan?' he asked as he poured her a glass of wine.

Cara fought to remember a single word of his conversation and came up blank. 'A who…what?'

Adam's eyes narrowed. 'Cary Grant. Chris's favourite actor? He's in *The Philadelphia Story, His Girl Friday*…'

Cara shook her head hard to clear out the soft and fuzzies that had gathered therein. 'Sure. Of course. I love Cary Grant. I think he's marvellous. I can even do an impression if you'd like.'

'No need. Really.'

She fully deserved Adam's bemused smile.

'So to recap, Chris is a great guy who loves Cary Grant, collects bells—'

'Shells,' Adam corrected, pouring himself a glass of wine.

'Shells,' she said without missing a beat. 'And shells… sells telephones for a living.'

Adam nodded slowly. 'In a nutshell, yes. And he deserves a toast, don't you think, for being the one to bring us together for this lovely lunch?'

'Who?' Cara asked, the soft and fuzzies winning hands down. 'Cary Grant?'

Adam laughed, his head shaking, his eyes bright with amused confusion. 'Why the heck not?' He lifted his glass. 'To Cary Grant.'

Cara had had enough. Another second of this conversation and she would probably forget her own name. She stood, dropped her napkin to the arm of her chair and then didn't know where to put her hands. 'You've been a fantastic help, but it's time for me to be…elsewhere. Thanks for lunch. And I guess I'll…see you 'round like a rissole!'

Before she could plant her foot deeper in her mouth Cara took off. She weaved through the tightly packed restaurant tables with her mind on the task ahead. Get to the television station. Meet Chris. Do the best job she could. Keep said job. Take home pay. Own St Kilda Storeys. So long as she kept that mantra going through her head, she was unstoppable. Surely?

Adam Tyler and his dreamy, distracting blue eyes did not come into the mantra once, so the bigger the distance between the two of them, the better.

Adam remained seated, debating internally whether it was better to watch her walk away, her lithe hips swinging as she mastered her outrageous shoes, or to watch her from front on, her lovely face so animated, her hands forever moving with nervous energy, and that huge flower bouncing about atop her head.

He dragged his interest away with some regret.

So, it looked as though Chris was going to be *The Billionaire Bachelor*. He cringed again. But that would have to be the last time. He had no choice. He was going to have to join bloody Chris on the set for the next two bloody weeks and act as babysitter to his bloody best friend.

'Sex sells,' Cara had said. He knew she was spot on. And if that feisty employee was anything to go by, he had the unsettling but mounting feeling that this show was going to produce fireworks…and that it would be in Revolution Wireless's interest to be seen to be lighting the match.

CHAPTER THREE

CARA went home to St Kilda Storeys, her beloved apartment building that would very soon be truly hers. There was a note from Gracie on her apartment door. She took the steps, two at a time, to Gracie's top-floor apartment and knocked.

Cara heard scuffling and snuffling as Minky got to the door first. Gracie was looking after the fluffy, almost-white, Maltese Terrier while their fellow Saturday Night Cocktails gang member Kelly and her husband Simon were out of town visiting friends in Fremantle.

Gracie finally opened the door with a wriggling Minky in her arms. 'Well?' she said.

'I got the job.'

Cara was lost in hugs from Gracie, and tiny lapping kisses from Minky.

'I knew it!' Gracie said. 'Or at least I wished and hoped super hard!'

Gracie grabbed Cara and steered her toward the small old couch that took up half of the tiny lounge. 'I have ten minutes before I have to be at work. So tell me all about…everything.'

'I can't, actually. It's all seriously under wraps.'

'Even to me?'

'Especially to you.'

Gracie had the good grace to nod. 'Good plan. I can't keep a secret to save my life. Keep it to yourself. So tell me something else. Who did you meet? Anybody famous?

How about that guy who hosts the movie review programme? He's a bit of a hottie.'

'Wrong channel.'

'Oh, yeah, right. Anyone else I can brag about?'

'Umm, not really. Though you'll be pleased to know that I did have an interesting lunch with this one guy...'

Cara went on to fill Gracie in on the important points of her lunch date—no names mentioned, of course: the ominous stare, the powerful grace, the serious good looks worthy of a menswear catalogue.

'Armani or Target?' Gracie asked, using their usual scale.

'Armani, without a doubt.'

Gracie nodded in pleasant surprise. But either way the truth about this guy was immaterial. Cara was going to be holed up in a hotel for the next two weeks with way too much else to occupy her to care.

Adam went back to work.

Dean, the third partner in the Revolution Wireless giant, was pacing behind his desk. Where Chris was the ideas guy, and Adam was the salesman, Dean looked after the day-to-day blood, sweat and tears side of the operation, and it showed. His tie was long gone and his shirt sleeves were rolled up, his hands flying about him as he yabbered away into a telephone head set.

Adam took a seat at the desk and waited for the one-sided staccato conversation to finish.

'Adam, my man,' Dean said, giving his friend a hearty handshake, before resuming his pacing. 'What's up?'

'It's about Chris.'

'And this dating show deal?'

Adam nodded.

Dean flapped a dismissive hand across his face. 'Let him be.'

'Are you serious?'

'Sure. It's been over a year since he last took a holiday, so think of it that way if it helps.'

'It doesn't help. I have worked my backside off to sell Revolution Wireless as a serious company, as serious competition against the giants who have cornered the market for years, and just as we've made the leap Chris is about to go and make us all look like amateurs.'

'Not amateurs,' Dean said, eyeing Adam down. 'Human. And human ain't such a bad angle to give a company this size, if you ask me.'

Adam blinked and Dean cocked an eyebrow at the move.

'So you back him on this?' Adam asked.

'A hundred per cent. I think he's a brave, brave fellow. He's putting it all out there and that takes guts. And I don't see why Revolution Wireless should suffer for showing that one of our leading lights has guts to spare.'

Adam let the idea wash over him. He was being shot down from all angles and he knew it would not do anybody any good if he fought against such diminishing odds.

'OK, then. If that's your decision, I want us to sponsor the show.'

Dean stopped his pacing at once. He ran a hand through his sandy hair, though it fell back into the same shambles instantly. 'You want us to sponsor the show?'

'Well, it certainly looks like I can't stop the show, so why not make the most of it? Why not take advantage of the fact that it will be a significantly supported prime-time television event with the opportunity for intensive branding that is set to rake in viewing numbers like none other has done before?'

And that way he could wangle his way onto the set, insist

that he be able to stay in the hotel with the cast and crew, because only then could he keep an eye on Chris. Make sure his magnanimous friend did not lose his heart and along with it his wallet to some conniving, manipulative schemer. Because for the life of him he could not see how the whole episode could end any other way.

Dean's smile dawned slowly. 'Sure, why not? You're the marketing guru, my friend, so if you think it will float, you have my vote.'

Adam nodded. Decision made. 'So will you be OK with the two of us AWOL for the next couple of weeks?'

'Of course. So long as you're on the other end of the phone. I mean, if *we* couldn't run our business by mobile phone and email we would be in a heap of trouble!'

Adam could not help but smile. 'Too true.'

Three of Dean's phone lines lit up almost simultaneously.

Adam stood. 'I'll leave you to it.'

Dean nodded, and his pacing resumed. He gave Adam a brief wave as he left the room.

Cara had her assistant offload the couple of jobs she had pencilled in for the next fortnight. But she called her main client, Maya Rampling, the editor of *Fresh* magazine, herself.

'Cara, darling! I hear congratulations are in order!'

'Maya, you are the darling. I know you're half the reason I got this job. Even though it means I have had to pass the styling of your lingerie shoot onto a colleague.'

'I will miss your light touch, Cara, but don't give it another thought. This job was simply made for you.'

'Did they call you or did you call them?'

'Darling, they would be afraid for me to find out *any-thing* after everyone else. Just take this one piece of advice.

Watch your back. TV jobs are notoriously precarious. Half the crew will be turned around by the end of the shoot. It's like the big boys are so scared of losing their jobs themselves, they have to keep everyone else on their toes.'

'OK...' Cara felt the brick in her chest grow a kilogram heavier.

'So be good. Keep your head down. Don't cause trouble. Do your job with a minimum of fuss and you'll be fine. Above all have fun, and I'll see you soon.'

Then Maya hung up.

Have fun? Cara thought. With those last pieces of advice hanging over her she would be afraid to smile at the wrong person in case she did the wrong thing. No. She would keep her head down and do her job. She would keep her job and she would pay off her mortgage. Her mantra well and truly re-established, she felt ready again.

She showered, changed into cut-off denim jeans, a white collared T-shirt and white flat Mary-Janes, closed her suitcase, checked all the electrics at home were shut off, and then left.

A big black limousine awaited her at the front door. She wound down the window so she could have a good look at her old red stucco building. A smattering of coloured perennials swayed lightly in the front garden. Lights shone from most of the windows. Music spilled from a second-floor apartment. The next time she would see it, she would own it outright.

The car took off, its engine humming softly. They drove past girls in G-string bikinis parading the beach. Boys lined the walkways, acting as though they were simply pausing to check out the ships in the distance, but the girls in the G-string bikinis knew better.

It drove Cara to wonder about the mysterious Chris Geyer, putting himself on the line for love. She wondered what it would take for someone to go to that sort of length to find themselves a partner.

She, who had never considered going on a dating show, had never looked up an internet dating agency, had only gone to nightclubs for the dancing with her friends, simply could not see herself in his shoes. When it came down to it she knew she was actually spending a good deal of time *not* looking to find herself a partner.

Still, no matter what Chris's reasons were, they had afforded her the opportunity of a lifetime and for that she would be for ever indebted to his romantic nature. So long as the anti-romantic nature of his friend did not turn the idea sour.

As the big car turned towards the city, Cara sank back into the soft seat feeling as if the rest of her life were waiting around the next corner.

'It's a done deal,' Adam said as he shook hands with Jeff of the unironed clothes and the too much hair gel. 'Revolution Wireless will be the main sponsor of this series of *The Billionaire Bachelor* and as such I will be allowed access to all areas of the set.'

'So long as you stay at the hotel,' Jeff qualified, 'and are bound by the same rules as the rest of us for the next two weeks, that's fine.'

Adam shot the younger man a wry smile. 'Of course. That went without saying.'

'Yet I said it anyway,' Jeff said, returning the smile. 'So if you can be at the hotel by eight o'clock tonight we will have a room for you—'

'On the same floor as Chris.'

'You will have the suite next door,' Jeff agreed. 'So here is a copy of the schedule, a timetable of the events that will occur within the confines of the show.'

Adam flicked through the document, which had no header and no front page. If anyone on the street found it they would think it a terribly dull, unimportant business memo, not the breakdown of the best-kept secret in Australian television.

'*The Billionaire Bachelor* is going to be huge,' Jeff promised. 'You won't regret this.'

No matter that Adam was now officially one of the gang, all the connotations implied by that title still made him fume. Chris sure needed him if he was going to come through this ordeal unscathed. And if Adam had anything to do with it, his friend would come out of this a billionaire and a bachelor still.

The front doors of the Ivy Hotel were guarded with big burly bouncers and a metal detector. They scanned the bar-code on Cara's pass and let her through the doors. Once inside, a whole other set of security guards searched her luggage for recording equipment and found only a Polaroid camera, which was listed against her name as an allowable item. The place was really locked down tight. And she was being let through to the inner sanctum. Her whole body hummed with excitement and she hoped it had nothing to do with the metal detectors.

And then her suitcase began to ring.

The security guard, whose nametag read ''Joe Buck, licence number 2483'', had been about to pass over her case and let her through. But at the ringing he tightened his grip. 'I'm sorry, Ms Marlowe, but mobile phones are not allowed as per your contract.'

They had a brief game of tug of war before Cara let go. 'But I didn't bring my phone,' she said, sure she had left it at home on her ironing-board.

Her case stopped ringing.

They looked at each other for a moment, both kind of hoping the other would agree that maybe they had imagined it.

'OK, then, Ms Marlowe,' Joe the security guard said. He handed the suitcase over again before the ringing resumed. 'Ms Marlowe, I'm terribly sorry, but—'

Cara felt herself blushing to her toes. 'I know. I know. I'm sorry. Just give me a second. I really do not remember packing it.'

With Maya's words—*keep your head down, don't cause trouble, minimum of fuss*—ringing in her head, she wanted to get this spectacle over with as quickly as possible. She lobbed her suitcase onto the ground, bent from the waist, unzipped the case, peeked around her neatly folded clothes and found…nothing.

A distinctive murmur invaded her ears. She glanced between her knees and saw a line had formed behind her. What a fantastic first impression she was making on her new colleagues: bum in the air, being searched for contraband.

The ringing stopped. She shook her case and the ringing began all over again. Not having any luck with checking under her clothes with care, she began to scoop them out in a flurry, hanging them messily over her shoulder. Her just-washed hair kept hanging in her eyes and she had to constantly blow it out of her face. Added to that she was getting hot from the unusual lifting movements that felt agonisingly like exercise. She was in first-day-on-the-job hell.

'Is everything all right here?'

At the sound of the familiar deep voice, Cara stood up so fast the blood took longer than necessary to reach her head. She held out a hand to steady herself as the world turned fuzzy and black. Since Adam Tyler was the closest pillar to hand, he had to do.

Her vision slowly cleared. She looked into her nemesis's dark blue eyes and bit back a self-effacing groan. He would hardly want to talk seriously about his time as Australian Businessman of the Year with a woman who could barely put one foot in front of the other without something going awry.

It just wasn't fair that she had to be at her most klutzy around someone so smooth. Her last words to him had been 'see you 'round like a rissole,' for goodness' sake! Who said that bar eight-year-olds and grown-ups with limited sophistication?

It only made him all the more intimidating and she did not stand for feeling that way with anyone. She was talented. She was sought after. She was focussed. She was ambitious. She was self-made. She was leaning against him, her hand splayed across his unexpectedly sculpted chest, with half her clothes strewn over her shoulder and a pair of plain white cotton panties hanging from her finger.

She whipped her hand away and tucked it behind her, shaking madly until the underwear plopped back into her suitcase.

'Are you OK?' he asked, reaching out to take her by the shoulder as though he was afraid she might collapse atop his shiny shoes.

Finding herself flummoxed, she pulled away, crouched down and began to pile her clothes back into her suitcase.

'Low blood pressure,' she said, frantically shoving her entire collection of cotton pants that had managed to make their way out of her suitcase back into her suitcase. 'Stood up too fast. Should have known better. Gives me blackouts.'

'Ah, Ms Marlowe,' Joe the security guard cut in. 'Your mobile phone?'

She threw the rest of her clothes atop the suitcase and stepped away. 'You look for it. Please. Be my guest.'

The guard looked to Adam as though hoping perhaps he would prefer to rifle through her intimates instead. Adam backed behind Cara. But then the ringing sound returned and the guard took a deep breath and went searching.

As Cara watched in mortified silence, it finally occurred to her that she was once again in the vicinity of the man she had been looking forward to never seeing again.

'What are *you* doing here anyway?' she asked under her breath.

'You're the one who needed the leaning post,' he said from right behind her.

'Not here. But *here*, in the hotel.'

At that moment Joe the security guard came up with something jingling in his hand. It was not a mobile phone. It was a card. It had a huge 'CONGRATULATIONS!' scrawled across the front. And when the guard opened it the card played a very good imitation of a mobile phone ring tone.

Cara, Adam, and a good number of those in line craned over the guard's shoulder for a closer look, to find the long gushy note Gracie had written and hidden in her case before Cara had left.

Every one of the big burly men turned to Cara with mushy looks on their faces. Cara just tapped her foot and held out a hand. Blushing, Joe handed over her private mail.

'I am terribly sorry, Ms Marlowe.'

'That's OK, Joe,' she said, swallowing down her indignation and embarrassment. There was no reason to make him feel bad. He hadn't done anything wrong, though Gracie would receive a tongue-lashing along with a hug for this particular stunt. Cara gave the guard a pat on the back and smiled until she sensed him relaxing. 'You were doing your job. And with impressive thoroughness. You are a credit to your post.'

Joe blushed and scuffed his toe on the carpet.

'Can I have my case now?' Cara asked.

'Sure. Of course.' Joe returned to his packing with extra special care.

Cara cleared her throat. 'Thanks, Joe, but I can look after it from here.'

Joe stood up, his blush growing by the second. While he went back to checking the bags of the growing line of guests, Cara continued to repack her case. But of course she could no longer get it closed. She looked about her for help. Joe was going through Adam's bag and naturally everything seemed to be going swimmingly for him.

Adam glanced her way. She bit back her pride and waved him over. 'If I sit, can you zip?'

A knowing smile lifted his mouth and she wanted nothing more than to slap it away. 'Of course,' he said.

She sat, having to lift her legs when he rounded the front, so that he could duck beneath them. Would there never be an end to her humiliation when he was about?

'Come on, say it,' she insisted.

'What?'

'Whatever it is you're thinking.' *Some smartypants comment about my backside, or falling into your arms, or about my white cotton underwear.*

'I was thinking you handled Joe's embarrassment brilliantly. You are one very nice lady, Ms Marlowe.'

'Oh.'

Adam tugged the zip through the last few centimetres. Taking a hold of her ankles, he pulled her feet back to the ground. 'There. All done.'

He kept a hold of her bare ankles for several long moments before releasing his grip with a final soft pat. Cara had to swallow to wet her suddenly parched throat.

'Adam, you never did say what you were doing here?'

'Not surprisingly, considering the floor show was a heck of a lot more interesting than anything I had to say.'

Cara felt a growl growing in her chest but Adam got there first.

'Revolution Wireless is sponsoring the show.'

Now that statement deserved a hesitant blink.

'Wow. That's some turn-round. At lunch I could have sworn you thought the show the most ludicrous idea you had ever come across.'

'I did. And I still do. But, nevertheless, people who know more about these sorts of things than I do tell me that it will be the biggest thing on television bar the Aussie Rules Grand Final. So I am here as Revolution Wireless's representative.'

'For the whole two weeks?' Cara asked, trying to rein in her hysterical voice.

He nodded.

'Mr Tyler,' the security guard called out. 'Mobile phone, laptop, printer, all on the list. You're right to go through.'

Adam watched her for a few moments longer before standing and returning to his bags without another word.

Seeing her chance to retire as gracefully as possible, Cara stood, and dragged her suitcase to the lift as quickly as she could.

Adam watched her walk away.

The woman was good entertainment value if nothing else. He watched her shuffle from one foot to the other as though the floor were covered in hot coals, and then as the lift doors slowly opened she bolted like a cat with her tail on fire.

Joe the security guard cleared Adam to go on through into the hotel proper. Adam sauntered to the lift recalling what a cute tail it was, squeezed into pale denim cut-offs that had been washed so many times they fit her like second skin. Though she was a slim woman, she certainly curved just where she ought. He had been well aware of that when walking up to the front door of the hotel and seeing those very curves wiggling so engagingly at him.

The moment he had realised just whose curves they were, he had instantly jumped in to help. Or, if he was honest with himself, he had instantly leapt to shield her considerable temptations from appreciative eyes other than his own.

Who needs security guards in this place? he joked to himself. *Adam Tyler is on the scene and he's ready and willing to protect everybody from themselves.*

CHAPTER FOUR

CARA was up early the next morning. She hustled downstairs to the buffet for some peace and quiet as she had the distinct feeling that it would be the last she would get for a good two weeks. It had nothing to do with avoiding one particular member of the crew, of course. She was happy to avoid all of them after her grand entrance the night before.

On her way back to her room, Cara passed by a young woman in sweaty gym gear who could not for the life of her get her door unlocked.

'Do you need a hand?' Cara asked.

The woman looked up, her pale blue eyes flashing. 'I can't seem to work this stupid card thing. I only arrived this morning and the guy who carried my bags let me in the first time.'

Cara held out her hand. 'May I?'

The woman gave it over as though it were a hot potato. 'Please. Otherwise I may be going about my day looking like this.' She pulled out a hunk of lanky hair, damp from an obvious session at the gym downstairs.

'Well, I wouldn't wish that on any of my fellow women,' Cara said, sliding the card through the slot. The door opened without a problem.

'You can't hardly tell I'm a country girl, can you?' the woman said with a self-deprecating smile, and her best hick accent. 'How's a gal like me meant to figure out one of these fandangled big city doohickies? Back home we don't even have front doors!'

49

'Don't worry about it,' Cara said with a smile. 'I've been here since last night so I've had time to master all the fandangled doohickies.'

'Practice makes perfect, then?'

'That's it.'

'Well, thanks…' The woman smiled at Cara with her head cocked to one side.

'Cara,' Cara said.

'Thanks, Cara. I'm Maggie. Anyway, I'd better get on in there and get my fire started so I can cook me some tucker.'

Cara could not help but laugh. The young woman was such a sweetheart. 'Put on a sausage for me.'

'Shall do. See ya!'

Cara didn't even make it to her room before Jeff was on the scene. She had already swiped her card so Jeff just bundled in after her, chattering away about the plans for the day.

'Do you mind if I go to the bathroom by myself?' she asked, half joking but half making sure he wasn't about to follow her in there.

'Go for it,' he said. 'Just listen up as you go.'

'OK, then.'

He sat on her bed and she was glad she was a naturally tidy person. The idea of this guy having to move last night's underwear from her bed didn't appeal. Especially since half the crew had already had a good gander the night before.

Cara did her make-up and cleaned her teeth as Jeff happily yabbered away. 'So today you get to meet Chris. Outfit him. Make him as hunky as you can. And tonight he meets the girls.'

She popped her head around the door to find him reading the last page of the book by her bed.

'Any good?' he asked.

She shook her head to try to keep up with him. 'Did you say we start shooting tonight?'

'Yep. So you'd better get cracking. Collect Chris upstairs in Suite 44, then straight downstairs to collect your credit card and limo. Shop, shop, shop. And I'll see you back by midday so we can dress him, mike him, and paint him.'

Then Jeff bounced off as quickly as he had arrived. Cara hastened her ablutions, then headed upstairs.

She knocked on the door for Suite 44 and a butler escorted her into a gorgeous suite five times the size of her own room.

The room opened up into a sunken lounge with a bar, and assorted gym equipment scattered across a raised platform by the ceiling-to-floor windows. The carpet felt so soft beneath her feet she itched to reach down and run her fingers through it. It would have been a great location for the underwear shoot she had been set to style for *Fresh* magazine, but she had to bite back that idea. Too late now. She had made her bed. She would simply remember the location for next time.

'Hello,' she called out. 'Anybody home?'

She stopped peering around corners and stood bolt upright when Adam Tyler, in his ubiquitous suit and tie, sauntered out of one of the opened doorways off to her right.

Her face warmed instantly under his unexpected gaze. Whatever for, she had no idea.

'Oh, I am sorry,' she said, backing away. 'I must have the wrong room.'

'You're looking for Chris?' he asked, his deliberate, sexy voice stopping her short.

'I am.'

He kept walking her way and she just stood there, rooted to the spot, as his personal magnetism washed over her in waves. She wondered if Chris would be such a terrible force. If so, it would make for a suffocating atmosphere.

'He won't be a moment,' Adam said, veering off towards the bar. 'Why don't you take a seat? Would you like a coffee?'

Cara shook her head. It took enough effort to keep her balance, mentally and physically, in the presence of this guy; she didn't think she needed caffeine to make it worse.

From behind Adam came a man of about the same age, mid-thirties or so. It had to be Chris. And Cara was infinitely glad to see that he was nowhere near as intimidating a figure as Adam: he was sweet and sandy-looking, like a day at the beach. He gave her a little finger wave then drew a finger to his lips, hushing her from alerting Adam to his presence. Cara bit her lip and drew her amused gaze back to Adam.

Sensing at once she had an ally, she felt her confidence return tenfold. She walked over to Adam, keen to keep his attention on her and not his silent friend.

'So, Adam, now we have established I am where I am meant to be, may I ask what *you* are doing here so bright and early? Don't you have somewhere else to be? Sponsorship deals to wangle? Million-dollar ad campaigns to oversee?'

Sensing Adam was about to turn and find Chris behind him, Cara dug deep for something that would make him stop. 'Or don't you have some buxom blonde to dump?' she asked.

That did it! Adam turned back her way with his usual slow grace. He watched her carefully, like a tiger who was not quite hungry enough to chase her down, but who saw her as a possible morsel for later just the same.

'Now where did you get that idea?' he asked.

'Oh, I don't know.' Cara flitted a hunted gaze to Chris

who gave an encouraging two thumbs up. So on she went. 'Isn't that what you are most famous for? Blondes first, billions second?'

After a few watchful moments, he shrugged. 'No blondes to dump right at this moment, so here I am.'

He turned away and for some reason it irked that he didn't seem to mind her comments in the least. She breathed deep, fortifying herself against his nonchalance.

'You really don't need to be, I'm sure. You'd think your friend couldn't tie his shoes without you.'

'Well, maybe he can't,' Adam said and Chris doubled over as though he'd been stabbed in the heart.

'Well, maybe you should give him the chance to try,' Cara said.

'Well, maybe it's best for him to keep his mind on more important details like running a multibillion-dollar business.'

'Well, maybe he thinks there are more important things than money.'

'Well, maybe your real concern is, with me here, you don't get to tie his shoelaces and that puts you out of a job. So who has the real money concern here, do you think?'

Electricity flickered across the room. She could feel it in every nerve ending. She was pretty sure she would be able to fling him across the room with a bolt of lightning shot from her fingertips if she really wanted to.

Then she pulled herself up. What was she doing baiting the guy like that? It had all begun as a little joke. All she'd wanted to do was keep him from finding out his friend was listening in.

She was a conciliator. She was a diplomat. She was the one to stop an argument, not to hold up her fists and shout, 'Bring it on!' Especially to a guy who looked as though he could wipe the mat with her. But there was just something about him that rubbed her the wrong way. He made her squabble muscles itch.

'Well, maybe you two should get a room!' Chris finally shouted.

Adam spun to face him and Cara was able to stand down. She unclenched her fists and rolled her shoulders, feeling ridiculously like a prize fighter. But there was no prize to be had from taunting Adam Tyler.

'I couldn't let you guys go on for a second longer or I would have had to put out a fire.' He slapped Adam on the back, then approached Cara with his hand outstretched. 'You must be Cara. I'm Chris Geyer.'

'Hi, Chris,' she said, pumping his hand. 'I'm your stylist for the duration of the show.'

'Fantastic! I'm colour-blind and fashion unconscious so my life will be in your hands. Though watching you handle my bodyguard here is such a treat, even if you had no function I would ask to keep you on for that reason alone.'

She flicked a glance to Adam, who had relaxed enough to lean against the back of the couch, watching them.

'Aside from that, you just saved me from a pack of monsters in the other room,' Chris continued, rubbing at his chest. 'I just had my chest hair waxed to prepare me for the microphone I'll be wearing. I didn't plan on torture being part of the deal.'

'So why did you let Adam tag along?'

'Ooh! She got you there again, buddy. This one's sharp. We'll have to be quick around her.'

Cara adored Chris in a heartbeat. He was a teddy bear. With his sandy hair, his sightly pink cheeks, his not-so-hard body, his slightly rumpled suit, he would be a dream. A nice guy who would take to her plans like a duck to water. Whereas she knew that in the same position Adam would fight her tooth and nail. Though she also knew Adam would never put himself in the same position. He was the type of guy who kept his heart for pumping blood and nothing else. Just as she did herself.

Maybe that was why she felt so strange around him—they were like two north poles clashing and repelling over and over again. Whereas Chris was a definite south pole, easily compatible with both of them.

Adam watched over Chris like a hawk and Chris seemed to take it with good humour and the occasional roll of the eyes. She could sense the camaraderie between the two in an instant.

'So, Chris,' Cara said with a decisive clap of her hands. 'Let's go shopping.'

'Rightio,' Chris said. 'I'll just grab my key card thingy…'

Adam stood and held the key card up, showcasing the fact nobody was going anywhere without him.

'Great,' Chris said. 'Let's go.'

'Is he coming too?' Cara asked over her shoulder, loud enough for Adam to catch the words.

'It looks that way.'

She leaned into Chris and whispered rather loudly, 'Is there some way you can get him to lighten up? Otherwise it will be a long day.'

Chris whispered loudly back, 'Tell him our stock price has hit an all-time high. That ought to do it.'

'Your stock prices have hit an all-time high,' she threw over her shoulder, but Adam didn't even flinch. At the door to the room, Cara turned and faced him down. 'Just don't get in my way, OK? I'm the best at what I do and if you want your friend here to be the best that he can be, you'll need me on his side.'

Adam just stood there. And she found herself faltering under his steely glare. She fought the urge to bite her lip, which was a bad habit and a dead give-away when nerves hit.

Finally he spoke. 'I'm not planning on fighting any professional decision you might have to make. Put the guy in head-to-toe pink if that's your bag. But I am here to stay, sweetheart. So get used to it.'

Adam watched as she fought to contain herself. He could see the strain building within her: the quickening of her breath, the flare of her dazzling green eyes, and the shoulders squaring back. She was itching to deck him. He was shocked to find himself preparing to block a swinging fist.

She was like a firecracker and he knew it took very little to light her fuse. She certainly had some temper lurking just below the surface and he was pretty sure that something about him brought it out in her. Though it was probably nothing more than the fact that he pushed buttons for a living and did it in his day-to-day life without even meaning to.

Then from nowhere, with a heck of an effort, she collected herself, rolling her shoulders and physically slowing her breaths. Then she licked her lips, drawing his rapt attention to her shapely mouth, which was withdrawn from his sight all too soon as she spun away from him and headed out the door.

Chris shot him a big grin. 'She's a keeper.'

Adam shut the door behind them, pocketing the key card. 'We'll see,' he said, finding the very idea a dangerously appealing one.

When Adam realised it was going to be a day of barbers, beauticians and boutiques, spent under the watchful blinking red eye of a camera crew, he was ready to throw himself from the moving car. The only thing that kept him along for the ride was the fact that he knew Cara was waiting for that exact reaction. She was waiting for the complaints. She was longing for them. She all but begged for them.

During Chris's manicure, her expression all innocence, Cara offered Adam the chance to join Chris, to make his friend feel more comfortable. Adam almost agreed, if only to wipe that cheeky smile from her face. Though when he turned down the invitation she sent him a saucy shrug and joined Chris herself. The movement was rattling enough to have him keep his mouth decidedly shut for the rest of the day.

The women he knew didn't rattle him as this one did. They were blissfully predictable. Yet he couldn't predict a step Cara would make from one moment to the next. It was disconcerting to say the least.

Later, when Cara had been choosing some appropriate underwear for Chris to put on under some fairly fitted trousers, one of the crew made a comment about Cara's known predilection for white cotton. News travelled fast in a small community and Cara's grand entrance the night before must have done the rounds and back again.

The whole room froze, waiting for Cara to fade away into embarrassment or fly into bossy hysterics, either of which would have been understandable. But she merely turned, hand on hip, pierced the boom operator with a steely glance, and said: 'Well, now you bring that up, since you've all seen mine, I think it's only fair I see yours too.'

Then she took one quick step his way as though she was about to chase him about the room with the intent to 'debrief' him. The boom operator flinched, his eyes wild with panic, and that was all it took. The crew lost it, erupting into loud fits of laughter that kept up for the rest of the day. Suddenly he was the one under the microscope. He was the one they would talk about at dinner. And Cara was instantly one of the gang.

Adam could have watched her work all day. In fact he quite happily did, even though the whole point of him being there was to keep Chris from the clutches of an unknown woman, and the last thing he needed to be doing was setting a bad example by obviously favouring one himself. But favour her he did. More and more every moment he was with her.

There was just something about her. Something in the way she managed to keep five guys doing her bidding without raising her voice. Something in the way she took care to keep Chris smiling all day. Something in the way her green gaze skimmed his way when she thought he wasn't watching.

So somehow it wasn't the most exasperating day of his life. Somehow with her impudent smiles and her teasing and her vivacious attitude, Cara made the whole day fly.

They hopped back into the limo a few hours later in good spirits.

'How are you holding up?' Chris asked and Adam glared him down. 'Don't look at me like that. I have never seen you look so morbid. You look like somebody died.'

'My friend Chris the man has gone. He has been replaced with Chris the dandy.'

'Anything for my little Cara,' Chris gushed. He took a hold of her face, squishing her cheeks between fingers and thumb, and remarkably she took the abuse. 'You just can't say no to this sweet face. You, who can charm anybody when you set your mind to it, were totally outclassed by this little lady today. If only we could headhunt her.'

'To do what?' Adam asked, his gaze lingering on the lady in question, who was hooking one foot beneath her in her seat, her companionable grin settled entirely upon Chris.

'Whatever she wanted.'

'This is plenty for me to handle just now, thanks,' the lady in question said.

'Have you worked for Jeff before?'

'Nope. First time for me too. But so far I like it and so far he likes me and I would like to keep it that way.'

'And by that you mean...?'

'They have enough faith in me to know that my work will be perfect. But that doesn't mean they can't sack me for any other reason they choose.'

'That's pretty tough.'

'Mmm. As I have been told, this is a tough business.' She waggled a finger at Chris. 'So be good. Don't cause me any trouble.'

Adam found her playful nature seriously attractive. Who was he kidding? Her porcelain skin, her long legs, her curling hair the colour of butterscotch, her cat's eyes, her luscious mouth, all were seriously attractive. She was a tough little chicken with confidence to spare, but her tendency towards the accident-prone seemed to bring out a strangely protective urge in him. She had him on constant alert, ready to whip out a steadying hand in case she stumbled.

All up she was a total mantrap and he was pretty certain she had no idea.

'So that's it for today?' Chris asked.

'Yep,' the mantrap said, mid yawn, her arms reaching across the expanse of the car as she stretched her whole body. Adam couldn't have dragged his eyes away if a gaggle of buxom blondes had sauntered by the car. 'And back to the hotel we go to prepare you for tonight. Are you excited?'

'I think so.'

Adam heard the uncertainty and his attention reverted back to exactly where it should have remained. On his friend. He pounced. 'It's not too late to turn back, mate. We can turn the car around, give those nice people back their fancy clothes, pay the hotel bill ourselves, and leave.'

'And why would you do that?' Cara asked, now fully alert, her smiles fading fast.

'Adam here thinks I am making a big mistake.'

'And what do you think?' Cara asked Chris. 'Are you ready to go ahead with this?'

'What do you care?' Adam asked.

The look Cara shot him was pure venom. The atmosphere in the car had gone from faintly prickly to toxic in an instant. It seemed those cat's eyes came with a matching set of claws. The faint sense of protective affection that he had been deluding himself he had been feeling throughout the day happily burst into a million imperceptible fragments.

'I care about what *your friend* wants. Chris?'

Chris nodded. 'Sure I'm nervous, but this is what I want.'

Cara turned back to Adam. 'So if you badger Chris into giving in now, that would mean he doesn't get what he wants. Is that what *you* really want?'

Adam clenched his teeth so hard his head hurt. And there he had been, feeling so clever that he knew how to push *her* buttons. 'No. It's not,' he admitted.

'Fabulous. Case closed. So let's do this thing and do it as best we can so that it works out for all of us.'

Cara shot a hand out the window and banged it twice on the roof. The driver got the message and took off back to the hotel.

Once there, Cara picked out Chris's clothes for the night, her movements so jerky Adam knew she was still none too happy with him.

'So what are you wearing, tonight?' she asked and, though she wasn't looking his way, Adam knew by the stern timbre of her voice she was talking to him.

'This, I guess.'

She shot him a look. Down and up, her glance travelled. Once it reached his face his whole body felt bombarded by her professional glance. If she had run a hand the length of the fabrics he wore, he would not have felt any less affected.

'I thought as much,' she said with a sigh and he knew that, whatever had been holding her at bay, he had been let off the hook. His relief was measurable. Substantial. Physical. Unforeseen.

She reached over and picked out one of the suit bags and all but threw it at him. He collected it in two hands. 'Adam Tux', written in large, strong handwriting on a white slip of paper, was safety-pinned to the outside of the bag.

'You got this for me?' he asked, feeling three steps behind her all the way.

'Mmm,' she said, with several pins poking out of her mouth. 'I heard the whole crew are getting dressed up tonight as well, to help get into the spirit of the thing, so I thought you might need it. Though after your little rebellion in the car I almost decided not to give it to you.'

She glanced his way from beneath lowered lashes and shot him a self-deprecating smile. Whoa. It rendered him speechless. He was never speechless. Sure, he wasn't a guy who talked people's ears off, but that was a cultivated mannerism created to get exactly what he needed from any conversation. He usually had plenty he could say on any given subject, he simply chose to listen instead. But on this occasion he was completely at a loss for words.

'Maybe after this you'll try to cut me some slack.' She

winked. Just once. And he felt it travel the room and lie upon his cheek like a feather-light kiss.

He took that as his cue to get the hell out of there. Without another word he took his tux, and his bafflement, and went to his suite to change. And to roll his incompetent tongue back into his mouth.

CHAPTER FIVE

THAT night, on the romantic, candlelit balcony of the Ivy Hotel ballroom, Chris set out to meet the woman he was going to marry, while Cara moved behind the scenes inside the ballroom proper in surroundings not nearly so romantic. Champagne glass in one hand, she used the other to hike up the heavy skirt of her slinky black dress so that she could better negotiate the light stands, cameras, and trailing cables stuck to the floor with heavy black gaffer tape.

She found Adam set up on a director's chair, which afforded a good view through the equipment to the scene outside. Despite the niggling tension she still felt licking between them, once the cameras began to roll she gravitated Adam's way.

'My stomach is curling as though I'm the one about to go out there,' she said, pulling up a chair.

Adam didn't even give her a glance, his focus was so fully on his friend. His whole body was clenched. He was like an explosion waiting to happen.

But it wasn't fair to say it was all him. She had been just as wound up earlier in the limo. At the talk of Chris pulling out of the show, the brick of fear inside her chest, which had been absent all day, had come back with a vengeance, so heavy it had threatened to pin her to the seat of the car.

The two of them were making their way through each day with the weight of the world on their shoulders and if she had to be around this sort of volatile energy for a fortnight, the finesse it would take to navigate him would eat her up inside.

She tried to get through to him again. 'Nerve-racking, isn't it?'

Nothing.

So she reached out a hand and placed it on his knee. He flinched so violently, she flinched in tandem. She could feel the tension radiating from him in waves. But what she saw in his deep blue eyes gave her pause. He wasn't being fractious. This wasn't some sort of manly power play. He was suffering.

She collected herself and placed her hand once more upon his knee. 'Are you OK?'

'You don't know him,' Adam said, his voice low and far away. 'He's too kind-hearted. Those women will eat him alive.'

She looked from him to Chris. Adam the confirmed bachelor, the playboy, the man about town, watching over his friend, the slightly younger, the sweeter, the less well travelled. They had made jokes earlier about Adam acting as Chris's bodyguard, but suddenly Cara knew it was no joke. For some reason, Adam felt he had to be there to protect his friend.

But why? As Cara saw it, the women, to a one, seemed to be even more nervous than Chris. She spied one other familiar face among them.

Well, what do you know? she thought. It was Maggie, the girl who had not been able to work her key card that morning. She was all dolled up in a pretty pink dress, her blonde tresses flowing straight and long past her shoulder blades. And Cara knew that if she was one to go by, the producers had picked good people. That girl would more likely build a campfire on the floor of her room than eat *anyone* alive.

'Give them a chance,' Cara said. 'If I think he's being taken advantage of, I will fight for him alongside you, OK?'

His gaze narrowed and she felt it focus on nothing but her. It was enough to sap her breath away.

'Don't play me, Cara.'

Her fluttery hand shot to her chest. 'I'm not. Seriously. I wouldn't even dare try. True, I barely know Chris, but I like him. And it's simply not in me to see someone like that be crushed.'

He nodded, slowly. Once. Twice. A deep breath filled his chest then released on a ragged sigh. Something in what she had said had hit the right note. His mouth kicked up at the corner. 'Allies.'

Her stomach clenched at that one small movement of his lips. He could be devastating when he chose to turn on the charm. But she had come into this conversation with one goal in mind, to make peace, and it seemed she had achieved her objective.

Cara held out a pinkie finger. 'Allies.'

Adam stared vacantly at her finger. Cara had to reach over, take his hand, and link his pinkie with hers. His hand warmed hers for a moment before the link was broken. The truce had been made. And too late Cara wondered if she had just made a pact with the devil and what sort of payment she would have to lay down to keep the peace with such a man.

'So are you taking notes?' she asked, lightening the loaded mood. 'So you can have your own show after this one?'

Adam laughed, the sound rumbling in his large chest. 'You got me. I'm pining to be out there myself.'

'Well, you're dressed the part, at least. And you do look pretty damn good in your tux if I do say so myself.'

He looked more than good. He looked absolutely edible.

Adam ran a hand down his white tie, but his eyes didn't leave hers. 'It's a perfect fit.'

Cara did her best not to blush, as beneath his words she heard him wonder how she had picked his measurements so well. 'It's my job, Adam,' she said. 'Don't get any ideas.'

His smile told her he was reserving judgment on her answer and she knew he had every right to. There would be plenty of women who could draw him from memory. He had that sort of magnetism that one could not help but stare if one had the chance.

'Or maybe you're not really planning to have your own show, maybe you are just here to ogle all the pretty girls,' Cara said, flicking a glance at the lovely ladies in evening dress fawning over his smiling friend.

He gave her a small grin, his eyes mercifully leaving her to rake over the other women before them.

But it wasn't long before his gaze drifted back to where it truly preferred to be, on by far the most beguiling woman in the room.

One minute she was sophisticated, with her dazzling red shoes and her portfolio, just the sort of woman he would happily spend a Saturday night seducing. The next minute she was the girl next door in her soft denim cut-offs and unbrushed curls, just the sort of *ingénue* he spent his waking hours avoiding.

Now tonight, with a dash of something dark about her eyes and gloss on her lips making them look as though she had eaten too many strawberries, she looked like sex on two legs and just the sort of woman who would surely be wearing something other than white cotton briefs beneath her clingy black dress.

Whereas he knew he had a Masters in the poker face, every thought flickered across her green eyes. Every blink told a story. Every twitch of her cheek said she had something to say. And if she nibbled at that full lower lip of hers a moment longer he would have to find out for himself how it tasted.

He knew it would be sweet. The longer he watched her nibble, the sweeter the thought became. He dragged his eyes back to face the same way as the cameras, but it was all he could do to concentrate on Chris.

After a couple more hours, day one of *The Billionaire Bachelor* shoot was over. The girls were herded out a back door while Chris trudged through the maze of cables and cameras to flop into a seat next to Adam.

'You looked great out there,' Cara said.

'Thank God that's over, hey?' Adam suggested.

Chris didn't move, his head flung back, his eyes closed. Finally he shook his head, slowly, back and forth. 'I could have stayed out there for the rest of my life.'

Cara felt Adam's whole body tense in response. His cheek muscles clenched and his knuckles showed white on his large tanned hands. If she had brought him to an uneasy peace earlier, the caged tiger was back with a vengeance.

Chris opened his eyes and Cara's breath caught in her throat. He was positively glowing.

'They were all amazing. Lovely. Sweet. Beautiful. I don't know what I ever did to deserve this. It's going to work. I can feel it in my bones. Within that group of women is the woman I am going to marry.'

If Adam was tense before, by that stage he had practically turned to stone.

'Was there any one in particular who caught your fancy?' Cara asked, trying to keep the spirit lively.

'Maybe. Possibly.' Chris thought about it, then his neck

began to turn pink. He sat up and shook his head. 'But it's too early to know.'

He seemed to just notice Adam, and Chris's expression went from delighted to grim in an instant. 'Adam, just relax.'

Cara blinked. She had not heard Chris so bothered before.

'Remember, they have no idea who I am. None of them know the title of the show is *The Billionaire Bachelor.* I am just Chris. There is no way they are in this for anything other than finding someone to love, just like I am.'

Adam laughed, or as much as it could be a laugh considering he looked fit to burst.

'You are going to have to get over this, mate,' Chris insisted. 'I'm here. I am doing this. And no matter your reservations and your history with relationships, you are going to have to suck it up and support me. Because I seriously can't do this without your cooperation.'

Cara could see that Adam was dealing with some pretty heavy emotions. There was a war going on within him so distressing even *he* couldn't keep it under wraps. He breathed deeply through his nostrils, stretched out his fingers and relaxed his shoulders. These were movements she knew all too well herself. The reeling back of one's temper, of one's true feelings in order to keep the peace. She wondered what it was about his 'history with relationships' that had him so heated.

Whatever else, she could see how much he cared for Chris. And for whatever reason he was torn between taking him by the ear and pulling him out of the hotel and all the way home, and letting him be. Adam was keenly afraid that Chris might fall for one of these women. Whereas Cara and every woman who would watch the show would hope for nothing less for sweet, fluffy Chris, it was the last thing in the world Adam wanted for him. And it was more than just wanting his friend to remain free and easy.

'So come on, Adam,' Chris continued. 'I need to know, here and now, that, despite your reservations, you will stick by me whatever decision I might make.'

Ever the diplomat, Cara ached to get between them and make it all OK. To do a little dance. Sing a little song. Anything to draw attention away from the tension. But she sensed that this time she wasn't needed. There was enough history, enough understanding between these two they could work it out and it wouldn't end in cold shoulders.

Adam finally dug deep enough to find what he was looking for. 'Fine. You know my feelings—'

'Unfortunately I do.'

'But no matter what you decide to do, I'm with you. Why else do you think I'm here?'

'To rouse at me?'

'To be your second. To be your shoulder.'

Cara wondered if the guys even remembered she was there. But she was used to sinking into the background while moments of high emotion rolled on by. She always felt it was better to live on an even plane—knock off the edges both high and low, and she would be much more content.

Chris gave him a lopsided grin. 'So you are.' He shook his head. 'Sorry, mate. I guess my head is just too full to take it all in. I'm used to figures and measurements, and not those concerning the ladies. We're all good?'

'We're all good.'

The two men stood and, where she would have expected shaking of hands, they hugged. Actually honest to goodness hugged. And she wondered again on the history that had brought them together. Such true friendship. A relationship built on rock.

Though she had spent her life rejecting the notion, for the first time in a long while she ached to be in the middle of the action. She yearned to reach out and take a little of that emotion before it rolled on by and out of her life for ever.

The next day, since the girls were piled into a couple of minibuses and taken to the local mall for their day of shopping and pampering, all under the watchful eye of a three-man location camera crew, everyone else had the day off.

But after the emotional invigoration of the night before, Cara could not stand being alone in her room. After an hour of channel flicking and floor pacing she was about to pick up the phone, and call Jeff and see if he wanted a game of cards, I-spy, whatever, when her room phone rang. She leapt across the bed to grab it.

'Good morning, Cara,' Adam's low voice coursed down the phone line.

'Good morning, Adam.' She sat down, her knees simply unable to hold her up. It was the voice, nothing else. He just had that type of voice that would kick at something deep inside any woman. She had been able to think of little else since the emotional display the night before. Zinging as if she had downed a carafe of coffee all on her own, she had nibbled away the fingernails on her left hand the night before in penance for imagining herself wrapped in Adam's arms in Chris's place.

'How does a day of fresh air and sunshine grab you?' he asked.

With him? Unexpectedly that grabbed her in all the right places.

'Don't tease me like that,' she said.

She couldn't give him an outright *no way* as that would

only mean spending a day alone, nibbling away the fingernails on her right hand.

'This is no tease, I assure you,' he said, his voice typically unhurried. It was almost hypnotic.

Cara lay back on the bed and cradled the phone under her ear. 'So what did you have in mind?'

'We have been given permission from the powers that be to have a day outdoors.'

'But I thought the idea was to keep us out of the light so that we don't remember what day it is, what time of day, what our names are, where we really live...'

Adam's soft laughter reverberated down the line and Cara was glad she was lying down. The mellow sound turned her whole body to jelly.

'We will be under strict supervision, of course,' he assured her.

'Sounds kinky.'

Cara slapped her hand across her forehead. Where had that come from? She waited for his reply and she had to endure several moments of humiliated silence before it came.

'Wear comfortable clothes and sneakers and meet me downstairs in fifteen minutes.'

'What for?' Cara asked, but Adam had already rung off.

She stared at the phone for a moment before her adrenalin kicked in. Tearing her clothes off as she went, she ran into her closet to find her most comfortable clothes and her sneakers, her mind reeling with ideas of what Adam could have had in mind.

Outdoors. Supervised.

Whatever it was she was giddy with excitement, and was out the door in ten minutes flat, lathered in sunscreen, wide-brimmed hat on her head, more excited than she was prepared to admit.

* * *

As it turned out she was to spend the day with Adam, the majority of the television crew and half the staff from the hotel for a game of baseball in the private park next door to a suburban hotel owned by the same chain.

Cara couldn't play baseball to save her life. It took her enough daily effort to navigate high heels without having to master the necessary coordination to play a team sport. The best she could hope for was that she wouldn't trip over her laces and land face down in the dirt. But here she was, in her cut-off jeans, sleeveless top and sneakers, her wide-brimmed hat long since laid aside to accommodate the blue cap that showed her up as a being on the Blue TV Team as opposed to the Red Hotel Team. It was to be a battle to the death.

She stood out in right field, bent at the waist, hands on knees, legs shoulder-width apart, waiting for someone to hit the ball her way so she could make the split-second decision to duck and squeal, or have a go and fumble it in front of everyone. Hmm. Nail biting suddenly seemed like a rather pleasant way to spend a day.

'How you going, Cara?' Chris called out from second base.

She gave him a hearty salute and by his ringing laughter she figured he had guessed just how she was going.

Cara turned her attention back to the game at hand. She punched her glove a couple of times as she had seen the players on television do, then hunched over, resting her hands on her knees, preparing herself for whatever came her way.

Adam, the pitcher for their team, looking resplendent in cut-off track pants and a loose-fitting T-shirt, lazily threw the ball into the air and caught it in his free hand as he talked behind his glove with his catcher, Mickey the boom mike operator.

Then he sidled back onto the mound, his long, loping strides catching at Cara. He was so effortlessly sexy that it created an ache deep in her stomach. Who knew that beneath those layered suits there was a body like the one working before her? The back of his shirt was stuck to his broad torso. He had a great pair of legs, strong, muscled and tanned, and in his loose shorts he gave her a prime view of the best masculine behind she had ever set eyes on. And she had seen some hunks. Most men she styled were models or actors, and kept themselves fit through many waking hours spent at the gym. But nevertheless this guy was a notch above. He was broad, and strong, and tall and had a simply pinchable behind. And she had no doubt it was all natural.

As he prepared to pitch, Cara saw that his beautiful hands came with a matching pair of beautiful arms. They were sinewy, bronzed and shaped like those of a swimmer. Those gorgeous arms stretched and twisted and threw the ball with such amazing power and grace it slammed over the home plate with ease and precision.

'Cara, it's yours, babe,' Chris called out.

Cara stood up straight, shielding her eyes with her hand, to find the ball was bouncing raggedly across the ground her way. She sensed her team all turning, facing her as the batter rounded first base and kept on going to second.

She flicked a momentary glance at Adam and knew she shouldn't have. If the view from the back was something, the view from the front with his shirt stuck to his muscular chest, his dark, damp hair curling about his face, his mouth open to rake in great dragging breaths, his eyes bright from exercise, his chest rising and falling... It was too beautiful to believe.

Cataloguing his features this way was suddenly no professional habit. This had nothing to do with any sort of professional survival mechanism. She was fast becoming bewitched by the guy.

Clearing her throat, she dragged her gaze away and waited for the ball. It bounced wildly at the final moment but she caught it, awkwardly, with her forearms.

'Straight to me!' Chris called.

Cara shuffled it into her hands and threw with all her might, meaning the ball took two bounces to reach him at second base. But reach him it did, just before the batter rounded it into second. He was tagged. Third man out. First innings; the Red Hotel Team nil.

Cara couldn't believe it. She leapt into the air and let out a great whoop, then ran infield to meet up with her team who were all jogging to the bench ready to bat.

Adam waited on the mound until she had reached him, his eyes on her, all but ignoring the pats on the back he received from his passing team mates.

Cara slowed to a walk and they headed off the field together.

'Well done, Ms Marlowe.'

'Please. We were lucky it came straight to me.'

'I kind of thought you might be more mindful of your new manicure.'

Cara blinked. 'Did you now? Well, that shows how little you know about me, doesn't it, Mr Tyler? Though I am a girl who likes a good manicure, I am a girl who likes winning more.' Point made, she quickened her pace until she strode away from him.

Adam was getting used to watching her walk away. Her head was held high. Her short curly pony-tail bounced as she walked. She swayed almost saucily. But he knew she was no sportswoman. Her perfectly white sneakers had been the initial give-away.

His gaze travelled up from her sneakers. Up long, smooth legs, over her denim-clad hips, over her dainty waist, and a back held ramrod straight just for his benefit. She was a spitfire, this one. Too damn impudent for her own good. And she was dealing with someone who could give as good as he got in that department. Didn't she realise that?

He kind of liked the fact that maybe she did realise it, yet it didn't stop her for a second.

As she reached the bench she sat down with a fresh bottle of water and glanced back at him from beneath her cap. Her green eyes shot fire. And he was suddenly thankful she was on his team. In her cute little outfit, meant more for a leisurely picnic than a rough and tumble game, she was distracting enough being on the same team. She would be one heck of a troublesome opponent.

Who was he kidding? She had been one heck of a troublesome opponent from the moment she'd got the job. But also the most fun he'd had being at cross purposes with a woman.

Though there was a seat right next to her, he took a space at the other end of the bench and he could still feel the daggers she was shooting at him with her eyes. It made him smile.

Chris was up first.

'Pitch to him carefully, mate,' Jeff called out to the hotel team's pitcher. 'If he gets a black eye I'll sue you and your hotel for all you're worth.'

The pitcher lowered his ball, his eyes growing wide.

Jeff leant over to Adam and through his teeth said, 'They're toast!'

The pitcher all but threw underarm and Chris hit an easy double. Then a grinning Jeff followed with a single.

Adam was third man up. He shot a look Cara's way as

he walked to home plate but she was steadfastly looking anywhere but at him. His smile grew bigger.

Standing at the mound, he swung his bat several times to warm his shoulders. He then positioned himself ready for the pitch. He was kind of showing off and he knew exactly who for: a girl who admitted she liked to win. But they *were* on the same team so why play down his prowess? Why not help her get her wish? Adam set himself up to hit the hell out of the ball. The pitcher pitched. Adam swung. And he missed.

'Come on, Adam,' Jeff called out from first base. 'Don't sweat it. Swing and hit, buddy. Swing and hit.'

Adam felt his cheeks warm and he knew it wasn't the weak spring sunshine that was doing it.

He could all but sense Cara smirking at his back.

He couldn't help himself. He had to see it for himself. But when he flicked a glance over his shoulder he found she wasn't smirking: she was leaning forward, her elbows resting on her knees, her chin resting on her fingers, which she had positioned as a steeple. Her cheeks looked as warm as his felt.

And her eyes were not on his face, but lower. The woman had been checking out his butt! She blinked several times, then her gaze finally locked with his and she all but fell off her seat when she found he was watching her.

He turned away. Readied himself for the pitch. Swung. And missed. But it was not pride that stopped him that time, but the fact that his thoughts were anywhere but on the game. They were on the pink cheeks and bright, telling eyes of the compelling woman sitting behind him, and wondering where those telling eyes were focussed at that moment. He was used to women eyeing him up as if he were a prime rib, but this was different. Perhaps because it was unexpected. She'd given his ego enough of a bashing he had thought she was immune to his attractions. And the fact that she was not immune shook him up.

Adam squared his shoulders and focussed his attention on the game.

The pitcher smiled as he lined up. Smiled! As though Adam were some sort of lightweight and it was only a matter of time before he beat him.

Adam smiled back. *Come on, kid,* he thought. *Give me all you've got.*

The kid pitched. Adam swung. And connected. It was only a single. But he made it to first base with tremendous relief.

The next two batsmen were caught out. But the bases were still loaded.

Cara was up next. She stood. She picked up a bat between two fingers and Adam knew she had never held a baseball bat in her life.

She stood at home base and swung the bat in much the same way he had, and he knew she had no idea why she was doing it. It was adorable. Then she set her feet apart, lifted the bat, turned to face the pitcher and swallowed hard.

'Come on, Cara,' Chris called out. 'Easy does it.'

Jeff called out, clapping. 'Whack it for all you're worth.'

Adam could see her considering. Easy does it, or whack it for all she was worth. And this to a girl who was still unsure she was holding the correct end of the bat.

'Cara,' Adam called out and saw her eyes swing wildly his way. 'If you manage to even hit the ball I'll shout you a new manicure.'

Her mouth dropped open. Then her eyes narrowed, and she wiggled her bottom and adjusted her stance. Her determination was palpable.

The pitcher pitched and Cara's eyes clamped tight shut

as she whacked the ball with every ounce of strength in her slender arms. The ball shot between the pitcher and the short stop and bounced past second base. Jeff jumped to let it between his legs and then he took off.

Adam watched as Cara opened her eyes, shock that she had hit the ball evident in her wide eyes.

'Cara, run!' Adam called out. She nodded then ran, the bat still in her hot little hand. Adam took off, his gaze swinging back to home plate to see that Chris had made it home.

The centre fielder misfielded so Jeff was able to follow Chris home. Adam rounded it towards third, jogging backwards the last few steps as the fielder picked up the ball. He stopped, turned, and saw Cara had made it to first and had pressed on. She was running towards second, and the second baseman had taken up residence there, awaiting the incoming throw.

It was tight. As tight as a race could get. Cara looked up and he saw the moment she knew it was going to be tight. She put her head down and ran.

The noise from the Blue Team bench was deafening. The fielder threw the ball, the second baseman readied himself and Cara was within reach.

The ball curved through the air in a beautiful arc. Cara saw it coming and, mustering every ounce of determination, she tucked one knee beneath her and in an all encompassing swirl of dust, and a great echoing crack, took a magnificent slide into the base, taking out the fielder in the process until they ended up in a tangled pile of dirt and arms and legs.

CHAPTER SIX

EVERYONE rushed to second base, but Adam got there first. That crack had sounded too ominous for his liking. He slid to his knees, dragging the fielder from on top of Cara.

'Cara,' he called, his voice tearing from him painfully. He reached out to her but couldn't touch her, fearing he might hurt her. What if that crack had been one of her bones? Or, God forbid, her neck? 'Sweetheart, are you OK?'

Cara twisted about until she was on her knees herself. She was covered in dust from head to toe. Her cap had fallen off and bits of her hair had escaped from her ponytail. Finally unable to stand it any longer Adam ran furious hands over her head feeling for lumps, blood, anything that might mean that she was badly hurt.

'Are you hurt?' he asked.

She winced and his whole body clenched as she reached beneath her and pulled out half her bat. Adam found a thankful laugh rising in his throat as he realised it had been the splintering bat, which she had carried with her the whole way, and not any bones that had broken.

Finding nothing else wrong, he grabbed her face between his hands and looked deep into her eyes, and the joy that spread through him when he saw her eyes were lively and focussed was not something he wished to dissect.

Then she looked up at him and spat a clump of grass from her mouth. 'Was I safe?'

'Excuse me?'

'Was I safe? Did I get here first?'

Adam looked over to the second baseman who was back on his feet. He held out his empty hands. 'Never even had the ball,' the guy admitted.

Adam ran one hand down Cara's face, his thumb wiping away a smear of dirt from her pale cheek. 'You were safe, Cara. Safe but now a total mess.'

She shrugged. 'I don't mind. I was promised a manicure so tomorrow I'll be fine.'

'You are one surprising lady, Ms Marlowe.'

She beamed at him. Her teeth showing perfect white from within her dusty face. 'I can live with that.'

After the third innings, they sat down for lunch, everyone grabbing what they wanted from an array of cold meats and salads laid out on a picnic table. Cara made herself a huge ham roll, then sat down on a patch of grass under a large gum tree.

'Do you mind if I join you?'

Cara squinted up into Adam's face. He was shrouded in sunlight, his face seeming dark and ominous in the over-bright sunshine.

'Of course not, Cap'n.'

Cara shuffled over so he had room on her patch of grass without them having to sit too close. Ever since he had caught her staring, she'd felt an awareness pulsating between them that she did not wish to encourage.

'Having fun?' she asked.

He took a bite of his roll and nodded.

'Thanks for today,' she said.

He shot her a quick salute.

'The crew all look like little boys in a toy store. The idea of fresh air and sunshine appeal a heck of a lot more than four walls and weekend television.'

He watched her without expression and nodded again.

That was all she could take.

'I don't get it. You are purported to be this great communicator. One-time Australian Businessman of the Year, who can change any person's mind with the use of nothing but his verbal skills. A man who can charm women out of their...inhibitions. Yet I can *still* barely get you to string two words together.'

Adam chewed, and chewed, and chewed, and then swallowed. 'I had a mouthful of food,' he finally said.

Cara was sure she heard a hint of cheekiness in his voice, but by the time she looked at him through narrowed eyes he had already tucked into his next mouthful. Since clenching her hands would only mean that the contents of her roll would end up on her lap, she had to settle for clenching her toes in her sneakers.

Cara took another mouthful herself and was careful to swallow just before he did.

'That has not been the reason in the past,' she persisted.

He continued to chew several times before swallowing his food. 'If all a question requires is a yes or a no answer, that's all you're going to get from me.'

'It's really frustrating.'

Adam laughed. 'OK, then. What would you like to talk about?'

Cara opened her mouth but had nothing in particular to say.

'Come on. You ask, I'll answer. This is your big chance to partake of my renowned "verbal skills".'

His last words came to her almost as a purr and Cara racked her brain for something to say but her mind was rendered blank. The longer she struggled, the bigger Adam's smile became, until slowly, slowly he raised his roll to his mouth as a sign that her time was running out.

'So why telecommunications?' she finally blurted, the relief she felt ridiculous.

But Adam, as promised, lowered his roll and talked.

'That was all Chris. We went to uni together. He was the studious guy with his head always in a pile of books. I was the party guy at uni, my majors being girls and beer.'

Cara felt a funny kick in her stomach. It felt a heck of a lot like a jealous stab, which was insane. She continued eating while he talked in case it was merely hunger making her tummy feel so tight.

'But we were always friendly,' Adam continued. 'He even got me my first real job, selling mobile phones and accessories in his uncle's store on nights and weekends.'

She couldn't quite picture him working in a shopping centre hocking mobile-phone contracts to innocent passers-by. Though she had the feeling that if he took it upon himself to try, he could do it without breaking a sweat. Any woman caught in that resolute blue gaze would be locked in until he chose to let her loose.

But as far as she could tell he had chosen to let them loose every time thus far. At that thought, her tummy problems eased considerably.

'My way through college was already covered so I didn't need the job, but Chris insisted that it would be good for me, and he was right. Unless you have worked your butt off for under ten dollars an hour, there is no way you can create sellable products for people in exactly that socio-economic bracket.'

'Born with a silver spoon in your mouth?' Cara asked, already knowing the answer but aware of a need to know how he felt about the fact.

'Diamond-encrusted platinum, actually,' he said with a wry smile. 'And you?'

'A wooden spoon, I'm afraid.' *And at least one foot.*

Adam blinked, sudden humour lurking deep beneath his dark blue eyes. 'And who is your mobile phone carrier?' he asked.

'You guessed it. Revolution Wireless,' Cara admitted.

'You are my bread and butter,' he said with a charming smile.

And the smile did it. Though he was just highlighting the fact that she was struggling and he was stratospherically wealthy because of people like her, his smile still made her toes unclench and her tummy flip over on itself. Her tummy needed a good talking to!

Cara managed to stop herself from snapping at him that she already had one of his bloody phones and he didn't need to sweet-talk her into making him more money. But she did say, 'I'll have you know I earn more than ten dollars an hour, buddy.'

He held up his hands in submission, his charming smile breaking into outright laughter. 'And I'm sure you're worth every cent.'

Cara could not help but smile either. So he was rich. She wasn't. There was no point in arguing the fact. It was empirical. Unchangeable. And such a nasty thing to get worked up over. She of all people should remember that.

'One day after work,' Adam continued, 'Chris approached me. He told me he had a business plan and only with the two of us working together could it be achieved. And I was hooked.'

'What was his plan?'

Adam smiled. 'It was fairly detailed and I dozed off through half of it, but when he hit the point about becoming a millionaire on my own by the age of twenty-five, I shut up and listened. He had me. He says that I'm the salesman of the crew, but he sure knew what would hook me that day.'

Abba had it figured out long ago. 'Money, money, money'—everything came down to money. But who was she to argue? The thought of living comfortably took up most of her waking moments, so why shouldn't Adam be the same? Her dad always said money made the world go around and he was right. Even if on the flipside it could turn people against each other, and make them bitter and cynical into the bargain.

Cara bit into her roll to show that the conversation was over. She could feel Adam watching her but she'd said and heard enough to think maybe she shouldn't have demanded so much information from him in the first place.

They sat for several long moments in conjoined silence. Keeping her eyes straight ahead, Cara tried hard to focus on watching the sunshine send dappled shadows through the leaves of the big old gum tree and listening to the crickets singing in the nearby underbrush.

Then finally Adam spoke. 'Was that what you were after?'

Cara sent him a sideways glance accompanied by a hasty nod. But he wasn't finished.

'Or were you hoping I might try to charm *you* out of *your* inhibitions?'

Cara swallowed too fast, and coughed and spluttered in response. She shot to her feet as gracefully as she could, her eyes searching wildly for an escape route.

'Looks like the game's about to begin again. So…see you there.'

And then she strode away as fast as her sneakers would carry her.

The rest of the game went pretty much the same. Though the hotel guys made a brief comeback in the next-to-last innings, the TV Team won easily: ten runs to three.

Everyone hopped back in the hotel bus in high spirits. Cara was the last one inside and the only spare seat was across the aisle from Adam.

She gave him a short smile before sitting down. Although she was well aware of every rise and fall of his chest, every flicker of his eyelids, every shuffle of his large frame in the small seat, she still got a fright when his hand landed upon her knee.

'You're bleeding,' he said.

She looked down at her calf where a trickle of dried blood was smeared. She watched in shocked silence as Adam rolled up the leg of her cut-off jeans to reveal a pretty nasty scrape on her knee. But Cara was less aware of that than of his hands creating a warm rush that reached deep within her stomach.

'Didn't you know you were hurt?' Adam asked, his brow furrowed in concern.

Cara shrugged. She was sore all over from that stupid proud slide of hers, and, though her knee had stung ever since, it was one of many bumps and bruises that would only look worse by the next day.

'Wait here,' he said before leaving her to walk up to the front of the bus to grab the first-aid kit from the driver.

When he returned, Cara held out her hands to take it but Adam ignored her. He sat down in his seat, his legs stretched out into the aisle so that he was facing her. He gently dragged her knee so that it was settled between his.

'Oh, no, you don't,' Cara insisted, all but scrambling onto her seat as far away as she could get. 'I can do this myself.'

Adam shot her a look from beneath his dark lashes that shut her up fast. It also caused the warmth in her stomach to spread to the rest of her body.

'You are not going anywhere near this scrape with those

filthy hands,' Adam insisted, going through the bits and bobs until he found some antiseptic, cotton wool and a bandage.

Cara hadn't really noticed how dirty she was. Compared with her just-as-dirty arms, her hands hadn't looked particularly bad, but, sitting in the clean air-conditioned bus, she suddenly realised how gritty she felt. Her hair was stuck to the back of her neck, her feet felt damp with sweat, and she could even taste dirt in her mouth. She must have looked frightful.

But then Adam touched her knee with a patch of antiseptic-covered gauze and she forgot all about how she must have looked as a sharp pain took the place of all other sensations, good or bad.

'Yowza!' she shouted.

Adam looked up, his spare hand moving to rest gently on her thigh.

'Did I hurt you? Am I too hard?'

He was doing the furrowed-brow thing again and she had to swallow to wet her dry throat. Besides which, his hand was still resting on her thigh. Gently. On her thigh, for goodness' sake! Pain gone. Good sensation back.

She shook her head. 'No,' she croaked. 'It's fine.'

Adam's brow smoothed out as he looked deep into her eyes. He didn't believe her for a second and she could see that he wanted to make sure she was not hurting in any way. She looked back, hoping beyond hope that he saw none of her deep awareness shining from her eyes. 'Really, Adam. It was just cold. That's all.'

He nodded shortly then went back to his job, which entailed running soft cotton pads lightly over her knee. Slowly. Softly. What was he doing being so tender? Adam was meant to be unsympathetic, gruff and unperturbed. Not delicate, and comforting, so much so that the sting was soon nothing compared with the sensation raging through her at his deft touch from his beautiful fingers. Those fingers that were as sure and as warm and as skilled as she had imagined.

This was bad. The last thing she needed was to find herself thinking such disturbing and ultimately distracting thoughts when she was meant to be focussed on her job. Maya had warned her to be good, but her imagination was being very, very naughty.

All the same Cara watched Adam's face as he went about his job. He was silent with concentration. Every fibre of his being was focussed totally on the task at hand. She had never met anyone who could focus so fully. Her mind was never settled. No matter which job she was on, she was thinking ahead to the next three. Yet this guy, with millions at stake in every conversation he had, could leave all that behind just so that her knee would be clean and germ-free.

He pulled out a bandage and wrapped it neatly across the scrape. Mission accomplished, his gaze travelled back to meet hers. There was a smile in his eyes. Simple pride at a job well done. What could she do but smile back?

'Thanks, Adam. That was very kind of you. Unnecessary, but kind.'

He rested both hands about her calf, encircling the width as he had encircled his baseball bat earlier, with familiarity and finesse.

'We can't have this leaving a scar,' he said. 'Your legs are too nice for that.'

She raised one eyebrow, careful not to let him see how his words and his touch were affecting her. 'Are you flirting with me, Adam Tyler?' she asked, trying to keep the conversation light.

His smile grew, kicking into a grin. 'What if I am?'

Now that was a question loaded with trouble and she had

been incredibly stupid to invite it. So it was up to her to bring it to a close.

'Then maybe you should stop.'

His smile stayed, but his hands began to move, slowly travelling down the length of her leg.

'All work and no play—'

'Means that Cara will take home pay.'

His hands stopped, meaning Cara's breathing could re-start.

Their gazes clashed. Held. Fought a battle of wills all on their own. Cara ached to look away but she knew she couldn't. This was no time to seem coy. No time to seem unsure. She did not want some sort of holiday fling with this guy—this guy with the sort of strong, sure hands that could take a woman's breath away. This job meant the world to her, and nothing and nobody was going to jeopardise that. No matter how unexpectedly considerate and unquestionably sexy and...

The bus suddenly slowed.

'We're home, guys!' Jeff called out and the crew groaned as one.

Cara and Adam still stared.

'But think of the hot shower and buffet dinner that awaits,' Jeff yelled, and the crew cheered as one.

Then finally Adam blinked. Slowly. But it was enough. His hands eased away, leaving a zinging trail of heat as they slipped off her leg. And as the crew tumbled down the aisle of the bus Cara was left to wonder if the strange, heady encounter had all been a heat-induced dream. Maybe she had concussion after all. Whatever she had, it made her feel hot and cold and breathless all at once.

That hot shower, followed by dinner *alone* in her room, sounded like just what the doctor ordered.

*   *   *

The next day, Cara spent the morning working hard following Chris and the girls around the glorious Melbourne Zoo. She primped, she preened, and she even helped out with the girls when she found the chance, anything to feel as though she was contributing as much as she possibly could. So by Sunday afternoon, happily tired from a hard day's work, she felt as if she had actually earned a little down time lazing by the pool.

After a quick refreshing dip, she was back in the shade of a large beach umbrella, lathered in sunscreen, damp hair tucked up into her wide-brimmed hat, and sheer white shirt covering her black bikini.

Lying on a sun lounger, she stared contentedly upwards, watching for long minutes as the small puffs of cotton wool clouds drifted across the wide expanse of beautiful blue Melbourne sky. The fat green leaves on the banana palms behind her rustled heavily in the warm spring breeze.

She mused over the fact that the night before was the first Saturday Night Cocktails get-together she had ever missed since the tradition began. While Kelly had been honeymooning, she and Gracie had kept up the tradition in her absence, meeting at Cara's for nights of cocktails and gossip. And the night before, tossing and turning in bed, she'd known if they had come together as usual she would have been the one asking for advice, not the one giving it. But by morning she was seriously glad the secrecy of the show had meant she'd had to forgo any meeting with Gracie.

How would she have explained her concerns, anyway?

'There's this guy. Don't know him well, or at all, really. Super rich. Dates models. Has eyes that I am sure can see right through me, and hands that make me blush every time I think of them. Glares at me more often than not but called me sweetheart when he thought I was hurt.'

No way. If she had said all of that Gracie would have raised one perfectly groomed eyebrow and told her to get a grip, or on the flipside would have goaded her incessantly and called her sweetheart in every conversation they had for a week.

Nope. Cara was seriously glad that, this weekend of all weekends, Saturday Night Cocktails had been postponed. Now she could rest easy that her disquiet had gone no further than her own sleepy head.

Instead Cara planned on enjoying her afternoon off spent with a book she had borrowed from the hotel library.

'Is this seat taken?' The deep, familiar voice that had invaded her sleepless night now invaded her happy alone thoughts.

She opened one eye to find Adam looking down upon her through a pair of dark sunglasses. 'What if I said it was?'

'Then I would say they should have left a towel upon the chair to bar it, else someone consider it fair game.'

Considering the provocative smile that kicked at the corner of his mouth, Cara felt the sudden urge to cover herself in a towel too. Their fleeting flirty conversations of the day before came back with such a rush she felt as if they were still mid-sentence—as though a whole day hadn't passed since they had last laid eyes on each other.

She wished she hadn't encouraged him to talk more in the first place. He seemed to have quite taken to the idea, and every second sentence that came out of his mouth seemed to be intended to charm her out of her indiscretions. She and her impatient ways.

Having had enough of him glaring down at her she fluttered a hand at the empty sun lounger beside her. 'It's all yours. I was just leaving anyway.'

As Cara made to sit up and gather her belongings Adam

rested a hand on her shoulder. She felt its warmth all the way to her curling bare toes.

'No, you weren't,' he drawled. 'Just stay, Cara. I promise I won't disturb you.'

Ha! He had no choice on that matter. That was the problem. But Cara did as she was told, sinking back against the chair more to shrink from his enclosed palm than anything else.

He dragged the white towel from across his shoulders and threw it down upon the lounger. It was only then that Cara realised he was wearing nothing but swim trunks. She looked away, hard though it was to drag her eyes from such a sight.

But when he ambled over to the water, her gaze was invariably drawn to him once more. He shook out his long limbs, the muscles in his back and arms clenching and stretching as he went. What a specimen. He was a supremely built man. Tall, sculptured, strong, tanned. Cara knew that beside him she would look like a scrawny, underfed, indoorsy waif. No wonder he was always photographed arm in arm with models, and Amazonian ones at that. Any other woman would be engulfed by his presence.

He dived in the pool with a sleek splash and it knocked Cara from her panting reverie. Now he was out of her eyesight, his presence only felt through the light slap of water as he swam lengths of the pool, Cara purposely lost herself within the pages of her book.

'I can't believe it,' Adam said half an hour later.

Cara lowered her book to squint at him. He was standing before her, dripping onto the pool tiles, his black swim trunks plastered to his lean hips, his torso sleek with water, his hair raked back and darkened from the pool water, his eyelashes clumped and spiky, his dark blue eyes bright and clear.

And for the life of her Cara could not remember what he had just said. 'I'm sorry?'

He pointed. 'That book. Where on earth did you find it?'

Aah. She had a good long look at the cover, which read, 'Unauthorised: Three Generations of Tylers'.

She grinned. 'Hotel library.'

'Meaning it was a book some discerning guest left behind in disgust,' Adam said, his voice deep with chagrin.

'Mmm. Makes sense to me.'

Adam raked a hand through his wet hair and flicked the gathered water droplets at her. She squealed, shielding herself with the hardcover.

'Why are you reading that trash?' he asked as he reached for his towel and dried himself down.

Cara half wished he wouldn't do that in front of her. But then she half wished he would do it in front of her for a good long time.

'Oh, I don't know. I was looking for something light-weight to read on my afternoon off.'

He stopped drying, swung the towel onto the sun lounger and lay his long frame upon it. His head turned her way, his deep blue eyes no longer clear, back to being dark and unfathomable. 'Lightweight, eh?' he said.

'Well, the subject matter is, of course, very heavy and important,' she said with a grin, 'but the manner in which it is presented is…lightweight to say the least.'

'Mmm,' he growled. 'So I have been told.'

'You haven't read it?'

'Hell, no.'

'Why not? It's a riot. Here, let me quote. This is from the chapter named: "The Son and Heir". That's you,' she qualified.

The smile Adam shot back was distinctly lacking in mirth.

'"*Stricken from an early age by his father's numerous nuptials and infamous infidelities, young Adam Tyler, son and heir, seemed intent not to follow in his father's large footsteps, choosing instead to date prolifically, not marry, and thus to keep his own self-made fortune intact. And yet the ladies in his life have been abundant and encumbered.*" See, I didn't make this stuff up about your infamy with buxom blondes.'

Cara looked up to find Adam staring at the sky, his jaw set tight. No wonder he was so protective of Chris, she thought. And of himself. His 'history with relationships' that Chris had once thrown at him was hardly littered with giggles and sunshine. Had his father's less-than-fine example numbed him to the possibility of enjoying a real relationship?

'Give me that,' Adam ordered, his hand suddenly shooting out to grab at the book. But Cara was quick off the mark. She shrugged out of his way, squirming and turning from his grabbing hand.

Adam sprang to his feet and, sensing failure, Cara did the same, rolling off the other side, her hat falling off her head and her air-dried curls tumbling from their makeshift constraint. They faced each other with her chair between them, their chests rising and falling in tandem, Cara with the book clutched tight to hers.

'Give it to me,' Adam ordered, his voice ominous.

'Or else what? You'll throw me in the pool?'

Adam shot a quick glance in the direction of the shimmering aqua depths. Then he turned to her with a lopsided smile that would have done strange things to her stomach if her pumping adrenalin had not already done the trick.

And this time, though he didn't say a word, he didn't need to.

'Don't you dare,' Cara whispered.

'Then don't tempt me, Cara.' His low, rumbling voice and his strong body spoke of all sorts of temptations that should have sent Cara running to her room.

'Give me the book and we both win,' he said.

Her pulse raced and she couldn't back down. 'No.'

His smile broadened. 'No?'

Letting temptation take rein, Cara again said, 'No.'

'Fine.'

His gaze raked over her body, which was trembling from an adrenalin overdose. She pictured her messy curls, her arms clamped over her chest, the sheer white shirt that stopped at her hips, leaving her black bikini bottom and bare legs available to his raking glance. She had no idea what was going through his mind, but no matter what it was she was struck still as a statue. But then when his hot gaze landed upon her knee it stopped. Cara followed the direction of his eyes and saw the scrape he had tended to the day before. It looked pretty raw. As did the massive bruise on her thigh that had come up overnight.

His gaze shot back to her face and she was shocked to see the raw alarm etched there. All evidence of playtime gone, he took a step around the sun lounger but she flinched, clasping the book to herself ever tighter.

He slowed, but kept on coming. 'Cara, don't be ridiculous. I'm not throwing you in the pool now. Just let me look at you.'

Cara stood stock-still as he rounded the chair and came to her side, his hands held in front of him as though to calm a startled deer.

'That bruise is just insane. Have you seen a doctor?'

She shook her head.

He reached out as though to touch it and Cara jumped back, the thought of those warm fingers running down her thigh sending her adrenal glands into overdrive.

'Don't tell me Jeff won't let you see a doctor,' he growled. 'If they won't bring in someone from the outside I'll sure have something to say about it.' His gaze whipped from her to flick to the hotel-suite windows high above them.

Sensing that he was about to scale the building to get to Jeff, Cara reached out and took him by the arm to garner his attention. His gaze swung her way. She could not fathom its intensity.

'Adam, please. I'm fine. It's a bruise. That's what happens when a human throws themselves at an expanse of hardened dirt. The human invariably comes off second-best. And it looks worse than it feels, I promise. If I bump into something, which I do often, I bruise. This, though larger than normal, is nothing unusual.'

Adam swallowed as his gaze once more sought out the black and yellow expanse. How Cara wished she were fully dressed. Having anyone stare so closely at one's bare thighs was never a pleasant occurrence, and having Adam in all his perfect athletic glory do so felt more uncomfortable than usual. His gaze was so focussed she could feel it scorching her bare skin. It was too much.

Her hand moved from his lovely bicep to take him by the chin so she could physically stop him from staring at her legs. 'Adam. I'm fine. OK?'

After several moments of intense concentration he nodded and she could feel the light stubble on his chin move against her fingertips. Suddenly aching to run her fingers over his cheeks and mouth to learn their texture, she pulled her hand away. Adam grabbed at it before she could get away, his long fingers easily encircling her skinny wrist.

He then used his grip as leverage, pulling her closer to him. Caught as she was in his dilated gaze, she could do little but acquiesce.

'Adam…' she started.

'Shh.'

She shushed.

He brought her hand around behind him so that it was locked against his back and her hips were flush against his. She could feel the smooth hardness of his waist along her forearm. Her breathing slowed to match his, until it was leisurely and lingering.

Then just as Cara all but gave into the idea that this big, gorgeous man was actually going to kiss her, the big gorgeous man's other hand reached up and grabbed the book from her slackened grasp.

Letting go, he sprung to the other side of the sun lounger, and out of her reach. He scooped up his towel and flung it over his shoulder.

'Count yourself lucky, Cara,' he said, his dark eyes flashing all the warning she needed. 'I might not be so noble next time.'

Mouth tingling with thwarted expectations, Cara watched him go, having no idea if he meant that next time their lips might meet as she had so much wanted them to do, or that she would end up in the pool.

Either way she thought she'd got away pretty lightly.

CHAPTER SEVEN

MONDAY, during the Luna Park date, Cara was again able to work herself ragged, but only because Adam had thankfully made himself scarce. Chris mentioned something about phone calls and workloads and Cara thanked her lucky stars that she was afforded the time to concentrate on her job.

But the day was all she was given. That night, as Adam once more accompanied her and Chris in their limo, it took a concerted effort to act as though everything were hunky-dory, even though her pulse beat more rapidly every time she glanced his way.

'How are you holding up, buddy?' she asked Chris.

'Pretty well.'

'Good.' She patted his knee. 'You are doing just fine. Do you know what they have in store for you tonight?'

'Karaoke,' he said, his face pale.

'I take it you're no virtuoso?'

'I don't even sing in the shower.'

'Think of it as an adventure.'

At the word adventure she saw Chris turn an even more sickly shade of green.

'The roller coaster at Luna Park was bad enough. Stick a microphone in front of me and I will be physically ill. I can't even do any public speaking, can I, Adam? That's why I roped Adam into Revolution Wireless in the first place—he can do anything in public without breaking a sweat.'

The word 'anything' conjured up all sorts of bad, bad

images that Cara had to squash deep down inside her impertinent imagination.

Concentrating hard on Chris, she took hold of his hands. 'Chris, most people live their lives within walls. Within confines. Within boundaries. But you have been given an opportunity to branch out, to try new things, test yourself. This is a privilege and if I were you I would go out there and sing like you've never sung before. Don't look back on this time with any regrets. OK?'

The car remained silent and Cara wondered if she had pushed too far. Then Chris nodded as though he were letting the idea wash over him, letting it seep inside his suit until it became a part of his armour plating.

By the time the limo pulled up to the bar, Chris was out the door, eager as a schoolboy to get onto the playground.

'Nice speech you made in there,' Adam said as he helped Cara out of the car.

She drew her hand from his as soon as was polite. 'Thanks.'

'What would you do in his situation?'

She shot him a sideways glance. 'Hide in the ladies' room all night. Without a doubt.'

Adam laughed. It was deep and resonant and infectious. 'Not such a bad plan. But it was still a nice speech. Chris will have a much better night because of it.'

Cara shrugged. 'It's my job. It's up to me to have the character be the person the producers need him to be. And Chris will be a much better hero for our show if he goes out there and has fun.'

'So that's why you gave him the pep talk? All for the good of the show?'

'Mmm hmm.'

'Sure it was.' Adam slipped an arm about her torso and

gave her one quick squeeze. 'You are all class, Ms Marlowe.'

When he let go and went into the club, Cara stood stock-still and stared at his departing back. It was ridiculous. Her whole body was shaking. One small, chummy hug and he had her nerve endings rioting for more. And the funny thing was, it didn't feel like flirting any more.

He had called her classy. And she knew instinctively it was not in the same joking manner her friends used the word. It was a real compliment and he was not a guy who gave compliments easily. It felt like a mark of…friendship. She felt as if she were skimming across the water in a speedboat, shooting through the levels of a relationship, all too fast. While on the job. With a guy who did not know the meaning of the word relationship.

Cara knew that Adam, son and heir to a history of failed relationships, had no such intentions. If he saw her as anything it was as a quick bedding before breakfast. And she had the funny feeling that, though it would be a pretty darned nice experience on its own, she would not come out of it with the same nonchalance. He did things to her senses that gave her fair warning not to take it any further than it had already gone. As such, for the sake of her job, for the sake of her plans, for the sake of her inexperienced heart, it would be up to her to nip it in the bud before it went any further.

When Cara made it inside the club, the show was up and running already. Cara looked around and found Adam. She gravitated to him, as she always did. There was one other seat at his table and it had already been pulled out. For her.

Then and there she decided to do her bud-nipping later. After allowing herself to enjoy his complicated company under the cover of forgiving darkness for a little while longer.

She sat, and gave Adam a small smile. He smiled back. And in the darkness of the club, she felt her inexperienced heart flip over on itself.

A couple of hours later the party was in full swing. Chris and the girls had enjoyed a sumptuous Japanese dinner, including enough sake to lubricate their vocal cords. And then the karaoke machine lit up, a spotlight showcasing the microphone that stood alone and lonely mid-stage.

'Here we go,' Cara said under her breath and Adam saw her hands clenching and unclenching upon the table.

He reached out and placed a hand over hers, their fingers meshing together, hoping to settle her. But she only stiffened all the more. She was desperately nervous for Chris; he could feel it. Sincerely worried for him. Sincerely. That was not a word Adam had had cause to use before when referring to a woman in his life. He gently massaged her palm until he could tell she was relaxing.

He had reason enough to keep her happy, to keep her comfortable, to sit with her, to tell her when he thought she had done a good thing. He had to be nice to her for Chris's sake. For Chris and for the sake of the company.

But even as he thought it he realised how ridiculous it sounded.

There was no way he was gravitating to the woman every time she was in the room for *the good of the company*. He was gravitating towards her because he was caught in her gravitational force. He was like a moon spinning around her planet. The day spent making phone calls and shouldering a workload he could just as easily have shuffled onto someone else proved that.

Where she was, there he wanted to be. Not because he wanted to keep her in check, or because she was the life of the party. Not just because he felt an uncontrollable need to touch her whenever he had the chance, but because he also felt a deep-seated need to protect her. And that was the worst reason he could possibly have.

Disentangling his fingers, he stood, his chair scraping against the polished wood floor, earning several severe glances from the television crew.

'Where are you going?' Cara whispered, her husky voice washing over him in the darkness, and he felt something tugging deep within him at her concern.

There was only so much sincerity he could take before it began to make a subversive impact, so he didn't answer her, merely walked away, not caring about the shaft of light he let into the set as he stormed from the room and outside.

He took off up the street, feeling the need for fresh air. He needed something other than the heady, disturbing scent of flowers that seemed to have filled his nostrils and addled his brain ever since she had joined them in the car.

It was intoxicating. He was intoxicated. There could be no other explanation for the sensations creeping through his body and mind. No explanation. No excuse. No reason to let them get any further. He was not the type to fall prey to such intoxication. He'd had his last drink of that delicious scent and he had to give it up before he became addicted.

'You are being absurd,' he said out loud. 'Control yourself, man. You'll be out of this Petri dish in a week and a half, and then back out into the big wide world where a dozen other perfumes, much more sophisticated than hers will grab you in just the same way. And you'll want to grab them right back.'

Back in the karaoke bar, Cara stayed put. The suddenness of Adam's departure played on her and kept her from paying full attention to the show, but, though she had wanted to leap from her chair and follow Adam, she knew Chris needed her.

After several songs had been sung, Chris turned to Maggie and begged her to give it a go. Maggie had been sitting back quietly, her face as pale as Chris's had been in the car, while the other women had sung and danced and writhed about the stage for Chris's benefit.

'Come on, Maggie,' Chris insisted. 'I know most of these girls can sing like angels, but I'm no Pavarotti. Give it a go. You'll feel like a million bucks afterwards.'

Cara watched as Chris smiled at Maggie, his face aglow with confidence and something else again, a need to shield the girl, to make her feel safe, to overcome his own embarrassment to protect her from hers.

He took her by the hand and led her to the mike. 'You pick the song,' he offered, 'anything you like.'

She nodded, her long blonde hair falling over her shoulders, her bright blue eyes so wide, but trusting, since she had her hand in his.

And Cara knew that, no matter the great speech she had given, Chris had never been more in control than now. Now that he had to be brave for someone more fearful of public humiliation than he was. And though Cara knew Maggie was no country hick as she joked, she looked as if she had never held a microphone in her life.

Chris picked it up for her, put it into her hands and then moved to sit with the other girls.

The first strains of her song began, and Maggie looked wildly out into the crowd beyond the bright lights. Cara stood and moved beside the main camera in the middle of the set. Maggie's gaze flicked straight to her and there was a glimmer of recognition. Cara grinned widely and gave the girl two thumbs up.

Maggie brightened immeasurably, then said into the mike, 'Practice makes perfect, right?'

Cara looked over to Chris, who was grinning at Maggie proudly, and though all the other girls were doing their dandiest to grab his attention, he only had eyes for the one on stage.

'So here goes,' Maggie said, 'the musical stylings of Maggie O'Laughlan. Seen for the first time outside of third-grade choir. Hold onto your seats.'

Then, with a big wink at Chris that had him leaning forward and watching her as though she were the greatest thing ever to hold a mike, she serenaded him with the most off-key yet passionate rendition of 'Stand By Your Man' that anyone had ever heard. And it brought the house down. The cast, the crew, even the waiters gave her a standing ovation. And in the end Maggie fell, exhausted, mortified and exhilarated, into Chris's waiting arms.

Cara turned to look into the smiling faces of the crew and found Adam had returned. He was lurking in the dark doorway, leaning on the wall, his arms and ankles crossed and he was the only one in the place not smiling.

She wondered what on earth could have him looking so sullen. But since he was so decidedly staring her way, and not at the tableau before her, she knew without a doubt it had something to do with her.

Her stomach tightened in response. It wasn't nerves. It wasn't hunger. It was awareness. Pure, unadulterated, sexual awareness.

He was watching her as a tiger watched its prey and she was petrified that, if the time came, she wouldn't run for her life. She would bare her neck, ready for the kind of torture she just knew his attentions would impart. Sweet, delicious, mind-numbing torture.

When the next song started, Cara broke free of Adam's

eye contact and turned to face the singers. And there she stayed for the remainder of the shoot, her feet planted, her legs shaking, her whole body stiff with the pressure of holding her ground and not turning to seek out the one person she knew she should not want to seek out.

Especially under the veil of forgiving darkness that she had found so secretly comforting not long before.

Tuesday morning, Cara stood atop the grassy lawn of the Flemington Racecourse, level with the starting line, a betting slip clutched in her hot palm, her spare hand shielding her eyes from the bright sunshine.

'Come on, number eight!' Cara cried out, her silver bangles clinking as she bounced up and down on her tiptoes to see over the dozens of heads in between her and the magnificent racehorses rounding the straight.

She had almost left her strappy white shoes behind on a number of occasions, the spiky heels all but disappearing into the moist turf with each step. And though the hat she had hastily created the night before—a simple conglomeration of mesh, white satin, a few feathers and netting, cocked jauntily to the side—matched her black and white lace dress perfectly, it created no shade whatsoever and she knew her nose would be spattered with freckles by the end of the day.

'Go, you good thing. Bring Papa home the bacon!' Jeff added, leaping up and down at her side.

Cara watched as both their hopes and dreams faded when number eight came home somewhere in the middle of the pack.

'Oh, well,' Jeff said, his frown turning upside down quick smart, 'at least he didn't come last. We are improving.'

'That we are,' Cara agreed. 'The odds are obviously on our side. By the time the Melbourne Cup comes around we're sure to come home with a win.'

Jeff nodded, satisfied. Then his finger moved to his right ear and Cara knew a message was being beamed down to him through his hidden earpiece. 'The girls are here. Is Chris ready?'

'Just about. I'll go make sure.' Cara headed to the back of their private marquee to find Chris, who was secreted away in his own little air-conditioned mini tent.

'Howdy, Chris.'

Chris turned, his face relaxing instantly at the sight of her. She leaned in, gave him a big kiss on the cheek, then continued to run both hands down his jacketed arms.

'How you feeling, buddy?'

'Fine.'

'Only fine? Because you are looking absolutely divine. Those ladies are going to go gaga when you walk out there looking so damn fine.'

She shuffled in behind him, her arms around his neck fixing his tie with adept hands, so they were both looking in the full-length mirror. She gave him a wink and a solid grin and felt her job was done when he smiled back.

It was only when her gaze moved from his reflection to her own that she saw they were not alone. She spun to face the man sitting quietly on a chair in the corner.

'Adam,' she said, her voice breathier than she would have liked. 'I didn't see you there.'

'That's the way he likes it, I'm afraid,' Chris scoffed. 'He would rather be the silent witness, looking down upon us all, than be in the game himself. Isn't that right, Adam?'

'Who am I to disagree?' he said, his face its usual hidden self.

'That surprises me,' Cara said, talking to Chris but with her gaze firmly fixed on the man sitting so casually in the chair. Maybe this was the perfect opportunity to call him out. To set some ground rules using Chris as an unknowing chaperon. 'From what I have heard and read, I would have thought Adam was a player.'

'Oh, he does well enough with the ladies. But they never seem to stick around too long.'

'Hmm. And why would that be, do you think?'

Cara could feel the heat emanating from Adam, even at her safe distance. His energy levels were growing exponentially as they talked about him. She just knew that he was dying to tell them both to lay off, but that would mean breaking down his permanent air of indifference.

'Well,' Chris said, 'that would be because our young friend has no intention of letting them stick around too long. The last of the confirmed bachelors, is our Adam.'

She remembered the passage she had read about in the 'Unauthorised' book. A guy from a broken home. A guy whose father had flaunted his lovers all his life. She had heard the reasons for his indifference to settling down too many times from enough sources not to believe it.

But the fire pulsing from those blue eyes became too much for Cara. She had the distinct feeling if she pushed much further she might get burnt. She turned away, bringing her attentions back to an easier target.

'Unlike you, hey, Chris?'

'Absolutely. I'm lookin' for love in all the right places.'

'That's my boy.'

'So, how about you, Cara?' Chris asked. 'Is there a man on the outside, avidly awaiting your return?'

Cara sensed a shift in Adam's posture. She flicked a glance his way and found he had uncrossed his legs and was leaning forward with his elbows resting on his knees. He wanted to know the answer and he was showcasing the fact. And now was the time to let him know it was never going to be any of his business.

'No, there's not, Chris. But I guess you could call me the last of the confirmed bachelorettes.'

'Really? That seems a dreadful pity. A girl like you could make some man very happy. Don't you agree, Adam?'

'Or not, as the case may be,' Cara bit off before Adam had the chance to even think about framing an answer. 'So long as I am not making someone out there unhappy, then that's enough for me. Besides, I am a woman with very specific plans for my future, and the last thing I need is something or someone coming along and messing up those plans.'

'What plans could a romantic interest mess up, do you think, Adam?' Chris said, his expression playful.

'Maybe she wants to be Miss Australia,' Adam said.

Cara shot him her most disparaging glare. 'You got me in one. I wanna be a beauty queen.'

'You'd get my vote.'

That shut Cara up quick smart. She turned back towards safer waters. 'OK, Chris. Enough mucking about. It's time to roll.'

She smoothed down the shoulders of Chris's jacket, flicked practised fingers through his hair and straightened the flower in his buttonhole. With a soft click of her cheek, she gave Chris a big smile.

'Looks like I'll be on clean-up duty for the rest of the day. I'll be following after those women out there wiping up their drool.'

Chris grimaced.

Jeff poked his head in the tent. 'OK, sports fans. Let's do it.'

Cara spun Chris on the spot and with two hands in the middle of his back gave him a nice shove towards the door flap. Once outside in the light of day, Chris was no longer hers as he disappeared into the swarming crew.

Cara felt Adam sidle up beside her.

'Looks like it's just you and me again,' he said.

Cara shrugged, more to give herself the chance to shake off the same old strain that always came upon her when he was so close.

Obviously telling him and herself the attraction resonating between them would come to no good simply wasn't working. It was like throwing a thimbleful of water on a bushfire. So then and there she made a decision to befriend the enemy, hoping it would make him less unnerving. Less intriguing. Less affecting. She would treat him as a mate, in the hopes it would make him as likely to sweep her off her feet as Jeff. Perish the thought!

'Looks that way,' she said, looping an arm through his. 'So I guess we'll have to bear it with what grace we can. Come on, you can buy me a drink.'

'It's an open bar,' he said, his feet planted, his tone even more stoic than usual.

She had no choice but to look him in the eye. 'The sun is shining. It's the Melbourne Cup. We are in a private tent, being waited on by men with weird food and goldfish bowls on their trays, so I am looking to take advantage and have an all-round fabulous day. Are you going to work with me here or not?'

His cool expression finally melted and Cara was rewarded with a hint of one of those rare, thus all the more enjoyed for the having, smiles.

And the reaction it caused in her stomach was almost enough for her to wish she could take back her little rant and keep to the other side of the tent alone all day. Almost.

'OK, boss,' he said, tucking her hand more securely through his arm. 'An all-round fabulous day coming up.'

*   *   *

When the big race came, the crowd moved forward as one. The Melbourne Cup had begun. Every person in Australia stopped what they were doing, turned to their televisions or their radios or the racecourse in front of them. Every person in the country stopped, watched and screamed their lungs out.

Every person except Adam, whose eyes remained steadfastly locked onto the back of the woman in the black and white dress, leaping about amidst the crowd of cast and crew before him.

She had been talking to him earlier, when she was chatting to Chris about not looking for romance, he had been sure of it. He had her running scared, before anything more had even happened between them than some light teasing and a few stray chances at touching one another. Cara was very determinedly trying to keep their relationship professional, even though she still flinched as if she had been burned every time they brushed within an inch of one another. And that sort of awareness should not be ignored. It had promise.

So what was the big problem?

The problem was Adam felt an attraction to her so strong he could all but see the ropes binding them together, but he also felt frustratingly disconnected. She was tough with Jeff, encouraging with the girls, a mate to the crew and a rock for Chris. But with him she was like vapour. Ephemeral, changeable, out of reach. And he knew there was no way he could stand another week watching her give everyone else exactly what they needed, except him.

The horses rounded the straight and the crescendo of noise and heat swelled around him. But Adam couldn't have cared less. He wanted nothing more than to drag Cara back into the private room at the rear. To have her all to himself. He willed her to turn, to look back at him, to smile, to understand. But she did not. She bounced up and down, her eyes firmly fixed on the race before her.

'Yippee!' a familiar husky voice called out, dragging Adam from his reverie. 'It only took all bloody day but I finally picked a winner! I've never won anything. Ever! Not even a school fête raffle!'

Weaving her way through the dispersing crowd, Cara tumbled over to him and threw herself so wholly into his arms her feet no longer touched the ground. Adam baulked. He finally had what he wanted. She was in his arms, but he didn't know what to do with her.

She felt so fragile and soft. So energetic and young. And he was completely overwhelmed.

'So how much did you win, Cara?' Adam asked when she finally stopped bouncing.

Cara stood on tiptoe, shielding her eyes from the sun as the final odds came up on the big screen. 'I won…twelve dollars and fifteen cents.'

After a brief pause Adam asked, 'That's it?'

'I only put down a fifty-cent bet.'

'And that's enough to get you into such a state?'

'I'm a girl who's learnt to take her joy wherever she can get it.'

Adam looked down into her smiling face and he knew she was also a girl who knew what she was talking about.

Her arms were slung casually around his neck, one hand buried deep in his hair, the other tucking under the collar of his shirt. Above the scent of her freshly applied sunscreen Adam noticed the mixed scents of cut grass and her usual floral perfume wafting on the warm air. And everything suddenly became clear.

If he was looking for a moment of joy to remember, to

cling to, to revisit, this was it. He took the time to burn the imprint of the moment onto his memory.

The desire to kiss her swept over him, and, for a guy who lived by the control he had over his faculties, the feeling was overpowering. No matter that it would have her running to the hills before he even had the chance to finesse her; her smiling face, her pliant, warm body, the sweet scent of champagne on her breath, the whole kit and caboodle inundated him to the extent that his head began to spin. His head that was of its own accord lowering to hers.

Then, before he could finally taste of those sweet lips, she was wrenched from his arms by a very insistent Jeff.

'Come on, my little winner, I need to rub you for good luck. Tell me who's going to win on the next race.'

Cara shot a forgive-me grin over her shoulder as she was bundled off towards their bookie.

It was the second time they had almost kissed, and the hundredth time he had wanted to do it. What on earth was happening to him? If he saw someone he wanted this much, he went for it. Always. So what was the problem? He knew with every faltering breath and every flicker of those expressive green eyes that she was just as attracted to him, no matter how much she was trying to tell herself she wasn't. So what? What was stopping him from simply taking what he wanted, consequences be damned?

She was nothing like the sort of woman his father kept; she preferred a flower in her hair to jewels around her neck and he would have put money on the fact that her caramel-coloured hair was as close to its natural colour as that of any woman he had met, and that those curls were all hers.

Still, she could be a wolf in sheep's clothing. But if that were true, would that fact make her less datable or more so? Adam could barely remember any more, he had put such strict and overlapping boundaries on himself when it came to his relationships with women.

With every step that his business grew, he added a brick to the wall around his heart. And this one, without even trying, made him care so little about the consequences of his actions he wanted to take a sledgehammer to the whole thing so he could just start afresh.

Adam shoved his hands deep within his trouser pockets and stormed off to find himself the greatest gulp of fresh air he had ever needed.

CHAPTER EIGHT

AT THE end of the day, all of the key crew ended up in Chris's suite back at the Ivy Hotel with Cara hanging onto Chris at the front of the conga line.

'Three cheers for the winner!' Chris shouted.

Cara gave the cheering mob a tipsy pirouette. 'Thank you. Thank you all. And I want to let you know that I plan on using my twelve dollars and fifteen cents only for the greater good. Money will not change me. I will still look down on you as ants to be crushed beneath my feet as I always have.' She gave them a nice deep curtsy, before collapsing onto the couch, her wide, multi-layered skirt puffing out around her.

Adam followed behind, ever the big brother, the watcher, standing on the outside looking in. He shut the door behind them, as the gang obviously had no thought for such sensibilities.

'Yet twelve dollars and fifteen cents does not a fortune make,' Cara said thoughtfully.

Adam pulled out one of the dining chairs and turned it to face the sunken lounge. He sat down, leant an elbow on the dining table, and rested his head against his hand. And he watched the interplay before him.

'True,' Chris said, smiling companionably at Cara. 'It will hardly pay off one's university loan.'

Cara fluffed a hand at Chris. 'All paid off.'

Adam paid closer attention.

'Really?' Chris asked, his voice also a little giddy from

113

champagne, sunshine and something else Adam could not put his finger on. 'OK, then, what about your car loan?'

'Paid off.'

'My, my. Home loan, then?'

Cara opened her mouth, then closed it. 'Not quite,' she finally said, grinning sheepishly. She then held up her hand, squinting through a tiny sliver of light that could be seen between her forefinger and thumb. 'But I am this close.'

She leaned over and in a loud stage whisper declared to the world, 'You know what else? My parents rented their entire lives. Never owned a house. Never owned a car. And in a little over a week, when I get my pay for this magnificent gig, I will have both. Not bad, eh?' She nodded, obviously mightily impressed with herself.

Chris nodded along with her. 'Not bad at all. And how old are you?'

'Not yet twenty-seven and not, may I add, a part owner in a multibillion-dollar company.'

Chris grinned back. 'Well, good for you. The styling business must be more lucrative than I thought.'

'Perhaps a very little,' she said with a self-deprecating giggle. 'I learnt early that, though twelve dollars will not quite get me my building, every cent helps.'

Chris nodded sagely, his head wobbling slightly on his neck. 'Makes sense to me.'

Adam ran a hand through his hair. The talk of money had him shifting in his seat. Her face took on a whole new look when she spoke of cents and dollars. It glowed with determination. He had seen something akin to that look many times over and it always made him uncomfortable.

But this was different. This one was determined to do it on her own. And that was what was making him itch. If she really came from nothing as she professed, then why the hell wasn't she throwing herself on his mercy? How much could she possibly be earning from the gig? A few thousand at most. A pittance to Adam. She had him so stirred up, if she played her cards right she could get pretty much whatever she wanted from him. At that nauseating realisation, Adam's itch got worse.

'Besides which, I wouldn't say I was the big winner of the day.' Cara pulled herself from her chair and shuffled over to Chris, plopping herself on his lap.

Adam sat up straighter at this sudden move. If he thought the talk of money made him uncomfortable, seeing Cara sitting on his best friend's lap made his jaw clench so tight he half expected to taste blood.

He wrenched himself from his chair and began to pace the room.

'I would say that young Christopher here was our big winner,' Cara continued, pinching Chris on both cheeks.

Jeff and the other crew, who had been more intrigued by the contents of Chris's mini-bar than by the conversation at hand, suddenly joined in.

'Hear, hear,' Jeff agreed, holding up a glass of something brown and alcoholic.

'What?' Chris said, his neck turning red.

'It is so obvious,' Cara gushed. 'You are a goner. You are in lurve.'

'Am I even allowed to talk about this?' Chris asked, looking to Jeff for help.

Jeff shrugged. 'So long as it's only between us, I don't see why not. Go for your life.'

'I know who Chris likes,' Cara chanted. 'I know who Chris likes.'

Adam stopped his pacing. He turned and watched. Waiting. Suddenly it didn't matter to him that Chris was falling from his protective reach. It just mattered to him that the conversation be finished as soon as possible so that Cara would disembark from his friend's lap.

Cara leaned down and whispered in Chris's ear and Chris blushed madly. He looked back at her, his face changed, filled with wonder and delight. And Adam stood stock-still with shock. Chris was not just falling. He had fallen. Chris was in love.

Adam's head began to spin. It was fast becoming too much to take on. But what could he do? Nothing. Just stand there and take it all in. Standing on the outside looking in had suddenly taken on a whole new meaning. He was simply out of the loop.

Adam cringed as a great rocking INXS song suddenly blared out of the hidden speakers. Jeff had found the stereo. The whole gang joined in, singing happily at the tops of their lungs. Cara leapt from Chris's lap and dragged him from the chair. They danced about the room, with each other, alone, as a group, copying each other's muddled steps. Cara, as the only woman in the room, had the most attention as the guys took it in turn to twirl her in their arms.

And though she was not the most coordinated person on a sporting field, and though Adam was more than sure that she walked extra carefully when wearing heels more than an inch high, she was one heck of a dancer. The music did something to her, gave her confidence, or perhaps some kind of shield so that she could just let go. Her lithe body spoke of the poise of a ballet dancer and it did not disappoint. She was graceful, and the pulsing tempo of the song sang through her limbs.

Then the music changed. A slow number ensued. The gents partnered up, stumbling, twirling each other about the room. Cara and Jeff joined in, both leading and both following in a ridiculous mimicking imitation of a ballroom-dancing exhibition.

That was as much as Adam could take. He stormed down to the makeshift dance floor and tapped Jeff on the shoulder. Jeff turned to him, and it took a few moments for understanding to dawn. Then he departed with a gallant bow leaving Cara standing, puffing slightly, her green eyes bright and dancing themselves. Adam reached out and took Cara into his arms. And without a word she came to him.

She rested her heavy head on his shoulder and swayed jauntily to the beat. Adam slowed her down, leading until she followed, her feet stopped jitterbugging and eventually she just swayed. She hummed, the sound vibrating through his chest, her sweet voice lilting and tripping across the chords of the song.

It was all he could do to stop himself from holding her tighter still. To wish that the room would clear. To have the sun set and leave them in the darkened space, alone.

'What did you say to Chris earlier?' he asked, his voice low and solemn.

Cara lifted her head from his shoulder. 'Hmm?' She looked at him with a blissful smile on her face.

And what a face. Pretty, pale, a smattering of freckles darkened lightly by their day in the sun, small upturned nose, long eyelashes framing her gorgeous green eyes, and lips that were made for kissing.

It took Adam more than a moment to recall his thoughts.

'Chris,' he remembered. 'I was wondering what you said to Chris that had him look so happy.'

'Oh. That.' She leaned in closer so as to whisper to him. Adam could smell the sweet scent of strawberries and champagne on her lips. It was about as much as he could bear. 'I told him I thought she was just lovely.'

'Who?' he croaked.

'The woman who makes him smile.'

'And who is that?'

She pulled back and waggled a finger at him. 'I can't say. It wouldn't be fair. Though I am a hundred per cent sure that I know who she is, it is not up to me to lead him her way. It is up to him to decide who the woman is who would make him most happy.'

'So how can you be sure you know who it is?'

She raised one eyebrow, one side of her lips kicking up in a wry smile creating the gorgeous smile line in her right cheek. 'Are you serious? Are you really telling me that you haven't seen the signs?'

'What signs?'

'The signs! The fact that he has slowed down immeasurably. He's not so nervous any more. He smiles for no reason. He looks at least half a foot taller. He doesn't whinge when we shave his chest any more. The signs!'

Adam had seen them all right, but he had been so distracted by…other things that they had passed him by.

'OK. So I've seen the signs. Which one is she? The chesty redhead? The blonde who laughs like a donkey? Don't tell me it's the cross-eyed brunette.'

Cara slapped him on the chest then her hand remained resting there, just above his heart, and it was almost enough to distract him anew. He swallowed hard.

'So what if it was one of those girls?' Cara asked. 'If they make him smile, make him relax, make him happy, does it really matter?'

'So long as they treat him well,' Adam said, and was shocked to hear the words spill from his own mouth.

'Exactly. And I know that this girl feels the same for him.'

'How?'

She rolled her eyes, then her hand slipped up from his

chest to take him by the chin, drawing his focus back to her face and nothing else. 'The signs, silly. The signs.'

The music stopped.

The sun had set.

The room had cleared.

They were alone.

Somehow in the last few minutes, while his attention had been so caught up in her alone, the crew had crept quietly from the room. Even Chris was nowhere to be seen and it was his room. Their swaying stopped.

'Where is everybody?' Cara's hand fell away, leaving his jaw cool where her fingers had made it warm.

'Gone,' he said.

'But why?'

Maybe they thought we might like some privacy! he ached to scream at her, knowing that would hardly help the situation.

'I couldn't rightly say.' He let her go and she leapt to a point far enough away that he could no longer feel her warmth. Her hands were wringing and she obviously didn't know where to rest her gaze.

'Would you like a drink?' he asked, already knowing the answer. She shook her head.

'I think I'd better go. I think I stayed long enough.' Her hand moved to cover her stomach. 'I think I drank and ate too much and had too much sun. And I think I had better lie down.'

Her face was beginning to look a little green.

'It's OK, Cara. Go lie down. I'll get Room Service to send you up some Berocca and dry toast.'

'Are you sure?' she asked. 'I'm sorry to have ruined your party.'

Adam looked around at the mess the crew had left in their wake. Finding the beseeching look in those green eyes too much to bear, he spun her on the spot and pushed her from the room. 'Goodnight, Cara. Sweet dreams.'

And the look she sent him as he closed the door showed him exactly what those dreams would be. The green around her dilated pupils blazed, and it was only her hand resting lightly on her aching stomach that stopped him from wrenching her back into the room and making those very dreams come true.

Cara spent the next few days as far from Adam's company as she could. It was bad enough hearing that the crew had a pool going to see who could correctly guess what had happened once they'd left Chris's room, but having to face him with the remembrance of swaying in his arms imprinted all along her body was even worse. But thankfully he seemed to have found a lot of work to do regarding the show's sponsorship, thus had turned up on set but rarely.

He had to know that he had her affections in the palm of his hand. She couldn't even perk up the courage to try to be mates again. She had blown that ruse all too quickly by melting into his arms the minute she'd had the chance. Distance was best. Distance would make her feelings ease away, eventually. It simply had to.

So, by Saturday night, Cara was overjoyed when her best girls turned up to her hotel room for Saturday Night Cocktails.

'Wow,' Gracie said as she trundled into the hotel room, her eyes bright. 'I can't believe the security in this place. I was all prepared for a strip search and everything. If we didn't have these little pass thingies you sent us, I fear we might have been shot.'

'You're not kidding,' Cara said, knowing she had at least one tale she could share with her friends without breaking any contractual secrecy. Her cotton underwear story would make the 'best-of' list, she feared. Especially since Gracie and her jingling card were mainly to blame.

Gracie then turned to the doorway and beat a drum roll on her thighs. 'And if that's not news enough for you, Kelly's back from her trip with Simon to Fremantle. Heeeeere's Kell-Belle!'

Kelly came through the door with a, 'Ta da!'

She gave Cara a much-needed hug and Cara hugged her back. 'You look great!'

Kelly smiled. 'And how the heck are you?'

'You first,' Cara said, carefully deflecting the attention away from herself. She hadn't yet figured what she was going to tell her friends about…her last few days. 'How was Fremantle, Kell?'

'Good. Simon had to head over there to do some business so I decided to tag along. We caught up with his best man and I had the chance to meet some of the friends he made when he lived there. We had perfect weather. We stayed in an amazing resort. It was simply wonderful.'

Gracie raised her dark eyebrows. 'Ahh the loving wife! All's well between you two then?'

'*Really* good.' Kelly said with a charmed sigh that soon dissolved within an accompanying blush.

Gracie squealed. 'Oh no, don't get too gooey on us now, Kell-Belle. Soon all you'll have to offer the Saturday Night Cocktails gang will be crochet patterns. Cara, I'm counting on you to keep us in the real world. Do you have anything to report? Or is the cone of silence still in place?'

'It is, I'm afraid,' Cara said. 'Despite the pass thingies. But I can tell you the experience has been…more than I even hoped it would be.'

'I am so proud of you, Cara,' Kelly said as Gracie gave up on the details and went to check out the mini-bar. 'Soon you will barely remember our names. We'll wave to you as you trawl the red carpets of the world and you'll look over, recognise us, almost, searching through your memory, clutching at the brief glimmer that you may have met us once.'

Cara finally stopped Kelly by placing a hand firmly over her mouth. 'Stop it! Seriously, though, it's really the same job with video cameras rather than still cameras.'

'And more money, I hope? Don't shoot down that fantasy, too!'

'And more money,' Cara agreed, her stomach warming at the thought of owning St Kilda Storeys entirely within the next few days. So far she had not managed to embarrass herself into losing her job, slow dance with the show's sponsor notwithstanding.

'High five to more money,' Gracie joined in, holding up a hand ready to be slapped. When she was rewarded as such she said, 'How are we going to do this? The mini-bar is stocked with enough to give us about half a cocktail each. Shall we order Room Service, or what?'

'I've seen enough of the inside of this hotel room to last me a lifetime,' Cara said, 'so I thought we would trawl the hotel bar. And I've checked with my bouncer friends and they said it's fine. No interlopers allowed so we can play there.'

'Good idea,' Kelly said.

'But do remember, I have vouched for you guys. Be good. Do me proud. And whatever you might accidentally learn while here is to remain top secret. This is really important to me so—'

'Yadda, yadda, yadda,' Kelly said. 'Lips shut tight. Besides I have something else to tell you that's a heck of a lot more interesting than some nameless television show. We have something to really celebrate tonight.'

The tone in Kelly's voice stopped Cara cold.

'And what's that?'

'Simon and I are going to have a baby.'

Out of the corner of her eye, Cara saw Gracie's mouth flop open and she knew she was doing just as good a fish impression herself. The two of them threw themselves at Kelly.

'Kell-Belle!' Gracie squealed. 'That's fantastic!'

'Kelly, that is the best news ever,' Cara yelled into Kelly's ear.

When she finally extricated herself from the octopus arms of her friends, Kelly said, 'All I can say is thank goodness for these pass thingies. If they hadn't let me in tonight I would have scaled the walls to find you. And I'm not sure that Simon would have been impressed.'

'Neither would I,' Cara insisted. 'By order of the Saturday Night Cocktails gang there will be no wall-scaling in your immediate future.'

'And no cocktails,' Gracie piped in.

'But still lots of celebrations,' Kelly said. 'Come on, girls, let's hit the bar. And the first round of apple juice is on me!'

'So everything's cool?' Chris asked, leaning back in the dining chair in the hotel restaurant.

Dean nodded. 'All chugging away nicely. The news about this show must be locked up real tight, as nothing has leaked at all. Our share prices are still steady.'

Adam nodded, soaking in the business talk like a much-missed elixir. It was trackable. It made sense. 'We'll know the minute the news hits the streets. There'll be a bump to be sure.'

'You mean you don't think the shareholders will think I've gone mad and all jump ship?' Chris asked, his tongue firmly planted in his cheek.

Adam had the good grace to grin. 'My sponsorship deal will make us bucketloads, mate, despite the fact that you are as mad as a snake.'

Adam, Dean and Chris all looked up as a threesome of laughing young women spilled from the lift and made their way across the empty foyer to the hotel bar.

But Adam's gaze slammed to a halt once it hit Cara. She looked amazing in a chic white sleeveless top, a black knee-length skirt that clung to every curve and those seductive red shoes that did disquieting things to her walk. Her hair had been blow-dried straight and pulled back into a low pony-tail, a flirty fringe stopping just short of her lashes. She looked so unbelievably lovely Adam's peaceful mood disappeared in an instant and his body began to twitch with discomfort.

'Tell me they are some of your choices, buddy,' Dean begged in a soft, distracted voice, 'and I'll be on your side against Adam come hell or high water.'

Chris laughed. 'Sorry, Dean. The taller one in the middle is my stylist for the show, the other two I don't know. Shall I call them over?'

'No, leave them be—' Adam began but it was too late. They had been spotted. So much for a night of business talk to get his head straightened out.

'Cara!' Chris called out, standing and waving.

Cara glanced their way and smiled. Adam was hit with that same light-hearted sensation that still took him by surprise every time she came into view.

Adam stood as the ladies approached. And Cara's smile faltered the instant it landed on him.

'Won't you and your friends join us, please?' Chris asked.

'Three girls, three boys. This is just trouble waiting to happen,' said one of Cara's friends, a curvy brunette in a tight red dress. The other friend in the denim jacket slapped her on the arm but could not control her indulgent smile.

'Good evening, Chris,' Cara said, giving him a great hug. When she pulled away her gaze remained resolutely anywhere but upon Adam.

'And you must be Dean,' she said, reaching over to shake the other man's hand. Adam watched as his friend all but melted under her sweet smile.

Finally she had no choice but to turn his way.

'Adam,' she said, leaning over to place a feather-light kiss upon his cheek.

He closed his eyes. He couldn't help himself. He was better able to breathe deep of the moment, to memorise the supple softness of cheek against his, her light floral perfume, the brief grip of her small hand upon his arm.

When he opened his eyes she was pulling away and he was startled to find her eyes were closed too. She blinked them open as though she were becoming used to a suddenly bright light. Their green depths sparkled, crinkling at the edges for a moment as though questioning…what?

Then she bit her lip and pulled away, physically and mentally, all but hiding herself behind her friends as she made her introductions.

'The one with the mouth is Gracie Lane,' Cara said. 'She's a croupier in the high rollers room at Crown Casino.'

'My advice is always choose red,' Gracie of the curves and tight dress said, giving a little curtsy as she shook hands with each of the gents.

Adam watched in amazement as quiet, workaholic Dean all but split a seam to get to her first. 'It suits you,' he said, his ears turning the same colour as Gracie's dress.

'Hey,' Gracie suddenly said, pointing an accusing finger at Adam.

'Yes?'

'You're not Adam Tyler, are you?'

Adam nodded, then shook his head, not sure which bit of the question to answer first. Then, to avoid further confusion, he said, 'I am he.'

'Wow!' She grabbed Cara's other friend by the arm and tugged several times. 'This is the guy who replaced you and Simon as the most photographed couple in *Fresh* magazine's social pages after your wedding. Though of course he was the only constant in the couple, changing the girl on his arm as regularly as he changed his tie.'

Gracie looked back at Adam, with one eyebrow cocked cheekily as though daring him to deny it. He shrugged his response, which earned him a huge grin from Gracie, who looked around the room.

'No new girl tonight?'

He shook his head and this time kept his mouth shut.

Her smile grew. 'Fabulous! Then this should make for one heck of an evening.'

'If you're done, Gracie…' Cara said.

Gracie linked her spare arm through Cara's. 'For the moment.'

Adam noticed that Cara looked a little flushed. It seemed these friends of hers were even more outspoken than she was. And that certainly did bode for an interesting evening. 'And this is Kelly Coleman,' Cara said. 'Ever since she got back from honeymoon a few months ago, she's been writing an insanely popular column called *Married, and Loving It* in *Fresh* magazine.'

'Coleman is her married name. She's married,' Gracie reiterated swiftly, eyeing off each of the men individually. 'And pregnant.'

Cara and Kelly both shot Gracie a look that said, *Shut your mouth now.*

'Sorry. But at least now we can celebrate in style without having to tiptoe around the issue.'

'You couldn't tiptoe if your life depended on it, Gracie,' Kelly said.

Introductions complete, Adam said, 'Dean, why don't you fix us up with a larger table? And, Chris, order some drinks.'

'Cocktails,' Gracie insisted.

'Apple juice,' Cara interrupted quickly.

'Apple juice it is,' Dean promised with a grin.

Once the table was set, they took their places, with Cara calling the shots. Boy girl, boy girl, boy girl, she ordered.

She had somehow managed to take the seat farthest from Adam, and he had the feeling it had been entirely deliberate.

CHAPTER NINE

WHEN their drinks arrived, *sparkling* apple juice with little umbrellas, no less, and they had ordered a round of potato wedges with sour cream and guacamole, the small spontaneous party settled into a companionable rhythm.

'Well, since we can't talk about the reason why we are all here, what can we talk about?' Gracie asked.

Chris piped up. 'How about you tell us all about young Cara here? She's a quiet one. Keeps herself under wraps. She must know every last detail about my life but I know nothing at all about her.'

'What do you want to know?' Kelly asked, her eyes sparkling.

'No, please,' Cara begged. 'I am seriously uninteresting.'

Adam blinked as she shot a glance his way. Even though the gang as a whole was relaxed, she was on edge. And by that glance he knew it was because of him. It was strangely comforting to know he wasn't the only one who felt as if he were teetering on the edge of some inexplicable abyss.

'Does she have a middle name? Did she have braces as a child?' Chris asked. 'How old was she when she lost—?'

'Yes. No. And none of your business!' Cara shouted.

'I was going to say when she lost her first tooth!'

'Sure you were.'

Chris reached out and gave Cara a chummy one-armed hug and she blushed adorably under the attention. Adam shuffled in his chair, knowing there was no way he could ever do that with her now, just reach out and hug her like that. It was as though as soon as their skin touched they were both scorched by the contact. He was achingly envious of his friend and his easy way with her. Even though he knew she saw Chris as nothing more than a friend, it was still a much more evolved relationship than the two of them had.

'What about her love life?' Chris asked, with his arm still casually draped over her shoulder. 'She tells me there is no one out in the real world, but I can't believe that. She's just such a doll.'

Adam saw Cara shoot her friends a death stare that would have stopped him in his tracks but they poked their tongues out in the face of such rubbish.

'Believe it,' Kelly said. 'But if there was someone, he would be a puppy dog.'

'All slobber and mess on the carpet?' Dean asked.

The girls cracked up, though Cara buried her head in her hands, obviously knowing there was no point in trying to stop her friends once they were on a roll.

'Oh, no,' Kelly said. 'That would be more trouble than they were worth. I mean that she goes for guys who are sweet and accommodating. Guys who do as they are told.'

'Come on, that's not true,' Cara said.

'Please,' Gracie said, shifting straight to the edge of her seat. 'Name me one guy you've dated who has ever said no to you and lasted another day.'

Cara's mouth opened, then snapped shut tight.

Gracie grinned. 'Yet, even though we have a distinct pattern in young Cara's preferences, she has never settled down with a puppy dog yet.'

'Right you are,' Kelly said. 'Maybe there's something in that. Maybe what she really needs is an anti-puppy dog. Maybe what she really needs is someone with the strength to tell her to *stay*.'

Adam watched as Cara's hunted gaze flickered from Kelly to Gracie before settling on him with a force that slammed him against the back of his chair.

He knew he was no puppy dog, far from it. And she obviously thought the same thing. And though she verbally denied the gist of the entire conversation, in that one look he knew that she knew they were onto something.

Cara was a woman who until now had dated yes-men.

Adam was anything but.

Cara was a woman who would unquestionably blossom in the arms of someone whose strength and will matched her own.

And Adam was such a man.

So what did she expect him to do about it?

Cara couldn't handle another second sitting across from Adam. She had placed him there thinking it would be more comfortable than having to avoid brushing against his arm as they ate. But having him sitting directly across from her meant that she had no choice but to make constant eye contact. And those eyes of his spoke volumes she had no intention of indulging.

'Since you guys are obviously planning on talking a lot, how about another round of drinks to wet your whistles?' she asked, and as soon as she received one nod she was on her feet and hastening to the bar.

She leaned against the bar, her fingernails digging into the cool wood surface. The barman was nowhere to be seen but Cara didn't mind. She was enjoying the moment's peace.

'Hi,' Adam said as he ambled up next to her, and Cara all but jumped out of her skin.

'Hi,' she said back, her voice instantly husky.

'I like your friends.'

That was not what she had expected. She turned to him,

checking to see if he was playing her, but he was casually checking out the labels on the bottles above the bar.

'So do I. They mean the world to me.'

'The sisters you never had?'

Cara blinked. Then nodded. He was right. More than right. His arrow had landed dead centre. 'How did you know that?'

He shrugged. 'It seems to be how the world turns nowadays. The friends we make as adults become our new family. Especially for we confirmed singles.'

He shot her a wry smile and Cara could not help but smile back. But then something began to shift in his eyes, and she felt him pulling away. She had to stop herself from reaching out and grabbing him by the chin, beseeching him to stay with her.

'It's the great marketing key,' he continued, his voice heading back from soft and friendly to professional and aloof. 'Aim to hook the urban family or the hometown family. Pick your mark and play for it.'

'And you guys picked the new urban family?'

'We did.'

'Because you knew about it, right? Because you and Chris and Dean are in the same boat? Finding more in common, finding more solace, and more support from them than from your actual relatives?'

He shrugged and stiffened, the light finally extinguishing in his eyes. 'We chose that as our market share as nobody else had.'

Cara could not help but stiffen in response. Her whole body, which had relaxed at the first sign of an intimate conversation, surged back to high alert.

It was agony. The moments where he seemed to come out of his shell were enlightening. They drew her to him like nothing else she had ever experienced. He was intriguing, sensitive, and riveting. And she knew that she opened up to that side of him without even trying. Her whole body melted and relaxed.

And then when he pulled away, emotionally and mentally, she became like a cat on a hot tin roof, skittish and anxious and ready to flee.

Probably best that way. As Gracie had so blatantly pointed out earlier, this guy was a playboy. He had even labelled himself a confirmed bachelor. He was a serial monogamist at best.

But then again, maybe that was even better. She was full to bursting with the thought of curving one hand through the hair at his nape, of running the other down his broad chest, and of kissing him. She had been sure he had been about to try on the day of the Melbourne Cup, until Jeff had foiled the plan. The mere thought of it raised her body temperature several degrees.

So maybe she should just clear the air, dispel all of that suffocating sexual tension that had settled about the two of them like a cloud heavy with rain. If she threw herself at him, it would get him out of her system. And she knew without a doubt that he would gladly let her go as soon as it was over.

Cara shot a glance his way and wished she hadn't.

He was leaning with one arm propped on the bar, and one foot propped against the bottom rung of a barstool. In his soft navy sweater and tailored tan trousers, he had such casual elegance, such pulsating charisma that even he couldn't keep it in check no matter how hard he tried. And just to top it all off, he was so damn handsome it ached.

And she knew that she could have him without a moment's hesitation. She felt her lungs close up and it took all of her effort to continue to breathe. If she said the word right then, he would ignore the company they had left back at the table and he would take her up to his beautiful hotel suite and he would lead her to his bed and—

'Sorry about the wait, guys,' the heretofore absent bartender said. 'What can I get for you?'

Cara dragged her eyes away and shot the guy a tight smile as she stopped herself from ordering a helpful bucket of iced water.

'Six sparkling apple juices, please.'

'Right! You're the cocktail gang,' the bartender said with a grin. 'Six of the most fabulous-looking sparkling apple juices you have ever seen, coming right up.'

Cara stayed facing the bar, firing up the mantra she had all but forgotten. *Be good. Keep job. Keep home. Anyone and anything not wholly linked to those ideals has to be disregarded unconditionally.*

Adam watched Cara as she watched the bartender. She was wound up tight as a spring. Her high-necked shirt, her tight skirt, her achingly flimsy shoes all supporting the fact that she was wrapping herself up tight inside.

He knew instinctively that beneath Cara's straight-backed outer shell lurked a volcanic heat. He had witnessed moments of it: a quick temper, a determined certainty about her talents, and a ferocious loyalty. And he could not help but wonder if that passion would extend as far as the bedroom. Who was he kidding? He hadn't been idly wondering. For several days now he had been mulling over the idea incessantly. Every time she was in his sight, and every moment she wasn't. This woman was taking him over.

He had to get her out of his system before the wondering became something more deeply ingrained. For a guy who risked ideas and money for a living, that was a risk he could not take.

So, decision made, and timing for once perfect, he leaned

over and whispered in her ear, 'I'm glad to see you're wearing your red shoes again.'

He sensed her control a deep, overwhelming shiver as his whisper tickled at her bare neck. After the moment it took to recover, she glanced down at her shoes, admiring their glossy curves.

'Yes, I am,' she said, her eyes now determinedly fixed on the bartender's back. 'I do tend to buy clothing with the knowledge that it will be worn again and again. I don't have the luxury of being able to use something once and then throw it away.'

Adam knew there was some sort of point she was trying to make but he wasn't totally sure what it was. 'Not many people do.'

'You do.'

That hit him for six. She was angry with him because he had money? That was certainly one to write home about.

'I guess I do have that luxury,' he said carefully. 'But that doesn't mean that I abuse it.'

Finally she turned his way and the inner heat he had been musing over hit him with the blast of an open furnace.

'Really?' she asked, one hand resting on her slim hip. 'You admit you have no trouble throwing people away once you are done with them. So why would you feel any differently about possessions? Some people work their whole lives to make a home for themselves only to have it all slip through their fingers. Most of us can't take it all for granted, you know!'

Her sudden forcefulness shocked him. He reached out and took her by the elbow.

'Hey, come on. What are you going on about?'

'Nothing.'

'Then where is this coming from? What has made you

suddenly so interested in what I do with my things and with the women I date?'

She opened her mouth, ready to breathe fire, but nothing came out. Her green eyes were wide and puzzled. She wasn't angry. She was something else entirely.

He was shocked anew. There was more than plain old heat lurking beneath the surface. She was churning up inside. About him. And not just about his relationships, or his bank balance, but about *him*.

She swallowed hard. Then licked her lips. And he wanted nothing more than to drag her into his arms and kiss away every wild thought that had her so mixed up. He tightened his grip on her arm and she didn't pull away.

'Here you go,' the bartender interrupted cheerfully. 'Six sparkling apple juices.'

The green eyes blinked and shifted away. And the anxiety that seemed ready to swallow her whole seeped slowly away. Adam let go. The moment had passed. In silence they grabbed three drinks each and headed back to the table that was noisy with chatter. But as each of their four companions took a glass the table eased into sudden silence.

Adam dragged his eyes away from Cara to find the others were watching them carefully. They were all smiling, cheekily, and he knew he and Cara weren't fooling anyone. The gang were as aware of the tension between them as he was. But he was pretty sure Cara had not given into the fact yet. She sat down, smoothing out her skirt, fixing her hair, looking anywhere but at him.

'How about a toast?' Gracie said, holding her glass aloft. The others followed suit.

Adam searched desperately for a way to seize Cara's attention. And he found it. He lifted his glass and, harking back to their first lunch together, he said, 'To Cary Grant.'

If only Mr Grant's famous charm could lend him a hand

that night, he would toast him for eternity. It worked. Cara's eyes flickered his way and held. And he read all he needed to know in her tortured gaze.

Gracie broke the searing silence. 'OK… I was thinking more along the lines of: to finding love. But whatever rings your bell. So how about: to Cary Grant *and* finding love?'

Chris grinned and clinked her glass. 'Hear, hear.'

Kelly held one hand to her tummy, her face glowing with a secret smile as she took a sip.

Dean blushed manically as he watched pretty Gracie from over his glass.

And after she had taken a decidedly small sip of her drink, Cara's hands slid to her table, where the pressure she exerted made her knuckles turn white.

Several torturous hours later, Cara listened with half an ear to Gracie and Kelly babbling like a couple of schoolgirls at a slumber party as they trudged back up to her room.

'That was fun,' Gracie said.

'What a nice bunch of guys,' Kelly said. 'That Chris is a sweetheart.'

'Isn't he?' Gracie agreed.

'And Dean had a little thing for you, I think.'

Gracie fluffed a hand in front of her face and became comically coy. 'Oh, he did not.'

'Please,' Kelly insisted. 'He laughed at every joke you made. You're simply not that funny.'

Gracie shrugged. 'Good point.'

'But that Adam is a hard one to figure out,' Kelly said.

Cara flinched, then bit her lip shut tight. There was no response she wished to make to that statement anyway. He twisted her in knots. So what? Nothing was going to come of it. Cara unlocked the door with one swipe of her card and the others followed her inside.

'No, he is not!' Gracie scoffed, flopping down onto Cara's bed. 'He's goo-goo over our classy young friend here.'

'Oh, that much is obvious,' Kelly said, flopping right down beside Gracie. 'The two of them are lit up like flood-lights. What I want to know is, why doesn't he darned well do something about it? Because we sure know how stub-born this one is.'

'Hang on a sec,' Gracie said, 'I somehow remember mention of someone she had met before coming in here. The ominous stare, the powerful grace, the serious good looks worthy of a menswear catalogue. That's Adam she was gushing about.'

Cara kept her mouth shut as she slipped out of the shoes and shuffled them into the closet, her unencumbered toes appreciatively scrunching the soft carpet.

'That's it,' Gracie said. 'Both as stubborn as each other, thus doomed from the start. Sitting back in their separate corners, trying so hard to work each other out, when if they were up close and personal the process would be a heck of a lot easier, quicker, and much more fun!'

Cara stood at the end of the bed with her hands on her hips. 'Hello? You two do remember that I am in the room, do you not?'

'Bah!' Gracie said. 'What difference does that make? It's not as though you are going to hear a word we're saying. It's not as though you're going to listen to your brilliant friends. You're going to tuck it all away somewhere safe and quiet and go about the business of buying your big home, keeping yourself to yourself and not turning into your parents.'

'What have they got to do with it?'

'Please!'

'Do you ever wonder why you only date puppy dogs?' Kelly asked, sitting up.

'And lap-dogs at that?' Gracie chimed in. 'Men who do as you say?'

'Because,' Kelly explained, 'you are so darned scared of becoming embroiled in fights the likes of which your parents lived for, you would rather split up than argue.'

Cara could barely hold her ground as the barrage hit her. Kelly's expression softened but she wasn't done yet. 'Cara, I don't think that big hunk of man out there would be the type to follow you around saying "yes, dear, no, dear, three bags full, dear". By the look on his face all night it looked like he was more than ready to give you some very specific instructions and if you aren't prepared to follow them, look out!'

Cara rolled her shoulders, easing out the rising tension. And then she stopped halfway. She was doing exactly what the girls were saying she always did. Preparing herself to moderate, negotiate, anything to bring about peace. Anything to stop the fight.

'OK. What if I agree that you're right?'

Kelly opened her mouth to say, I told you so, but Cara held up a hand to stop her.

'I am the queen negotiator. Always the diplomat. Fine. So be it. But this has nothing to do with my relationship with Adam.'

'Your relationship?'

Cara threw out her arms in exasperation. 'My friendship, my acquaintance, whatever you want to call it! We've been thrown together a good deal during the filming of the show, but that's all. Circumstances have pushed us together, nothing else. We might have developed an…attraction of sorts, but that's it. Certainly nothing to hang your hopes on.'

Kelly and Gracie sat on the bed staring at Cara, wearing matching grins on their faces.

Gracie broke the silence. 'I doth thinkest she doth protesteth too much.'

Cara grabbed a couple of cushions off her small couch and dived on the bed, doing her best to smother the cheeky grins from both friends' faces.

'So what's with you and Miss Cat's Eyes?' Dean asked as Adam and Chris walked him to his car.

Adam shot Chris a look but he held up his hands in surrender. 'Don't look at me. I've not said a word.'

'So there is something going on?' Dean asked.

'No. There most definitely is not.'

'Please!' Dean shot back. 'I've never seen you so withdrawn. I almost felt the need to poke you once or twice to see if you were still with us, while she fidgeted like she had fleas.'

'I'm amazed you could see anything past the impertinent brunette at your side.'

Dean's ears grew red instantly.

'Hey, don't change the subject,' Chris insisted. 'The whole problem is that nothing has been happening but he would like nothing more than for there to be lots happening. He's been impossible since the day he met her.'

'Which also happens to be the same day you told me about this show of yours,' Adam reminded him.

They reached Dean's car and Chris leapt on Adam, putting him in a head lock. 'Come on, Deano,' Chris said. 'Between the two of us we might be able to lock him in the trunk of the car and you can keep him away from me for the duration.'

'I'm not going anywhere,' Adam insisted, twisting easily away from his slighter friend.

'And why not? What are you achieving by being here? The show is almost finished, so you can't stop it now. Especially now you've seen the projections of the exposure it will give us. I win. I was right. The ideas man got it right. What a shock. So why stay?'

'Moral support.'

'Pfft. What? You'll miss my moral support of you?'

'Fine. Then let's call it unfinished business.'

'Between you and Cara, right?'

His friends watched him with bright eyes. They were smart guys and he could deny it all night long, but they wouldn't believe it for a second.

So he afforded them one short nod.

'That's more like it!' Dean said, giving Chris a sly low five. 'Wow, you guys are making me antsy. I feel like I'm missing out on something big.' Dean hopped into the driver's seat of his sporty number. 'I'll see you guys next week, right?'

'Three more days and this will all be over,' Chris said, his voice suddenly heavy with exhaustion.

'And has it been worth it?' Dean asked.

Adam watched from the sidelines as his friend's face lit up.

'More than I could have ever hoped.'

Adam knew without a doubt his friend was in love. Though the main reason why Adam had kept so close to Chris this whole time had been to make sure that he would be safe from the clutches of any of these women, Chris had fallen and he had fallen hard.

Adam was too late. He had failed. So why didn't he feel as torn up about the fact as he should?

Cara walked the girls downstairs and saw them off in the lobby. They waved frantically all the way through the revolving doors and Cara watched as their sprightly forms shimmied into a wavering mirage and disappeared.

Then through the doors came Adam, head down, hands in pockets, walking slowly, his attention a million miles away. He hadn't noticed her, and if she headed for the stairs they would not cross paths. But her slipper-clad feet were rooted to the spot.

Kelly was right; he lit her up. He made her think, he made her reconsider her opinions, and he made her want to fight back. And rather than having the battle eat away at her until she didn't know any other way to communicate, she felt all the more alive for it.

He was simply in an altogether different league from any guy she had ever known. Even from the producers who earned enough dough to wear comparable clothes. But he wore them better, he wore them as if he were born into them. Where others stood, he lounged. They spoke, he drawled. He was just the most attractive, disturbing man Cara had ever known.

When he was only a few steps from her, Adam looked up. She knew the moment he spied her. The perpetually crinkled brow smoothed away, and he smiled. His pace picked up and he stood straighter. It amazed her that she could bring about such a sudden change in the demeanour of a guy like him.

'Beautiful night for it,' he said as he approached.

'Mmm?' she said, flinching at his unexpected words.

A beautiful night for what? For falling for someone who would never have you? For putting yourself through growing torment just for one more moment in someone's precious company? For mad, debilitating terror that you were falling prey to something that would change you for ever?

'Beautiful night,' Cara agreed.

Adam shot her a sweet smile and she hoped she smiled

back, though it felt more like a panic-riddled grimace. Then as he came closer he looked to her feet and spied her slippers. His glance shifted back to hers, his beautiful eyes questioning but still smiling and creating the most wonderful tumbling sensation in her stomach.

What could she do? She was undone. The girls were right. She'd had enough of yes-men. She wanted a real man.

The moment that she had missed by the pool and the moment that had been stolen from her at the races were not moments she could live with missing entirely. She had insisted that Chris have no regrets in his life; it was only fair that she do as she preached.

So in the quiet, air-conditioned stillness of the hotel lobby at midnight, Cara took the final two slipper-clad steps and threw herself into Adam's arms, kissing him with every ounce of passion she harboured, as it would have to be her only chance.

Adam stiffened for only a brief, stunned moment before his strong arms wrapped her tight. This man spoke only when he had something important to say and his kisses held the same authority. Cara knew she was being treated to something special. Something significant. His indulgent, hot-blooded kiss told her he had longed for this just as much as she had.

Cara instantly buried her hands deep within his soft hair, as she had wanted to do since the first moment she'd laid eyes on him. She could feel the hardness of his chest through the softness of his expensive navy sweater, the fabric rubbing along her inner arms, the smooth sensation enough to make her melt her whole body against his. She delighted in the knowledge that his curves fitted against hers as though he had been carved just for her.

Waves of finally unbridled need crashed down on her

and she lost herself in Adam's luscious kiss as she never had lost herself before. Cara's head felt light and empty. She would have happily endured the exquisite kiss until it sapped away her last breath. But as though sensing her imminent collapse Adam pulled away, ever so slightly, the heat not easing but shifting, slowing, burning slower and hotter still, so that now she could take the time to experience every nuance, every variance, every sensation he afforded her.

Her whole body ached as it craved ever more. It flushed from his desire, his skill, his reverence. She was so immersed in the kiss, Cara's lungs felt ready to collapse. She had to take a breath. Though she felt willing to drown in the warmth of his lips, her lungs made the decision for her.

She pulled away, raking in great gulping breaths of air so cold it ached.

Adam looked down into Cara's wild eyes. Her pupils were dilated, the glittering colour surrounding them deep and mysterious as emeralds. He leant in and placed a kiss on the end of her nose. He felt so much tenderness towards her in that moment it physically hurt. Endorphins whipped through his entire body, both relaxing and invigorating every part of him. And his chest ached, as though he was using muscles within that he had never used before.

'We shouldn't be doing this here,' Cara whispered, drawing Adam back to the present.

Adam was infinitely glad she had added the word 'here'. 'There is nobody about,' he said, his voice eloquently husky. 'Everyone else is in bed.'

That word was enough for their combined temperature to rise. He could feel her heart beating through his chest, her beautiful, kind, heavily protected heart. But Adam felt her pull away, physically and emotionally. No! He wasn't about to let her kiss him like that and then retreat. He dragged her back into his embrace but she would no longer look him in the eye.

'I can't do this,' she said.

'And why is that?' he asked, running a hand up and down her straight back. He felt her shiver in his arms, the reaction flowing through him as well.

'Because working relationships amount to trouble. And this job is really important to me. It's a career maker and I can't let anything stand in the way of that.'

'From what I've heard you had a pretty darned good career to start with.'

She shook her head, refusing to listen to reason. 'I will not jeopardise this job to indulge myself with some sort of holiday romance. This may feel like a walk in the park for you, a bit of relax time away from the office, but this is it for me. This is a career clincher. This job means more to me than you can know. So don't make me blow it.'

She looked up at him then and her internal struggle shook him. It wasn't that she couldn't go to the next step with him, it was that she desperately wished she didn't want to.

'How can I make you do anything?' he asked.

'By looking at me like that. All sure and dark and brooding and strong and lovely and…'

He sensed her winding down as she went, as though with each word her desire became too much, piling up on itself, growing exponentially with every reason why she was attracted to him. Her words speaking less truth to him than her body, he leaned down to take up where they'd left off but she turned away at the last second.

'What's going on? You were the one who kissed me just now,' he said, knowing it was a low blow. But he couldn't help it. His body was singing and he couldn't fathom why she would even want to fight it. Or even how she had the physical strength to do so, because he sure didn't.

She swallowed. Hard. 'So I was. And that was wrong of me so I apologise. But that has to be the end of it. That has to be enough.'

It wasn't. Not nearly. But Adam was not one to push a woman past 'no'.

'Fine,' he said, his frustration making the word explode from his mouth. Something inside him wrenched as he saw the intense relief wash across her face and he knew in that moment that if he had decided to push past 'no' there would have been no further resistance.

But then he also knew that she would have hated him and herself in the morning and though that once would not have concerned him, with her it did.

'Come on,' he said, his voice deliberately sympathetic. He held out a hand, shepherding her towards the open lift.

Low on resistance, she fell into step beside him. She didn't look his way and he didn't make her. He felt the abyss at his toes once more and the only thing holding him from falling was the most tenuous of reasons.

His greatest fear had been realised: that one kiss would never be enough. Now that he had tasted of her sweetness, he wanted. He had to have more. Especially since it seemed it would be the only way to rid himself of the caving ache that had gradually taken up residence in the pit of his stomach.

Her kisses were honest, even if she was not. He knew she wanted more from him than one stolen kiss even if she could not admit it aloud.

The lift stopped on her floor. He led her to her room and when she couldn't for the life of her get the key card to work he took it from her trembling hand and unlocked the door for her.

She took a step inside the room, turned and faced him, her cheek leaning against the edge of the door.

The carpet in the hallway was different from the carpet in the room, the line where they joined taking on one hell of a significance. If he took that one step across that line, they would spend the night in each other's arms. If he kept himself on this side of that line, they could look each other in the eye in the morning.

The decision was suddenly easy. It was more important for her to like him than for him to seduce her. Not to help Chris. Not for the good of the company. But for him.

'Goodnight, Cara,' he said. 'Sweet dreams.'

Taking in a deep breath gave him the time to imprint her sweet, sleepy face on his memory. But that alone was one step too far. Before he could stop himself he took the leap into the abyss.

'I'm in Suite 45,' he said.

Cara's eyes flared with suppressed desire. Her lips disappeared as she bit down on them hard.

'Goodnight, Adam,' she said, her husky voice wafting over him like the caress it was.

And as Cara closed the door to her room Adam's whole body vibrated with the most intense, unresolved sensations he had ever experienced.

CHAPTER TEN

LYING in bed, still wide awake an hour later, Cara thought back to the promise she had made to the good fairies right back at the beginning of her adventure. If she landed the job, she would never want for anything else.

Her wish had been granted but she was not keeping up her side of the bargain. She had become greedy with her success. Her real potential was opening up before her as never before. She wanted the job and she wanted more. And she wanted it with Adam.

Gracie would tell her it was the age of safe sex. But Cara knew that sex would never be safe with Adam. To her, 'safe' also meant that she would come out of the episode unscathed. If she let herself be led into Adam's waiting arms, she would be anything but safe. She would be lost. And once gone, she did not know if she would have the strength to find herself again. For a girl who had done it alone for almost ten years, the thought was terrifying.

Cara all but fell out of bed as a loud knock sounded at her door.

Adam's sensuous voice saying the overloaded words, 'I'm in Suite 45,' reverberated with each of the continuing knocks.

Cara grabbed her delicate nightgown and wrapped it about her, looping the tie in a triple knot around her waist.

She opened the door, her expectant face switching to shock in an instant as Kelly's husband stood before her.

'Simon! What are you doing here? It's one o'clock in the morning!' She whipped her head around the corner, finding the usually bustling hallway magically devoid of crew. 'Besides which, if I'm seen talking to you I'll be sacked.'

Simon stuck his foot in the door so she couldn't close it. Cara looked up at him in bewilderment.

'Cara, it's Gracie.'

She no longer needed Simon's foot for the door to remain wide open. She was out in the hallway in a heartbeat. 'What? What happened?'

'It's her mother. This evening, in Sydney… Gracie's mother has been killed in a car crash.'

It took Cara half a second before she was off down the hallway to Jeff's room. She banged on the door until Jeff finally appeared looking as bedraggled as always. 'Do you have any idea what time it is?'

'I've just had some bad news. A friend of mine has had some bad news and I have to go to her.'

Jeff shook his head and yawned. 'Sorry, Cara. Can't let you go. There's only another three days left of the shoot. Wait until then.'

'Come on, buddy,' Simon said, appearing at Cara's side, 'don't do this to her.'

That brought Jeff awake like a slap to the face. 'Who is this?'

'This is Simon. Another friend. He came to tell me the bad news.'

'How did you get in here?' Jeff asked, all five feet eight of him trying to outmuscle the much bigger Simon, and all five feet eight failing miserably.

'That doesn't matter,' Simon said. 'What matters is I'm taking her home with me now.'

Jeff's eyes narrowed. 'Fine. But if you do she's not coming back. If you go, Cara, you will have broken your contract and we don't have to pay you a red cent.'

Maya's words tumbled through her mind. *TV jobs are notoriously precarious. Don't cause trouble. Do your job with a minimum of fuss and you'll be fine.* Having a stranger at Jeff's door so late at night while wearing nothing but a nightgown would not be classed as a minimum of fuss in anyone's book.

'Jeff, you're not shooting until this evening. I'll be back by then, I promise.'

'Sorry,' Jeff said. 'Just wait the three days and you're free as a bird.'

Cara stared through him, biting on her lip as her mind whirled with the pile-up of bad news blocking her way to a clear decision.

Then she turned and ran. She wrenched open the stair-well door and took the steps two at a time, not even waiting to check if Simon was on her tail. When she reached the next floor she went straight to Suite 45. She banged on the door. Adam appeared, still wearing the same clothes he had been in at dinner.

Adam took in Cara's attire. No matter his brazen invitation, he had never actually expected her to come knocking, especially decked out in such seriously gorgeous get up.

Her gown had slipped open, the tie dragging along behind her. Her hair was wild and curling about her face. And she huffed and puffed, her chest rising and falling as though she had run all the way to his room. He had never seen anything so sexy in all his life.

His body responded in an instant. He could feel a low growl of desire welling from within and he knew how the cavemen felt. He wanted nothing more than to reach out, grab a hold and drag her into his cave.

But only then was he able to see past his own desire to

the state she was in. She wasn't panting at his door in response to his invitation. Something was wrong.

He reached out and took her by the arm, his grip purposefully gentle.

'Sweetheart, what is it?'

'I've never asked anything of you before, and I wouldn't now if it wasn't an emergency, but you are my last hope. You have to convince Jeff to let me go.' Her voice was ragged and her eyes wild, the green flecks flashing. 'He won't and I have to and he says that I can't leave or he'll renege on the contract and he can't. I need that money. But if he does I'll go anyway. But I was hoping you could help.'

'Help what, sweetheart?' he asked, pulling the poor haggard girl into a soothing embrace. Anything to stop her from quaking. He couldn't stand watching her look so frightened.

'It's Gracie. You met Gracie.'

'I met Gracie,' he agreed, running one hand up and down her slender back, the silky fabric rising and falling through his fingers.

'Her mother...'

She stopped and he could feel her gulping down a breath.

'Her mother has just been killed on holiday in Sydney. Her stepfather is up there, and she never knew her real father, so she needs me. And there is no way that I am going to leave her alone tonight. There is just no way.'

'Of course you're not.'

Adam looked up the hallway to see a man he did not know striding towards them. Thinking the big guy was a security guard, he whipped Cara around behind him, putting his own bulk between her and any trouble.

'Cara?' the man said as he approached, and Adam knew

by the care in his voice that this was no security guard. This guy knew her. But still, Adam kept her shielded.

'What can I do for you, mate?' Adam asked, his voice coming out so low and ominous it surprised even him.

'I'm Simon. A friend of Cara's. Kelly's husband.'

At that news Adam relaxed immeasurably. Suddenly he had himself an ally, not a challenger. He put the thought of what that meant from his mind. There were more important things to do before that could even hope to be tackled.

'Great,' Adam said. 'Take her back to her room for me and help her get what she needs. Then have her downstairs in fifteen minutes. OK?'

Simon paused for a brief moment and Adam knew he was being sized up. They were like two stags looking out for the same doe, though he knew instinctively that their motives were very different.

Obviously getting all he needed from Adam's silent entreaty, Simon gave him one curt nod, then took Cara by the hand and, with one arm wrapped about her slim shoulders, herded her to the lift.

Adam whipped inside his room long enough to grab his key card, then he headed off to do what he had to do.

Fifteen minutes later Cara was in a limousine heading back to St Kilda Storeys. Simon sat next to her, watching over her like a protective older brother as she stayed on the phone with Kelly the whole way. Kelly, who was at Gracie's side back home.

As they pulled into the driveway Cara had the same view of her home as she'd had less than two weeks before. But rather than coming home and running up and hugging the warm stucco that belonged to her, and her alone, her heart ached with the knowledge that she would have to wait a good while longer.

But no matter.

Though it shocked the hell out of her to realise it, there were more important things in her life than a pile of bricks. And one of those things was upstairs nursing a broken heart.

Simon opened the door and went to the back of the car to get her luggage. Then as Cara stepped out she smacked into the large frame of Adam Tyler.

Momentarily forgetting where she was and what she was doing there, she simply stared into his big blue eyes.

'I…I was up front,' he said, his voice quiet and uncertain. 'I didn't want to crowd you. But before I head off I wanted to make sure you were going to be OK.'

'I'll see you upstairs,' Simon said and Cara followed his voice. She saw the brief nods that Adam and Simon shared, then realised that Adam had done this all for her. He had organised the car. He was under the same contractual stranglehold she was, and likely had a hell of a lot more to lose from the deal than a few thousand dollars, yet he had left the hotel to make sure she was all right. She had asked for help and without argument he had come through for her. He had put in danger his company's position with the station to help her.

The moonlight created a halo of light around his beautiful face and she found herself reaching out and taking a hold of his large hand and saying, 'Please don't go. Not yet.'

They stood like that for a few moments. He finally gave her hand a quick squeeze, then let go and bent to chat to the driver. Cara saw the light on in Gracie's top-floor window. With a deep ragged breath she headed up to her friend, feeling secure in the knowledge that Adam was right behind her, supporting her all the way.

She opened the unlocked door to Gracie's apartment and, by the look of pure relief on her friend's red face, she knew without a doubt she had made the right decision. Cara ran to her best friend, and card-carrying member of her urban family, and wrapped her tight.

Hours later Adam stretched out his neck as he filled the kettle in Cara's downstairs apartment.

Cara came back from the bathroom where she had gone to splash cold water on her tired face. She then flopped into the large leather sofa with all the coordination of a rag doll and remained where she landed, lying across the couch, one leg dangling onto the floor and one arm flung across her tired eyes. She looked so small. But hours of hugging and consoling a devastated best friend could do that to a person.

Through the night, Adam had witnessed exactly the sort of emotional involvement he had sought to avoid in trying to talk Chris out of this whole escapade in the first place. He had seen his father rise and fall with the women in his life so many times that he had come to the conclusion that any such grief and loss was self-inflicted. It was simple. *Don't care and you won't find cause to grieve.*

But when Cara had asked him to stay, the thought of simply not caring had been inconceivable. And even when the tears had been flying thick and fast in Gracie's apartment upstairs he had not been able to drag himself away. The desire to be there if Cara needed him had been stronger than the desire to shield himself from the potency of the enshrouding emotions. It had been quite a night.

Once the kettle was boiled he poured a cup of black instant coffee for himself and a sweet white for Cara. He carried the cups over, resting them on the big wooden coffee-table as gently as he could as he sat in the chair opposite hers. But the smell must have reached her just the same.

'Mmm,' she said, her arm shifting just enough to reveal her lovely eyes, which blinked slowly, sleepily, at him.

He couldn't move. He was frozen in time, mesmerised by that lush mouth of hers curling into a slow, appreciative smile. Then she stretched, her whole lithe body yielding and unwinding before him. Finally her face erupted into a great gaping yawn and she pulled herself into a sitting position. Blinking sleepily at him some more, she grinned.

'What are you grinning at?' he asked and sat back, enjoying her first smile all night.

'I feel like I'm playing hookey,' she whispered.

'Private school girl, hey?'

'Yep.'

'Were your parents doctors or lawyers?'

She shook her head vehemently. 'Good Lord. Neither. Scholarships all the way for me.'

'So you were a brainiac.'

Her eyes smiled at him from over her mug of coffee, their emerald depths glistening back at him.

'And you weren't?'

He shrugged. 'I did well enough. So why didn't you become a doctor or a lawyer? Can't stand the sight of blood?'

That earned him another grin and he found he was amassing quite a collection of them, and they were that good he had the feeling he would be keeping them with him to bring out on cold, lonely nights.

'Oh, I like action well enough. There's plenty of bloodshed in my business but at least there I am the decision maker; I'm the end of the line. What I say goes. I brook no arguments, or I walk.'

'I saw that tonight. When I happened on Jeff he looked

like he didn't know what hit him. He must have thought he'd bought himself a lap-dog when he took you on.'

'Then he didn't do as much research as he originally professed.'

Adam nodded. The conversation had hit a natural lull and for several moments they sipped on their coffees, simply enjoying each other's company. He watched as Cara tucked her feet beneath her, shuffling her bottom until she was comfortable, her slight frame sinking happily into the large seat.

Adam glanced around the apartment. It was stylish and homey at the same time. Cosy. Comfortable. 'I like your place.'

Cara followed his gaze and he saw her face light up again but the brightness diminished as though someone had snuffed out a burning candle.

'Me too. It's almost all mine, you know. The whole building.'

'I'm impressed. You did it without having to be a doctor or a lawyer…'

'Or part-owner in a multibillion-dollar company,' they said in tandem.

Adam could not believe he was making jokes about money with a woman. It was just surreal.

She nodded, her mouth twisting as she bit at her lower lip. Adam knew this meant she was disconcerted. By now he knew what pretty much all of her little idiosyncratic expressions meant. It wasn't as though he had purposely studied them, they were just that memorable, and just so particular to her.

OK, so he had studied them too.

'With this job I could have paid it off. But now I have run out on the production…' She finished off on an expressive shrug.

He remembered her saying in amongst her earlier ramblings in the hotel how important this pay-cheque was to her. And then for the first time in his life he found himself uttering the words, 'If you need the money—'

Cara held up her hands, stopping his words short. 'Don't even think it, Adam. There is nothing more likely to ruin a relationship than money.'

And he was so relieved at her words he wanted to throw himself into her arms and bury his face in her warmth and never let go.

It was enough to have him leap to his feet and ask, 'How about breakfast?'

Adam looked suddenly lost. As though he didn't know what to do with his hands. Cara figured he had every right to be antsy. He'd put up with a lot that night, more than she would have expected of anyone. Even Kelly and Simon had headed home some time after three. Yet Adam had stayed.

Cara glanced at the closed pantry doors, imagining the delights within. 'It'll have to be cornflakes or two-week-old eggs, I'm afraid.'

'Sit,' Adam insisted. 'Stay here. I'm going out for a walk and I'll bring something back.'

Cara nodded. He wanted to leave. He needed fresh air. But she didn't blame him. He hadn't asked for this. Hadn't asked for a night comforting practical strangers. If he had reached his limit she couldn't blame him at all.

He didn't even turn at the door when he left. She wouldn't be surprised if he didn't come back, if he made some excuse and ran for his life. And though she tried to pretend she was OK with the thought, it sapped the last of her resolve. She slumped back into her soft couch, the last remnants of her energy finally leaving her as tranquil, heavenly sleep took her over.

*   *   *

The smell of store-bought coffee laced with cinnamon invaded her senses. And croissants. And jam. And something else... She sniffed the air and peeled open an eye.

Adam was back. She could see him silhouetted against a wash of morning sun streaming through the small side window. Her heart grew so that she could barely breathe.

On the dining table she saw the something else. A huge bunch of fresh flowers took pride of place as a centre-piece. Adam had obviously not been able to find a vase so they resided in an unused spaghetti canister. Daisies, her favourite flower. The same scent as her favoured perfume. She had a feeling he knew it, too.

Cara sat up and only when Adam turned her way did she realise the creaking groan she had just heard had come from her.

'Good morning, sunshine,' he said.

Cara ran a hand through her tumble of short curls. 'How long have you been gone?' she asked, hiding the burgeoning tenderness from her voice under the mask of a yawn.

'Half an hour at most.'

'Are you sure it's not really tomorrow?'

He raised an eyebrow.

'Are you sure I haven't just had the most delicious, rejuvenating twenty-four-hour sleep?'

A smile kicked at the side of his mouth. 'Pretty sure. Sorry.'

Cara peeled herself from the chair, her joints aching, her whole body heavy with exhaustion, and her heart singing that he had returned to her. She realised Adam must have felt pretty much just as achy and exhausted, but instead of hotfooting it back to the hotel for a couple of hours of much-needed sleep, or running for the hills and out of her life altogether, he had returned to her with flowers and breakfast.

Her heart ached with the perfection of the scene: the mouth-watering display of croissants, muffins, pancakes, sausages and eggs, the thoughtful flowers, a man she adored seated at the head of the table. She had to take the edge off before she burst into tears.

'Wow!' she exclaimed merrily as she sat.

'What?'

'Are we having company?'

'Not that I know of.'

'Do I look like the sort of girl who can wolf this lot down?' With that, Cara's tummy let out a groan to match any in history. She couldn't help but laugh. 'OK. So maybe I am just that sort of girl. Load me up a plate.'

'All I ask is that you leave me a bite.'

She shot him a smile, feeling warm and fuzzy with tiredness. 'We'll see.'

Adam filled up Cara's plate as asked. He was famished and he could tell she was too. So only once she was satisfied did he take a seat and grab some food for himself.

'What do you think Gracie will do now?' he asked.

Cara looked up at her ceiling as though curling out her thoughts to her friend a few floors above.

'I really don't know. Her mother became pregnant with Gracie when she was in her late teens. Gracie never knew her father. I don't think he's even Australian. And her mother married Gracie's stepfather when she—Gracie—was in high school, so her half-siblings are still pretty young. Her stepdad's a lovely guy, so I'm sure if Gracie decided to go and stay with him and her half-brother and sister that would be fine.'

'But will she? She doesn't seem the type to lean on people too easily.'

'She's not.'

'Which is why you had to come. You knew she would lean on you. Her urban family.'

'Exactly.' An amazed smile grew on her face and it kicked at something deep inside him. 'You are too astute for your own good.'

'It comes in handy.'

'In your work, sure. But it must be hard to give people a second go if you know that your first impressions are usually so bang on.'

Cara smiled up at him and he couldn't for the life him remember what she had just said. She was all warm and rumpled with sleep. Her cheeks were pink, her hair ruffled and curling about her face, which was long since devoid of make-up. Her smattering of freckles stood out on her sweet nose.

She must have thought she had not explained herself well enough so she rephrased her question.

'I mean, if someone makes a bad first impression, how could you ever trust them again?'

She shook her head sadly, then tucked into her breakfast and Adam relaxed once he realised that her conversation had become rhetorical. He was thankful when they settled into a companionable silence.

It was halfway through the meal before Adam wondered how long it had been since he had eaten breakfast in companionable silence with anyone.

His rare breakfasts with his father were anything but companionable. They were always fraught with disappointment on Adam's side, and resentment from his father that he'd had to fall back onto his son's fortune since losing all of his own.

And breakfasts with Chris or Dean were anything but silent. They were always noisy and energetic as the three of them sparred back and forth with new ideas.

But this breakfast experience was new to him. It was leisurely, it was peaceful and it was pleasant. And to add to the conundrum, he was eating this delicious, companionable, comfortably silent breakfast with a woman. He could not recall a time when that had ever happened.

He watched Cara from beneath his lashes. Her gaze was aimed towards the window, but, with nothing more interesting in her path than the neighbour's garage wall, he knew her mind was far away. She bit into her croissant vacantly, chewed slowly, her wide green eyes blinking slowly into the sun.

Without warning she turned his way and he was caught staring. She sent him a warm sweet smile that spoke of comfort and sunshine and all things nice.

His heart flipped in his chest.

Again she had blessed him with a moment of simple joy that he did not want to ever forget. In fact this was a moment he did not want to have happen only once in his lifetime. He wanted to experience again and again. And not just with anyone.

But with her.

CHAPTER ELEVEN

'So YOU only date puppy dogs?' Adam said out of the blue.

Cara blinked and drew her attention from her daydreams to the man who had been featuring in them. *Where had that statement come from?* she wondered. But then, when her sleepy focus snapped back into place, she knew. There was more than just friendly interest in his eyes.

In an instant her heart rate doubled, and, for someone who saw exercise as something other people did, she felt that doubled heart rate in every limb.

'And you only date brainless bimbos,' she lobbed back, her voice unfortunately heavy and languorous.

The twinkle in his eyes showed he knew just how he affected her. 'And so far how do you think that has worked for the both of us?'

She slowly lowered her fork, her gaze unable to disentangle from his. 'Not so well, obviously,' she admitted. 'Or else we would both be settled with toddlers scampering about our feet by now.'

He nodded. Slowly. 'Maybe it's time we break the mould. Try something new.'

Was he saying what she thought he was saying? Was the gorgeous, emotionally unavailable, confirmed bachelor, billionaire Adam Tyler saying that he would like for them to try each other on for size?

If Cara had felt the double heart rate in every limb, the shortness of breath that suddenly hit her like a sack of flour to the chest was a whole other sensation. The brick in her chest that she had felt for so long was nothing in comparison. She gripped a hold of the edge of the dining table so as not to swoon from her chair.

Adam watched her with his usual quiet patience. Well, he would have to wait. Her answer would be one of the most important of her life.

Think, Cara. Think!

Gorgeous—God, yes.

Emotionally unavailable—surely as much as ever. But aren't you the same?

Confirmed bachelor—meaning he would never try to change you so as to keep you. Isn't that perfect?

Billionaire.

That was where it all fell apart. Money ruined everything. Her parents hadn't had enough to keep them happy. But since then she had seen where too much could cause just as many squabbles and levels of mistrust. Adam was as damaged as she was by his parents' failings, and that was the last thing she needed to be reminded of every day.

Relax! This is no marriage proposal. He is not asking you to move to the other side of the world and become his love slave. He has just thrown out the idea that two consenting adults who find each other appealing might want to consider the idea of dating.

Who was she kidding? They didn't just find each other *appealing*, the two of them could run a small town on the electricity they produced between them, so any sort of affair would be…unforgettable.

But then she knew. It would not only be unforgettable, it would be unbeatable. If she ever had Adam, she did not think that any other relationship would compare.

Along with the face Adam presented to the world was the Adam she had come to know over the last several days. He was extraordinarily perceptive, doggedly loyal, and infinitely lovable. So he wore suits that cost ten times as much as her one pair of Kate Madden Designs shoes, but he didn't flaunt his money in any way that she had seen. He used his powers for good, to look after a friend in need, to give some exercise and sunshine to a group of virtual strangers whom he thought might like it, and she had no idea who or what he had threatened to get her out of the hotel the night before and to Gracie as quickly as he had.

And the fact that he didn't speak unless he had something to say just showed what a good listener he was. Cara had not had too much experience with people who actually listened. Her parents had screamed their opinions at one another without ever answering one another's questions. Any way she looked at it, he was a good man.

The fact of the matter was, she had fallen deeply and longingly in love with him. So, contrarily, the answer had to be no.

No matter how much he seemed to care for her, he had never given her any indication that his thoughts on long-term relationships were anything other than exactly as his biography suggested. And any sort of dalliance with him would be so unforgettable she could very well not get over it. It would be unforgettable and bust.

She peeled her fingers from the table and sat forward, her answer fixed. 'Or maybe we stick to our guns so as not to fall prey to outside forces telling us what they think our lives should be like.'

He did his blinking thing. 'There is always that argument.'

Cara took the several beats of silence to meditate her beating heart to a more manageable pace.

'So how has it been working for you?' he asked.

'Hmm?'

'Sticking to your guns.'

Pretty well. Fantastically. I love my life.

Those were all perfectly reasonable responses to his question. But Cara knew in that moment that they were not true.

Her life was nice. Busy. Ordered. But that was hardly the message she wanted written on her tombstone. Outrageous. Hectic. Abundant with love. Now those were descriptions to be proud of.

She looked up to find Adam watching her. He was nodding.

'Yep,' he agreed, though she had not said a word out loud. 'I thought as much.'

'Did you now?'

'I did. Because it's pretty much the same for me.'

Cara knew they were talking in circles and she knew what they were talking in circles about. But though Adam was doing his thing, leaving big great gaping holes for her to fill, she could not drag the words from her mouth. Instead she bit at her bottom lip.

'You do that a lot, you know.'

'Hmm?'

He leaned over and, taking a hold of her chin, ran his thumb over her bottom lip, which grew soft and pliant in his caress. 'You nibble at your bottom lip.' His hand pulled away.

'I used to suck my thumb as a kid and since I stopped it has become a sort of makeshift habit.' Cara's hand reached up to rub away the tingles Adam's thumb had left behind.

'Mmm. And there I was thinking that you do it especially when you're holding something back.'

Of course she did. And of course he would know it too.

'You don't have to hold back, you know,' he offered. 'Whatever you have to say, I can take it.'

Cara ached to drag her lip between her teeth. 'You're one to talk,' she said.

Adam laughed, a low rumbling sound that Cara felt in the pit of her stomach.

'You have a point there,' he said. 'It seems we are two very similar creatures, Cara. Obstinate. Opinionated. Closed to possibilities that we might be wrong.'

'Well, I guess there's no hope for us, then, is there?'

Cara knew he could have taken it one of two ways. That there was no hope that either of them would ever really change, or that there was no hope for the two of them to come together. Either way she felt she had made her point. He had asked her not to hold back, and that was as close as she could come to telling it as it was without hurting herself or him.

She waited for his response.

Would he sigh and say, *I guess you're right?* Or would he stare deep into her eyes and promise to show her how wrong she was? The longer it took for him to reply, the harder Cara found it to breathe. And the more she hoped it would be the second response.

By the time Adam cleared his throat Cara was so stiff with concern she flinched. She looked into his deep dark blue eyes to find them glancing over her face with concern, and with a modicum of humour. A tolerant smile had settled upon his face.

'There's always hope.'

He stood up and began clearing the plates and when he reached her side he bent to place a soft kiss atop her head. She bit her lip so hard she drew blood. But she had no choice. She had to stop herself from throwing herself into his dish-laden arms and letting him know the extent of her secret hopes.

* * *

Later that morning Adam helped her from the limo. As they looked up at the beautiful façade of the hotel it looked more like a fortress than ever.

'Are you sure you want to go in there alone?' Adam asked. His guiding hand resting softly at her back felt so like a brand.

'Absolutely,' Cara said on an outward breath.

'You do realise Jeff is going to eat you alive. Beneath all that strange hair lives a real-life television executive and a more ferocious beast you will never hope to meet.'

'Even so.'

As they entered the lift together Cara realised that the job did not mean to her what it once had. There was something more important in her life. Something that had always been there, but only after last night had she realised how important it was.

Friendship. The people in her life were bigger than the things in her life. If she had nothing, if for some reason she lost St Kilda Storeys, Kelly, Gracie and, yes, even her beloved Adam would take her in and give her the shelter she'd thought she so desperately needed. She waited for that same old sunken feeling to take up residence in her chest, but it never came. A smile eased across her tired face.

So her parents had fought. So her father had not earned enough money to keep her mother happy. So her mother had spent too much money to keep her father happy. They had had each other. That was why they'd stayed together through the lean years and through the fights. They had known that having each other was more important than anything else. To them love had been enough.

As they readied to part ways, Cara ached to prolong their time alone together. 'Thanks again for last night,' she said.

'Any time.'

She leaned in and gave him a thankful kiss on the cheek. She could not help herself. It hardly rated against their impassioned clinch the night before but she still felt blessed to be able to feel his warm cheek against her own.

With a deep intake of breath Adam turned and left her on her own. Cara knocked.

'I could fire you, you know,' Jeff said, hanging up his mobile phone as he opened the door. Cara almost laughed. His hair was spikier than she had ever seen it. It was almost a parody of itself.

'There is nothing to smile about here, Cara. You broke our contracted agreement. And as such I could kick you out on your bony ass without paying you a cent.'

She waited for the cold lick of fear to take her by the throat but it didn't come. Realising that in the grand scheme of things it did not matter made her feel free. She felt peace wash over her. She would pay off her building. Maybe not this month. Maybe not this year. But she would get there. By her own blood, sweat and tears, her own late nights and weekends, she would do it.

Besides, she had long since proven she was not built to keep her head down and be good.

'So fire me,' Cara said, eyeing him levelly, and enjoying immensely the look of utter shock on his young face.

He coughed and spluttered and sought meaner words until Cara cut him off.

'Just hold up there, Jeff. You know I want this gig, or else I wouldn't have gone after it. I want the exposure that will come from having my name on the credits. And, yes, I want the pay-cheque. But I am the best damn stylist in town. I am highly sought after, I am paid well, and I am as good as it gets. So keep me, don't keep me. It's up to you. Keep me so that on the final episode your bachelor, who adores me as I adore him, and would be pretty miffed to know I have been treated badly, will look better than you have ever seen him. Or let me go and see how your precious show turns out without me.'

Jeff stared her down, but the wind had well and truly gone from his sails. 'Well, actually, I have just been talking with the station manager and we have decided that your leave of absence was understandable and we would like to keep you on. With full pay.'

'Glad to hear it. Oh, and I'll need the afternoon off on Tuesday for my friend's mother's funeral, OK?'

Jeff gritted his teeth and nodded. 'Fine.'

'Well, then, I'd better get back to work. Chris will be wondering where I am.'

Then she stood, smoothed down her cargo pants and T-shirt, shook his hand, then left the room with as much stature as if she were wearing Chanel couture, not merely the only clean clothes she had managed to find at home.

The next few days went by in a blur.

Cara had to prepare Chris for the big day as well as wanting to be on the phone to Gracie as much as she could be. And Adam had disappeared. Cara had no idea if he was even staying at the hotel any longer. She should have been frantic, she was so busy, but her mind was only half on the job. She had all the distance she had so recently craved and it made her feel worse than ever.

She missed his company, his face, even his argumentativeness terribly. But how could she have been surprised? He had obviously run for the hills the first chance he had. And why not? A guy like him didn't need to be caught up in the small-time problems of a suburban girl like her. He had gone above and beyond for her and for Gracie. And for that she would love him for ever.

Tuesday afternoon, Cara left the hotel once more to join

Gracie at her mother's funeral. And she was amazed to find that Gracie, the flippant airhead of the crew, had become a grown-up overnight. Her stepfather was inconsolable, and her half-sister and half-brother, who were so much younger than she, were a mess. But Gracie held it all together beautifully. Cara was amazed at her friend's fortitude.

She half hoped Adam would be there. But he never showed. Though he did send the most beautiful spray of gardenias, Gracie's favourite flowers. How he had ever known that, Cara had no idea. Even though she was finding herself becoming more and more desperate to know where he was and what he was doing, the flowers represented a small ray of hope.

Afterwards, Maya Rampling, the editor of *Fresh* magazine, insisted Cara accompany her in her town car back to Gracie's stepfather's house for the wake.

'So how is the big gig going?' Maya asked. 'Is television everything you imagined it would be?'

'Everything and more,' Cara joked.

'So what's Chris Geyer like?'

'Who?'

'Come on, Cara,' Maya said, a thin silver eyebrow rising in disappointment, 'Jeff Whatsit from the TV station has already been in touch in a mad panic to make sure I realise the fact that I know every detail means I will not say a thing now, but can have the exclusive in two weeks. He's like a terrier. Ferocious yet kind of cuddly all the same. I like him.'

'Despite everything, I kinda do too.'

'From what I hear, young Chris took quite a shine to you as well. Did you outshine the other lasses in his eyes?'

'Oh, no. At least one of them has outshone the lot of us.'

Maya sighed. 'So true love reigns in the end.'

Cara bit her lip and nodded. 'I guess it does.'

'So you haven't been having a mad fling with a grip? I always liked the sound of that job title: Grip.'

'No,' Cara laughed. 'I didn't have a mad fling with a grip.'

Maya flicked a telling glance Cara's way and she fought to smile calmly back.

'Don't mess with me, darling, I'm too old and too frosty to sit here and pretend to believe your hogwash. If a grip didn't steal your heart, somebody did. You're all pale and sickly and it's not just young Gracie's loss that has made you look this way.'

Cara chose her words carefully. 'You have to admit, my being in that atmosphere for the last couple of weeks can't have helped the situation any. The whole set-up has been put in place to create the perfect location in which two people could fall in love.'

'Bah! People fall in love in factories, in diners, on tops of mountains. Location is a small part of the story, what matters is the people. So, tell me, my sweet, *did somebody steal your heart*?'

Cara shrugged, but not with much effort. Her whole body felt bruised, way more than after she had hurt herself during the baseball game. They were just superficial injuries. For some reason her whole body ached. Maybe she was getting the flu.

'Maybe a little,' she admitted. 'But it doesn't matter. I was there to work and you know me. It's always about the job. Not about me.'

'Well, it's damn well about time it is about you, Cara. You don't always have to play the good girl. You're all grown up now; you've been away from the familial home for nearly ten years. It's time you gave yourself a break.'

'I don't think I have it in me to play the bad girl, Maya.'

'Don't be bad, be true. True to yourself. Not to some

perfect vision of yourself. Listen to your heart and do as it tells you. It pumps your lifeblood through every inch of your body, so it certainly should be given a lot more credit than you have given it to date.'

Cara had nothing to say to that. She stared out the window, watching the trees swaying with the hot, humid wind that had been buffeting the city all the day, signifying a change was in the air.

That night Cara took her time smoothing down Chris's tie as he readied himself for the final day of the shoot. She wanted to savour every moment of this, her last day.

'Are you ready, buddy?' Cara asked him for the final time.

'More than I ever thought I would be,' Chris said, his voice steady. He turned to her and grasped her hands in both of his. 'And a great deal of that is thanks to you. Without your support I could very well have been turned to the dark side by my solemn friend.'

Cara noted he did not use Adam's name. And she knew that Chris knew exactly what she was going through, a slow, sure but necessary breaking of her heart. Cara braved a smile and clasped a tight hold of his hand, amazed that she had found herself such a firm friend under such unusual circumstances.

'Did you think you would find what you were looking for from this process?'

Chris thought about it a moment. 'I did. But in the end I found more than I ever imagined I would.'

'You really love her, don't you, Chris?'

'I really do.'

Cara threw herself into Chris's arms and gave him a huge bear hug. 'I can tell. You're glowing.'

'That's what the power of love will do to a guy.'

Cara nodded. 'It suits you.'

Chris held her at arm's length, his eyes narrowing as he took her in. 'Along the same lines, what's with all the sunken eyes and stooping walk? You look like the world is on your shoulders.'

Cara moved away and headed over to the clothes rack, and began flicking blindly through the suits and shirts. 'I think I'm getting the flu. Or something. I've got the whole aching-muscle-sleepless-night thing going on.'

'I guess that's what the power of love can do to a girl.'

Cara pretended she hadn't heard him. She picked out a tie and held it up to him. 'Do you think this would be a better choice?'

Chris held a hand over hers, and her panicky gaze flickered to him.

'You should tell him.'

She opened her mouth to ask who but thought better of it. Instead she gave him a weak shrug. 'Can't.'

Chris let forth an expletive that she hadn't imagined such a sweet guy would have in his repertoire. 'The two of you are as bad as one another. And here I am, having the most exciting time of my life, yet at the same time caught in the middle, watching the two of you pine away for one another.'

'I'm not pining,' Cara insisted. But her mind was off and running in a whole other direction. *He's pining? Wherever the guy is, he's actually pining?*

But Chris glared back at her.

'Sorry,' she said. 'I was supposed to be the one giving you a pep talk.'

'I don't need a pep talk. I know what I want and I am going out there to get it. Can you say the same for yourself?'

She couldn't give him a straight answer so, borrowing a

move from someone she knew, she just shrugged and let him fill the silence.

'Just don't take too long to figure it out, Cara.'

And then, without a doubt in the world, Chris walked out of the room, more than ready to propose to the woman he loved.

But he was stopped the moment he hit the hallway by Adam on the fly. Chris held up a hand to fend off his friend and just kept on walking. 'Where the hell have you been these last couple of days?'

'Working. Wheeling. Dealing.'

'Pfft,' Chris scoffed. 'Hiding, more like it. And whatever you have to say can keep until after the filming.'

Adam settled into a slow walk a few feet behind his friend. Wow. He had never seen Chris so determined. He walked with a purpose. His usually fuzzy edges were clear and crisp. He even looked taller than usual. Adam told him so.

Chris wasn't in the mood. 'I said don't.'

'But it's true.'

Chris stopped only to press the button on the lift and Adam was able to catch up.

'I only came up here to wish you good luck today.'

Adam flinched under his friend's silent wary gaze.

'I mean it, Chris.' Adam placed a hand on Chris's shoulder. 'I can see how much this experience has changed you. Helped you. Made you happy. And for that there is no way I can make any sort of complaint.'

'Are you joshing me?'

'No, I'm not. I am here to shake your hand and to wish you all the best. Treat her well and I'll leave it up to you to make sure she does the same for you.'

Chris was still not completely convinced.

'I can't complain that you are a total romantic, mate,'

Adam said. 'You need to be at least a little fanciful to be a really good inventor. And you're the best I've ever seen.'

Adam held out a hand in conciliation but Chris would have none of that. He grabbed the hand only to pull Adam into a hearty bear hug.

'Thanks, mate. That means the world to me.'

Adam gave Chris's back one last slap before pulling away.

'I could offer you some pretty similar advice right now, Adam,' Chris said with a sympathetic smile playing about his mouth.

Adam blinked.

'Please,' Chris said. 'You can try to pull the strong, silent method on me but it will never work. I've known you too long. But you have shown me today you can stay out of my business when it is warranted so I will show you the same courtesy.'

The lift binged and the doors slid open.

'Saved by the bell,' Chris said, stepping into the lift.

'Now go get her, mate,' Adam said, acting the jovial friend again. 'Make sure one of those kisses she gets is from me. And tell her so.'

Chris nodded. And as the doors closed Adam could sense his friend leaving him as his thoughts reached out to someone else. A woman waiting for him to reveal himself to her. Adam only hoped that woman knew how good she was about to have it.

He looked back down the hallway and saw Chris's closed suite door. He knew Cara would be behind that door. Alone. And after having sat with Chris all evening she must have been thinking along much the same lines that he was.

They had been thrown together under such odd circumstances and neither had any idea if what they felt would survive in the real world. So he had left. He had gone home. And it had killed him not seeing her.

He could only wait and see and hope that she had felt the same way.

CHAPTER TWELVE

CARA watched in rapt amazement as Chris and Maggie declared their love for one another on the balcony where they had first met. If the rest of the shoot had felt like some sort of hyper-reality, this felt like a fairy tale, pure and simple. The candles, the star-spangled night sky, the trailing ivy, it was more beautiful than anything she had ever seen. How could a girl refuse a proposal in such surroundings?

But she knew that Maggie would not have refused Chris's hand if they had been sitting across from one another in some dingy milk bar instead.

Cara wiped away a tear. While she felt so excited for Chris, her own heart was breaking. This was what she was giving up. But if she did as Chris suggested and told Adam how she felt, she would only be setting herself up for ever worse heartache. Adam had it in him to feel as strongly as Chris did, she knew that without a doubt. But she was not sure that he was ready to admit it.

She sniffed back her sadness and concentrated on the scene in front of her. Chris was about to drop the second part of his bombshell and she could not wait to see how Maggie would react. Would she jump for joy, would she faint, or would the news hit her as it did Cara and make her want to run for her life?

Chris took a deep breath and squeezed Maggie's hands. A small shy smile flitted across his face. 'Oh, and by the way,' he said, 'I am a billionaire.'

The whole crew held its collective breath.

Maggie's response could not have been more unexpected. With a big grin, she slapped Chris on the arm and said, 'Well, good for you!'

As Chris wrapped Maggie up in a delighted embrace the whole crew burst into spontaneous laughter and applause.

Cara stared at the couple in shock. What a response. *Good for him. He's rich. Now let's get on with things.*

The simplicity of it all hit her like a kick to the stomach. Her heart rate struck up a solid rhythm as she suddenly realised what she had to do.

Adam leant against the doorway, his chosen spot affording a view through the cameras and assorted equipment to his friend who stood on the balcony of the Ivy Hotel.

But more importantly, it afforded him an unimpeded view of Cara. She stood by the central camera, ready to be a rock of support to Chris in this, the most important moment of his life.

She was dressed down in jeans and T-shirt, obviously making sure she was not about to outshine the woman of the moment, the delightfully unshockable Maggie.

As the sweet blonde girl was released from Chris's embrace, she stumbled. Chris reached out to catch her, and the two of them faced each other with matching blushes. Adam's heart jerked in his chest. Damn it! He even felt something akin to tears burning the backs of his eyes.

Maggie whispered something that had Chris and the crew laughing. Adam moved away from his hiding spot and quietly eased closer to the action. He slowly walked around the outside of the room until he found a spot at the far right of the cameras. He was still in the shadows, but from there he could see Cara's face. Her hands were covering her mouth and she had tears pouring down her face.

With her heart on her sleeve she looked more beautiful

to him than she ever had before. Adam wanted to go to her, and hug her and kiss the tears from her cheeks.

Who was he kidding? He wanted to do more than that. He wasn't looking for a date for Saturday night, he wasn't looking for a month-long fling. He wanted to wake up looking into those bright green eyes, he wanted to kiss those beautiful lips, and he wanted to caress those soft curls every day for the rest of his life. He wanted to introduce her to his father, for heaven's sake!

He finally realised that all the signs led to one thing. He was head over heels in love.

At that moment, the rain that had been threatening to wash down on the city all day finally hit. It rained with such unceasing force it would have drowned out the couple's voices if it had come but a minute earlier.

Everyone on the balcony sprinted inside the ballroom. Jeff grabbed every spare guy to help shut the balcony doors to shield their precious equipment from the rain buffeting the outside of the hotel.

Cara went straight to Chris and Maggie, making sure they were OK. She all but hugged the life out of each of them.

Then once the rain was no more than a steady hum against the windows, Jeff called out, 'And that's a wrap! See you all at the wrap party at Lunar on Friday night!'

The crew exploded into raucous cheers, hugging and clapping and generally whooping it up. Then as quickly as they started, they stopped, and with happy chatter they began to pack up the equipment. Before Adam had time to catch his breath, one by one they began to leave. Almost immediately the room started to clear. He watched as Cara gave everyone a hug, saying goodbye. It was over. It was all over.

They were leaving. Cara was leaving. And if he wanted

to do those things with her for the rest of his life, it would be up to him to tell her so. Adam remembered back to the Saturday Night Cocktails dinner where Kelly had professed that was exactly what she needed.

'Cara. Stay.' The words wrenched from him with such power the whole set went quiet. The grips slowly lowered their bags; the sound guys stopped their unplugging; Adam felt every eye swing his way, but there was only one set of eyes he cared about. A pair of glittering cat's eyes that belonged to the woman who had long since awoken his dormant heart.

Cara turned, her expression puzzled. 'Adam?'

She had every right to be confused. He had avoided her for days. But since he no longer had an ounce of confusion remaining in his body he got on with what he had to do.

'I said, stay.'

She blinked and it took all of his strength not to run to her and drag her into his arms and kiss that gorgeous puzzled look from her face. Instead he sent her his most encouraging grin, lifted a finger, and beckoned her to him.

What the hell does he think he's doing?

Cara looked about her. The whole crew had stopped packing and were watching in smiling silence. Whatever Adam was up to, there was no way they were going to miss a minute of it.

Cara hastened to Adam's side.

'What do you think you are doing?' she asked through gritted teeth.

'Something I should have done a long time ago.'

Adam grabbed her hand and tugged her to him so fast her breath released on a shocked sigh. He tipped her back and planted a long, hard kiss upon her mouth. Over the sound of angels singing in her ears Cara heard whooping and catcalls of two dozen crew members.

Finally, when Adam deigned to release her from his liquefying embrace, Cara pulled away and brought a shaking hand to her mouth.

'Cara,' Adam said. 'I'm asking you to stay. With me. I'm asking you to be mine.'

She had barely recovered from his delicious kiss, and any words he had to say came to her as outright gibberish. Surely he couldn't have said he was asking her to be his?

'But why?' she asked.

He offered her a lopsided smile that had her smiling right back. 'Are you really telling me that you haven't seen the signs?' he asked. 'For a guy who is a professed bachelor, have you not seen that I have had eyes for no one but you since the moment you walked into my life on your sexy red shoes?'

Cara swallowed, unsure, uncertain, desperate for him to tell her what she needed to hear. Then he smiled at her and her knees turned to jelly and she was glad she was wrapped tight in his arms. He shifted his grip so that she was moulded so perfectly against him she could barely breathe. His words then came to her, low and alluring, and soft enough for only her to hear.

'Hmm. Not a good enough reason? How about because no two people ever tried so hard to deny what was best for them? And only if the both of us take the leap can we ever see if what we feel is real.'

Somebody gave a great big sniff and Cara came back down to earth with a thud. The two dozen others in the room came back into sharp focus.

'Why couldn't you be the one with the fear of public speaking?' she asked through gritted teeth.

Adam turned to the crew and said, 'Would you guys mind giving us a minute?'

'Change of plans!' Jeff called out instantaneously. 'Wrap party is in my room, right now!'

The crew hustled as though a whip were cracking at their backs. Chris and Maggie blew the pair of them a big kiss before heading out a hidden side door together.

When Adam and Cara were alone, with nothing more than the sound of steady rain on the balcony as a companion, Cara asked, 'Do you know what you are asking?'

'Mmm hmm,' he whispered against her ear.

'But are you sure you're ready for this? Ready for me?'

'More than ready.'

'And what do you think this is exactly?' His breath against her neck was making her giddy.

'I don't know if I can put it into words,'

'Mr Tyler, I thought your special gift was words.'

'It is. This is bigger than words. But whatever this is, I don't ever want it to go away. So what do you say, Ms Marlowe?' Adam said, burying his face beneath the hair curling at her neck, his hot breath sending pulsating shivers down her back. 'Do you promise to be mine for as long as we can stand each other?'

Cara suddenly could not have cared if they were standing in the middle of the Melbourne Cricket Ground with a packed stadium looking on. This moment was too important to worry about such trivial details as location.

Now was the time to swallow her own fear and be true. She felt a calm come over her as she said, 'I promise to be yours for ever.'

Adam stopped nuzzling. 'Say that again,' he demanded softly.

He waited until she lowered her gaze and looked directly into his eyes. He held his breath and had no desire to take another until he had heard those words again.

'Adam,' she said with a vulnerable shrug, 'I am hopelessly in love with you. And if you will have me, I promise to be yours for ever.'

He hadn't been able to put the feeling into words, but she, ever the strong one, had. She deserved as good as she gave. He took her face in his hands and said what had to be said.

'Cara, sweetheart, there is nothing hopeless about a love that is returned to you tenfold.' He swept her into his arms once more, bruising her lips with as much passion as he could give.

'But I want you to know I want nothing from you,' she said when she next had the chance.

'Tough. You take me, you get everything I have to give.'

'Adam, no.'

'OK, then. So long as you promise not to give me anything of yours either.' He had her just where he wanted her. With a rising smile he added, 'I will never want your strange little apartment block. You can keep *it* for ever.'

Cara slapped him on the chest. 'You rotter! St Kilda Storeys is a fantastic piece of real estate, I'll have you know. It's worth twenty-five per cent more now than the day I bought it.'

Adam grabbed Cara by the hand to stop her struggling. 'I don't care what it's worth. But I want you to know *I* know how much the place means to you. How much your independence means to you. So, though I am never going to let you out of my arms for another minute, I want you to keep your building,' he reiterated. 'For you alone. As a safety net.'

She believed him. He saw it in her eyes. He felt it in her touch as she melted against him. Then just as suddenly she threw herself wholly into his arms and Adam rocked back at the force.

'Whoa, sweetheart,' Adam said. 'What's that for?'

'It's for being an amazing man.'

She pulled away and looked into his eyes, the love she felt for him hitting him in waves, and it was all he could do not to wrench her back and kiss her for all she meant to him.

'Adam, don't you understand?' she said. 'You have no choice. What's mine is yours. You get me, you get too many clothes in your closet, you get Kelly and Gracie on our doorstep at least once a week, and you get my old place.'

He screwed up his nose. 'And what am I meant to do with it?'

She slapped him on the arm. 'Don't you screw your nose up at my beautiful building. Or I'll make you live in it.'

Adam made to pull away, his feet shuffling on the spot as though if she let him go he would bolt for the hills like the Road Runner. It made her laugh and that sweet tinkling sound was the final straw.

He stopped pulling, he stopped shuffling, and he wrapped his arms so far around her he was almost hugging himself.

'So we'll live in your cosy little building, then.'

Her beautiful eyes narrowed. 'Are you serious?'

He shrugged. 'Wherever you are, I am. Whether it be in my nice, new, air-conditioned home with its guest rooms, its salt-water pool, its billiard room, its acres of tended gardens, or in your St Kilda Storeys apartment where Gracie will pop in every morning with her news of the previous night's marriage proposal.'

Cara bit at her lip and he knew he almost had her.

'So there we'll stay,' Adam continued. 'No sleeping in…together. Scenic views of the next-door neighbour's garage wall. A spare couch for Kelly and Simon to sleep on after a late night DVD jag—'

'OK, stop!' she finally acquiesced. 'Stop. You've made your point.'

She hugged him tight back and he couldn't believe how wonderful he felt.

'And a good point it is,' she said. 'I will move in with you instead?' He could hear the uncertainty in her voice so he kissed her sweet nose.

'Sweetheart, you are coming home with me as of today if I have to carry you over my shoulder kicking and screaming to get you there.'

She grinned back at him with such force he knew he had her.

'And so what will we do with St Kilda Storeys?' he asked.

Still wrapped tight in his arms she looked up at him. 'I think we'll keep it for ever and ever. It has served beautifully as a place for young strays and I wouldn't want to take that opportunity away from the next generation. If I sold it they'd probably tear it down and build gleaming new condos. Nope. St Kilda Storeys stays.'

'Fine.'

'Besides, where else would Gracie go?'

A month later, Cara went back to her bottom-floor apartment of St Kilda Storeys to spend one last night. And she went with a bang.

Kelly and Simon came over bearing a cask of sparkling apple juice. Chris and his fiancée Maggie joined them, neither of them remembering to bring the bags of crisps that had been sitting on their kitchen bench. Gracie arrived late, but had managed to pick up an industrial-sized box of Belgian chocolates from a visiting gentleman who had given them to all the cute young croupiers in the high rollers room as a tip.

While Kelly set up the room with borrowed cushions from Gracie's couch upstairs and beanbags from another neighbour, Simon moved the television from Cara's old bedroom into the lounge, and Adam made caramel popcorn.

'Wow,' Cara whispered in Adam's ear as he piled the snack into a big bowl. 'The man can cook. I am impressed.'

'Dad's third wife. She lived on the stuff.'

'And you said they gave you nothing. Caramel popcorn is not nothing.'

Adam caught her around the waist, pulling her to him and placing a kiss upon her nose. 'My little eternal optimist. You are too good for me.'

'Not too good. Just about perfect.'

'Come on, guys!' Kelly yelled from her seat in the lounge. 'It's starting!'

Cara grabbed the first full bowl and took it into the lounge where she was greeted with a mass of flailing arms reaching for the popcorn.

'Turn it up,' someone demanded and Gracie did the honours.

Then as the first episode of *The Billionaire Bachelor* lit the screen a barrage of popcorn hit the television.

'Hey,' Cara called out, 'I just had the carpet professionally cleaned.' But the popcorn merely flew thicker and faster.

'Look, there's Maggie.' Chris shifted so quickly in his beanbag Maggie all but rolled off his lap.

'Wait up, cowboy, I'm right here too, you know,' Maggie said, her bright blue eyes glinting.

Chris's ears burned red. 'So you are.' Then he gave her a light, lingering kiss on the mouth.

Cara sighed as she watched them. Two young people in love. Two young people who had found each other under the most trying, unusual circumstances, and it was obvious to all how right they were for each other.

As though picking up on the romance in the air, Kelly and Simon snuggled closer on the couch, Simon's hand reaching out to rest on Kelly's tummy as she laid her head on his shoulder.

Cara's gaze was immediately drawn to Adam, his bulk taking up so much of the small kitchen. He was leaning back against the kitchen counter, and his arms were crossed, but the latent frustration that had blazed from him since the day they had met was gone. His relaxed pose was all real as he watched the gang with a smile on his face. It was a smile full of understanding and hope.

Then, as though sensing she was watching him, he blinked and turned his eyes her way. And his smile changed. Where it had been lit by hope, it was now lit by the fulfilment of that hope. She knew, as if he had whispered the words in her ear, that he owed it all to her. Cara's breath caught in her throat, the impact of his loving gaze was so great. So great but so beautiful.

With a slight flick of his head he beckoned her. And without argument she went to him, burying herself in his solid embrace, breathing deep of his glorious scent and feeling more than safe enveloped in his amazing warmth. After several long moments feeling as if she were floating on air, she heard the voices of her friends cut in.

'Come on, guys! Come join us!'

Adam pulled away from the kitchen bench and, with his arms still wrapped about her, led Cara to the leather couch. Simon and Kelly shuffled up. And Cara tucked her feet beneath her as she snuggled against Adam on the couch.

Gracie shot them a big grin from her spot lying on the cushions on the floor.

'So I'm taking bets,' Gracie said as the show went to its

first ad break, half of which was taken up with Revolution Wireless's new campaign. 'Who do you reckon our bachelor is going to choose? And how long until they break up?'

The popcorn that had been flying thick and fast at the television earlier now came pelting Gracie's way along with a barrage of not-nice words. She squealed and covered her face with her arms.

'Hey, no fair. Don't pick on the single girl. I'm trying very hard not to be sick, there is so much schmaltz in the air right now. So I think I deserve a little leeway for bitterness.'

'It's your turn next, Gracie,' Maggie predicted.

'What about Dean?' Kelly asked. 'He thought you were a bit of all right.'

'So where is he now?' Gracie demanded.

'Yeah,' Chris said, 'where is Dean? I thought he was coming too.'

'Working,' Adam said. 'Always working.'

Gracie shrugged. 'Well, there you go. I'm a player and he's a worker. It's just wouldn't work. Seems you guys are stuck with me. Just keep an extra set of clean linen in the house in case I need some company and I'll be a happy girl for ever.'

Cara grinned. Simply enjoying the moment. Her friends all together, all smiling and happy, all helping her give her old home a grand send-off. The man she loved keeping her wrapped safe in her arms.

She was one of a bunch of decision-makers in the house and she didn't care a lick. She was happy to sit back and let someone else make the decisions right now. She would just go with the flow. If she had to give up the remote control in order to have this abundance of hope, and love, and excitement for the future, then so be it.

Adam could have the remote control, as he had her heart. And as far as she was concerned he could do with them as he pleased.

Cara clinked against her glass with beautifully manicured fingernails. 'I would like to make a toast.'

The gang noisily fought over mismatched cups and glasses until they were all ready.

'To Cary Grant,' Cara said, shooting Adam a glance full of meaning.

'To Cary Grant,' the rest of the gang mimicked cheerfully before gulping down their apple juice.

Adam's eyes softened and she leant in and kissed him, not caring who in the world was there to see it.

'Who's Cary Grant?' Maggie asked in a loud whisper and received a barrage of cushions thrown at her face.

'You really are a hick, aren't you?' Chris asked, and received a cushion wallop across the face for his efforts.

'Wait. It's back on!' he shouted, his face lighting up in amazement and blushing furiously at the same time as he watched himself on television.

The others settled into their positions and Cara snuck out of her seat. She beckoned to Adam, who came to her all too readily.

'What is it?' he whispered as she took him by the hand and led him out the front door and into the communal hallway at the front of the building. He kept looking over his shoulder back towards the gang inside. 'We're going to miss it.'

'We were there, doofus. I can even tell you how it ends if you're that worked up about it.'

On the word 'doofus' she had him hooked. He grabbed her around the waist and walked her backwards out the door and into the open air.

'Doofus? Is that any way to talk to the man you love?'

'Who says you're the man I love?'

'You do. And often. And if you keep pretending it's not true, I'm just going to have to torture you.'

He trudged down the big cement front steps and she had to stand on his feet so as not to lose her balance.

'OK. Stop! I give up. If you go any further I am going to fall.'

'I won't let you.'

Cara stopped her complaining and looked into his gorgeous blue eyes. Of course he wouldn't let her fall. She'd fallen only once in their relationship and she intended staying that way, especially since he had caught her in his strong arms.

'Now you've got me out here,' Adam said, his eyes dancing, 'what are you going to do with me?'

Cara grinned and stood high on her toes so she could kiss him. She could feel the smile on his lips as he kissed her back. And it wasn't the kiss of a passion they were afraid might extinguish if they did not drink of it desperately. It was a kiss that held the remembrance of many kisses gone, and the knowledge there would be many more kisses to come. It was a kiss that matched the steady heat and delicious languor of the long, hot summer that stretched out before them. It was a kiss that held all the time in the world.

Locals in shorts and T-shirts trailed the path in front of the old red St Kilda Storeys building and off to the beach, to nightclubs and to local restaurants. But Cara and Adam were exactly where they wanted to be.

The location was entirely irrelevant, so long as they were together.

BOUGHT AND BEDDED BY THESE PASSIONATE MEN WITH POWER!

At the Prince's Pleasure

Three ordinary girls will be wedded – and bedded – by royal command!

Available 5th June 2009

At the Tycoon's Command

Three innocent girls will be seduced for revenge – and for pleasure!

Available 3rd July 2009

At the Billionaire's Bidding

Three beautiful women will be bought with cold, hard cash – and bedded with red-hot passion!

Available 7th August 2009

Collect all three!

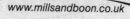